Kisatchie Voices

J.C. Oliver

Kisatchie Voices

Copyright © 2023 by J.C. Oliver
All Rights Reserved

Introduction

Kisatchie is a name derived from the Kichai Indian tribe.

In the late nineteenth century, large areas of Louisiana were covered by virgin forests of yellow pine, much of which was magnificent longleaf pine.

Ruthless lumber harvests raped the land in what came to be known as 'cut out and get out,' leaving a few families to scratch out a living by any measure except lumber. Many sawmill towns were literally picked up and moved, house by house, to other locations, other forested areas, and other dreams of wealth.

Such ghost towns still stand today, a postmortem symbol of greed and harsh ambition.

The Kisatchie National Forest was established in 1930 and occupies 604,000 acres of public land in multiple Parishes of Central Louisiana and is protected land under the watch of the U.S. Forestry Service.

This story is based on the author's knowledge of the area and its inhabitants during the time the story takes place. Many things have changed since then. Examples of the poverty found there have since found redemption and courage. The names and events in this story are fictitious but carry a distinct flavor of how it was in that place and at that time in history.

Chapter 1

It took a certain kind of person to live there. Mostly, you had to be born there. Back in those days, as it is now, Kisatchie was a small country town right dead in the middle of Louisiana, not too far from Alexandria, the biggest town in that part of the state. The population in Kisatchie was always questioned, but the 1940 census was at around 327. The count was never verified. It didn't matter, but some folks wondered who was included in the tabulation. Census takers were not on the list of trusted folks because they asked too many questions. One would think that it would be easy to count the population. In fact, that's what some families did; They just sat around the table after dinner and wrote down everyone's names. A decade later, the number seemed unchanged for the most part. A few folks had died; a few babies had been born.

The old bread delivery box in front of Rucker's store was still the same one from three previous owners before, maybe further back than that. Nobody remembers for sure. There was a time when the bakery in Alexandria delivered bread before the store opened. The box was strong and waterproof with a large lock, not that it really needed one. Years ago, when the deliveries began coming later in the day when the store was open, the current owner considered getting rid of it, but the box had taken on the properties of a park bench. There were always a couple of old men sitting on it, spittin' and talkin', waving at the occasional car that went by. The post office was next door, so after most folks came by to check the mail and say 'hello' to Mr. Rucker, there wasn't much else to do but hang around and see who else came by. Life had no sense of urgency. All the town's news eventually drifted past the breadbox. Besides the school and the post office, the only other public buildings in town were two churches; one was Methodist, the other Baptist. The breadbox, though, was the center of town — it held the soul of Kisatchie. There was a hidden community strength beneath the apparent lethargy — the strength to endure, to be timeless, to remain unchanged. Change had passed through once, had been there and gone, leaving a scar.

Shortly after the turn of the century, prosperity stood at the door with the look of a fresh bride, but after the honeymoon, the tarnished soul of a harlot. Parts of Louisiana were struck by ruthless lumber empires whose aim was to cut out and get out, leaving barren land and floundering economies. In the beginning, whole towns appeared almost overnight as logging crews settled their families and descended upon beautiful long-leaf pine and hardwood forests. The rapists of the forest were large companies that built sawmills and constructed company-owned towns to support their greed. Kisatchie was situated between two such mill towns, only a mile or two from each one. Both mills were owned by the Whitmyer family. When their father died, the mills were divided between the family's two sons, Doyle and Steven. The old man would have wanted it that way. The towns had taken on the names of Pittman and Bushnell, based on some family names from long before the Civil War — names that had made an indelible mark on the map perhaps because of a trading post, a boarding house, or maybe even a stable. No one ever took the time to remember exactly what it was. Neither town was ever incorporated, but control of the respective towns by each Whitmyer son was never questioned. Plenty of votes and money for the parish elections originated from these two blind, faithful congeries of humanity. Crime was never a problem in either town. The punishment for even rumored wrongdoing was the loss of a job and the house that came with it. Doyle and Steven stood as judge and jury over their separate kingdoms, answering to no one. They could hold court any time, any place. Compliance was the only option, and grace was an orphan.

Kisatchie was a little different than its two sister towns in that it was much older, and private citizens owned the properties. Although there was some electric utility, and some had wells, most house lots included underground cisterns that collected rainwater from the rooftops. Chicken yards and vegetable gardens were commonplace. Some had milk cows. The mills poured money into the local payroll, which made business ventures materialize and flourish. Kisatchie drew its life and strength from the two mill towns, and everyone knew it. About thirty miles away in Alexandria, car dealerships saw a ripening market in and around Kisatchie, and soon the sounds of Fords and Chevys appeared amid the clop-clop of horse-drawn buggies and wagons.

Folks say World War I started the decline. Like a monstrous wave, it beckoned many men away from their families and the work at the mills by appealing to their sense of duty and inviting them with the promise of adventure. But it was the Whitmyer brothers who, after ruling their own private domains for twenty years, steered all three towns down a gradual pathway of suffocating collapse from within that was almost imperceptible at first. It began with friendly competition between the two mills, then greed, and then hatred between the two brothers. What had been a gentleman's agreement to honor the other's lumber rights became a claim-jumping war that resulted in frequent clashes between logging crews. Payroll deliveries were intercepted by opposing sides, mule teams were sabotaged, and log piles were set afire. Both brothers foresaw the eventual withering of their own empires and had been wisely investing heavily in outside ventures, particularly other untouched timber areas of the South. Both were determined to exploit the land as fast as possible, doubling then tripling their output. Residents of all three towns saw the momentum gathering, but their conscience was deaf and blind to the clear signals of an impending barren, hollow future. For the moment, folks had more money than their wildest dreams could imagine, and the contest between the two brothers seemed to fan the fires of prosperity.

Joshua Parker was one of the lucky ones. Since the inception of the two opposing camps, he had been the strong arm of Steven Whitmyer of the Pittman mill, a man with no compunction toward distasteful work. Compassion and justice can be the road to greatness despite obstacles, but for Joshua, intimidation made the pathway straight and short. He was good at it. It came naturally. He ruled all the work crews with an iron hand and carried out his employer's orders to the letter. By the end of the war in Europe, men were returning home to find work. Most of them preferred Pittman because many of the wells and cisterns in Bushnell had become mysteriously fouled without explanation. To work in Pittman required two things: Joshua's approval and a willingness to do his occasional dirty work.

In his younger days, Joshua could drink with the best, but he always managed to keep his wits about himself. It was safer that way. For a man with few friends and a thankless job, he had to be careful. Although no one could ever prove it, there was always an element of danger and suspicion hanging over him concerning a series of small fires near the Bushnell mill. And then there was the accident when a saw blade chewed into an iron spike that had become embedded in a tree trunk many decades ago. It could have been part of an old gate hinge left in a small tree at the woods' edge. No matter how it got there, the metal was swallowed up by the cambium and the bark until the day that all would blame Joshua. Bits of jagged steel from the five-foot whirling saw blade exploded like shrapnel, injuring several men and killing the crew foreman. Gossip traveled like an evil cloud that enveloped good men and bad. Joshua did it, they assumed, but no one could figure out how. If not, well, folks just knew he must have had something to do with it, so it all equals out. To Joshua, such rumors only strengthened his position. He was a man of few words. His reputation set the stage, and the town followed the script.

As a matter of survival, Joshua had to stay sharp. He held one weapon more powerful than any gun — the mill. To get a job, he held the only key. To keep your job, you marched in step with him. Given a task by Joshua, no one argued. His mere presence spoke the message of propriety.

Deep-set hazel eyes and dark straight hair were the gifts of his mother, a Cajun woman from Ville Platte. The face had not a hint of compassion, a gift of his father, a Texan who never spoke of his own childhood. By deed and example, he taught young Joshua the use and effectiveness of intimidation as a manner of control. Joshua learned fast. One noxious look from the old man could bludgeon anyone into submission, emasculate any man, and the fruit didn't fall very far from the tree.

Only one person held sway over Joshua. Marcia Patrick, considered by most to be the best catch in town, first noticed him in 1918. It was a rare, warm November day during a spontaneous town gathering celebrating the news of the end of the First World War. He was the most handsome man she had ever seen. She saw him standing on the edge of the picnic grounds outside the First Baptist Church of Kisatchie, quietly watching the festivities. He had a way about him, so casual and arrogant with his hat slightly cocked and the brim turned up front and back. A pencil line mustache and his tanned complexion seemed to add the finishing touches. Any man who happened to come near him would suddenly grow quiet, speak politely to him, and keep walking. Occasionally, small groups of women would whisper and look in his direction. He seemed to have what all men wanted and what most women desired. He was in control. Marcia, in a stroke of boldness, said 'hello' and could feel her fate sealed with the first words he said to her. She was a vibrant strawberry blonde with a contagious personality. Beautiful and almost twenty, she was not bothered by his age, ten years her senior. If anything, he made her feel more adult. Somehow all the rumors about him didn't seem possible. She found nothing bestial about him.

They courted for only a month and married. As a wedding gift, Steven Whitmyer built his gatekeeper and new bride the largest house in Pittman. It was on a gentle slope with a barn and ten acres. The house had a high peaked roof and a porch that wrapped around two sides, allowing Marcia an unrestricted view of both woods and meadows. The kitchen was enormous and built to Marcia's wishes. If walls could talk, one would hear the laughter and joy that came from the gatherings of Marcia and her friends in the mornings over coffee and teacakes. She felt certain that Joshua had a domestic thread within him and set out on a campaign to find it. She never finished that search, but she did learn to control him as sure as the touch of a spur could turn a horse. In fact, Joshua once had a five-year-old stallion named Jupiter that no one else could ride. He always claimed that Marcia kept a tighter rein on him than he did on Jupiter. She never asked for much because Joshua saw that she never did without. The evenings belonged to Joshua — to the privacy of his home — and Marcia never questioned it. She was the only person he trusted, the only human he ever really loved. Soon after they married, she began to see reasons to believe some of the rumors about him, but she denied they existed. She was seeing how the lumber industry was abandoning their town, and she heard the lies he offered to the townspeople about the eventual return of prosperous times. However, his charm blinded her from the obvious; she saw only the love, shelter, and protection he provided. To her, he was immortal, unsinkable. She was dazzled by his clever wit, the promise of a new life, and a swift climb up the company's financial ladder.

No one could have known that the Whitmyer brothers had managed to secretly agree on one thing despite all the conflict. No one would have guessed that a date had been set — a funeral date. A date in September 1920, which marked the beginning of the slow strangulation of all three towns.

It was the day both mills began closing down.

At midday, without forewarning, over half the workers of each mill were sent home. Those remaining would be randomly dismissed over a six-month period, giving time to fill remaining lumber contracts. Joshua was allowed to collect his pay as Steven

Whitmyer's watchdog while equipment was dismantled for sale or to be transported to another location. As the work scaled down, it was his responsibility to fire those no longer needed. A bonus was promised to him for efficient use of the diminishing money and resources. He was assured there would be a new position waiting for him at a new mill somewhere in Georgia.

Of the three towns, Kisatchie was the only survivor, but not without visible wounds. The mills' closure began an immediate exodus of the labor force. Some stayed — skilled workers looking for any job. Farmers around the area and others not-so-dependent on the lumber industry continued to do business with a few of the merchants in Kisatchie, but the pulse of the town beat at a greatly diminished rate. Gradually, the population of Kisatchie dwindled to a dismal level with abandoned storefronts and warehouses. The train schedule was absent of any freight deliveries and only one passenger run per week. Most passengers were of the outbound type.

At least there was measurable life in Kisatchie. Pittman and Bushnell had become ghost towns, images recorded only in the minds of those who had been there. Vacant, lifeless houses fell into disrepair as time, wind, and weather brought decay and rust. Most were torn down and used for second-hand lumber. Many of them were sold, lifted off the ground and moved to other locations by groaning mule teams, leaving only the crumbling foundations, overgrown rose gardens, and the wind whistling through empty clotheslines as a hint of the lives that once filled the streets there.

With all his cruel and unforgiving ways, Joshua still knew that a facade of compassion could sometimes motivate employees better than fear. His brand of compassion was unique but unconditional. Two days before Christmas that year, he had a visitor in his office.

In the doorway stood a mountainous colored man in grey wrinkled pants and a faded brown and tan plaid shirt with the collar buttoned. He wore a poorly fitting old suit coat. In both hands, he held an old, tattered hat. His name was Oscar, Oscar Carter.

Oscar had been in the mill business for as long as Joshua had and possessed an uncanny ability to keep things running. Joshua knew he would need someone with unwavering loyalty as he went about the unsavory business of firing and evicting. Someone loyal yet expendable in the end.

Joshua had called Oscar there to tell him he was due for a pay raise and the promise of continued employment until the last worker was gone. After that, he promised he would put in a good word to the Whitmyer family on Oscar's behalf, although he knew it was an empty promise. In return for all this, Joshua would ask for his loyalty without any questions asked.

Thinking of his wife, Lavenia, with their house full of children and another one on the way, Oscar knew this was a crucial decision. He knew what Lavenia would say. She was a hard-working, slender woman almost the same age as Oscar. She kept her house in order with calloused hands and the tenacity of a bulldog. She had her own brand of tough love. It took Oscar only a split second to agree to Joshua's terms.

Oscar and Lavenia never moved again.

Joshua got his expected bonus. It was the promise of a pauper's monthly pension and free title to his house and the land it stood on. Nothing more.

As the mills slowed down, he lost the leverage of control provided by his position and eventually lost his coercion over the community. The few ruffians he usually cavorted with left for more fertile ground. He would have left as well, but Marcia stood her ground. The house was theirs, free and clear, and she intended to make a go of it, despite many who wanted Joshua gone. It was difficult being the wife of the most hated man in town. Late one night, they woke to the sound of a single gunshot. Jupiter was found dead in his stall.

While his income declined, Joshua and Marcia both worked odd jobs when they could find them. She sang in the church choir, but listening to the top tunes on the radio was her favorite source of music. *Red Sails In The Sunset* was her favorite. Joshua could hear her softly singing to herself as she moved about the house each day. Their first child was born in 1930, a son that lived only two weeks. It was the first time she had ever seen him weep. Five years later, when Marcia was thirty-five, a daughter was born who grew up knowing only empty streets, a father with a weakness that controlled him, and a mother who taught her daughter to sing as soon as she was old enough to talk. Marcia took her last breath at age forty-five.

The daughter's name was Emma. She was ten years old when her mother died in 1945.

Emma's vague childhood memories included hearing her mother complain of not feeling well. Her occasional remarks of discomfort to Joshua were so subtle; he didn't find much significance in it. She was too much of a proper lady to give him a graphic description of the changes she felt. It was the first time he had neglected her. In contrast to Joshua's lack of companions, Marcia still had plenty of influential lady friends who lived in Kisatchie. A few of the bolder ones approached Joshua and tried to tell him that Marcia's illness could not be ignored, but to no avail. He did not see the urgency. Two months later, she convinced him to take her to a doctor. His life was in an emotional freefall as they left the small clinic. How long did the doctor say she had left? Only a few months?

Marcia died in one of five beds in the small Kisatchie clinic. Joshua would not allow any of the clinic staff near her body. Scooping her withered, lifeless figure up in his arms, he walked down the hallway past astonished onlookers and out to his pickup truck in the parking lot. A small homemade oak casket lined with material from her wedding dress lay in the truck bed. Placing her in it, he tearfully and carefully proceeded to adorn her with every piece of jewelry he had ever bought for her. He moved slowly to position each appendage of her body as though not to inflict pain on the dead. Several rings were placed on every finger. Strings of pearls and gold necklaces were wrapped one by one around her neck. He clipped ten jeweled pins and brooches on the front of her dress. In her right hand, he placed the Bible given to her by her grandfather. All the while, he mumbled softly to his dead wife. No one could hear the words, but from his expression and the way his lips moved, it was as though he expected her to answer. Someone later said they thought they could make out the words, 'I'm sorry.' A man in the crowd tried to approach him compassionately, whereupon Joshua jerked a pistol from inside his shirt and fired it into the air, screaming obscenities. He then loudly nailed the coffin lid shut, once more oblivious to the throng of people gathered around.

Marcia's favorite spot had been on a small, wooded hill overlooking Little River, just outside of Pittman. The name of it was Oak Point. The drive there took twenty minutes. Knowing the end was coming, Joshua had prepared a secret grave site in advance with the intent that no one was to know where her final resting place would be. She was his alone in life and would be forever his in death. With Marcia in the ground and the grave closed, he went home to his young daughter and a bottle of whiskey he had been saving.

Many tales were told about ghost towns in the old days, but few people have ever really seen them. Pittman was a checkerboard of streets and vacant lots. When the houses were eliminated, nothing remained, not even an outline of any house except for the pattern left on the grass. Most yards had Saint Augustine grass that would spread quickly across a bare surface, obscuring flowerbeds, sidewalks, and anything that could be clues to the past. A few houses once had brick foundations around their perimeter. For most of these, only a pile of bricks remained. Seedling trees germinated voluntarily, helping to swallow up history.

Occasionally, souvenir hunters would pass through. Stooping beneath his dignity, but out of necessity, Joshua had established himself as the self-appointed guide for treasure hunters, making sure not to show them all the potential dig sites on the first visit. And he still had enough of his old coercive ways to convince outsiders that the heavier the tip, the better the tour. Their favorite spot was the site where the drugstore once stood. A wealth of old fashion medicine bottles of various colors and shapes lay in wait less than an inch below the surface. Someone once discovered an old mortar and pestle by the fence line at the back of the property. It brought a nice price at auction. The town dump held countless treasures if one's curiosity was strong enough and if one knew where it was. Joshua knew. Over the years, however, discarded artifacts of a past era gradually became so scarce that interest dwindled, and so did the slow trickle of cash that came with it.

Across the hard-packed dirt road in front of Joshua's house, the tracks of the rusted railroad spur were visible through the tall weeds and blackberry bushes that grew up from the gravel rail bed. What had been a straight linear ribbon of open space, cleared by men for their steam-powered machines, was being slowly reclaimed by nature as though plant life had acquired a love for steel, creosote, and aging wood.

Six tall ancient red oak trees formed a rough circle around the house, two in front and four in back, their limbs coalescing into a canopy of shade in the summer and a naked barrenness in the winter. Time was when there were seven such trees in the yard. A stiff wind had uprooted one and sent its massive branches plunging through the side of the house just below the peak of the roof. The damaged part now looked like a quilt; a patchwork of shingles, corrugated tin, and scraps of lumber held over the splintered hole in random disarray by countless nails. Somehow the effort kept the rain out, but the wind still whistled through the cracks and ill-fitted gaps. Far from a masterful repair job, it satisfied Joshua. With time, the weathered wood and rust were beginning to match the rest of the house, both inside and out.

Chapter 2

There is a point in the darkness, just before dawn, that the stirrings of a new day start not on the horizon but in the subconscious visceral depths of those who will rise to meet it. As with every summer morning of her young life, Emma Parker rose and felt the heavy, clammy night air that held the silent promise of another muggy August day in Louisiana. She and her father used two corner bedrooms in hopes of a cross breeze at night. Joshua insisted that Emma lock all the doors when the sunset. Occasionally, he even locked his bedroom door, a habit from the old days when he knew he had an abundance of enemies. Real or imagined, they were still out there. Years before, in the yard outside his bedroom window, he had begun a collection of empty paint cans, scrap metal, tractor parts, and anything else that would prevent someone from silently approaching the window at night.

Emma pulled the cord on the naked light bulb hanging from the ceiling of her bedroom. The low wattage gave a dim, shadowy look to the room that swayed and danced as it swung a few inches back and forth. She sat back down on her bed and rubbed her eyes, feeling perspiration trickle down her face to the corner of her mouth. The skin of her long legs seemed stuck to the sheets. Her wheat-colored hair was long, stringy, and hung across part of her face. Draped over a wooden chair next to the bed was a faded sleeveless cotton dress, drying from the hand washing she had given it the evening before. The fabric was a cheap grade but durable. Weeks before, the dress had been a cloth sack of chicken feed in Rucker's store where she worked. With what she was learning from Lavenia Carter, she had become very resourceful with the aging foot pedal-operated sewing machine that once was her mother's. Lately, more and more of the feed sacks were paper, and her source of fabric was becoming scarce. In one motion, she slipped the dress over her head and walked barefoot in the dim light toward Joshua's bedroom.

She remembers enough of her mother to know what it's like to be a half-orphan. When Joshua's mood turns dark, she knows the feeling of being a full orphan.

Her morning ritual began with emptying her father's chamber pot if the bedroom door was not locked. The leaning, rotting privy in the backyard was not convenient for him at night, especially after a day of heavy drinking, which was most days. This morning, she had access to his room. She quietly entered and tiptoed toward the bed, thankful that he had remembered to put the lid back on after using it during the night. She recalled, as a matter of routine, that several boards on the back porch were loose, but she knew where they were and avoided them, gingerly stepping as though treading on slippery rocks in a stream. At the steps leading down, she stayed near the edge of the framing where the support was the strongest. The yard was devoid of any grass. Grass had to be mowed, and she kept it carefully plucked out. The path to the privy was paved by a line of wide rough-cut lumber, placed end to end, an absolute necessity when the yard was nothing but mud after a rain. Experience had taught her the wisdom of not returning the pot to his room immediately because he would use it and fall back to sleep. The walk to the outhouse helped him wake up and take inventory of his whereabouts, a fact she had learned from her mother.

Her next task was to light the gas oven, which was always a challenge. The pilot light hadn't worked for years, and she had to lie on the floor to see where to aim the lit match. Sometimes, the ignition would delay for some unknown reason, followed by a whoosh of flame. Years before, it had been her mother's pride among other kitchen appliances, most of which now fell into disrepair and wound up in the front yard. They rested where Emma used to play house with them as a child. Shortly thereafter, a wringer washing machine in need of a new motor joined the junk pile. In 1951, however, the stove remained, adorned with an assortment of spare parts from her father's attempts at repair.

Just as the sun began to pierce the morning, Joshua stumbled out of his room, his eyes hiding behind the grey hair hanging down on his face.

His voice was husky like oatmeal, full of phlegm, "Coffee —"

"Go ahead, Papa. It'll be poured when you get back."

She glanced out the back door to make sure he was headed in the right direction. Not seeing him immediately, she started toward the door but stopped when she heard Joshua utter a quiet belch from the other end of the porch. A soft trickling sound on the sandy soil told her this morning he had chosen a spot more convenient than the privy. Emma was used to it. He returned in less than a minute and sat at the kitchen table, staring across the room and rubbing the stubble on his chin. His hands shook as he tipped the cup and dribbled a small amount of coffee into the saucer.

"Here, Papa. Let me do it for you."

Steadily, Emma poured a few spoonfuls of the strong brown liquid into the saucer and helped Joshua hold it steady as he raised it to his mouth. Pursing his lips, he carefully gave it a long, slow puff of air to cool it, then took it down with a loud, prolonged slurp. She dispensed another small measure into the saucer and repeated the process. She had learned not to engage in much conversation with her father first thing in the morning.

"Okay, can you handle it from here?"

He nodded and looked toward the stove.

"Don't worry, biscuits are coming. Papa, we're almost out of some things in the kitchen. I made a list. Kin, you go by the store and talk to Mr. Rucker?"

Again, he nodded silently.

After about thirty minutes, Joshua's senses were beginning to focus.

Emma sat down across the table from him, "Don't forget, you said you'd do some work at the school," she looked at him intently, "You remember me tellin' you about Mr. MacArthur, don't you? Mr. MacArthur, the principal, remember? He says he wants to get the school building cleaned up for the beginning of classes. That's just a couple of weeks from now, Papa. I told him you needed work, and then I told you what he had said. You didn't show up there yesterday, and if you don't go in today, he'll find somebody else."

"Oh - yeah. I didn't feel good yesterday," his words ended in a weak cough.

"I know, Papa. But the light bill is due, and I can't make enough at the store for both of us. Groceries ain't cheap, and Mr. Rucker isn't going to give us credit any longer."

"I said I'd go."

"Okay. Papa, when you got to the store —"

Joshua sat up a little straighter in his chair, but his voice was still raspy, "I don't know why his daddy gave the store to him. Whinnin' little turd! Makes me think of a sick, skinny dog, like he has worms in him or something. His daddy always gives me credit! I could count on his daddy in the old days. Who does that little shit think he is? I'd just as soon hook him in the jaw as to look at him."

Emma stood next to her father's chair with her hand on his shoulder, "Yes, Papa. Everyone gives you credit back in them days, but things ain't the same now. No one wants to talk about credit, 'cept on big things like cars and houses. Papa, you just gotta go to work today. I'll be back in school soon, and I won't be able to do as much, so you gotta go. Okay?"

She had long since known how to melt her papa's heart, but only when he was sober. And when he was drunk, she had learned to filter out the words that came from an inebriated brain. But there was a tiny thread of truth in much of what he said, and Emma knew what to listen for, much like her mother had. She hugged his neck as she spoke to him. His whiskers were long enough to be beyond the prickly stage and felt soft against her arms.

"Ain't you had enough school yet?" he said through his daughter's embrace.

"No, I gotta' finish."

"So, finish. Then what? I never did," he looked down at his cup and swirled the coffee before taking another sip.

"I can get a better job. I can't spend the rest of my life sweepin' floors at Mr. Rucker's store," She nodded at the sound of her own words.

He squinted his eyes at her, "How old are you now?"

"Sixteen, Papa. I'm sixteen. My birthday was three months ago."

Joshua wasn't listening. He took a bite of biscuit and began talking as he chewed. Crumbs fell from his mouth onto his lap, "Aw hell," he said with a mouthful, "You'll just get married like all the other girls. Stop worrying about a damn job."

Emma stepped around the chair and looked closely at him, "You seen any fellas comin' around here lately?" She thought before she continued, "Papa, when are we goin' to do something about this house? There's things that need fixin'."

Joshua stopped eating and stared at her, "What's wrong with it?" He followed Emma with his eyes as she sat down across from him. "Your mama was proud of this house. It's ours, free and clear. I know every board, every nail, every inch of this house. I watched 'em build it and made 'em do it right. The framin' is all cypress. It'll last forever. Your mama drew pictures of the rooms and the roof and the porches and—"

"That's not what I'm talkin' about."

Joshua sat up straighter and his voice suddenly had a twinge of clarity. He had a faraway look in his eyes, "We had the well dug, so it would come up right there by the kitchen sink," his words suddenly became focused, "Them sonsabitches was gonna' to put it clean out there on the back porch where your mama would have to walk all the way out yonder for water and carry it back, but I made 'em tear down what they done and start over," he got up and walked toward the window. Staring out, he said, "Your mama really loved this house. She loved every inch of it," his gaze was fixed on a memory off in the distance, "But hell, I'm just no good at fixin' things anymore," he had never been, only at making others do it for him.

He peered through the screen at the side yard where Marcia's flowers used to grow. Once, Joshua had erected a low picket fence around her vegetable garden. Hardly any of it stood now. A few of the smooth round rocks she had used for borders around her flower beds were still visible through the weeds, but the rain and the years had erased the whitewash that he once painted on them. In all the things Marcia undertook as a wife and mother, there was a labor of love, affection and vision. She never did anything halfway. She had been the heart and soul of the family before she became ill. All Joshua saw now was a jumble of thickets and brambles, as though nature was trying to hide the pain of remembering.

Emma stepped up beside her father and saw the far-off fixed stare in his eyes, one she had seen often before. She slipped her hand into the crook of his arm and gave it a squeeze.

He offered a weak grin and started a chuckle, which quickly became a horrendous gagging cough. A thin trickle of blood showed at the corner of his mouth.

"Papa, you're bleedin' again," she tried to look closer, but he had wiped his mouth on his sleeve and turned away.

"I'm fine. I better get goin'," his graveling voice trailed off. He started for the door but changed his direction suddenly and headed for his bedroom. He reappeared moments later, still swallowing and wiping his mouth with the back of his hand. He glanced at Emma and hesitated. "Just a little to get me started," he said.

Shoe leather was Joshua's sole means of transportation. The family vehicle was the same truck he owned when Marcia died. It had found its own grave in the far corner of the yard where he left it three years ago, the day it refused to start.

As Joshua stepped onto the front porch, Emma yelled from the kitchen, "See if Oscar will give you a ride."

He quietly mumbled to himself, "I don't need no favors from nobody."

Oscar Carter had worked for Joshua at the mill years before. He and his wife Lavenia now had six children and were the only other family left in Pittman. Oscar was younger than Joshua and eventually found a job with the Missouri Pacific railroad when the mills finally shut down completely. He had proven himself to be a very capable member of any work crew, and shift leaders would manipulate their schedules to have him on their crew. He learned quickly, and his sawmill knowledge of mechanical devices served him well. Folks quietly counted on Oscar in emergencies, like the time a ninety-car freight train derailed just outside of Alexandria. Oscar had privately told his young foreman exactly where to place the cranes that would lift the damaged cars off the tracks and precisely what signs of track damage to look for. Because of his quiet discretion in times like that, many folks owed Oscar a multitude of favors. Unassuming, he never kept score. Regardless, he remained as a simple laborer on the payroll - he and the other colored folks. Maybe he was just happy with what he was, but he never spoke of it. That was all behind him now. He had invested just enough continual employment to qualify for a railroad pension.

Emma walked to the front of the house and stepped onto the porch. She called out, "Hey, Papa, Mr. MacArthur said he'd feed you lunch if you came in today, okay?"

He waved an acknowledgment without looking back. There was small change in his pocket. He had never told Emma about his meager retirement income from the sawmill. She never thought to ask. To him, it was drinkin' money.

She watched her father slowly shuffling along the shoulder of the road toward town, his body swaying a few degrees to each side and his feet kicking up dry dust beside the crumbling pavement. The early morning sun had already begun its punishing glare. Running her fingers through her hair, she watched until he was out of sight and then went back inside. As the woman of the house for the last six years, she had a morning routine that seemed to work. First, find Papa's dirty clothes and put them in a tub of soapy water to soak on the back porch. Second, straighten up the house as much as possible, which included her father's bedroom. Third, mop the kitchen if it needs it. Usually, it did. By then, the clothes were ready for a hard scrub on the rub board. They would be dry on the line when she came home that evening.

The last thing she did each morning was talk and sing to Marcia. Over the years, Emma had forged a maze of lumber-lined walkways through the woods that lay between the house and the mill. Closure of the mill had made this part easy. Rejected pieces of rough-cut lumber were left behind in huge piles. Some were culled out because of being miscut, others warped in the curing process. They became her sidewalk upon which she knew each fork and turn of this tree-canopy world and managed to travel every inch of it at least once each week. Blended seamlessly with the spirits of woodland plants and animals, both living and dead, her world of thoughts and imagination floated and undulated unbridled by concerns of the rational world and carried her to havens of abundance, of harmony, love, and contentment beyond words. Alone here, she could see, touch, smell, and remember. Marcia's face was a vague image from a dream, but her words were in the trees, in the wildflowers that would bend toward the sunlight, in stories Marcia had told during their long walks under the pines and oaks. When Emma wasn't singing *Red Sails In The Sunset,* she found herself repeating the conversations out loud from memory, interjecting what she knew her mother would have said. The visits usually lasted almost an hour.

Emma had an unwritten agreement with Mr. Thomas Rucker in Kisatchie. She would work in his store at whatever hours she had available, and he would pay her thirty cents an hour in merchandise or sometimes in cash. The store was first built by Mr. Rucker's grandfather, Isaiah Rucker, around the year 1890. It was passed on to the son, who welcomed the opportunity during the depression, and later to the grandson, Thomas, who took it reluctantly. He was middle aged, thinly built, and carried a worrisome attitude about everything he encountered. He had worked with his father in the store all his life. His goal had been to escape from Kisatchie, but family pressures came to be more than he could resist. As the owner of the store for the past eight years, it had become a millstone around his neck, leaving him imprisoned with a bitter outlook on life that touched everyone around him. Emma appeared one day at the age of eleven, not long after Marcia died, wandering through the store barefoot and dirty-faced. After a moment, Tom Rucker's wife, Flora, realized who she was and that she was alone. Her eyes were scanning the rows of cans, reading labels as if to memorize every detail. Flora watched her wander about the store for almost an hour, whereupon she finally came to the register with a candy bar and one potato. She spread a small fistful of pennies on the counter and mumbled something about fixing supper for her father. Before taking her money, Flora asked what else she was fixing. Getting no answer, she led Emma to a shelf of canned goods that could be easily heated in a pot. Emma's visits to the store became more frequent, and her choice of food items broadened. She didn't come in every day, leaving Flora to wonder what she did eat each day. About a year later, Flora asked her if she wanted to make some pocket change doing odd jobs around the store and running errands, much to Tom's disapproval. From that point on, Emma came to depend more and more on her job for the bare essentials, while Joshua's drinking increased, and his reliability diminished.

With her morning routine at home finished Emma started walking north on the road in front of her house, which made a slow, gradual turn to the right and headed east, past Oscar's house and on toward Kisatchie. Before the turn, there was a cross street that went past the old mill on the right and all the mill's machine shops on the left. The paved, cracked surface of the cross street ended just beyond the mill, and wagons and trucks from decades before had worn a path of wheel ruts that continued into the woods. The ruts were now barely discernible through the years of undergrowth. This had become Emma's shortcut. It took her through the abandoned mill yard to a narrow, wooded trail that eventually came out only a block from Rucker's store. She never saw anyone nor evidence of anyone along this route, and as a small girl she began to think it was her own private wilderness. By most definitions of ownership, it was hers. Along the way, she would pass the mill pond and imagine what her mother used to tell her about the oxen and mule teams and then later, trucks that would haul huge loads of logs to the edge of the pond. 'The ground would shake beneath your feet,' she would say when the chains and binders were loosened from the wagons, bringing tons of tree trunks crashing down and rolling toward the water. She remembered hearing her father talk about times when carelessness would result in the pond being totally choked with logs. Private woodcutters, sometimes paid by the competing mills, would create a diversion, then pop loose the binders when no one was looking. The mill pond was big enough for the workmen to move the logs around with long poles, guiding them onto the waiting conveyer that pulled them into the mill and the whining saw blades. But too many logs in the water prevented them from floating freely, and all progress would stop. Unjamming the logs was dangerous business for those who had to venture out onto the entanglement. One wrong move and the jam would shift, sending men into the water where they risked drowning or being crushed between massive logs. Some had died. No longer just a simple muddy body of water with trampled shoreline, the pond was now a piece of natural artwork. Long grasses obscured much of the water's edge, and islands of lily pads floated across the surface. Years before, ducks had made it their refuge during cooler weather on their flights south.

A stretch of Emma's path followed a small creek that emptied into the pond. The small spring-fed trickle of water had been dammed up almost a century before, interrupting its normal journey to Bayou Boeff, which was five miles away in deep woods. Bayou

Boeff made a slow, lazy journey to drain into Little River in the next Parish. The weight of hundreds of trucks had compressed the dam into a structure that would never erode or fail with age. The springs had almost dried up over the years, which meant rainwater could only replace what water evaporated from the pond. During heavy rains, though, when the trickle swelled and the pond filled to its limit, the overflow would find the original creek bed downstream and renew its marriage to the bayou and the river.

But there was no rain today. It hadn't rained for two weeks, and the hot sun made heat waves on the road, even at this early hour of the morning. Most of Emma's shortcut was in the shade, however. In fact, the woods were delightfully cool in the early morning. When she was younger, there always seemed to be time to stop and explore along the creek. The woods were full of shapes and colors, secret hiding places, small clearings, and countless other magic things to stir a child's imagination. In her woods, Emma found that she could sing and yell at the top of her lungs, and no one would hear her. Being alone never alarmed her or conjured up visions of danger. The woods, the vacant house lots, and the empty buildings around the mill were all hers. Single-handedly, she ruled over the biggest kingdom in Grant Parish. But that was then.

Now, her daily journey to Rucker's store was more than just following an attraction. Her mother was gone, her aging father had lost his spirit, and she felt responsibility shifting more and more onto her shoulders. Even when school was in session, she would go to Rucker's in the early morning hours and make herself busy for several minutes by sweeping the floor or wiping off shelves. If nothing else, it kept her in line for future employment when school was out for the summer. It also gave her the rare chance to see Flora.

Emma came into the store through the back door, as always. She stopped in the storage room to grab an apron and walked toward the front, tying the strings behind her. Over the years, the old store had taken on the smell of old leather and molasses.

"Morning, Mr. Rucker," she called out.

From behind a row of shelves, a man's voice answered, "Emma? That you? C'mere a minute."

She followed the voice to the other side of the small store and found Tom trying to clean up something on the floor. Next to him was part of a ten-pound bag of sugar lying on its side, the bottom seam split open. Most of the contents were around his feet.

"Emma, don't just stand there! Go get another broom and help me clean this up before customers start coming in!"

As he spoke, the bell tied to the front door let out a loud jingle as several men entered, their voices filling the place with robust laughter and conversation. Emma could feel the old floor tremble faintly from the heavy stride of the men's work boots.

"You go ahead," she said, "I'll take care of this."

She heard the men greet Mr. Rucker with gusty tones. She recognized the voice of Jack Spears, a man close to her father's age whom Joshua spoke of with lethal hatred. Spears had been the strong arm of the Bushnell mill, which put Joshua and him on a collision course many times. Before Emma's mother died, there had been a flurry of rumors flying around town about Jack Spears. Emma was too young to understand why her papa was so mad over something Jack had said about Marcia. What she did understand and vividly remembered was the image of her father in a fistfight with Jack that was serious enough to require help from the mill doctor for both men. Joshua had left his supper uneaten that evening and gone to Jack's house, where he screamed obscenities from the middle of the road in front of the house. Emma and her mother had followed at a safe distance. Jack answered the challenge, and the two of them dove into each other like two hungry dogs fighting over a scrap of meat. The sheriff, who was seventy-five years old, arrived alone and decided his role should be crowd control rather than trying to separate the two combatants. When it was over, everyone went home undecided about who won. From that time on, the two men never crossed paths, and Jack Spears never uttered Marcia's name again in public.

Emma was frantically sweeping the spilled sugar as fast as her arms would move, trying to finish so she could disappear into the back room. Squatting down carelessly with her knees touching her chin, the hem of her dress had pulled up while she worked feverishly. She glanced up to see a strange young man at the far end of the aisle, kneeling with his eyes just inches off the floor, looking at her indiscretion and grinning. She then turned and gasped when she saw a pair of boots encased in dried mud only inches behind her.

A familiar voice spoke before she could look up.

"Girl, look at the mess you made."

The face standing over her came into focus, and it was not Jack Spears but his son, Woodrow, who was close to Emma's age. The other fellow from the end of the aisle strolled over and said, "Ain't that like you, Woodrow. You are never in the right place at the right time. Who cares about the mess? You shoulda' seen the squirrel shot I had from back there!"

Both of them laughed. She stood and took several steps back, clutching the broom in her hand. Woodrow was wearing greasy jeans and a sweat-stained cotton shirt. From the looks of his hands and face, he hadn't bathed in a week. Nor had he seen the inside of a barber shop in a while. His companion had a large wad of chewing tobacco wallowing in his mouth.

"You want some help?" The young stranger asked.

"I don't need no help. Thanks."

"I need some of these," Woodrow mumbled through a half-grin, grabbing several boxes of Cracker Jacks but never taking his eyes off her. As he stepped forward, his boots slid across Emma's neat pile of spilled sugar, scattering it. Pretending to look for more merchandise, he made several more sliding steps through the spillage, his boot soles sounding like sandpaper on the sugar-coated floor. When he seemed to be finished browsing, he winked at his friend and looked at Emma, who stood motionless nearby. Her heart was beating faster.

"You got any eggs?"

She simply pointed to a cooler box in the corner. Woodrow walked to the cooler door, opened it, and grabbed one egg. Walking back to her with a slight swagger, he pursed his lips and asked with a smirk, "Gal, you know anything about eggs? Huh? Now tell me, is this a hen egg or a rooster egg?"

Each time Woodrow came into the store, he always went out of his way to tease and taunt Emma. She had been able to ignore him the past few times, but he seemed more persistent today. She tried to brush him off and go back to her cleaning.

Woodrow's friend chimed in with a clown-like expression. He stepped closer to her, "What's the matter? Hey Woody! She don't know the difference!"

Both boys looked at each other and laughed with gaping mouths. Woodrow took a small step toward Emma, putting her between the two of them, "I'll show you a way how I kin tell," he said in a low, breathy tone. She saw a grimy fingernail rub across the end of the egg and quickly puncture a hole in the shell. Slowly he brought it to his mouth, tipped his head back, and sucked out the contents with a loud slurp. When he lowered his head, his lips parted, and some of the raw egg ran from one corner of his mouth, dribbling over the stubble on his chin.

"Don't taste like no rooster egg to me," he said in a sultry tone, "I'll bet you knew that, didn't you? I'll bet you know a lot more'n you let on."

"Did it taste like someone you knew?" his friend asked.

They both laughed again.

Emma shook her head in disgust and resumed her sweeping, "Woodrow, you are crazy, you know that?" Said Emma, "You plum crazy." She tried to step away, but suddenly, "Rooster egg, who ever heard of—"

Woodrow interrupted, "Wonder what you taste like?"

He moved closer toward her, beckoning with a subtle motion of his fingers. His grin widened, and his eyes seemed to dance. The other boy stood behind him, watching the drama develop.

Emma backed up until her shoulders bumped into the shelves. She felt her heart start to pound but planted her feet and didn't budge. When Woodrow was less than arm's length away, he smacked his lips softly, reached out, and touched her arm. His eyes were half-closed. In a flash, the end of her broom handle pounded the arch of his foot. He silently winced and hopped a few steps on the other foot, chuckling.

"I bet you like to play rough, don't you? You even smell better when you're mad."

"Woody, I don't think she likes you."

It was all a game to them. It wasn't the first time, and they never seemed to tire of it. She quickly walked around to the other side of the store, where Mr. Rucker was still talking to the group of men.

Jack Spears cut his eyes toward Emma and chose to ignore her. Woodrow came around the end of the aisle, limping slightly.

"You git what you come for?" Jack asked his son impatiently.

"Naw, but close enough," he said with a toothy grin. Reaching into his pocket, he grabbed some change and tossed it on the counter without bothering to count it.

Emma stood beside Mr. Rucker as the group walked out. Woodrow continued to talk to his friend with one arm draped over his shoulder. They hesitated at the door and glanced back at Emma. Woodrow whispered something to his buddy, and they laughed.

Tom asked, "Emma, is everything okay? What'd you say to those customers?"

"Everything is fine, Mr. Rucker. It's just a little game they play with me sometimes."

"Game? That isn't what I asked."

Apologetically, she said, "No, sir. I didn't say nothing to 'em."

She retrieved her broom and finished her cleaning task.

Later that morning, Alton MacArthur, the school principal, came in. He was a tall man, well over six feet, with lean, sinewy features. His hands were huge. A balding man in his late fifties, he was known to be very soft-spoken and gentle. He had moved to Kisatchie from Mississippi about ten years before after accepting a teaching job there. Soon thereafter, the principal of Kisatchie High School retired, and Alton was awarded the job. His reputation had preceded him as older men in the community sometimes told stories they had heard about him as a younger man with a long temper, but one who backed down from no one. Rumor had it that he had left Mississippi because of an altercation with an unreasonable father who thought his son was entitled to special treatment when caught cheating on a test. The details of the rumor seemed to change over time. Whether true or not, the legend and his physical size made powerful weapons to maintain discipline in the school.

Occasionally, students would witness a hint of his past. Last year, several boys had been caught in the act of some minor Halloween vandalism at the school. In deciding their punishment, he determined it was time to begin removing an old stone foundation in the far corner of the schoolyard. The concrete fragments were too large to handle, but a small gang of rough and tumble-high school boys armed with sledgehammers might make it more manageable. As he walked them toward the huge pile of rubble, there was obvious disbelief on their faces. Alton MacArthur was a great organizer and began dividing the boys into smaller work groups. When their response was not as rapid as he had expected, he simply showed where he wanted each group to work, using one of the sledgehammers like a four-foot pointer, gripping it with one hand by the end of the handle, and indicating what was expected. He made his point, and the reaction was immediate. He quietly asked if anyone had any questions, then turned to leave. For one hour each day that week, the boys worked on the rock pile in lieu of their gym class and the rubble was hauled away the following week.

He had the respect of the entire student body and the town, who affectionately referred to him as 'Mr. Mac.'

In the store, Mr. Mac was rummaging through a box of screws and washers. Emma normally didn't wait on customers, but this was someone special.

"Can I help you find something?"

"Oh—hi there, Emma. Good to see you."

She broke into an immediate, intractable smile that seemed to split her face. Her world always glowed brightly when Mr. Mac was around.

"Maybe you could help me," he continued, "I'm looking for faucet washers. Every fixture in the schoolhouse is leaking. By the way, this is what I've got your pa working on today. He's a good man with a wrench."

"Mr. Mac—"

"Yeah?"

"What, uh, what time did he git there?"

"Oh, he was right on time today. You know Emma, it's nice of you to worry about your pa all the time. Don't think for one minute that such responsibility goes unnoticed."

"Yes, sir. Thanks."

He returned to his box of washers and fumbled through the pile for several seconds while Emma stood by silently. Hard of hearing, he hadn't realized she was still standing there, watching him closely. A few seconds later, he gave her a slightly startled look, thinking she had gone.

"I'm sorry, Mr. Mac. Did you find what you wanted?"

"Oh, well, no. Not exactly. These are the wrong size."

"Look up yonder on the top shelf. In the corner. I think there's some bigger sizes there."

He peered upward with a curious tilt to his head. "Damn bifocals," he muttered, trying to adjust his glasses.

"Here, lemme' git 'em for you, Mr. Mac." Emma was already pushing over a wooden step ladder. Alton was trapped between

Emma and the corner shelves as she climbed quickly. In her eagerness, leaning sideways and reaching upwards, she was oblivious to the fact that her dress was in the man's face, dislodging his glasses from the bridge of his nose. Emma was well beyond her adolescent years, and it was impossible to ignore the bulges and curves of her body in such close quarters. Without looking down, she quickly started handing boxes down to him.

"Try these, Mr. Mac."

Politely, he had endured the event like a gentleman and said nothing.

"Yes, this is what I need, these right here."

"Let me have the box. We'll count 'em out at the counter."

"That's okay, I can—"

Emma was down off the ladder and had already snatched the box from his hands and headed for the register. Tom Rucker was standing at the end of the aisle, watching the scene and shaking his head.

"Mr. Rucker," she announced, "Mr. Mac needs some of these. I'll bag 'em up for you," Alton was just arriving at the register.

"Will that be all Mr. Mac?" Mr. Rucker asked.

Rubbing his chin and looking first at Emma, then at Tom, he said, "Emma, you count out about four dozen of these, and I'll look for some other things."

Emma ducked her head with a blush. Tom gave her a stern look and walked to the far end of the store with his customer.

Alton MacArthur had known Emma since she was in the second grade. She had idolized him from the first day of school. He learned quickly that she was one of those kids who refused to be ignored by those she cherished. The year she started high school, she had been selected to compete in a regional art contest in Alexandria, which she won. In front of the whole student body, she received her award from her beloved principal. She drank in every word of congratulations he uttered that day. He waited a few days and called her to his office, telling her that she had been a model student and was possibly college material and if not, she certainly should look for some reputable school of art. If she desired, he would help her look for a scholarship and grant money. She had thanked him but secretly saw no way she could leave.

"Alton, I'm sorry if she got in the way," Tom was offering quietly, "I keep thinking it was a mistake to hire her, but she keeps coming back, and my wife has this tender spot, you know."

"Think nothing of it. Honestly, I admire the girl very much. She's really the only responsible figure in her house. Whatever her dad was before, he's —"

"I know all about Joshua Parker," Tom blurted out. My family's been in this town for almost a hundred years, and we've seen it all."

"Have you seen Joshua lately?"

"No, but I hear he's still mean as ever."

"Actually, he's working at the schoolhouse right now, doing some plumbing work for the school board. He doesn't look too mean to me."

"Maybe so. Well, maybe he'll pay on some of his bills then. You know, my daddy gave him a line of credit years ago when he was working for the mill, and it hasn't been paid off since then. I hear he stays drunk most of the time."

The two men walked back to the register after Mr. Mac had picked up a few other items. The washers were neatly stacked on the counter. Emma was nowhere in sight.

"Let me count those for you."

"I'm sure Emma knows how to count, Tom. How is she doing, by the way? You know, working and so forth?"

Tom Rucker spoke while looking at the floor, his arms folded, "Well, she shows up every day."

"So, you feel good about having her here."

In a whisper, he said, "Well, yeah, I suppose. But, you know, it does look like she could…"

"What's that?" Mr. Mac reached for the volume control on his hearing aid.

Tom spoke a little louder, "I was saying she could try to look different or something. I mean, she wears the same dress practically every day, and you see how dirty it is. I just hate to have the customers see her."

"Have you said anything to her?"

Tom actually blushed, "No, I don't know how to bring up stuff like that."

"And yet, you keep her around."

Tom glared at the ceiling, "*Flora* keeps her around!"

"So, where's Flora?"

"At home!"

"Doing what? Something Emma could be helping with?"

"In my house? That girl?"

"Well, your wife likes her, and she'd be supervised, wouldn't she?"

"I guess so, most of the time."

Mr. Mac's mouth turned up ever so slightly at the corners as a small twinkle came in his eyes. Heading for the door, he spoke over his shoulder, "Thanks for the hardware, Tom. Just put 'em on the school bill."

He was barely out of the door when he heard Tom Rucker's high-pitched voice from inside.

"Emma, c'mere for a minute! I got an idea."

Chapter 3

Emma had carried two large cans of trash to the old stone incinerator behind the store. No one remembered which generation of Ruckers built it, but the mortar holding it together was still as solid as Gibraltar. About once a month, Emma would shovel the ash into a cut-down oil drum in the back of the Rucker's Chevy pick-up truck. Then she and Tom would drive to a dumping spot in the woods off the main road with Emma riding in the back. He would stop back up, and Emma would struggle to push the barrel off so it would flip itself over as it hit the ground. Sometimes, it would land right-side up, and she would have to lift one edge and heave it over to empty it. This usually required Tom's help, which he never gave without a long string of verbal reprimands. He usually just sat in the cab of the truck. Today, the incinerator was almost full.

She was just returning to the back door when she heard Tom call her. Wiping her hands off on her dress, she entered the store and hurried toward the front.

"Yessir?"

"Emma, I want you to go over to my house for the rest of the day. Mrs. Rucker has some things she wants you to do."

"Yessir, okay … things like whut?"

"I really don't know. She'll tell you."

"Well, I'll just finish up the …"

"Don't argue with me, girl! Git on over there … she's waiting on you right now!" He made a subtle sweeping motion with his hands, urging her toward the door.

Silently, she took a step backward and turned toward the back door. The thought of seeing Flora again after so many months and spending the whole day with her made Emma's spirits soar. The house was just a few blocks away. She walked fast for the first few seconds, then broke into a dead run with a broad grin on her face.

As soon as Emma was out of sight, Tom reached for the phone. Flora answered after three rings.

"Hello …"

"Hi. It's me. Listen, I've got to ask you something."

"What's that, dear?"

"Could you use some help around the house, you know, like today?"

"Well, I don't know, I suppose there's some …"

"Listen, I'm sending Emma over there, and she's …"

"You're what?"

"I said I'm sending Emma to help you around the house."

"What brought this on? When did you decide I needed help?"

"It's just that Emma needs something different to do, and I know you always spoke kindly of her, so maybe she could …" His voice trailed off.

"Tom, I asked you to hire that girl because she needed the money."

"I know, I know. And she's been here for a long time, hasn't she? But Flora, honey, she's getting older now. There's lots of people coming in the store every day, and they're starting to notice her and … you know, I think she needs some talkin' to."

"Talkin' to? Like what?"

He looked around the empty store before answering. He could picture his wife holding the phone with one hand and the other on her hip, "I don't know what else to call it. She's getting to be a young woman now and, you know, stuff like that."

"Now, Tom, wait a minute. Slow down. What are you trying to say?"

"When was the last time you saw her? Well, when you see her, you'll know what I mean."

"I admit, it has been a while."

Tom waved his hand and continued, "And you know, there's this thing with men."

"What thing?"

"Uh, I'm not sure she knows what to do with them."

"What do you mean, DO with them?" Flora stammered.

"Wait a minute, I didn't mean that the way it sounded. See, there was a bunch of young fellas come in here today, and now, I'm not sure about this, but I think they were teasing her. And then Mr. Mac came in, and he …"

"Mr. Alton MacArthur? What did HE do to her?" She said sarcastically.

"Oh, he didn't do anything …"

"Well, I should think not; he's the nicest man!"

"Yeah, I know. Emma thinks so, too. But listen to me. She followed him around like a puppy here in the store."

"Why?"

"Well, she just likes him, I guess. He's always nice to her and - but look, I didn't call to talk about Mr. Mac. I mean, she bends over sometimes like … and that dress she wears all the time … well, you can see right through it!"

There was a heavy silence. Tom sensed that his wife was getting the message, so he said nothing.

"What you're saying is that she needs to be told about men and their trashy thoughts."

He smiled and said with a chuckle, "Flora, you have such a direct way of putting it."

"And when I tell her about men and their inclinations, should I mention you and Alton MacArthur as well?"

Tom's face suddenly dropped. Flora could picture him as they talked, and she owned the grin now.

"Flora, you know EXACTLY what I'm talking about! Now, stop trying to make me feel uncomfortable. Men just got a cravin' that she doesn't understand, and she needs it explained to her."

"Oh. So, the next time I see Alton MacArthur, I'll ask him how his cravings are doing. Sounds like the natural thing to talk about."

"Flora, stop it! I'm asking you to help this girl in a Christian way!"

"Oh, I'm sure that's what you had in mind, Tom," she said flatly, "Okay, you say she's going to come over here for a day, and I'm going to keep her busy and talk to her about woman stuff. Is that what you want?"

Tom breathed a sigh of relief, "Yeah, That's it. And, you know, it may take more than just one day. I don't know how bright she is on things like that."

"Things like what, like sex?"

"Flora!"

"Tom Rucker, you can't even hear the word, much less speak it," *Or do anything close to it*, she thought.

"Flora, this is a party line telephone!"

"Send her over, Tom," she hung up the phone without another word.

Out of breath, Emma stood on the steps leading up to the front porch. The screen door rattled slightly on its hinges when she knocked. She could hear footsteps approaching the door. When Flora stepped out of the living room onto the porch, she was momentarily surprised to see Emma standing there.

"How did you get here so fast?" Flora said.

"Mornin' ma'am. I guess I did run part way."

"I can see that," Emma's face was streaked with perspiration and grime, "When did my husband tell you to come over?"

"Um, 'bout ten minutes ago?"

"Wha…? I just got off the phone with …" Flora realized she was almost shouting.

Emma ducked her head, "Miss Flora if this ain't a good time, I can come back later."

"No, child. Your timing is priceless. I guess Mr. Rucker didn't know how fast you could run. You sit here and cool off for a few minutes. I'll bring you some water."

"Oh, no, ma'am. I'm ready to go to work!" She seemed to be bouncing.

"SIT!"

"Yes'm."

Emma sat on the porch swing, looking at the expansive front yard of the Rucker home. Within seconds, Flora was back with a glass of water.

"Just sit for a few minutes. I'll be back."

From within the house, Emma could hear Flora talking on the phone. She was unable to make out the words, but there was definite venom in her tone.

The house had been part of the Rucker family for three generations. In the boom days of the sawmills, Tom Rucker's father and grandfather were practical men and often exchanged credit at the store for merchandise or goods of any sort. Lumber was often an accepted currency. It was plentiful, and consequently, the house grew over the years. The latest count was ten rooms, according to the town rumor. Since no other relatives seemed interested in staying in Kisatchie, the house was left to Tom and Flora, who, for thirty years of marriage, lived there using a mere fraction of the space under the roof. Several huge, towering red oak trees made a canopy of shade that covered most of the front yard. Around each tree was a wide azalea bed with bushes almost as tall as Emma. She remembered walking by the house in the springtime when all the yard was an explosion of colors clearly visible from the main road. She had always wanted to see it up close, to be in it, to touch it. It was Flora's yard, more like Flora's child, make no mistake. In spite of the heat, the sheer beauty and tranquility seemed to draw Emma off the porch to walk on the deep turf of Saint Augustine grass. It felt like a pillow under her bare feet. She sat down and leaned back on her elbows, looking at the heatwaves rising from the main road, some distance away. Large grasshoppers made a whirring sound when they flew. Beyond the edge of the yard was a stand of tall, long-leaf pine trees that seemed to whisper when even the slightest breeze sifted through their branches.

"Emma ..."

She jumped to her feet, feeling like a trespasser. With her head lowered, she walked quickly back to the porch where Flora stood waiting for her.

"Miss Flora, I'm sorry. I know you told me to stay on the porch, but everything looked so purty out there. I just had to go see. I was just ... I'm sorry."

"Emma, come sit with me in the swing."

Flora was middle-aged, slightly graying at the temples, wearing moderately priced clothes that were color-coordinated and freshly pressed. Her appearance sharply contrasted with Emma's. She sat beside the girl for a few moments, letting her thoughts settle. The soft, refreshing breezes had dwindled to nothing. The heat of the day, although not yet risen to its peak, was unmistakably climbing. As they sat, Flora began to sense a barely perceptible yet nauseating sensation in her nostrils. The more still the air became, the more noticeable it was. She directed Emma's attention to something out in the yard, and when the girl turned her head, Flora leaned toward her. The source of the pungency came as a revelation, and the right words for the situation became strongly apparent. She was surprised at her own candor.

"Emma, first things first," she paused to make her declaration effective, "Let me show you where our bathtub is."

"Yes, ma'am. I kin have it clean in no time."

"That's not what I had in mind. Come on, I'll show you."

Taking her by the hand, Flora led Emma to a far corner of the house to a spare bathroom, one of the rarely used rooms in the house. While the tub was filling, she parked Emma in the middle of the room with instructions to disrobe and get in. She left and returned with soap, washcloth, and towels in hand, only to find Emma still standing, fully clothed, right where she had left her.

"You want me to git naked? I thought I was comin' here to work."

Her perplexed look told Flora that things were moving too fast.

"Trust me, you'll love it. You know how good a hot bath feels, don't you?"

"No, ma'am, not really. We don't have any runnin' hot water, 'cept what we can boil on the stove. I wash clothes and dishes with it for my paw and me, but it takes a lot of boilin' to fill up a whole tub."

Flora instantly felt a sting of embarrassment. She started toward the door.

"Well, you go ahead and try it," she said over her shoulder, "I'll come check on you in a few minutes. I'll leave the door open so the room won't get too steamy. Don't worry; there's only the two of us in the house."

About ten minutes later, Flora returned with rose-scented shampoo and a plain cotton dress, which she rescued from the back of an obscure closet. She hung the dress on the doorknob and peeked over the girl's shoulder. The bathwater was a dingy brown, and Emma was far from finished. She told Emma to pull the plug and refill the tub which she did promptly. When she came back the second time, she had clean underwear and a pair of slippers. Emma was trying to wash her back.

"Here, let me get that for you."

Emma picked up a fingernail brush. As Flora knelt beside the tub, she saw what delicate, fine features the girl had. Lifting her hair off the back of her neck, the youthful bloom and texture of her skin began to show itself as the thin layer of dirt came off. There was a definite resemblance to Marcia Patrick, someone Flora had known from childhood. Marcia, two years older than Flora, had the poise and character that Flora's parents always used as an example for Flora to look up to. That is until she married Joshua and became Marcia Parker. Many of the girls in the town were glad to see the marriage take place because now Marcia had a flaw that made her as fallible as the rest. Her choice of men was used as a backdrop to find fault with any and everything else she did. After all, look where she lived! She could have had her pick of any - including Thomas Rucker. Several of Marcia's friends remained loyal, however. Not many, but enough.

Working the washcloth across Emma's shoulders and down her back, Flora sensed how empty her house was.

"Emma," she said quietly, "Do you remember your mother?"

Emma turned to look at her, "A little. I know her name was Marcia."

Flora felt a quick tightness in her throat, "Yes, I believe you're right," She stopped scrubbing for a moment, then continued, "I didn't know her all that well. She was a couple of years older than me, so we weren't in the same grade in school. We each had a different set of friends."

"I remember her teaching me some things about keeping house," Emma said.

"Like what?"

"Oh, like makin' beds and settin' the table."

"How old were you when your mother died?"

"I'm not sure. I remember how mad Papa was when it happened."

"Who cooked for you then? I mean, until you were old enough to learn how."

"You know Lavenia Carter?"

"The name's familiar. Who is she?"

"She's a colored lady in Pittman. Her husband used to work at the mill with Papa. She helped us out 'til I could take over," there was a touch of pride in her voice.

"I see," Flora realized how engrossed she was in what Emma was saying. Coming back to reality, she suddenly felt guilty for prying into another family's troubled past, "What about your hair?" she asked.

"Ma'am?"

"Your hair. Want some help washing your hair?"

"Yes'm. I suppose so."

"Okay, lean forward and shut your eyes."

It took three washings before the rinse water came clean. Emma pulled out the plug and watched the water swirl around the drain as it disappeared. Flora dried her hair, wrapped a towel around her head, and handed her another towel to dry off with. She was about to leave the room to afford the girl a little more privacy when she stopped and looked back. Turning around, she saw the body of a beautiful young woman stepping out of the tub, rubbing the towel vigorously on her arms.

"Miss Flora," she asked, "What did you mean when you said not to worry about the door bein' open? You said there was only the two of us in the house. What'd you mean?"

Astonished at this sudden display of innocence, Flora felt herself groping for words.

"I just didn't want you to be embarrassed, that's all."

She looked up from drying her legs, "About what?"

Tom was right, she thought.

"I don't know, Emma. I really don't remember what I was thinking at the time. Look, you go ahead and get dressed and meet me in the kitchen."

"Yes, ma'am. You know, you was right. This really does feel good," her broad smile showed beautiful white teeth in perfect alignment.

"My pleasure, Emma, any time."

Flora's kitchen was a homemaker's dream. Aside from a walk-in pantry, there were more cabinets than Emma had ever seen. Over a large butcher block table hung a huge rack with pots and pans of every description. The double sink gleamed with white enamel, and the plumbing fixtures were all chrome. The gas stove was in the middle of the room, a concept that mystified Emma. The kitchen table sat next to a large bay window that flooded the room with sunlight.

Emma entered the room wearing what Flora had given her. It was a simple, pale yellow cotton dress tied around the waist with large pockets. Her hair was gathered back with a ribbon at the nape of her neck.

Flora handed Emma a brightly colored floral apron.

"Put this on. We'll make Mr. Rucker some lunch. He'll be coming home directly to eat." She took a large ham from the refrigerator, "You start slicing this, and I'll cut up some tomatoes."

The two women fell into a synchronous rhythm, preparing lunch like they had been doing it together for years. Tom came home exactly on time, as always. Emma heard the brand new '51 Chevy stop out front. The screen door squeaked and slammed. Then footsteps came through the house into the kitchen. His eyes darted back and forth between Flora and Emma. He gave a feeble attempt at a weak smile.

"So, ah, I come home to two women in my house. What's for lunch?"

"Emma and I have fixed cold cuts and some salad, and there's apple pie for dessert if you want it."

He nervously rubbed his hands together as though he had walked into someone else's house and didn't know what to expect next.

His nervous mood changed to indignation when he realized Emma was setting three places at the table. After a few seconds of indecisiveness, he made a beckoning motion to his wife with his finger, "Flora, could I speak to you for a moment?"

She followed him through the French doors into the dining room. He turned and closed the doors.

"What is she doing in our kitchen? I didn't send her here to cook our food! She might have all manner of disease!"

"Tom, I got the distinct impression that you sent her here to get her out of YOUR store! You sent her to me, so what I do with her now is MY business! In my kitchen, nothing gets past me, and you can rest assured, Thomas, that she doesn't have any DISEASE or any other manner of unpleasantness that will affect your meal. And if you had any power of observation AT ALL, you would see a definite difference in her since she left YOUR store!"

Flora's eyes were blazing as the two of them stood glaring at each other.

"Fine. But I don't want to sit at my table where I have to look at her. I just don't want to be around her anymore!"

"Thomas, hold your voice down!" she whispered through clenched teeth.

"I'll say what I want in my own house! And if you can't be firm with her, then I've had lots of practice." He opened the doors to the dining room and re-entered the kitchen, where he found Emma sitting on the floor, huddled in a corner.

"Emma, stand up and come here!"

The girl rose to her feet and timidly walked toward the man, taking small steps. The first thing he noticed were her ears. He had never seen them before because the stringy blond hair always covered them. It was fine and silky and tied back with red ribbon. Her tapering neckline had a sculptured look to it. Then his eye caught a hint of freckles. Nothing prominent, just a faint band of them across the bridge of her nose and under each eye. Her dress fit with just the right undulation at the hips, waist, and breasts.

Suddenly realizing that he was staring, he asked quietly, "Emma, may I see your hands?"

She held them out for inspection. The thin line of black she always had under her nails was gone. The palms remained calloused and tough, however.

"I can see you two were busy this morning."

"That's right," Flora chimed as she slid a plate across the table in his direction, "All that and fixed lunch, too."

He found it hard to make eye contact with Emma. He stood shuffling his feet and silently gesturing with one hand in the air, searching for words. He finally found his voice.

"I think I'll take my lunch back to the store with me. Flora, would you wrap it up?"

Emma reached for the plate, and he quickly stopped her, "Emma, let Mrs. Rucker do it, please."

Flora silently went about wrapping her husband's lunch in waxed paper, which he took and left without a word. Emma stood with her hands clasped behind her, watching him leave. It was she who finally broke the cold stillness.

She said, bouncing gently on her toes, "Ain't Mr. Rucker the nicest man?"

Flora had thrown together a list of small tasks. She took Emma from room to room, explaining each item on the list, only to find the girl was comprehending a mere fraction of the instructions. They stood in the doorway to the living room.

"Emma, are you remembering any of this?" she said finally, "Emma, are you listening?"

Startled, Emma's attention was suddenly jolted back to the woman who was talking to her.

"Yes, ma'am."

"Yes, ma'am, what?"

"What you said …"

"What DID I say?"

"I'm sorry, Mrs. Rucker. I just ain't never seen so many things in such a house like this." She stepped quietly into the living room, almost inching forward as though the floor might protest her undeserving foot on its hardwood shine. She carefully skirted around a large oriental rug and reached down to caress the fringe.

"My husband's father was given that rug by someone long ago. I never could find out where it came from. It needs cleaning. Would you like to start in here? I'll show you how to use the sweeper."

Flora left the room with a promise to return in a few seconds. Emma marveled at the pictures on the walls. In one, a man with a hat and a beard was rowing a small boat in a pond surrounded by a beautiful park with flowering trees. In the boat with him was a woman holding a parasol bordered by lace around the edges. Another picture was that of two young girls on a beach, frolicking in the low tide. She stood close and examined the pattern in the wallpaper. She was astonished to find she could actually feel the scrolled pattern beneath her fingers. Flora returned, sounding all business.

"This is the sweeper, Emma. Just hold it by the handle and push it back and forth. Like this, see?"

Emma took the carpet sweeper and slowly, gently moving it as Flora had shown her. She glanced up at the woman, looking for approval, and blossomed into a smile when Flora nodded her head.

"I'll be in the kitchen, Emma. Tell me when you finish."

Mesmerized, the girl gazed around the room, captivated by the richness of her surroundings. A porcelain cloisonne figurine beckoned to her from the end of the mantle. She reached out to touch it, then withdrew her hand. The spell was broken when the large Regulator Clock in the middle of the mantle chimed one o'clock.

She immediately went to work on the rug. Her first few strokes were very tentative, then became bolder as she realized the rug was not fragile tissue. Kicking off her slippers, she walked on her tiptoes as she worked across the middle of it. The pattern in the rug was almost hypnotic.

"You're doing fine," proclaimed a voice from behind her, causing her to inhale suddenly. Estimating the amount of time it should have taken, Flora had returned and stood in the doorway watching, almost amused, at the painstaking effort of her new housekeeper, "Here's a dust rag. Let me show you what to do with it."

And so went the rest of the day. Flora instructed, and Emma followed her motions exactly. By five o'clock, she had done three more rooms. They met in the kitchen.

"That just about does it for today, Emma."

"Yes, ma'am. Any time you need more help ..."

"Oh, yes ... well, what about, ah, tomorrow?" She stood thoughtfully with her hands on her hips, looking around the kitchen.

A small look of creative inspiration came across her face, "Eight o'clock tomorrow morning. Okay?"

"Yes'm. Oh, where's my dress … the one I come with?"

"That? We'll talk about that tomorrow." She looked at Emma's bare feet, "I may have some shoes …"

"No, ma'am," she replied quickly, "I don't want no shoes from you. Not 'till I earned 'em."

"If that's what you want. But why don't you take them anyway? Let's just call it a loan. I think you definitely earned the dress, though."

Emma's face beamed as she uttered a shy half-giggle.

"What about Mr. Rucker and my work at the store?"

"Let me take care of that."

"Ma'am?"

"Never mind. Tomorrow … bright and early. Right here."

Smiling from ear to ear, Emma left the house first at a fast walk, then at a slow trot toward Pittman.

As she watched Emma leave, Flora felt something stir from a place deep within her, something she had not felt in a long time.

Chapter 4

Emma arrived home about twenty minutes later. The distance home from Flora Rucker's house was slightly longer than her usual trek to the store. Approaching the house, she saw Joshua on the front porch sitting in an old, faded pink stuffed chair with thread-bare arms, staring off into space with a large chew of tobacco bulging in his mouth. He had long ago stopped using anything resembling a spit can, made obvious by the brown stains on the floor beside the chair. Emma had complained only once about emptying it, so Joshua had found a quick remedy. He could usually give his spittle enough velocity to clear the edge of the porch, but not always. In his lap, he held a tall, thin brown paper bag that stood upright, the top of it crimped and narrow. A circular rim of glass barely protruded from the opening. She saw him start to lift it to his mouth and then stop when she came into his view. After the few seconds it took to make his eyes focus on his daughter, he returned to his bottle and took a long swallow.

"You're late," he said, a string of brown drool hanging from his mouth.

She saw some of his tools lying beside the walk. They weren't there the day before. He was always talking about trying to repair the appliances that cluttered the front yard. Ignoring his inebriated state, she asked, "Did you bring home the stuff I asked you to git?"

"You were at the goddamn store, weren't you?"

She walked up the steps without looking at him, "Only for a little while, Papa."

"So, where'n hell you been?" he growled, "Look at me when I'm talking to you!"

She turned her face toward him, "I been at Miss Flora's house."

"Doin' what?"

"Workin' … Papa, you didn't git none of that stuff like I asked you to, did you?" She was standing next to his chair, looking down at him.

"Don't give me that look, girl!" He shifted his wad of tobacco to the other side of his mouth and asked, "What's for supper?"

She ignored his question, "Papa, where'd you git that bottle? You were supposed to be workin' at the school."

"I asked you a question, girl."

"I heard you, Papa. Where'd you git it?"

"Mr. Mac sent me to Marlin in his car to pick up some things, so I made a little side trip," he ended his comment with a scoffing snort. He picked up the bag for another long pull on the bottle. The liquor dribbled down the front of his shirt as he was tipping the bottle away from his mouth, "What's it to you, anyway?"

"You already have one in your bedroom."

"I finished that one off this morning."

"Why the bag, Papa? Ain't nobody here to see it but me. Mr. Mac know you bought that?"

"Hey, girl! I asked you what's for supper?"

"Whatever you brought home from the store, Papa!" She was shocked at the tone of her own words.

Joshua rose from his chair and had to catch his balance before taking the first step, "Damn, Tom Rucker's a whining little piece a' shit anyway," he mumbled, "His daddy, now there was somebody that …"

"Lemme' get started," she said with a deep breath and a sigh. "I think I got some flour and bakin' powder."

"Goddamn biscuits," he mumbled, "Is that all you can make?"

"It's all we got, Papa! I didn't try to get nothin' else 'cause I thought you were goin'…"

The old man brushed past her, uttering a soft belch. Emma followed him to the kitchen and pulled out a mixing bowl as he continued onto the back porch. A few seconds later, she heard the squeaky door of the outhouse.

She walked to the back door, down the steps, and continued around to the far side of the house. On the ground beyond the small fence and faded whitewashed stones were a series of gentle undulations left over from the furrowed pattern of a garden abandoned years before. Tall weeds rimmed the edge of the garden, and creeping vines covered the center. As a child, Emma had planted vegetables with the help of Lavenia, who introduced her to simple gardening that required little in the way of tending. Three years ago, Emma had tried to plant another garden, but a long dry spell put a stop to it. The shallow well that supplied the house also suffered, and she couldn't risk overusing it to haul buckets of water to her garden. Most everything died, but a few stubborn plants lived long enough to go to seed. Each year, a few seeds would voluntarily germinate from the previous year. The rains and change of seasons gradually flattened out the ground, like a story that fades away without really ending. All that was left now were a few turnips, the last hope of an edible crop. Fortunately, she remembered which corner of the garden she had reserved for them. She found four.

Her father's voice startled her, "What was you doin' at Rucker's house?"

Emma straightened up quickly and turned around to face him, then slowly started brushing the dirt off the small turnips, "She had some stuff for me to do in the house. I might be workin' there for a few more days. It's a nice house and …"

"Stuff, what kind of stuff? Does this mean you goin' be comin' home late every day?"

"I can't help it, Papa. I need to work, and Miss Flora …"

"Where'd you git that dress?" His words slurred.

"She gave it to me. She said I could keep it."

"So, keep it! What do I care? You think I want to wear it?" His words slurred even more as he returned through the back door and into the kitchen, "Biscuits again. Shit! Biscuits and turnips! Ain't no damn meat in this house?"

Emma heard pans and kitchen utensils clattering and bouncing off the walls. Wisely, she walked around to the front of the house and came in through the living room. She knew to keep her distance when Joshua's rage took control of him, but this time, she braved a quick peak into the kitchen. Joshua had a chair raised above his head. Her scream was blotted out by the crashing sound of the old chair coming down on the kitchen table, which still had dishes on it.

"Papa, STOP IT!"

He staggered backward at the sound of her protest. The way he looked once again reminded her painfully as to why he had been the most feared man in town years ago. His tired voice now had a faint, quivering tone.

"Listen to me, girl! When I come home," he spat out, "I want dinner on the table! You come home with a new dress for yourself and not a goddamn thing for me to eat! Who'n the hell d'you think you are? I been cleanin' floors, skinin' my knuckles on monkey wrenches all day for that candy-ass school teacher from Mississippi, and look at this house! Looks like shit! Why can't you do nothin' right? Wait till I tell your mama!"

Emma knew what was coming. She had it memorized by heart, even though she never got used to hearing it. Joshua would get drunk, loosen his rage, destroy whatever was in his direct line of vision, and start talking about Marcia as though she were still alive. He would walk through each room and then sit for hours talking to the silent walls of the house. Once, when Emma was a child, she had innocently laughed at what appeared to her as a grown-up game of play-acting. Emma remembers her reward was a hand across the face that left a bruise for several days. Joshua had immediately recognized what he had done and tried to apologize, but Emma would not come near him for two days. No one at the school seemed to notice it. Ever since, Joshua Parker's classic drunken transformation was a clear signal for her to disappear, usually to Lavenia and Oscar's house. She never told her father where her sanctuary was, and it never occurred to him to look for her there.

Within a few hours, he would be passed out cold somewhere in the house, and she could safely come home while he slept it off. The last time was about four months ago. On that occasion, the dining room, Marcia's pride and joy, which included a china cabinet, sideboard, and a table large enough to seat a dozen people, was reduced to rubble. It didn't matter, though. To destroy what was no longer useful was no big loss to him.

Oscar and Lavenia lived on the main road to Kisatchie. The house had a low roof line with a screen porch across the entire front. The siding was old clapboard lumber that had once been painted white, but the brightness of that luster had faded, peeled, and chipped away until only bare, grey wood remained. It was a metaphor for the whole town of Pittman. The roof was tin, like Emma's house. Hydrangea bushes with big blue balls of blossoms lined the front and were so tall they obscured most of the porch screens. They made great hiding places for children to play games of hide and seek and to peek and spy on one another. In the front yard was an assortment of small wooden pinwheels, windmills, and cut-out figures of ducks, all with rotating wings, pitched to catch the wind. On a fence post near the gate was a large cypress board with the name 'Oscar Carter' carved into it. The Carters had five children, the youngest of which was four years old. The oldest, Earl, was the same age as Emma. He had come to the Parker house when Lavenia cooked for Joshua a few years ago after Marcia died. Earl and Emma had a conditional friendship that always hinged on who else might be watching. On those occasions when they saw each other in town, neither would make eye contact. Earl made a mistake once of yelling and waving to Emma from across the street, only to get a hard jerk of the hand and severe words of warning from Lavenia.

Emma's arrival was announced by Duke and Luke, the two large mongrels in the front yard. Oscar had named them thusly, so he only had to call one, and both came, "Why call 'em twice? I just say 'Uke!' and they always come together," he would say.

Earl heard the dogs barking, came around the corner of the house, and saw Emma.

"Hey, Miss Emma! How're you?" A warm smile naturally came to him.

Emma had her arms folded across her chest and her shoulders held in a seemingly permanent shrug. She stood at the gate staring at the sidewalk with one of the turnips still in her hand. Earl's expression slowly changed.

"You okay, Miss Emma?"

He cautiously walked to the fence and looked closer. Her blank stare and lack of response brought a concerned look to the boy's face.

"Hey, Mama!" he yelled through the screen while never taking his eyes off Emma, "Come see."

Lavenia appeared on the porch, "What is it, Earl? Oh, look, Emma's here."

"Yeah, Mama. She got that look again."

Lavenia leaned forward and peered closely at Emma.

She asked, "Yo' papa, where he at?"

Emma kept her gaze on the ground and spoke slowly in a quiet voice, "At the house."

Lavenia straightened up with her hands on her hips, "Drunk?"

Emma nodded.

"Probably pitchin' another fit."

Another nod.

"How come, this time?"

Emma shrugged.

"Lawd, he gotta' temper. Earl, git them dogs away from here! Come on in, Emma. Child, you look plum scared to pieces," she guided Emma toward the front door, "Oscar! Oscar, c'mere!"

Oscar sat in the front room of their small house, reading the local paper. Thick smoke hung over his special corner with the overstuffed chair. He folded his paper down and withdrew the cigar from his mouth, patiently waiting to hear what would come next.

"Oscar! Did you hear me call you?" Lavenia had a scolding tone, but he knew he could safely ignore it.

He retrieved a shred of tobacco from his tongue, "Yeah, I heard you. But why should I get up when I know you comin' back in?"

Lavenia led Emma into the small front room.

"Whut's wrong?" He waved his hand through the smoke. "Oh, hi, Miss Emma," He looked hard at the girl, and his face began to wrinkle, "Aw hell, Joshua's crunk again, ain't he? You okay, honey?"

Her tears finally started flowing, "I'm fine, Oscar. Papa's havin' a really bad one this time."

"Did he follow you?"

"No. He's too busy tearin' up the kitchen," Lavenia handed her a clean dishrag, and she wiped her eyes.

Oscar asked, "What got 'im goin' this time?"

"She don't know," Earl chimed in.

"Be quiet, boy!" Oscar bellowed. Gently, he asked, "You had supper yet?"

"No."

"Mama, we got enough?"

"Always enough for Emma," Lavenia said, "Come on in the kitchen, baby. We can sit and talk while I finish up making supper."

Everyone left the room for the kitchen except Oscar, who sat deep in thought. Joshua had stood by him when others would have let the Carter family go hungry. But that was many years ago. Before she died, Marcia Parker had transported the entire Carter family to the doctor when influenza hit their household and Joshua had not objected to her generosity. On the other hand, whenever Joshua sent Oscar to carry out some unpleasant task, such as give someone a notice of eviction from one of the mill houses, Oscar always called around first to other mill towns, checking on openings for those who were about to be displaced. Each time, Oscar would try to soften the blow and give Joshua the credit by saying, 'Mr. Parker hate to tell bad news, and he heard there's more work over at ....' Most folks saw through it and knew Joshua wouldn't go to such trouble. Oscar had been cleaning up behind Joshua for a long time. Loyalty aside, he was getting tired of it. Looks like today would be another mess to take care of, and after each time, feelings were never the same. He knew someday he might have to confront Joshua and it would be a white man's word against his.

Lavenia had an ease about her that could make any child forget what might trouble a young heart. There was clear communication in her silence. Her premature grey hair gave the impression of someone with wisdom and understanding. The rhythmic *thump, thump, thump* of Lavenia's mixing bowl where cornbread batter was taking form seemed to replace any need for conversation. As the woman moved about in her kitchen, her soft humming filled the room, gave gentle texture to the evening. It made Emma feel safe. At last, when the simple meal of pork, cornbread, and greens was ready, Lavenia finally spoke in a soft tone like Emma was one of her own.

"Emma, go call everybody. Supper's ready."

Eight sat at the crowded table with Oscar at the head. Lavenia sat in the chair closest to the kitchen. All heads bowed as Oscar mumbled a three-second blessing. Emma couldn't understand a word of it, except the last part, "… in his name, Amen!" The last syllable was more like a hard grunt to add emphasis. There may have been a mystery as to what he had just said to God, but there was no mistake about when it was time to stop praying and start eating. The only sounds from around the table were those of muffled satisfaction and forks and spoons clinking against dinner plates. Oscar said to the seven-year-old, "Eat your greens, Gloria." His voice was deep, kind, and powerful. It made Emma think of how a lion might sound when it purred.

After a few minutes, Emma spoke up, "I worked at Miss Flora's today."

"You mean at the house?" Earl asked, "That's a big house."

Emma answered with a mouthful, "Yeah, I cleaned the rugs and dusted the tables, and … well, first, she gives me a bath!"

Oscar, Lavenia, and the kids all stopped eating and stared at her. Emma continued eating, unaware of the family of eyes suddenly fixed on her. Gloria uttered a soft giggle, and the other kids joined in. Emma joined the laughter, unsure of the reason.

"What else did you do?" Lavenia asked.

"I helped make Mr. Rucker's lunch. He came and got it. Took it back to the store with him. You know, he and Miss Flora shore do fuss a lot."

"What they talk about?" young Preston asked.

She was about to answer when Oscar looked up from his plate, "Boy, what white folks say in they own house ain't none of our business." It was tough being one of the kids in the middle.

"That's right," Lavenia said, "And speakin' of baths, I know a bunch of you what's going to take one tonight. I'm glad Emma reminded us of it."

"Kin I help?" Emma asked with a gleam in her eye.

"Help who?" Earl asked cautiously.

"The little ones, I meant."

"I hope that's what you meant," Earl said with a smirk.

"What's wrong with that anyway? I kin wash their backs. Miss Flora done mine."

Earl leaned over toward his father and whispered, "I can wash my own self."

Oscar's face widened into a slow smile, "I don't think she meant you, son," Oscar said out loud.

"No, but I could," Emma said with a twinkle, "There's that spot right back there where you can't reach," she extended her hand toward Earl, who leaned away from her until he almost fell out of his chair. He finally jumped up and stood at a safe distance.

Oscar came to his rescue, "Come on the porch with me, son. We'll let these women take care of the children."

As the two of them left the room, Emma spoke out, "Earl, later, you kin help me read to the little ones, okay? You want to do that?"

"Yeah, sure. I guess so."

Turning back to Lavenia, Emma saw that she was stacking dishes. Emma joined in and asked, "I don't know what gets into Earl sometimes. I never seen him act so touchy 'bout things."

"Well, he ain't a little boy no more. Once they start growin' up, they slow about talkin' on some things in front of women."

"Like what?"

"Like bathin'."

"Why?"

"Well, child, bathin' their self is personal stuff."

"Why?"

Lavenia's voice turned to a whisper, "Did you bathe wid' all your clothes on?"

Emma got the point, and Lavenia nodded in agreement.

"I seen Papa naked once. But I just seen him from the back."

Lavenia almost dropped a stack of dishes she was carrying.

"I wasn't tryin' to peek or nuthin'. He just left his door open one night when it was real hot, and I just … seen 'im. Weren't nothin' to it, really."

Lavenia's mind was in a whirl, trying to cope with Emma's unabashed candor. She could only sigh and shake her head, "Somebody got to talk to you about this. It may as well be me. But not tonight! I got to think on this first!"

Emma and Earl had finished reading to the smaller children when Oscar came back inside from the porch.

"Emma," Oscar said, "Let's see if it's okay to get you back home."

He had the keys to the old Plymouth in his hand. Emma thanked Lavenia for the supper and started toward the door with Oscar close behind. The topic of baths was history. On the front porch, she hesitated a moment to say goodbye to everyone. Earl glanced at her, took a step back, and bid her good night with just a wave.

In the car, Oscar turned the key, stepped on the starter pedal, and the old Plymouth coughed and came to life. The gears slightly clashed as Oscar found first gear. He muttered something about getting a new clutch someday.

Within minutes, they were approaching Emma's house. Oscar turned off the headlights and the engine and coasted to a stop at the corner of the yard. They sat for a minute and listened. No lights were on inside.

"Sho's dark around here," Oscar declared, "I thought you had a streetlight."

"Used to. It burnt out a long time ago. No one comes to fix it."

"You stay here," he said, "Lemme' go look."

"It's okay, really."

"Good. Then I'll feel safe leavin' you here while I go look. You stay put."

Emma sat in the car with the windows down, listening to the night sounds. It seemed there was more life in Marcia's woods at night than in the day. Millions of frogs were making a continuous background of groaning and croaking. It all melted together in the thick night air like soup in a pot until no single sound could be picked out except for one that stood out with a rhythmic bass note that all others seemed to follow. Bass frog, first chair. The moon shone through the pines behind the house, outlining the wings of some night bird that passed by, a ghostly shadow on a mission of hunting. Sometimes, when the mosquitoes weren't too bad, Emma would sit on the back porch and give herself a soothing dose of the contentment that came to her ears. Tonight was no different, even while she was sitting in Oscar's car. The effect was the same. Her mind wandered, thinking first about the men at the store that morning and how delighted she was to have worked at Flora's house. For some reason, her mind kept settling on the pattern in that oriental rug.

She heard the faint crunch of gravel on the shoulder of the road, looked up, and saw Oscar approaching. He had turned on a light in the back of the house, and the faint glow filtered and reflected through the living room to dimly outline the front door.

"House's tore up pretty bad. He's asleep on the sofa," he said with a sound of relief, "I'll walk to the house with you."

"That's okay. Thanks, Oscar."

"You ain't seen the inside of your house yet. I'll stay and help for a while. Lots of stuff to clean up."

The two figures walked into the house past the sleeping Joshua, who was snoring loudly. The kitchen looked like a tornado had passed through. The table was on its side. Parts of chairs were scattered on the floor, mixed with dishes, utensils, and shards of glass. All the cabinet doors were open, one hanging by only a single hinge. The shelves were empty.

"Lemme' go back to the house and git Earl. We can help you."

She walked around the edge of the room with her arms folded, looking at the destruction and stepping over pieces of it, "No ... thanks, anyway. He might wake up. You wouldn't want to be here if he did," It was the voice of experience.

"What about you?" he asked as they both slowly walked toward the living room.

"I'll be okay. I've done this before."

The shuffling of feet from the living room caused them both to freeze. Joshua slowly ambled past the kitchen door and headed for his room. He stopped and peered into the kitchen through squinting, blood-shot eyes, looking directly at first Oscar, then Emma. Seeing but not acknowledging the two of them, he continued in his unsteady gait to his room and shut the door.

Oscar spoke first, "That's it. You're comin' back to the house with me."

"No need. He won't remember any of it. Thanks anyway."

"Now, Miss Emma ..."

She gave him a gentle pat on his bulging arm, "Like I said before, this ain't the first time. You just never seen it before. You're a good man to think of me, though."

Although Joshua frequently had fits of anger, only two or three times a year was it too severe for Emma to endure, forcing her to find refuge. Over the years, the Carters had always welcomed Emma into their home when such a crisis erupted, Oscar always escorting her home afterward. This, however, was indeed the first time he had gone inside with her. Reluctantly, he went home after helping her right the table and sort through some of the rubble.

It was close to midnight when she finally stopped putting things into some semblance of order. The night was hot and sticky. Crickets sang through the open window of her bedroom. Unable to sleep with her thoughts racing, she found her drawing pad in the closet and a box of colored chalk, a gift from Mr. MacArthur. He admired her apparent natural artistic gift and still dropped gentle reminders that she had a possible future in it if she applied herself. Drawing doodles and meaningless shapes on the page, the pattern in Flora's rug flashed by. For the next two hours, she sat on the edge of her bed and escaped into a swirl of colors and shapes that talked to her, sang to her, held her hand, and ushered her into the safety of another world. She leaned back finally and fell asleep.

Morning came like a cymbal clash, like a blessed sacrament delivered rudely by an evil priest. She jolted and sat up in bed, realizing she was still wearing the dress Flora had given her. Her drawing materials were on the bed beside her, and her fingers were covered with chalk dust. As she gradually recalled the night before, she stood and walked down the hall to the kitchen, remembering the scene as she had found it a few hours earlier. Previous tantrums from Joshua had destroyed all the drinking glasses in the house, leaving Emma with no alternative except to save old jars she found during her journeys through the old town. After last night, there were only three left. She knew where to find more, though. There was also a possibility of some other items from the old town dump. Souvenir hunters had picked the obvious places clean, but this was Emma's town. She knew of hiding places where no one else would think to look. She would find time later.

She went into Joshua's room to see if he could be roused. Twice, she gave him a nudge on the shoulder, then gave up. She would be expected at the Rucker house soon. It would only take a few minutes to boil some water and start the coffee dripping. Joshua liked it somewhat cool, anyway. Two leftover biscuits had survived in the food safe. He'd find it all when he woke up.

She was almost out to the gate when an idea occurred to her. Quickly, she went back to her room and gathered the drawings she had done the night before, then hurried down the road toward Kisatchie, anxious to feel approved, loved, accepted - to see Flora again.

Chapter 5

The second day at the Rucker house seemed more structured than the first. Flora had had time to plan for the day with Emma. Most of the morning was spent in an enormous, neglected room of the house, a venue that was seldom used. When Flora opened the door, the stale air greeted Emma like the inside of an old tobacco pipe. Against the walls were bookcases made of heavy dark wood with ornate patterns carved around the edges. In one corner was a monstrous desk of the same finish. A large couch flanked by two matching over-stuffed Queen Anne chairs filled the center of the room. Each chair was guarded by a tall floor lamp. Emma noticed the light bulbs were missing in both. Three large area rugs blanketed most of the hardwood floor between the pieces of furniture. The wall opposite the desk was graced with a wide fireplace. She stopped once to page through an old book about World War I after first blowing the dust from it. On the inside cover was a handwritten note directed to Isaiah Rucker, Tom's grandfather. The note carried the date of 'Christmas, 1918'. The dust on the furniture and the other furnishings served as evidence that Tom and Flora made little use of this portion of the house. Despite the tedium of removing all the books, dusting them clean, and replacing them exactly as they were, she finished the room quickly and moved to another bathroom Flora had pointed out to her. She was bent over under the basin, polishing the bulky porcelain base, when Flora walked in.

"Oh, there you are. Did you already finish in the library?"

Emma raised up and said, "Yes, ma'am. I done it like you said. I was gonna' clean out the fireplace, but there weren't no ashes or nothin' in it."

"I guess I'm just not accustomed to your pace yet. Are you sure you've never done housework like this before?"

"No, ma'am. This here's the first nice house I ever been in. Here … I'll show you what I done in … wha'd you call it?"

"The library."

"Good idea, callin' it that. You read all them books?"

Flora was about to answer, but Emma was already out the door and moving at a fast clip down the hall. As she tried to follow, Flora said, "I'm sure you did a good job, Emma. You really can show me later," Oblivious to the older woman's comment, Emma closed the distance to the library and pointed out what she had done before Flora could catch up to her.

"See," she said, "I done took all them books off'n the shelves and dusted them, and then I done the floors like the ones I done yesterday. I got the rugs and the tops of all the lampshades."

Flora noticed a strange pile of papers on the desk, "What are these?"

"Oh, that's my drawing stuff," She stiffened and spoke with hesitation, "I hope that's okay. I thought I'd work on 'em a little while I took a break later today. I ain't finished any of 'em yet."

"No, that's quite all right," Noticing Emma's sudden state of apprehension, Flora said, "I really don't mind," Her voice trailed off as she leaned over the desk and picked up the first drawing, then the second.

"You did this with chalk?" she asked slowly.

"Yes, ma'am. It's all I had," she paused and seemed to be searching for words, "Miss Flora, I brung 'em because Papa don't like to see these around the house. I don't know why. I guess it would be best to just throw 'em away," There was a shy hint of disappointment in her voice.

Ignoring the girl's last few words, Flora turned the sheet of paper at different angles, "It's a ship … the picture, I mean … that's what it is, right?"

Emma felt a twinge of excitement at Flora's interest in her work, "They're all ships. I know it's hard to tell, but chalk is all I had."

"No, it's fine, actually. Did you say you were going to finish these?" She held up the first one, "This looks finished to me. The sails are all red."

The question caught Emma unprepared, "That one? Oh no, it needs more gray in the waves. I'll get to it later, I guess, maybe … I dunno'."

Realizing how long they had been distracted and now regaining her full business-like composure and awareness, Flora said, "Yes, I'm sure you can do that later. I'm sorry I interrupted what you were doing. Let's see, back to the bathroom."

"I'm almost done in there."

"Fine. When you finish, please come to the kitchen. We can wash the breakfast dishes and straighten up the kitchen together."

Emma beamed. Flora never ceased to be amazed at this young girl who seemed to be at her happiest when given direction and orders … so eager to please. As Emma hurried back to the bathroom, Flora returned her attention to the stack of drawings, carefully lifting them up by the edges.

Steam rose out of the soap suds in the kitchen sink. As Flora handed a dish to Emma to be dried, she asked, "Why sailing ships? Have you ever seen one? Most girls would draw flowers, or trees, or still life, something like that."

"Well, I just draw what I'm thinking about. And last night, I thought about goin' somewhere on a ship."

"You did all those last night?"

"Yes, ma'am. Papa was asleep, and that's when I kin do it without him knowin'," she stopped and gave Flora a quick look of panic. "You won't say nothin', will you?"

"I don't understand. Why does your father object to this? I think it's wonderful."

"I don't know why, but it makes him fightin' mad. I found a stack of pictures one time in an old drawer, and he took 'em away from me and burned 'em."

"Who was the artist?"

"Ma'am?"

"The drawings your father burned. Who drew them?"

"I dunno'. I asked Papa about it, and he just got mad all over again."

"So, what do you do with your work? I mean, you obviously have others, right?"

"I hide them in a special place."

"Well, I just think it's a shame that you must hide to do all this. So, you drew all this last night?"

Emma nodded, "Yes'm. 'Course, I was up kinda' late."

"My God, child. How fast can you draw?"

"It really ain't hard; I just draw what I see."

"You saw ships?"

"Once, in a book," she paused, "Miss Flora, what was that thing you said before … still life? What's that?"

"Still life, like a bowl of fruit or a vase of flowers."

"Is that what you call it?"

"Here, dry your hands. I'll bring you a pencil and some paper. There's a bowl of apples right over there on the food safe. Take a look at it. I'll be right back."

Emma studied the bowl carefully, and Flora returned in a few seconds, pencil and paper in hand.

Without either of them saying a word, Emma went to work, her hands making wide sweeping motions across the paper. In less than a minute, the bowl of apples appeared on the page.

"It really don't look good without no color," she said, "If I had my chalk …"

"Don't move, I'll get it."

Emma took the chalk from Flora's hands as soon as she returned to the kitchen. Silently and quickly, she brought new life to the page with dark red fruit, green leaves, and a blue porcelain bowl.

Mesmerized, Flora watched as Emma added to the picture. Gradually, the bowl sat on a table covered by a flowered tablecloth. A candle appeared from behind the bowl, complete with dripping wax and a small yellow flame. The bowl cast a shadow on the table beneath it.

Without pausing a moment to look away from her work, Emma said quietly, "Someone's at the front door."

"What?"

Emma looked up and repeated, "I heard a car pull up. Someone's at the front door. You want me to go see?"

"Yoo-hoo! Flora!" The voice of Reba Longford cackled and squeaked through the front screen like an old bucket handle. It was unique and could belong to no other person. Reba had been born and raised in Kisatchie and had lived in the same house, which was the boyhood home of her late husband. One could see Reba's house from the Rucker's, no more than one hundred yards away, through the trees.

"Come on in, Reba," Flora said loudly enough to be heard from the kitchen. Pulling herself away from Emma's emerging creation, she walked toward the front of the house and met Reba in the living room.

"I brought you that catalog you were asking about the other day," said Reba.

"Catalog?"

"Yes, remember you asked about it – oh, maybe it was a while back!" Reba allowed a small grin to peak through and couldn't stop her eyes from glancing in the direction of the kitchen.

Flora said vacantly, "I'm sure it was a while back. More like last Easter," she flipped through some of the pages politely, wondering about the real purpose of the visit. Since her husband died and both her children had grown up and moved away, Reba's life was rather uneventful, and she made other folks' lives her business. In her early eighties, she had an unbridled curiosity about anything or anyone within her radius of detection. Nothing, absolutely nothing, happened within a stone's throw of her house without her knowing about it.

Hearing feet shuffle and a chair scrape on the kitchen floor, Reba said, "Oh, I'm sorry. You have company. Maybe I should come back at a better time," She made a half-hearted motion to turn around but continued to look back.

Giving in to the inevitable, Flora said flatly, "No problem, Reba. Come on in," she headed back toward the kitchen with Reba close behind, who was craning her neck to see beyond the kitchen door.

Reba entered the room, her eyes bright and darting, a weak smile on her lips. Her view immediately tunneled in and locked on Emma, bent over the drawing. Confused, she glanced back at Flora, then again at Emma.

Flora folded her arms and let Reba cogitate on the matter for a few seconds. She correctly surmised that Reba had seen someone come to the house that morning and probably had spent most of the morning trying to think of an excuse to come over and see who it was. *Couldn't stand it, could you?* She thought.

After a few seconds, Flora spoke, "Reba, you know Emma, don't you?"

Emma hadn't looked up yet, and Reba stared hard at the girl, trying to invoke her sputtering memory.

With one final stroke of her hand, Emma laid her chalk down and calmly looked up at Reba, "Good mornin', ma'am. I ain't seen you come in the store lately."

Reba's recollection suddenly made a connection with the face looking at her, "Oh, Emma! Joshua's child! Yes! My husband used to work for your father. Now let's see, your mother …

"She's dead, Miss Reba."

"Yes, God rest her. What a nice lady she was. I remember one time when …"

"Why don't you have a seat, Reba," Flora said, admitting defeat.

"I ain't met too many people who remember my mama."

"She was such a pretty thing. No one could understand why she, uh, well …"

Flora quickly interrupted, "May I get you a glass of iced tea, Reba?"

"No, thanks, I'm fine."

"Well, I do thank you so much for the catalog.

For several seconds, no words were spoken by the three. Reba finally broke the silence, "So, I guess I better go for now. Looks like you're busy with other things." She rose from her seat and took a step away from the table.

"Bye, Miss Reba."

"Goodbye, child. I'm sorry I didn't recognize … you're … well, you don't look the same as I remembered."

"Oh, it ain't nothin'. Miss Flora give me this dress, and yesterday I took a ba—"

"Reba! Look at the lovely picture Emma just drew for me!"

Momentarily, Reba looked puzzled, then slowly tilted her head to see the picture better. Flora stood by cautiously, hoping that nothing more would be said about yesterday's event in the bathtub.

After a few moments of closely examining the sketch, Reba shot a quick glance at Flora, questions written on her face. The silence was broken by the sound of a car in the driveway, and Reba began to move toward the front door. Flora quickly offered to escort her in that direction and expressed inflated, hollow regrets that she couldn't stay longer. The front screen door squeaked opened, and heavy footsteps came onto the porch.

"Good morning, Thomas," Reba said to Tom Rucker as he came into the living room.

"Miss Reba," Tom answered with a polite but nervous nod. His eyes were snapping and darting, "Haven't seen you in the store lately."

"Well, I'm still around, Thomas. I guess I do need to do a little shopping. So, ah … I better be going."

Reba started toward the door at the same time Tom was about to say something to his wife, but Flora was firmly preoccupied with politely saying goodbye to her visitor. Tom stood aside, shifting his feet.

"Don't mind me," Reba said, "I can find my way out. You two look like you're busy."

Facing Flora again, Tom opened his mouth to speak when Reba's voice crackled once more. She was looking back toward the kitchen and said loudly, "Goodbye, Emma."

Emma came bouncing out of the kitchen in her bare feet and stood in the door, waving. Tom finally had Flora's attention and was talking to her in hushed tones. Emma approached the couple and stood mere inches away from them. Indignantly, Tom stopped in mid-sentence and glared at the girl. Softly touching her arm, Flora said, "Why don't you finish what you were doing, Emma? Mr. Rucker needs to talk to me."

Emma skipped back into the kitchen as Tom stared at the floor and shook his head.

"Okay, start over, Tom."

"Like I was saying, my sister called from Houston. They have to go to Europe for ten weeks on business, and they want to send Hugh here to stay with us while they're gone."

Out on the main road, they could hear Reba's '46 Plymouth shifting gears as the old woman headed for the center of town.

"Their son, Hugh? Ten weeks? Tom, that's almost three months. He'll miss the start of school!"

"She was hoping he could start here and return home when they got back."

"That poor boy. They certainly don't have his best interest at heart. Who was it they farmed him out to last year? They went to San Francisco, didn't they? How old is he?"

"He's just turned seventeen, and never mind about last year. That's none of our business."

"Well, they certainly want to make it our business THIS year! I presume she called you at the store. Why didn't she call here?"

"She probably knew you would give her a heavy dose of your opinions, Flora. Look, she's not looking for a lecture on child-raising, just someone to take care of Hugh for a while. She knows we have the room for him."

"Yes, and she knows we NEVER have any plans of our own!"

She was right. The store was a millstone around their necks. Sounding defeated, he said, "Fine, I'll tell her you said no."

"Oh, great! Lay the blame on me! That's not fair, Tom."

Exasperated, he sighed and said, "I'm sorry. That just slipped out. Okay, I'll give her some kind of excuse."

"So, what will they do with him?"

Tom looked at the ceiling and said, "She mentioned a military boarding school in Virginia. They had been thinking about sending him there, anyway."

Flora's eyes widened, "Tom," she said, "Are you sure about that?"

"Yes," he said firmly, "She's mentioned it before several times."

"So, they would send him there before school started? If he's seventeen, this will probably be his senior year."

"Yeah, I suppose so."

She tilted her head, "Is he a bad kid?"

"You know he's not. You've seen him."

"Yes, but how many years ago was that?"

Trying to sound positive, he said, "I could give him stuff to do at the store."

"Well, he is YOUR sister's child, and I certainly wouldn't know what to do with a teenage boy around the house!"

Flora walked back toward the kitchen, deep in thought. Tom followed a few steps behind, sensing a glimmer of hope but feeling like a teenager himself who had just asked for the car keys.

She turned and said, "Tom, call your sister. Tell her to put Hugh on the train. We'll meet him in Alexandria."

She saw a wave of relief come over her husband's face. Flora never could understand what power Tom's sister seemed to hold over him. She wondered what would have happened if he had called back and declined to take the boy.

"Thank you so much, darling. You really will like him."

"Of course, you would say that. When was the last time you saw the boy?"

"Trust me, it'll be just fine. I'll call her as soon as I get back to the store."

"Call her from here."

"But I need to get back," He started for the front door.

"And I need to be polite and say a few words of assurance to your beloved sister while you have her on the phone."

"You really don't need to."

"Yes, I do. I also need to be sitting right here so I can hear what you're telling her. NOW MAKE THE CALL!"

When the call was finished, Tom and Flora walked into the kitchen. Emma was still at the table with her artwork, but her chair was turned to face the door. She sat cross-legged with her dress pulled up above her knees. Tom's line of vision immediately focused on the obvious.

"Good God!" he said, jerking his head toward the ceiling.

Emma looked up with an innocent smile.

"You see," he said with a grimace, shaking his finger at Flora, "This is what I've had to put up with at the store! She has no idea! Not a clue!"

"Tom, remember your manners!" she hissed through her teeth. Flora then turned and spoke softly, "Emma, why don't you finish the hall bathroom? I'll be making lunch soon."

Tom looked at his watch, "Yes, it is getting on toward noon. I'll fix something for myself at the store."

"Nonsense. I can have something ready for you in no time."

Reluctantly, Tom sat at the table and was about to push Emma's stack of papers aside when the top page caught his attention.

"What is, I mean, WHO is … this?"

"What do you mean?" asked Flora.

"This picture. The face in it looks familiar."

"Let me see."

Flora studied the pencil drawing for a few seconds, and her face widened in amazement.

"It's Reba!"

"Reba? From next door?"

"Exactly!"

"Where did this come from? What are all these other pictures?"
Flora looked at her husband with a devilish twinkle in her eye.

"Ask Emma."

"Emma? When did she do it?"

"She certainly hadn't started this one of Reba before you came
home. Apparently, she did it just in the length of time it took us to
talk about Hugh coming and make the phone call."

Tom continued to scrutinize the drawing, "But that wasn't more
than a few minutes. And Reba was gone by then. How did she do
it?"

"From memory, I guess."

"Reba hasn't been in the store in weeks. How long was she here
this morning?"

"Only about ten minutes. Look, every wrinkle, every line in this
picture is Reba. Even the way she smiles. She's caught every detail.
It's like a photograph!"

"I didn't know she could do stuff like this," Tom said.

"Neither did I. Until this morning."

Tom sat in silence for almost a minute while Flora studied the
drawing. He asked, "Could she do more?"

"More, like what?"

"More, like more people."

"Who?"

"Oh, folks in town. You know, the ones that come in the store."

"What did you have in mind?"

He paused, "Just wondering, that's all."

Flora's eyebrows raised, and she gave him a skeptical look. She
shook her finger at him and said, "Tom Rucker, she's nothing but
an ignorant little urchin to you. Those are your own words. What are
you scheming up now? I know that look you get when you think you
have a money-making idea."

"Well, dear, think about it. If she can sit here and draw from memory, I could sell these in the store on consignment and ..."

"I knew it! I knew it! Five minutes ago, she wasn't worth a plug nickel, and now you want her to have an artist's corner in your store so you can ..." Flora's face was beginning to look flushed.

"I said nothing about an artist's corner. No, I said she could sit here."

Flora looked astonished, "Ah, you don't want her in your store, just her pictures!"

"You don't understand! I can't have her back in my store! She's too disruptive to the customers."

"You mean male customers."

"Isn't that enough?"

"Has anyone complained?"

"No, but I don't want them to come in just so they can gawk at her."

"Oh, so now they gawk at her!"

"No, this isn't a new development. It's been a problem for about the last six months or so."

"Make it eight months, Tom! Sounds better!"

Looking at his wife with defiance, he continued in a louder voice, "They don't come in to buy anything. It's just to see the sideshow. I feel like I'm running a carnival. Actually, worse than that! Flora, if she ever comes back to my store for anything, it won't be to meet the public. I still may need her help on occasions, but I don't want her meeting customers."

"Now, wait a minute!" she said, slapping her hands on the table, "Either you want her at the store, or you don't! Which is it?"

Feeling himself begin to wilt, he rubbed his chin and said, "I just can't have her mixing with the customers."

"Fine. So, she stays in the back until you need her?"

"That's right. Out of sight. No contact with the customers. I simply will not have it."

"And you can simply forget about selling any of her pictures. Go fix your own lunch!"

With few exceptions, Flora usually kept her word when her mind was made up.

Chapter 6

Three days passed uneventfully. Emma worked with Flora at the house until late afternoon each day and then walked briskly to the store where, from closing time until a few minutes afterwards, she swept the floors, replenished what stock she could on the shelves, and straightened up the loading dock in back. One day, she decided to sweep the front sidewalk, but Tom told her not to stand in front of the store. He didn't want her in plain view of anyone passing by.

On the fourth morning, Emma arrived at the Rucker house earlier than usual and slowly opened the front porch screen, attempting to avoid making any noise. She wasn't sure what time Flora began stirring each morning and hadn't been given a definite start time at the close of the day before. Her caution with the screen only made the hinges squeak even louder. The door slipped from her hand, and it slammed shut with a muffled bang. The response from the back of the house was immediate.

"Emma? That you?" Flora's voice sounded welcoming.

"Yes'm," she called through. "I hope I ain't too early."

"No, dear. Come on in," Flora continued talking to her as Emma tiptoed through the immense living room, where she stopped to flatten out a wrinkle in the corner of the large area rug. Continuing through the house, she walked toward the sound of Flora's voice in the kitchen. "Mr. Rucker left several minutes ago," Flora said, "I never can sleep when he's up and about early in the morning like this."

Flora sat at the kitchen table holding a cup of coffee. Emma stood just inside the kitchen door, hands behind her, gently shifting her weight from one foot to the other.

"Well, I'm here," she announced proudly.

Flora sat for a few moments with a faint smile, holding her cup with both hands and gazing at this amazing bundle of energy and youth.

"Somethin' wrong? Did I come too early?" Emma asked with a concerned look.

"No, child. There is absolutely nothing wrong. I was honestly looking forward to your coming today."

Flora thought Emma's face would split from the broad smile that suddenly erupted. A narrow bridge between them had been forming over the past week, and today, it seemed very apparent for some reason. The bridge beckoned to be crossed. Flora felt a strange, fleeting, warm glimpse of years past. The bright, young face looking back was silent but spoke in terms beyond words.

"Why don't we just sit for a few minutes before we get started?" Flora said.

The smile on Emma's face seemed to invade her whole body as she quickly pulled out a chair and sat across from the older woman. For several seconds, she remained speechless and radiant, as though someone had just given her a million dollars.

"Emma, sit like this," Flora positioned herself with her knees together. Emma closely studied what she was doing and tried to emulate.

"Like this?"

Flora nodded and offered no explanation. She finally broke the silence.,"Would you like some coffee?"

"No, ma'am, thanks."

"You sure? How about a pastry?"

Emma's face became more serious at the suggestion of food.

"Well, if it ain't too much trouble," she said, wiping her nose with the back of her hand. Flora instinctively looked away.

"Good. And how about a glass of milk? We've got plenty of time."

Emma's eyes sparkled. She ate the pastry in two bites and chugged the milk without stopping to breathe.

"More?"

Emma shook her head while catching her breath. She released a quiet burp and said, "That was good. Lavenia makes stuff like that."

"Lavenia. Lavenia. Oh, yes—the woman you spoke of the other day. You're saying she cooks like I do?" Flora looked toward the ceiling and felt herself stiffen, "How interesting."

"Oh yeah, Lavenia's a good cook. She taught me lots of stuff about cooking. The only thing is, we ain't never got much in the house to cook with, so I don't get to practice much. I do most of it at her house."

"At—her—house? Does she live near you?"

"Yeah—well, there ain't much to our town, so nothin's too far from anything else."

Flora looked around her own kitchen with all its porcelain and chrome. She asked slowly, "Is her kitchen like this one?"

Emma shot a few casual glances around the room and replied, "Yes'm. Sorta' like this one, only smaller. You know, she's got a stove and a sink and an icebox. Stuff like that. But it ain't never this clean."

Sitting up straighter in her chair, Flora asked, "Why do you suppose that is?"

"Oh, it's them young'uns of hers. She's got a house full to cook for, and the kitchen never has time to get all shined up like this one."

Shifting uneasily, Flora said, "Yes, I suppose her family does keep her busy."

Seconds passed. Surprising herself, Flora said, "Would you like to do some of that here?" She immediately regretted her words.

Emma's mouth flew open in amazement, "Me? Here?" Sensing no response from Flora, she exclaimed, "You sayin' I kin cook in this kitchen?"

Her mind racing and realizing there was no retreat now, Flora said, "Uh, yes—here. We could make—"

Emma was out of her chair and in the middle of the floor, her eyes darting from one side of the kitchen to the other and her arms waving like disjointed wings. She blurted out, "We could make fried chicken, and biscuits, and sweet potatoes, and—and—" Her eyes suddenly fell on the plate of pastries. "And I kin make those!" she said, pointing to the plate.

"Emma, Emma, slow down. I didn't mean to cook a whole meal. We have lots of time. Look, later today, we'll start with something simple."

The rest of the morning, Emma was like a child waiting for Santa Claus. Three times, she asked Flora if it was time to cook. Finally, Flora said, "How about we do it together after lunch?"

"So, when do we have lunch?"

Almost laughing, Flora said, "We will eat in one hour."

Dust rag in her hand, Emma left the room humming.

The lunch hour arrived, and while they were eating, Flora said, "Let's start with something easy. Something like, uh—"

"Cookies," Emma said, still chewing her last bite.

"Cookies?"

Emma bolted from her seat and hurried across the room. As she began to poke her head into one cabinet door after another, she almost shouted, "You got everything here. I don't need much space, so I won't dirty up the kitchen much." Speaking with her head inside one of the cabinets, her voice sounded like it was inside a bucket.

Flora suddenly had visions of a disaster. Collecting her thoughts, she said while pointing, "Okay. The mixing bowls are over there. No, that one's too big. Try the smaller one."

Looking confused, Emma reached for the smaller bowl, "This ain't near big enough."

Flora chuckled, "How many cookies did you plan to make?"

"I never did stop to count, but this here bowl just won't work."

"Whatever you say. What next?"

"I need four cups of flour, about a half pound of butter, three eggs—"

"Whoa, how many cookies are we making here?"

"Like I said, I don't know. I just know this is what Lavenia does when she makes 'em."

"Can't you just cut it in half? Or less?"

She looked at Flora with a blank expression, "I wouldn't know how to do that."

"Just half of everything. That's easy."

"How do I do half a mouthful?"

"What?"

"The milk. Lavenia just pours it in and says to use about three mouthfuls of milk."

Puzzled, Flora said, "She pours it from - oh, you don't really mean a—I mean, you're not going to—"

Before Flora could say anything else, Emma had retrieved a bottle of milk from the refrigerator and was holding it over the bowl. Realizing she had taken Emma's words too literally, she just shook her head and said, "Go ahead. You seem to know what you're doing."

"You got one of them aprons I kin use?"

An hour later, a huge platter of sugar cookies sat in the center of the table. Flora and Emma had washed, dried, and put away the last of the utensils. About mid-afternoon, the phone rang. Flora answered.

"Hello. Yes, Tom. I remember. Uh-huh. They said—but - when - today? When did he leave? Why didn't they call us? Well, maybe they DID think that - don't they ever talk to one another? So, both your sister and her husband thought the other had called us two days ago!"

Flora paused to listen. Emma, standing in the doorway, could hear a man's muffled voice coming from the receiver as Flora held it away from her ear. A minute elapsed, and without uttering another word, she hung up.

Emma stepped into the room, "Everything okay?"

Half-startled, Flora turned and answered, "Why, yes. Just a little—ah, yes, everything's fine," She collected her thoughts for a moment and continued, "You know, it's a good thing you're here today. It seems we have a little unexpected work to do."

Flora stood thinking for a full minute, then led her down to the darkened end of the hallway and through a door that opened with difficulty as though time had sealed it shut like a healed wound. The air that issued from the small room was stale, and a thin layer of dust covered every surface. A double bed with a plain white spread stood against the far wall. A dresser and an armoire occupied a position on either side of the only window in the room. Flora stood in the doorway, partially blocking Emma's view. Eagerly, the girl squeezed past her and entered the room.

"Wow! This is great! I didn't know this room was here. You never showed me this—"

"Emma!" Flora said, almost shouting, "Please, this room is very special."

Startled, bewilderment momentarily gripped Emma as she froze in mid-sentence. The older woman's sudden, visceral outburst made Emma want to withdraw and disappear into the woodwork, but looking closer, she saw tears welling up in Flora's eyes. The woman pulled a handkerchief from her dress pocket and tried to compose herself. Emma saw Flora slowly look around the room, her eyes resting on each piece of furniture, every picture, all the sundry items on top of the dresser - a pocketknife, a watch, a set of keys, a baseball, a small pewter sailing ship. Flora picked up the baseball carefully and gazed at it with a distant look.

Patiently, Emma waited and, in almost a half-whisper, said, "Mrs. Rucker, I'm so sorry. I didn't mean to bother you none. I just thought it was a nice room, that's all."

Taking a deep breath and exhaling slowly, Flora said, "Thank you. Yes, it is a very nice room. Todd always thought it was."

"Todd? Who's Todd?"

Flora formed her words slowly, "You mean, who was Todd? He was our son. He died at a place in Hawaii called Pearl Harbor."

Emma bowed her head like a scorned servant and said, "I'm so sorry. I don't know where that is, but it must be a horrible place."

She paused, "No, it's actually very beautiful. He sent us pictures."

"Why was he there?"

Flora covered her mouth with the handkerchief and spoke, "Our son was a proud sailor. He had a boyhood love for ships and the ocean even though he had never seen either one until he joined the navy."

The detached gaze in Flora's eyes became even more distant, and she seemed suspended in mid-thought.

"How old was he?"

Flora opened the armoire, revealing a young man's wardrobe. Tucked in the back was a stiffly pressed navy uniform.

"They never found him."

"Ma'am?"

"He was eighteen, and they never found his body."

Wide-eyed and at a loss for words, Emma shook her head in disbelief. Not knowing what else to do, she slowly and gently touched Flora's arm.

Flora patted the hand that touched her and said, "It'll be ten years this December. That's a long time, but sometimes it seems like just yesterday. Don't worry, I'm okay. I just hadn't planned on coming in here today."

"So, why—"

Flora suddenly tried to look more in control and finished Emma's question, "So, why are we here? Okay, I'll tell you. Thomas has a nephew who is coming to visit, and he needs a bedroom. The other bedrooms are full of clutter, and I don't have time to straighten them out. So, he gets this one."

Crossing the door's threshold, the bare hardwood floor creaked softly under their feet.

With a minimum of words between them, they put clean sheets on the bed and cleaned out the armoire and the dresser drawers. Emma made the dust disappear quickly. She watched Flora gently take the artefacts from the dresser top and wrap each one in tissue paper before they went into a box in the closet. The window hadn't been opened in years, and it took the strength and perseverance of both women to finally break the seal.

The rest of the day went by in slow, lazy fashion. Flora knew she didn't have enough work to keep Emma busy all day. Thomas normally didn't want Emma at the store until almost closing time, so the two women passed the time in silent communion with one another, moving from room to room, trying to make menial tasks seem essential.

Looking at the clock, Flora said, "Emma, why don't you go on to the store now? We're just about through for the day."

"Mr. Rucker, don't want me there until five."

"Mr. Rucker isn't there right now, so it doesn't matter."

"Where is he?"

"He went into Alexandria to pick up our nephew at the train station. He'll be back around six. You go ahead now. Thanks for your help today. I have some cooking to do."

Emma seemed to bounce as she spoke, "What ya' cookin'?"

"Banana pudding. That's our nephew's favorite, from what I hear."

"Banana puddin'. Ain't never made that before. Kin, you show me how to someday?"

"Oh, it's easy. Yes, certainly—one day when we have time."

Quietly, Emma put her shoes on and left.

Tom had left the store in the hands of Lonnie Ray Campbell, a young man who had graduated from high school two years before and had worked at the store since he was fourteen. Lonnie worked two jobs now, claiming he was saving to go to college. He had been a star basketball player, but colleges didn't pay much attention to small high schools like Kisatchie. Patricia Marshall, his girlfriend of the past four years, had let it be known he didn't need a college education to marry her. Emma had seen Patricia's car parked out front as she approached the store. She entered from the back and could hear voices whispering in the rear storage room. A giggle came from the shadows as Emma reached for the pull chain on the bare bulb hanging from the ceiling.

"Hi! What ya'll doin'?" she asked in earnest.

Startled, Lonnie and Patricia quickly released their embrace. They both were speechless for a few seconds.

"Emma, don't ever sneak up on us like that again!" Lonnie said in a hushed, angry tone. Patricia immediately began pulling at her dress and smoothing out wrinkles. She tried to act casual at first, then looked hard at Emma as though a bolus of bile had just risen into her throat.

Speechless for a moment, Emma finally spoke, her hands on her hips, "Lonnie, I didn't sneak up on you! I come through that door every day! I didn't know you were back here," she took a step closer and leaned toward Lonnie, "So, what was ya'll doin'?"

"Nothing!" Lonnie said in a forced whisper, waving his arms, "Why are you here an hour early?"

"Miss Flora ran out of things for me to do at the house, so she sent me here."

By now, Patricia had walked out of the storage room and into the main part of the store, obviously headed for her car. Lonnie was trying to catch up to her.

She turned, walked back to Lonnie and spoke through her teeth, "You make sure that little dirt clod forgets everything she saw. You're not going to lose your job because of her! Do you understand?"

"She won't say anything, don't worry."

The two walked to the front door and said a quick goodbye. Patricia gave Emma a glaring look over Lonnie's shoulder and whispered something in his ear.

Standing at the back of the store, broom in hand, Emma waved cheerfully and immediately went to work, humming to herself.

After about a minute, Lonnie walked slowly toward Emma, trying to look appealing.

"Emma? Could I ask a favor of you?"

Emma stopped sweeping and looked at him seriously, "Yeah. What is it?"

"Just what did you see when you came in?"

She went back to sweeping. She followed the broom with her eyes and said, "Lonnie, that's a question, not a favor."

His eyes widened, "Hey! Don't give me none of your shit today! I got too much at stake here to take something off a little … Wait, I'm sorry, I'm sorry. Okay, first a question, then a favor."

Emma had stopped and looked at him warily, "Okay."

Lonnie looked at her in anticipation.

"Well?"

"Well, what?"

"So, what did you see when you came in?"

"You mean back there in the storage room?"

"Yes."

"When I first come in?"

"YES!"

"Nothin'. I didn't see nothin'."

A look of satisfaction spread across Lonnie's face, "Good. That's good. There wasn't anything to see, right?"

"I don't know. It was dark when I first came in. That's why I said I didn't see nothin'. Can't see in the dark, you know."

Lonnie took a deep breath and let it out slowly, "Emma," he said slowly, "You turned the light on, right?"

Emma nodded.

"And what did you see?"

"You and Patricia."

"Doing what?"

"I don't know. I was going to ask you about that later - what WAS ya'll doin' back there? Why are you worried about it?" Emma looked back down at the floor and made a few half-hearted sweeping motions with the broom, "But you were going to ask me a favor."

"Uh, yeah. Listen, Mr. Rucker is kinda' funny about her coming here while I'm working and maybe, well…could you just not mention it to anyone?"

Emma started sweeping more vigorously, "Lonnie, she's a customer just like lots of other folks. I just saw her in the store, that's all. Ain't nothin'."

Relief emerged on Lonnie's face at Emma's words. She worked her way down the aisle, sweeping as she went. Lonnie wiped his mouth with both hands and turned back toward the cash register when Emma continued, "You know, you ought to tell her to park in the back next time. Everybody in town know'd she was here," she stopped and pondered for a few seconds, "But I ain't sayin' nothin' to nobody."

The smile on Lonnie's face vanished, and his jaws tightened, but he remained silent.

The two of them closed the store at six.

The weekend came like all weekends. Saturday, Emma worked a couple of hours at the store and about the same amount of time at the Rucker's house. She hardly saw Flora at all that Saturday. She had a routine and needed little if any, supervision.

As she walked home, she decided to cut through the woods next to the mill pond. Her mind was floating aimlessly, concentrating on nothing yet taking in everything. The hot sun beat down on the road, but the deep woods around the mill pond were always cool from the shade. The air stirred ever so slightly. The weather had been dry for a few days, but that morning, a brief shower had awakened the myriad of miniature woodland kingdoms and had given the forest a renewed fecund smell of all things natural, of plant and soil making new green succulent shoots, of wild honeysuckle responding to the soaking nourishment coming up from its roots; the unfolding of tiny blue Johnny Jump-Up blossoms. Crossing into the shadows, Emma entered this world of which she was an ordained member, dues paid in full, embraced by her friends, both animate and inanimate. The cool water of the pond came to mind, especially the east end, farthest from her house, where the shady creek sand lay undisturbed and smooth on the bank. The pond was just around the next turn, and as she walked, she stopped to remove her shoes, thinking about the feel of the sand between her toes. She crossed her arms in front of her and gathered a handful of her cotton work dress in each hand. The neckline had just slipped over her face as the dress was half off when she heard sounds coming from the pond. Dropping the dress back down onto her shoulders, she froze on the path. Had she heard it? There it was again. Splashing, then soft laughter. Her movements became slow and cautious. She tiptoed to within sight of the pond, where a broad span of bushes hid her presence. In the distance, she heard a car engine start and drive away. On the edge of the pond were three boys, all about her age. She immediately recognized two of them, Jeff Carmichael and Scott Turner. She had known them from school since first grade. The third one was a stranger. He was a little taller than the others and seemed willing to laugh at anything his two companions said. The sunlight bounced off his uncombed blond hair. She strained to hear what they were saying, but each time she tried, the breeze hummed softly through the tops of the pines, blotting out details. She knelt to watch and suddenly realized that Jeff had taken his shirt off, and Scott was not far behind. Bare-chested, they both spoke to the blond stranger, who finally began unbuttoning his shirt as well. Quickly, the first two had their pants unzipped and stripped off while encouraging the third to follow along. Finally, Emma saw the stranger give a surrendering shrug and unbuckle his belt. She was so focused on this one that it took a moment to realize that Jeff and Scott were completely undressed and headed for the water, their backsides showing a pale lack of suntan on their buttocks. They were knee-deep in the water when both turned around in full view of Emma and said something to their friend, who was shyly lagging behind. Emma had never seen her father so totally undressed, but she had a vague notion of male anatomy from seeing Lavenia's boys as infants. She remembered hearing the hushed whisperings in the girls' locker room of the gym, not knowing what the intrigue and apparent fascination were all about. Now, in full view, she was shocked by the pendulous size of everything, surrounded by the dark fringed halo, much more prominent and visible than she had occasionally imagined. Finally, all three boys were in deeper water, and for some reason, Emma felt relieved that they were. Why did she feel unwelcome and intrusive in her own woods?

She rose from her secluded spot and crept back to the main trail. She followed the path instinctively, her thoughts focused on this new discovery, as though she had seen a blue cow with green polka dots. And not one, but three! Her mind quickly pictured all the boys at school, all the men she had seen come into the store. She had seen pictures of naked statues and hadn't paid much attention to the details of manhood, but it came back to her now so vividly. Her father! Did they all look that way? The revelation was stunning. Then, she thought of Woodrow Spears and felt an unexpected wave of repulsion.

But who was the tall one? It was her last fleeting thought before turning into her yard and heading for the back door.

Tom Rucker was at the store early the next day, and breaking with routine. He hailed Emma as she walked by on her way to the house. His words had a hint of a sharp tone.

"Emma, could you come inside? I need you here this morning. Mrs. Rucker and I talked about this last night. Just a couple of hours, then you can go on to the house," she followed him into the store, "Right now, I need you to fill the soda machine, then bring all those boxes from just inside the back door … yeah, those … bring 'em over to that far aisle and fill in the gaps on the shelves. I thought I told Lonnie to do that yesterday; well, maybe I didn't. Anyway, put the new stuff in the back and the old stuff in the front. You know how to do it, now git going."

An hour later, she had the shelves stocked and all the cans turned so the labels faced the aisle. Her knees were grubby from kneeling on the floor. Finding a push broom, she began sweeping, only to have Mr. Rucker stop her.

"Did I tell you to do that?"

"No sir, but I always do it when I see it needs doin'."

They both heard the front door open and bang shut. "Don't argue with me. Just go on to the house now. G'wan, now. Miss Flora's waiting," he made a shooing, upward motion with the back of his hand as though she were a pestering child, all the while looking toward the front of the store.

Emma started in the direction of the back door when she heard Tom speaking to someone. His voice sounded hurried and concerned, as though someone important had just entered. She peeked around from behind a display of mops and saw him talking to a teenage boy. He wore a yellow short-sleeve sports shirt and brand-new crisp jeans. Peeking out from under the cuff of his jeans were sharp-toed cowboy boots with a deep luster. He smiled when he spoke and seemed very comfortable with Mr. Rucker. His voice was rhythmic and almost musical.

Noticing that Emma was still lingering in the back of the store, Tom directed the boy's attention to something out the front window, a line of vision away from Emma, then motioned to her again and mouthed 'Hurry up' with a scowl.

In a few short minutes, she was at the Rucker house. Flora was rushing about, seemingly preoccupied with her own thoughts. When she finally spoke to Emma, she was quickly walking through the kitchen and said, "I'm going over to Ruby Forester's for a couple of hours. She's coming to get me shortly. I'll be back before lunch."

Emma was standing by the sink in the kitchen, putting away pots and pans which had been washed and allowed to drip dry. Flora continued from the hallway, "There's a load of wash on the line already and another one in the machine. You'll need to run that load through the wringer, remember? Then run in the rinse water. Remember how I showed you? You can do that, right?"

"Yes'm."

Flora finally came to a stop in the kitchen doorway, holding three purses, "There's a list on the table of a few other things I want you to do before lunch," she hesitated and asked, "Which purse do you think I should take?"

"The one in the middle," Emma said quietly, only glancing up.

"Think so? Maybe I should change my shoes then."

Flora finally left when a car horn beeped a single staccato note in the driveway. The purse, the shoes, and the dress all matched.

Emma had never been left alone in the Rucker house before for this length of time. She had been working there long enough to know the house like her own, and Flora trusted her. She caught on quickly and soon had established her own routine, as she had at her own house, of putting the things back in order from the evening and night before. Per Flora's instructions, she made the bed in the master bedroom, although Tom would have objected to the idea of her going into his and Flora's bedroom had he known. The kitchen usually had to be cleaned up after breakfast, although on this morning, Flora had already done most of it. She spent several minutes over the washer, feeding clothes through the wringer and into the spinner. Done with that small task, she carried a basket load of wet sheets to the line in the backyard.

Propping the empty wicker basket on her hip, she came back into the house humming softly. She hadn't heard the car pull into the front drive and stop, nor had she heard the front screen door quietly open and close. What she did hear was the sharp footfall on the hallway floor, which made her gasp just as a tall figure emerged from the side kitchen door. The first thing she noticed was the boots, then the yellow shirt.

"Hi," he said, "I'm Hugh."

Chapter 7

"You're who?" Emma asked with alarm.

"Hugh. Hugh Giles, from Houston."

"Nobody told me about no one coming in here today. I don't know nobody named Hugh!" She was shifting her feet and trying to avoid making eye contact with him.

"Well, I'm sorry. I was just looking for something," he started down the hall toward the guest bedroom.

"Hey! Where're you going? You ain't supposed to be in here. I'm going to call Mr. Rucker!" She quickly picked up the telephone, "You better git outa' here!"

He turned around and came back to the kitchen door, "Look. I'm not trying to scare you, and I'm not lying. I'm Hugh Giles from Houston. The Ruckers are my Aunt Flora and Uncle Tom," he said as Emma's trembling fingers dialed the phone.

Her breath was coming in gulps as she heard Tom Rucker answer the phone, "Mr. Rucker! They's this guy in here! A fella' just come in the house, and he won't leave! No, he ain't done nothin', but he's just standin' here lookin' at me!"

On the other end of the line, Tom spoke firmly, "Emma, calm down. Is he about six feet tall, blonde hair, yellow shirt?"

"Well, yessir. But he just comes in the house while I was out back hangin' the—"

"Emma, did he say his name was Hugh Giles?"

For a moment, she was stunned, "Uh, yessir—he did."

"Calm down. That's my nephew, Emma. He's supposed to be there. I sent him to get something out of the garage, but - let me talk to him."

Emma laid the phone down and stepped back. She kept her arms folded tightly in front of her, "he wants to talk to you," she said firmly, nodding her head at the phone.

Hugh took a step toward the phone, and Emma took another one back. Half-smiling, he kept his eyes on her as he picked up the receiver with his fingertips and spoke into it, "Uncle Tom, it's just me. I looked in the garage and … no, it wasn't there. The bumper jack with the big handle? No, I only saw a small one. I don't think it'll fit the truck. Wha—I just came in to get something. Something from my room. No, you didn't tell me to stay out of the house. Yes, I was listening to you, Uncle Tom," he held the phone from his ear while Tom Rucker said something Emma couldn't make out. She made a gesture for him to give her the phone, and Hugh interrupted his uncle, "Wait, this girl wants to say something to you," he gently tried to hand the phone to her, then decided the best move was to lay it down as she had. He took a step back, and she picked it up.

"Mr. Rucker, you looking for the jack to the truck? It's in the truck bed, right behind the cab. Did you see them feed sacks back there? It's under them. Yessir. You put them back there last week. No, sir, you never told me to clean the truck. Yessir, I'll do it first thing tomorrow. Okay, tonight, then. Yessir."

Feeling safer, she handed the phone to Hugh and returned to the laundry room. She heard Hugh talking to Tom as the conversation ended. Something about hurrying back to the store. He stuck his head in the door as she was sorting laundry.

"Sorry if I scared you," his voice was soft and warm, "By the way, you know my name now, but I don't know yours."

"Emma," she said decidedly, "My name's Emma," she spoke without looking up from the basket of clothes she was holding.

"Okay, I'll be seeing you later—Emma. You know, maybe at the store or something," he paused and looked at the back of her slender figure. Her feet were bare, but her toenails were red with nail polish, "You go to school here? Looks like I'm going to start the year here while my folks are away," he paused, waiting for a response, "So, that's in a few weeks, isn't it?"

"There 'bout."

"I'll be a senior. How about you?"

"Junior," she said curtly.

Hugh leaned against the doorframe, "Well, that's good. I mean, maybe you can introduce me to some folks. I don't know anyone here," he paused for a moment and said, "Well, I do, sort of. Uncle Tom and Aunt Flora introduced me to some family friends a couple of days ago, but that's all."

Emma turned her head, cut a quick glance at him, and said, "Sure, maybe. I stay kinda' busy, though," she lifted the heavy basket of wet clothes and spoke without looking at him, "You better go now."

"Okay, I'll be going. Talk to you later, Emma. You need some help with that?"

"No," she said over her shoulder, trying to sound uninterested in further conversation. Her steps quickened toward the back door and the clothesline.

Hugh left through the front door, and Emma waited until she heard the car door shut and the engine start before she walked back toward the front of the house. She peeked through the curtains to see out the window. The car's rear wheels spun slightly in the loose gravel as it left the front gate.

So, that's Hugh, she thought. Overwhelmed by curiosity, she quietly walked down the hall toward Todd's bedroom, then suddenly realized she was the only one in the house to hear her own footsteps. He had been back there doing something when she came in from the clothesline. She carefully opened the bedroom door and noticed a black baseball cap hanging on one bedpost. It had the letters 'NY' on the front. The closet was open, and several pairs of jeans and an array of shirts were neatly hung. On the dresser was a picture of a baseball player taking a full swing with a bat, his legs in an awkward twist from the exertion. He had the number '7' on the back of his jersey. The hat he wore looked like the one on the bedpost.

Suddenly feeling like she was being watched, she backed out of the room and shut the door.

Throughout the rest of the morning, she tried to stay focused on what needed to be done for Flora. The image of Hugh kept coming back to her as though it controlled her thoughts. Details which she hadn't noticed earlier came into focus. His voice had smooth tones when he spoke to Mr. Rucker on the phone. He seemed so sure of himself. Tom Rucker had seemed more upset than Hugh. And there was that look he had when he was listening intently. It was gentle strength, unwavering patience. But there was something else.

The more Emma's mind became engrossed with thoughts about Hugh, the faster she worked. She suddenly realized she had finished all her morning list of chores and had time to spare. She retrieved her cigar box of drawing materials from the library closet where Flora had said she could keep them. In a quick fifteen minutes, she had a fairly accurate picture of Hugh Giles sketched out with pencil and colored chalk, complete with the blond curls, one of which fell limp-like over his forehead. His eyes were sky blue, and that subtle little wrinkle at the corner of his mouth seemed to carry a message. She remembered small beads of sweat on his forehead, brought on by the summer heat. It had trickled down while he talked. He had looked like he needed - something cool! A swim! That was him! Her thoughts immediately flashed back to the woods, the pond, and three boys in the water. She suddenly felt embarrassed by what she remembered. It hadn't been her fault, though. Nobody had asked if they could swim in her pond! She couldn't help it if she saw them. They couldn't help being, well, what they were. Should she have stayed as long as she had? Should she have watched as closely as she did? What if they find out? But how could they know?

"This is silly," she finally said out loud. Her attention turned back to the drawing.

In bold strokes that took about twenty seconds, she added the collar of the yellow shirt. She had gathered all the chalk and charcoal back into the box and was returning it to its place in the closet when she heard Flora saying goodbye to her friends on the front steps. Quickly, she closed the closet door.

Flora walked into the library, mopping her forehead. She kicked off her shoes and flopped ungracefully into one of the large chairs, "This is one of your favorite rooms, isn't it?" she said to Emma, who responded with a quick nod, "C'mon, let's go fix lunch for the fellas. You can run it over to them."

In a few short minutes, Emma was walking at a brisk clip toward the store. Her heart was in her throat. Hugh: He was not what she was used to seeing in Kisatchie. He was more like what she had seen in magazines: a square chin and a smooth complexion. There was something about the way he walked, the way he stood, the way he talked. His personality was like an invisible magnet. *So, what!* she thought. *He's just a guy. Why can't I stop thinking about him?*

Entering the back of the store, she heard Hugh and Lonnie talking. The topic seemed to be baseball, although Emma could only hear fragments of the conversation. On those days when Flora asked her to bring Tom's lunch to the store, she had always placed it by the cash register and simply left. This time, she was intrigued by the dialogue between Lonnie and Hugh, not so much the words but the mannerisms. Lonnie had always been her image of a confident young man, minimally attractive but nevertheless someone out of her league. He was no longer a boy but not yet a man with wrinkles of wisdom. Standing next to him was Hugh, whom she figured to be two years younger if he was a senior, and yet he had the look of a mature, young man. When the two of them looked in Emma's direction, she got two completely different reactions. Lonnie scowled, looked at his watch and said, "Hey, it looks like it's time to eat. I'm going to meet someone for lunch," he started untying the apron he was wearing.

Hugh's face broke into a smile that seemed to reach out and envelope her. His eyes spoke as clearly as words ever could. Emma felt her cheeks begin to flush, then burn ever so slightly. The back of her neck tingled, and she suddenly realized she was staring intently at him.

"I brung your … I brung your lunch," she finally managed to say. She stole a quick peek in one bag and said, "This 'uns yours. Miss Flora showed me how to make that puddin' you like. It's back at the house. I couldn't put it in no lunch bag," she uttered a shy giggle.

"Why, thank you so much, Emma. That was very kind of you," he was about to continue when Mr. Rucker walked in carrying mail from the post office next door.

"Hugh, you ready?" He looked at the lunch bag by the register, "Emma, I forgot to tell my wife, Hugh, and I are going to Haverty's tavern for lunch," Lonnie was coming out of the storage room when Tom stopped him, "Lonnie, you mind eating your lunch here? We won't be long. You can have mine. Flora makes a good lunch."

Lonnie was caught in mid-stride when Tom spoke. Not knowing what to say, he simply nodded and walked back to the storeroom.

Hugh was still looking into his open bag, "I'll keep mine in the cooler," he said quietly to Emma, "I always get hungry in the afternoon."

With that, he turned and followed Tom to the door. He hesitated just long enough to turn and give Emma a wink.

She thought she was going to burst. Never had she felt so drawn to anyone. She understood none of it except that the whole world seemed like a whirlwind with her caught up in it. One smile, one small wink, and her self-esteem went soaring! She had always been the one no one ever paid attention to—avoided, in fact. The image of him going out the door was permanently etched on her mind. She felt captured in a pool of joy where nothing else mattered.

Lonnie's voice startled her, "That's three days in a row that sonofabitch hasn't let me off for lunch," Angry, he perched on a stool behind the register and dumped the contents of the lunch bag on the counter, "Hadn't been but four people in here all day! Patricia's gonna' think, well, I dunno what she's gonna' think!" He looked back at Emma. "What are you all smiles about? Huh?"

Lonnie's intrusion into Emma's thoughts was like a rude awakening from a euphoric dream. Embarrassed, she felt like Lonnie could read her thoughts. She started to leave when he stopped her, "Hey, wait a minute! Did you tell Mr. Rucker that Patricia was here the other day? Is that it?" He paused for Emma's answer. Seeing her flushed appearance, he drew his own conclusions, "You little bitch! You know, Patricia said it right. You really are just a filthy rag!" Leaning his face inches away from hers, he said, "If I find out you said anything to him about me and Patricia, I'm gonna' beat your little tattletale ass!"

Emma felt herself flinch and backed away, "Lonnie," she said, "I told you I wouldn't say nothing. Why would I say anything?" She felt herself begin to bristle, "I'd be in as much trouble as you if I started blabbin' about things! You ain't never heard me open my mouth about anybody before, and I ain't startin' now! And if you gonna' whup anybody's ass, it ain't gonna' be mine! Mr. Rucker went to Alexandria for the last two workdays. That's why he left you here! And today, he's gone to lunch with Hugh!"

Lonnie's anger shifted but didn't subside, "Okay, so I guess I gotta' call Patricia. Maybe tomorrow'll be different." He stopped and glanced at Emma, "His name is Hugh, huh? How'd you know his name? I didn't think you knew him."

"He come by the house this morning. He come looking for Mr. Rucker's bumper jack to the truck. Besides, Mr. Rucker called him by name as they was leaving. Didn't you hear him?"

"Came by the house, huh?"

"Yeah, scared me half to death. I was in the backyard, and I came in the back door, and there he stood. Miss Flora was off at another lady's house, and I didn't know what to …"

Lonnie interrupted, "Ah, I see. You were all alone in the house, and this new guy comes in to see you."

"Lonnie, he didn't come to see me. He—he come for the …"

"Yeah, now I'm getting the picture. Musta' been nice. I think I know what you're smiling about now. Hey, girl, you really think he's interested in you? You must be crazy. His family is loaded! Oil business back in Houston. His papa owns three cars and two airplanes," he leaned toward her for emphasis, "Flies 'em hisself. His mama is Mr. Rucker's sister. She went off to Texas to go to college and met this rich oil family. Married right into it. They got a whole crew of housekeepers. People just like you! That's what you are, you know. You're Mrs. Rucker's housekeeper. Miss Flora's little white nappy girl. And now you got your eye on the rich stuff! Lots o' luck, sweetie!" He finished with a howling laugh.

What little remained of her composure was slowly losing strength. Her chin started to quiver as she backed away. Rarely had any bully made her cry. Her thoughts were returning to reality, and she felt like a fool. Lonnie was right. Her only option was to leave as fast as possible.

"Yeah, go on," Lonnie said, taunting her as she half ran to the back door. In the back parking lot, she could still hear Lonnie's haunting laughter.

As she walked back to the house, she knew she had to talk to Hugh. Somehow, she had to find the time to know more about him. He was like an unsolved celebrity puzzle. Was he just flirting with her? He seemed friendly enough to Lonnie. Did that make him the same as Lonnie? Maybe he was just nice to everybody. Maybe she meant nothing to him - just another person to be polite to. He was looking to meet more people. Was he just some fake guy? Blinking away tears, she pulled up the hemline of her dress and wiped her eyes. As she approached Flora's house, she took a quick detour to the backyard, where she knew there was an outside faucet. For several seconds, she filled her hands over and over with cool water and rubbed her face. Not until she was sure all traces of distress were gone did she enter the house.

The next two weeks went by quickly. Joshua was on better behavior than usual. He still drank every night, but he seemed satisfied with smaller quantities. The school board was keeping him busy with an assortment of work. He even found time to dig up some old relics for an antique dealer who was passing through town. It always amazed Emma how he could leave just before dark with a slight stagger in his step and come back a few hours later with a wheelbarrow full of old dishes, bottles, and kitchen utensils. But then, that's what had occupied the shelves of their kitchen for years. Some of Emma's kitchenware was well over one hundred years old and would have brought a rich price at auction. Emma had brought home some more clothes that Flora had given her, a partial payment for her work in preparation for the opening of school. Flora knew that too much cash might find its way into Joshua's hands, which translated into more liquor. Emma saw only glimpses of Hugh at the house or the store. They were usually going in opposite directions and had time only for a few words. Each time was the same, though. The muscles of her face seemed to have a mind of their own and blossomed into a broad grin from the time he came into view until well after he departed. Each time he did most of the talking, her answers were usually of the one-word variety, but it left Emma glowing inside each time. Hugh, on the other hand, seemed the perfect gentleman with everyone, including Emma, which made her sometimes wonder if he felt the same as she did when they were together. If so, he must be good at hiding it, she thought.

The first day of school had its usual confusion. Mr. MacArthur held a special afternoon assembly of all twelve grades and talked about the events of the coming school term and how the high school students were expected to set an example for the elementary grades. Although the lunch break was staggered so as never to mix more than three grades at a time in the lunchroom, the younger children had opportunities to mix with the older kids before and after school as well as on the buses. The student population was about 350, including all twelve grades, which meant that Kisatchie practically doubled in size during the school year. Students above the ninth grade were allowed to leave the campus during lunch, so Rucker's store always stocked up on dessert items like popsicles and ice cream cups. Many of the older kids came with lists of things to buy for younger brothers and sisters or any other youngster who knew how to negotiate a favor from an older friend.

Hugh was quickly forming a circle of friends by the end of the first week. His personality was contagious. While many of the students were from farms and came to school barefoot and in coveralls, Hugh had a disarming manner which soon erased any fear of social distinction. Every day after lunch, he would take his shoes off and play softball with any or all of them. He never spoke of his home in Houston. He was just *Hugh from Texas.*

On Friday of the second week, Hugh was walking on the school grounds during lunch with three others when he spied Emma going in the same direction but by herself.

"Let's see if Emma wants to go with us," he said. The others slowly turned and looked at him in disbelief.

Beverly Towers, who had personally taken a shine to Hugh from the first day, asked, "Don't you know who she is?" Before he could answer, she walked closer to Hugh so their shoulders rubbed.

"Well, I know she does some work for the Ruckers," he said with a glance at Beverly.

"That's not it," said Ellis Carmichael, "What we're talking about is who she is, what she is, and where she lives."

"I don't follow what you mean."

Beverly started to say, "Her father was the foreman …"

Ellis interrupted, "She lives in a shack over in Pittman. Her old man's a drunk, and her mama's been dead for a long time. She never bathes. One day last year, she smelled so bad the school bus driver made her sit in the back, and everyone else crowded up in the front. There's a colored family not too far from where they live, and Emma spends a lot of her time at their house."

"So, what's the deal with her father? What does he do for a living?"

"Not much of anything," Ellis continued, "He used to be the foreman at the Pittman sawmill until it closed. The only friend he ever had was his wife."

"And Oscar Carter," said Beverly.

Hugh looked puzzled.

"Oscar and Lavenia," she continued, "The colored family we just told you about."

"So, tell me, how does she smell this school year?" Hugh asked with a chuckle.

"You're missing the point again, Hugh," said Ellis.

"No, I think I see the point exactly. Look, I'll catch up with you guys later," he split away from the group and started around behind the gym where Emma had disappeared a few seconds before.

She was walking through a small grassy area behind the maintenance building next to the gym and was startled when she heard someone coming from behind. Hugh was slightly out of breath when he reached her.

"Emma, where are you headed?" he asked.

She shoved her hands into the pockets of her dress. "Nowhere. I just walk around the schoolyard during lunch."

"Yeah—say, I was wondering … some of the others were going into town. You want to come?"

"With all of y'all? Like who?"

"Well, Ellis and Beverly and …"

"No, Hugh, I don't think so," she said firmly.

"Why not?"

"They don't like me that much."

"I don't see why," he said.

"It's a long story."

"Uh-huh."

"I'm just waiting to finish school so I kin get a job in, maybe, Alexandria or Jena or somewhere. Just something away from here."

"I don't understand. Why don't they like you?"

"You ask a lota' questions," she paused and continued, "Nobody in this town likes me or my papa. And now, I suppose you're going to ask about that part, too. Ain't ya'?"

That familiar infectious smile spread across his face and invaded her gloom, "So, why don't we sit down, and you tell me about it? We've got some time before class starts again."

Emma looked around to see if they were alone. For the next several minutes, the two sat on the ground, leaning against the building with Emma talking and Hugh listening.

"Papa was a foreman at the mill. He always told me that the only way he could get people to work was don't let 'em get away with nothin'. 'You got to MAKE people work. Don't never trust nobody,' he'd tell me. If you wanted a job in his town, you had to go through him. He was in charge of everything."

"You remember this?"

"Naw, it's what he told me. But listen to what I'm telling you. Everybody in town says the same thing, so it must be the gospel truth. Anyway, nobody liked Papa, and then he went and married my mother, and they tell me that just about knocked the daylights outa' everybody. I've seen some pictures of her one time. She was real purty. But she died when I was little. By then, Papa had done lost his job with the mill, and, well, there weren't no mill by then, so he started drinkin', and he still does," she stopped and pulled at a blade of grass, "Sometimes his drinkin' gets bad, and I have to get out of the house."

"Where do you go?"

"Lavenia's house."

"Oh, that's … yeah, I heard about them."

She looked away as she spoke, "Yeah, I bet you did. Anyway, we ain't got much, and I don't fit in for all kinds of reasons, so—"

"So, how did you get to know the Ruckers?"

Emma folded her hands, "Miss Flora? She took a shine to me when I was a little girl. Right about when I needed a mama the most, but it ain't like she's trying to be my mama; she just does nice things for me sometimes. She fixed it up with Mr. Tom so I could work in the store. He's awful cross all the time, though. I don't think he's very happy."

They both sat silent for a few seconds.

"I heard you like banana puddin'," she said.

"Yeah, I do. My favorite," he picked up a small rock and tossed it.

A bell rang, "God, look at the time! I think my watch stopped," Hugh almost shouted. They both jumped up and ran to the science classroom, bolting through the door just as the tardy bell sounded. Everyone in the class looked toward the door when they came in.

When school was over that day, Hugh caught up with Emma.

"Emma, how do you get home?"

"I take the bus. Sometimes I walk."

"Where do you live?"

"It's about two miles from here—that way," she pointed south.

"Well, I've got Uncle Tom's truck. I could give you a ride."

"I—I don't know."

"Actually, I wanted you to finish what you started telling me during lunch break today."

"Not today. Maybe some other time."

"How long does the bus take?"

"About thirty minutes."

"To go two miles? No wonder you walk. Look over there at those clouds. I'll bet it's going to rain."

"No, it ain't. Hugh? Them purty white clouds? That's miles away, and they ain't even dark. Besides, I kin smell it when it's going to rain, and it ain't," she felt herself beginning to relax.

"Well, you can't blame me for trying."

"Why're you trying to be so nice to me?"

"I just want to hear the rest of your story. Look, the buses are ready to leave. Everyone's going home. Now, you gotta take my offer."

She paused for a moment and looked away from him. It was as though looking at him robbed her of the last shred of self-control she may have. She was trying hard to keep a tight rein on her by herself.

"Straight home?" she asked.

"I had nothing else in mind," he said with a harmless shrug.

A few more seconds passed before she said, "Okay. But I gotta' tell you how to get there. Where's the truck?"

"Over there."

Again, she waited to answer. She gazed off in the distance and finally said, "Okay, bring the truck around beside the maintenance building and meet me back there. Nobody'll see us."

"What's with all the secrecy? Let's just get in the truck and go."

"Never mind, I'll walk."

"Wait, wait. Okay, whatever you say. I just feel a little clandestine."

"Beside the building, okay? Give me a few seconds to get there."

"I'll be there."

Hugh casually strolled over to the truck and looked back over his shoulder. Emma was nowhere to be seen. He was about to slide in behind the wheel when an authoritative voice spoke from behind him.

"Have a nice day, Hugh?" It was Alton MacArthur.

Surprised, Hugh turned quickly and bumped his head on the open door of the truck.

"Hugh, I'm sorry. I didn't mean to startle you."

"Mr. MacArthur! Oh, hi! Uh, it's okay … I'm fine. Actually, I've had harder bumps in football," he placed one foot on the running board and one hand on the steering wheel. He was halfway into the truck as Mr. Mac talked.

"Yes, I heard you played back in Texas. Too bad we don't have that here. School's too small. One team would take up most of the senior class, girls included!" Mr. MacArthur chuckled slowly.

"Uh, yessir. That's right. But nothing wrong with being small, though," he turned and again started to climb into the truck.

Mr. Mac continued, "I remember when I was in college, we had a team. I played some. I wasn't quite the athlete that some of the others were. The jocks were always popular. That's why I tried, I guess. So, how big a school do you have in Houston?"

"It's a lot bigger than this one. Mr. Mac, I gotta' …"

"Yes, well, I hope our small size doesn't hinder you any when you transfer back. When do you suppose that will be?"

"Yessir, about ten weeks. Mr. Mac, I really …"

"Well, don't forget about us when you go back. You seem to have made a few friends rather quickly. Lots of good people around here. But even good people can be swayed by something that dazzles them. You know what I mean?"

Hugh was puzzled by the last comment but tried not to show it, "Yessir, I think I know what you mean."

"You've made good friends here, so I've heard. Remember, it's a small town. A small, neighborly, loving town. But sometimes, small towns can be a little nosey, too. I guess it's because folks don't have enough to keep them busy. I try to keep my finger on the pulse of what's going on. Especially with my students, I've established myself as a good vantage point in more ways than you can imagine. For instance, I know of a couple of kids who almost missed class after lunch today. This quiet little town isn't as quiet as one might think."

Hugh could only look at him. For the moment, nothing worth saying came to mind.

"Hugh, in case I've got you totally confused, just let me tell you this. You're a newcomer. Things you do will be very visible. Just don't lose perspective. You have a nice weekend."

Mr. MacArthur walked back toward his office as Hugh said goodbye. He started the truck and slowly backed out of the parking spot.

Turning the corner, he saw Emma's head quickly pull back behind the corner of the building. He pulled up even with her and opened the door.

"Where have you been?" she asked anxiously.

"Mr. Mac. He stopped me as I was trying to leave and wanted to talk."

"What about?"

"Oh, uh—football!" Hugh put the truck in gear and started moving.

"Football?"

"Yeah, of all things. Wha—Emma, what are you doing?"

"Doing?"

"Why are you hiding your face under the dashboard? Your chin's on your knees!"

"Just drive and tell me when we're off the school grounds."

"Are you hiding? You're hiding! From who? Why?"

"Are we off yet?"

"Almost. God, I can't believe this! You don't want to be seen with me!"

The truck rattled across the cattle guard at the school gate, "Okay, we're off! Now, what's this about?"

She carefully raised up and looked, "I told you people don't like me," she said with her eyes quickly darting from side to side, "It ain't that I don't want to be seen with you; it's just that you shouldn't be seen with me. Then they won't like you, neither. By the way, what was that word you used back there?"

"What word? Good Lord, you're acting spooky all of a sudden."

"Clan, it was. Clan—something. We were talking about meetin' behind the building."

"What, oh—you mean clandestine?"

"Yeah. What's that?"

"Secretive, sneaky."

"Well, I guess that's us, huh?"

"Yeah, but why? Hey, which way do I go?"

"I told you before, south."

"So, where's that?"

Emma was practically bouncing in the seat now, "Hugh Giles, you don't know which way is south?"

"I'm not believing this!"

"I ain't believing it either! You don't know which way is south. Ha!"

"No, that part, I believe. I don't believe what's come over you! Do you always get this crazy in a vehicle? Do pick-up trucks do it to you? C'mon, which way is your house? Just point, kiddo, or I'm going right down the middle of town telling everyone I've got Emma with me! By the way, what is your last name?"

"Go ahead, it's your funeral."

"Tell me what your last name is!"

"You also said you were going to drive down through the middle of town. Go ahead. One more year, and I'm leaving this place."

"Well, I'm leaving in nine weeks! What do you think about that?"

Emma was suddenly silent. She looked out the open car window and chewed her thumbnail. Finally, she spoke, "I know you're leaving, Hugh. I'd rather not think about it. And it's Parker. My last name is Parker."

Hugh slowed the truck down to a crawl. "Wait a minute. Did I say something wrong?"

"Look, this was a bad idea. My house is just up here a ways. Let me out. I'm sorry I was acting so crazy a minute ago. I don't know what came over me. Just feeling a little silly, that's all. I kin walk from here."

"Wait, just hold it a minute. Why would you be upset about my leaving, " he turned himself in the seat and looked at her intently, "Do you have a crush on me?"

"I'm not upset about anything. What's that?"

"What's what?"

"Crush. What's that?"

"A crush? Why, that's when you meet someone you really like. It's a boyfriend-girlfriend kind of thing. Is that what's on your mind?"

Emma just stared out the window.

"Oh, God! Not that. Emma, we just met. How can you be already thinking, well, whatever?"

"You sure did seem interested in me."

"But you should know how it is. You know, you meet someone; then, you take some time to get to know them better and, well, you know!"

"No. I don't."

"I mean—you've been through this before, huh?"

She just shook her head. Hugh took in a long breath and exhaled slowly. The truck rolled at a snail's pace along the road.

"You said you lived along here somewhere."

"I said it was up there a ways. Hugh, let me out."

"Emma, I will. But not until we get some things straightened out. I gave you this ride because I wanted you to finish your story. Now, I think we have something more important to talk about. Look, I'm only here for a short while. I like people. I really like people. I like to hear their stories, like yours. I like to hear about their lives. I like to hear about people and who they are, what they do."

"I guess I thought you liked just me."

"But I do."

"But not enough to have one of those, what'd you call it—a crush. You like me just like you do Beverly and Ellis. Well, you better stick to them because if they see us together, you won't even have them for friends."

Hugh brought the truck to a stop. They seemed to be in the middle of nowhere. All around him were vacant foundations of houses. Patches of sidewalk peeked out from under the overgrown grass. Up ahead, a lone figure trudged along, going in the same direction as the truck, away from Kisatchie.

"What is this place, Emma?"

"This here's Pittman. This is my town. This is where I live, where I grow'd up."

"What happened to it?"

"Everybody left, 'cept us."

"I think I've been here before. Isn't there a pond around here? Like a mill pond?"

"Yeah, why?" Emma felt herself starting to smile.

"What? Now you're smiling. Wait a minute, I don't understand. What is it?"

"Never mind."

Hugh just shook his head in disbelief, "Okay. Whatever you say. So, tell me, why did your family stay?"

Emma's face darkened. She pointed ahead of them at the stooped figure walking south, "It was mostly 'cause of him. That's my papa up yonder. I better walk from here. He might git mad if he know'd I was takin' a ride from anybody."

"Emma, I'll be glad to get you to your house."

"Naw, this is far enough. Thanks."

She opened the truck door and hopped to the ground, "I'll see you later, Hugh. Thanks for the ride."

Hugh noticed she didn't completely close the truck door. When he considered doing it himself, he realized she didn't want her father to hear it and know she was behind him. Hoping the gears wouldn't grind, he put the truck in reverse and slowly backed into a side street and waited about two minutes before securing the passenger door, then drove back to town, finally realizing the smallness of her life.

That night at supper in the dining room, Hugh mustered up the courage to ask about Emma.

"Aunt Flora, tell me about this girl, Emma. I've talked to her several times, but folks seem to avoid her."

Flora cleared her throat, "Well, she was once part of a well-to-do family, although the theme of that family wasn't exactly fitting with the genre of our town. Joshua Parker sold himself to the devil long before he came here. He charmed that poor Marcia Patrick into marrying him, and her life was never the same afterwards. She was from a good family here and could have had her pick of all the young fellows we had to offer. But she had a bit of a wild streak in her, and she thought Joshua was a challenge. So, she married him."

"So, what was so bad about him?"

"He set the hours; he set the working conditions; he took the bribes; and he carried out the orders of the Whitmyers. They were the owners of the mills. Joshua had no compassion at all. You had to work for a whole year before he'd give anyone a day off. If anyone got hurt at the mill, they may or may not have a job when they recovered. If anyone got killed, well, they better schedule the funeral on a Sunday if you wanted anyone to come to it. No, sir, he wouldn't give anyone any time off for any reason. He was just a mean old, well—"

"He was a sonofabitch is what he was," Tom Rucker chimed in.

"Thomas, I'm telling you this," she continued, "But anyway, he married Marcia, and they had a child that died right after birth, and then they had Emma. Now, later comes the part that troubles me and most of my friends the most. His dear wife got sick, and he would not take the time to get her to a doctor. By the time he did, she was just riddled with a cancer like I had never seen before. And would you believe he blamed the doctors? He certainly did!"

"So, what about Emma?"

"I'm getting to that. You see, Emma is a product of all of this. After Marcia died, no one would dare approach Joshua and ask about what he was going to do. I mean, the man was like a powder keg! He got into fights in town, and nobody comes out of a fight with Joshua Parker, win or lose, without something being changed. Broken bones, cut faces, ears bitten off, you name it."

"Flora, I'm trying to digest my dinner," said Tom.

"Well, we just need to face the facts. Thomas, if it bothers you, then go start cleaning up the kitchen. So anyway, the only people he could trust was a colored family named Carter."

"Yes, ma'am. I think I heard something about them."

"Well, the woman, Lavenia, started coming over to cook for him and his little girl. I guess he paid her a regular salary until a few years ago. Word has it that he said that his daughter could take over from that point, but I think the man just ran out of money. It's no wonder the way he drinks all the time. A few people in town have shown some Christian charity and given the poor man some odd jobs," Flora sat up straight in her chair and cleared her throat, "I, myself, have taken the girl under my wing. We must help the poor in spirit, you know."

Flora leaned out of her dining chair and peered toward the kitchen, "Well, let's see if your Uncle Tom has finished cleaning the kitchen, or is he going to try to weasel out of it tonight."

Flora and Hugh walked into the kitchen to find Tom sitting at the breakfast table with a large piece of paper in front of him. He slowly looked up at his wife, then his nephew.

Turning the paper towards them both, he said, "Hugh, I found this in the library closet. It was next to some things Emma left here. This is a picture of you, isn't it?"

Chapter 8

Flora and Hugh both leaned toward the drawing to look closer. Hugh reached for it, but Tom pulled it away and looked at him warily.

"Just answer my question," he said.

"Uncle Tom, I've never seen this before."

"And you, Flora? Have you been encouraging this?"

Flora glared at him, "Thomas Rucker, what's gotten into you? That's a fine drawing. Yes, it does look like Hugh. No, I haven't been encouraging it—I just—well, the girl has raw talent, and I just recently found out about it."

"I wasn't talking about her artistic talent. I'm talking about the way she has decided to put her sights on Hugh. This isn't just any picture; it's a picture of Hugh."

Both looked at him in astonishment and started to speak at once.

"Save your breath. I have it from a good source. Several good sources, in fact."

"About what, Uncle Tom? I really don't know what you mean."

"And from what I've heard, you're very much in the middle of it, young man. I'm talking about this puppy-love thing you've struck up with that little clod."

"You're calling Emma a clod? Uncle Tom, that's -"

"Did you or did you not give her a ride today in the truck?"

Hugh looked at Flora before speaking. "Well—"

"For what purpose, I might ask?" Tom's arms were folded, but one finger was constantly tapping. "Your mother told me to take care of you for a few lousy weeks, and you go and start associating with white trash like this; I just won't have it."

Flora had held her tongue for as long as she could. Firmly, she pulled Hugh back away from Tom and stood in front of her husband.

"Thomas, I am shocked at you! What are you implying? Is our Hugh some slick city boy who is coming here to take advantage of a poor, disadvantaged, ignorant little country girl? Do you think he hasn't an ounce of sense or decency in his head?" She turned to Hugh. "You didn't give her a ride today, did you?"

"Yes, ma'am, I did."

Flora was about to continue, and Hugh's response caught her in mid-breath. A smirk spread slowly over Tom's face.

"Uh, well, okay," said Flora. "And I'm sure you had a good reason."

Boldly, Hugh spoke up. "The buses had already left. It would be a long walk home for her."

Tom piped up and said, "The school's just down from the store. She walks to the store every day in the summer and home again. It's even farther to our house, and she walks here as well."

"Every day? With books?"

"And why was she late for the bus?" Tom continued.

"She was talking to me."

"Exactly. And did she start the conversation?"

"No sir, I did."

Flora interrupted, "Tom, you seem to know quite a bit about Hugh's day."

"It's one of the advantages of having a busy, successful store. I talk to lots of people."

"Like who?"

"Flora, I'm not on trial here."

"And neither is Hugh. Who did you talk to about Hugh?"

Tom began to shift uneasily. The body language was not lost on Flora. "Well, Mr. Mac came in," he said.

"So, Alton MacArthur came by to share some juicy gossip, huh?" Flora said.

"I didn't say that. I just said he came in."

"And you talked about what?"

"Flora, don't change the subject on me. Mr. Mac is a very discreet man."

"Did you talk about me?" Hugh asked.

"I'm talking to your Aunt Flora!"

"Answer the boy!"

"Yes! He said you were a popular figure in school and that you made friends very quickly, and you were late for class today. So was Emma."

"How did THAT come into the conversation?" Flora asked.

"Look, both of you. I'm just looking out for Hugh's welfare. He's a typical young man and—"

"And God knows what typical young men might do!"

"Flora, when I asked Mr. Mac how Hugh was doing, I really had his best interest at heart. Really."

"Go on."

"We talked about different schools in the parish, subject matter, class size …"

"A regular PTA meeting! How honorable."

"And when I asked, uh—when I said—"

"Wait. When you asked what? You were going to say, 'You asked'. What did you ask?"

"Okay. Look! Lonnie at the store told me something."

"Now, who's changing the subject?"

"I'm getting there. Just hold on. Lonnie told me he had a conversation with Emma, and he suspected that Emma had taken a liking to Hugh. And I was just following up on it. Then I hear about being late for class, the ride home in the truck, and now this picture. Hugh, you still haven't told me when or where she drew this."

"Uncle Tom, when she did it isn't important. Or where, for that matter. It's more important for you to know that I didn't even know she was an artist. How could I tell you anything about this picture? You know as much about it as I do."

Flora chimed in, "Well, one thing I can tell you, it's a darn good picture. Come to the library, Hugh. I'll show you some others she's done."

The two of them walked out of the kitchen, leaving Tom shaking his head. In the library, Flora glanced over her shoulder to see if

Tom was following. Assured that he wasn't, she whispered to Hugh, "Listen, part of what your Uncle Tom is saying is good advice. Don't get mixed up with her. She's a sweet girl, but she's about as refined as a, well, I don't know how to say it. There's plenty of kids here for you to be with. My husband, if he had his way, would get her out of our house and out of the store completely. I won't have him doing that. So, I couldn't let him get started on the topic of Emma tonight."

"Would he use me to get rid of her?"

Flora just raised her eyebrows.

The next day was Saturday. Everyone's world underwent a shift in schedule. For the most part, it meant less strain, less urgency, and more leisure. Hugh woke at the crack of dawn, however. He had laid awake several hours the night before thinking about Emma. He reflected on what Aunt Flora had said, and it bothered him. And yet, Emma had an innocent sincerity that penetrated through that exterior. The way she smiled was genuine. That wide grin and the way the tip of her tongue barely poked out between her teeth had a strange appeal. She didn't hide her gloom or her delight about anything. She didn't know how. The tiniest little gestures done out of simple politeness, not as a favor, were received as if all the holidays in the year had been rolled up into one and handed to her on a platter. Special delivery for Miss Emma Parker. He wondered what she was doing this morning.

With the sun barely over the horizon, Hugh strolled through the woods behind the Rucker house. *This is crazy*, he thought. *I'm leaving in a few weeks. Maybe Uncle Tom is right.* As he emerged from the trees and walked back to the house, he heard familiar sounds coming from the kitchen. He smelled coffee and hoped breakfast wasn't far behind. Softly whistling, he casually stepped up onto the back porch and headed for the kitchen door.

"How you like ya' coffee?" a cheerful voice called out.

"Emma? That you? What are you doing here? And so early!"

"Well, my neighbor friend, Lavenia, remember I told you about her? Well, she brought me a message that Miss Flora had called and wanted me to come today—see, we ain't got no phone, ain't had one for years, but anyway, she wanted me here this morning to help set up some kinda' social thing she was havin' with some of her lady friends. The message just said, "Come early." Didn't say exactly when. So, I woke up this morning before the sun came up. I did what I had to do for Papa and hurried on over. The rest of the house probably ain't even up yet, are they? Well, I know Miss Flora's an early riser, and I know how she likes her coffee fixed, so I figured I might as well get on over here. I bet she wants me to polish silver today."

Hugh sat at the table, listening. Authentic, that was the word he was looking for. She was just authentic, no facade, no pretense, no games, all suchness. Just pure Emma."Is that coffee okay? Want some more?"

"Where's that pudding you made?"

Hugh was reaching for the refrigerator door when a coarse cough came from the hallway. Tom Rucker appeared at the door in his bathrobe. "Aw shit," he mumbled when he saw the two of them in the kitchen. With that, he turned around and shuffled back to the bedroom. Flora materialized a few seconds later, equally surprised to see Emma already in her kitchen.

"Well, no one can fault you for being late to work, can they?" she said.

"No, just late to class," Hugh murmured loud enough for only Emma to hear. She covered her mouth and giggled.

"So, what you want me to do for you today, Miss Flora?"

"Drink your coffee, child. I have to get my thoughts together before I can organize anyone else's."

"Emma, Aunt Flora showed me some of your drawings last night. Hey, you're really good! You ought to put on a show sometime."

Emma cocked her head. "A show?"

"Well, you could draw pictures of people while they're acting natural, not posing. You could be a real centerpiece for any type of gathering or, you know, like a social function. People like to see pictures of themselves. I've been to art shows in Houston."

"You mean, like, to sell? Nobody wants my old pictures. It's just scribbles."

"How do you know? You haven't tried, have you?"

"But where would I do something like that? I don't go to Houston or places like that."

"Emma, people are people everywhere. You could do it anywhere folks are gathered." He took a long sip of his coffee and looked straight at Flora. "Believe me, anywhere."

Flora caught Hugh's expression. She stirred her coffee and thought. "Emma, the first thing I need done is dust the library and fill all the vases with cut flowers. You remember how I showed you."

"Yes, ma'am." Emma went on her way, humming.

Flora let a few seconds tick by and then shot a glance at Hugh. "You are wicked, Hugh," she said with a devilish gleam. "Pure wicked. I can't have her at my party drawing pictures of folks!"

"Does she serve at your parties?"

"Yes. But she doesn't talk to the folks. She just serves refreshments."

"Last night, you seemed quite proud of the changes she's made in herself. Now, it sounds like you share a little of Uncle Tom's opinion about her."

"Hugh, remember who we're talking about. That would be like inviting, well, I don't know what! It's just too ridiculous to imagine!"

"Aunt Flora, what's the party for? What's the occasion?"

"Why, we're going to plan our next gumbo supper at the church. We do the suppers to raise money for our missionaries overseas."

"So, the purpose of the soiree today is to plan another one later on, which is to raise money for the mission."

"Hugh, start over. What did you call it?"

"Soiree. Party, Aunt Flora. Formal party."

Flora was momentarily befuddled. "Uh, yes. That's what we do. We have one party to plan for another. What are you driving at?"

"Show some of her drawings today. Maybe there could be some interest. If so, let her draw a few, sell them, and give half to the missions."

"And the other half?"

"That's for EMMA, Aunt Flora. She can't be your housekeeper the rest of her life."

"You mean sell pictures in my house? How vulgar!"

"So, sell them in the store!"

"Oh, God no! Thomas has already asked to do that, and I flat turned him down."

"Asked to do what," Tom said from around the corner.

Flora just waved him off with a shrug.

"No," he said. "I want to know what you were just talking about. What did you turn me down on?"

"Oh, lots of things, Thomas," she said with a smirk.

"Could I please have some attention here? What were you talking about?"

Seeing that Flora wasn't going to elaborate, Hugh spoke freely. "We're talking about Emma and her pictures."

"Oh, gad! Yeah, what was she doing here so damned early? Why is she even here on Saturday? Wait a minute, what about her pictures?"

"We were talking about selling them."

"Selling them? Didn't we talk about that before? Oh, yeah! You did shut me up about that one. So, now you want her to do it?"

"No, Hugh does."

"Me? Aunt Flora, I suggested it as a money-making idea for your ladies' group. I didn't say I wanted a part of the action. Emma's a good artist, but I wouldn't know how to manage something like that." He paused. "And neither would she."

"Something like whut?" came Emma's voice from the doorway.

The three seated in the kitchen turned in unison and then looked at each other. A full ten seconds went by before anyone said anything. It was Flora who broke the silence.

"We were discussing your potential future as an artist. Hugh seems to think you could do well at it."

"You mean, like, sell stuff?"

All nodded in agreement.

Emma twisted the dust cloth in her hands. "No, my Papa won't let me do that. If he knew I had any drawing stuff at all, he'd be really mad."

"Why?" they all asked in a chorus.

"Well, I don't remember much about my mama, but I remember she loved to draw. She showed me how, and when she died, Papa got rid of all her drawing stuff. I found some of it one time that he didn't know about, and when he saw me with it, he got fightin' mad, threw it all out, and then he got real drunk. That's when he broke the couch in the living room. Now, I don't think we ought to do it."

Hugh was amazed. "He—he broke the couch? How?"

"Picked it up and threw it. It just broke one of the legs. We still use it, though. I put a stack of books under it to make it level."

Silence fell over the group again. Emma returned to the library, and the others just stared at the table.

Finally, Hugh spoke. "We ought to do something for her."

Tom answered quickly, "Hugh, that's just what I was talking about last night. Don't get involved with that girl! I know there's lots of poverty and hunger all over the world, but you can't save everyone. You have to be practical and work where you can fit in."

Hugh thought for a few seconds. "Aunt Flora, why do you support missionaries?"

"Why, they spread the gospel to those in need of it," she said with an air of righteous pride.

"Yeah, that's what I thought. You know, sometimes you don't have to go too far to find the ones in need, do you? Excuse me, I think I'll go wash the car."

Tom and Flora silently watched as Hugh walked out the front door.

"Well," Tom said slowly. "This is one hell of a way to start out a Saturday morning! I guess I better go open up the store."

Two hours later, Hugh walked into the store whistling and approached Lonnie.

"Heya', Lonnie, what's the latest on the Yankees?"

"Latest, like what?"

"Are they going to make it to the series?"

"Probably. Red Sox won't. I think the Dodgers will. Giants ain't bad, though."

"You by yourself today?"

"Yeah, I don't know where that girl is."

"You mean, what's her name, Emma? Oh, she's at the house. I needed to get out, so I came over here. Uncle Tom around?"

"He's next door at the gas station. What's she doing at the Rucker's house on Saturday?"

"Aunt Flora's got something going on with her ladies' group, and she has Emma helping her get ready for it."

Lonnie was about to walk away when Hugh took a deep breath and spoke up. "Say, I wanted to ask you something."

Lonnie continued walking and said, "Talk to me while I'm sweeping. I gotta get done here. What is it?"

Hugh followed behind, talking to the back of Lonnie's head. "Well, Uncle Tom said something last night that I needed to clear up. Did anyone say something to him about Emma? I mean, you know, about Emma and me?"

"Emma and you? How would I know?" Lonnie had stopped and was looking cock-eyed at Hugh.

"He just said it was something he heard at the store. He didn't mention a customer saying it, so I figured maybe you …"

Lonnie continued sweeping. "Naw. Can't think of nothing. Why?"

Hugh took another long breath and let it out before continuing. "Well, he actually said that you told him that Emma had, well—you know, that she sorta' had eyes for me, you know what I mean?"

Lonnie looked at him again. "Yeah," he said. "Come to think of it, that could be. She does look at you kinda' thick-eyed. I bet if she ever got turned loose, she'd probably go after anything. Probably like a sow in heat, you know. I wouldn't worry none. It'll pass."

Hugh rubbed his hands nervously on the back of his jeans. "What I asked was, did you say anything to him?"

Lonnie shook his head as though the conversation was a nuisance, "No, I didn't say nothing to Mr. Rucker 'bout you and her."

"That's funny. I might have misunderstood him. I'll have to ask him again about that. I just don't like loose ends, you know."

"Yeah, me neither." Lonnie stopped sweeping for a moment. He realized that Hugh was standing right next to him.

"Loose ends. I hate 'em," Hugh repeated. He was moving a little closer, uttering a slow chuckle and feeling braver.

"Hey, look! I don't know what goes on between you and your dear uncle," Lonnie said with a snort and tried to make another stroke with the broom. Hugh was still chuckling almost silently, pulling on his ear. He put his foot on the corner of the broom and held it fast to the floor.

"Yeah," Hugh continued in almost a whisper. "I'll have to check with him on that. Because when someone doesn't have enough balls to tell me the truth, it really chaps my ass. That really puts me in a bad mood, you know?" By now, his voice had diminished to almost a hissing sound as their faces were just inches away from each other.

Lonnie took about three chews on the wad of gum in his mouth and smiled weakly in return. He was three inches taller than Hugh. "Yeah, Hugh. I know what you mean. I truly do. Unless you think you got a problem with me. Then you got real problems."

"That's a two-way street, Lonnie. I'm sure if you happen to hear anything I need to know about, you'll be sure and look me up. I'm easy to find."

"That's what I hear."

Hugh was starting toward the door when Lonnie said, almost as an afterthought, "Come to think of it, I believe I did tell someone your choice in women ain't too swift."

Hugh stopped dead and turned around. "Now we're getting somewhere. That's exactly what I came here to find out about. I didn't think you could come clean right away, but now that you did, remember what I said. Next time you got something to say about me, say it to my face, not behind my back."

"Ain't you forgetting something?"

"What?"

"That chapped ass of yours."

Hugh half-laughed and tried to act casual, "You know, you're right. Tell you what, I think I got a little something out back that can fix it. Care to see it?"

"Any time, little fella'."

Lonnie took his apron off, leaned the broom against the wall, and started for the door. Hugh followed, perspiration already forming little beads on his upper lip. They rounded the corner with the sun to Hugh's back. Outside, Lonnie turned quickly and pointed a finger at Hugh.

"Now, look. You ain't from around here, but –"

He never finished his sentence. Hugh landed two quick left jabs and a right, all at the point of Lonnie's chin. The big guy went down like a tree.

Lonnie got up and shook himself, took one look at Hugh, picked him up from under his arms, and tossed him like a sack of feed. Hugh bounced back up and feigned to the right. Lonnie took the bait, and Hugh decked him again. As Lonnie got up the second time, he grabbed Hugh's legs and jerked them both out from under him. Off balance, Lonnie fell over Hugh, who then promptly planted a right and left below both of Lonnie's eyes while the two of them were sprawled on the ground. The next few seconds were filled with gouging, kicking, dust flying.

They finally came to rest on their backs, propped up on their elbows, looking at one another, both out of breath.

"Where'd you learn that?" Lonnie wheezed.

"Houston."

From inside, they heard Tom Rucker, "Lonnie? Lonnie! Come gimme a hand here!"

"You want to finish this later?" Hugh asked.

"I'll think about it."

"Don't think too long."

Lonnie started toward the door and then turned and said, "You still got a lousy choice in women."

"Women aren't the problem, Lonnie."

Hugh slowly felt the muscles in his back relax. But the tightness in his jaw remained. He got up and started down the road back toward the house.

Emma and Flora were busy in the living room. Hugh walked past them without saying a word. Both women just watched him go by and glanced at each other. The phone rang, and Flora became involved in a long-winded conversation with someone. Emma stepped into the hall just as Hugh came out of the bedroom.

"Hugh? Hey, puddin' man!"

Before she could get an answer, he disappeared into the bathroom and closed the door. Patiently, she stood outside in the hallway. Hugh reappeared seconds later.

"You okay?" she asked.

"I'm fine. I'm—I'm fine." He paced back toward the bedroom and turned around again.

"Where'd you go?" she asked. "I heard you out front washing the car, then you just disappeared."

"You keeping track of me today?" He rubbed his neck nervously.

"Whoa, what's got into you? How'd them jeans git so dirty?"

"Stop worrying about my jeans. They're fine."

"Uh-huh. Ya' jeans is fine. Right! Ya' shirt's tore. Yeah! Look at the pocket! Give it to me; I'll sew it back. Nobody'll notice. Leave your jeans on the trunk in the bedroom, and I'll wash 'em for you. What have you been doing?"

"I … I got in a fight."

"Fight?" she almost yelled.

"Be quiet! Just … be quiet about it."

"With who?"

"Never mind. It's all worked out."

"What's worked out? Look, Hugh, you don't want Miss Flora to know this, so you better tell me."

"What are you going to do? Tell on me? That'll make two people talking about me now."

"Talking about you? Like who?"

"Leave me alone about it. I mean it, don't nag me. I gotta go change."

Hugh came out of the bedroom a few minutes later in clean clothes and holding his dusty jeans and torn shirt. Emma was still standing in the hall.

"Don't give them clothes to me," she said firmly.

"But you just said you'd do … whatever!"

"And I also asked you who you was fightin' with."

"Is it really important? Look, I've really got to go back to the store. Help me out here, please. C'mon Emma. Don't tell Aunt Flora." His voice was pleading.

"Give 'em here," she said with a tone of defeat. "I'll put 'em under your bed. Then, I'll think about it."

Hugh smiled broadly and planted a big kiss on Emma's cheek. She blushed noticeably and returned the smile.

Hugh had turned away but stopped his exit and said, "Lonnie was looking for you. He seemed in a hurry to get away from the store."

"Yeah, He's got a girlfriend. Her name's Patricia. He's always trying to get away to go see her. If he does today, it won't be 'cause I'm there to cover for him. Miss Flora wants me to stay and help with her party."

"Great! I won't be long. I'll see you when I get back."

Hugh hurried out the door with Emma watching him go. Flora was saying goodbye on the phone, and Emma hurried to Hugh's room to hide the evidence of today's battle.

About an hour and a half later, the first of Flora's guests began arriving. The library was replete with several flower arrangements and platters of cookies, pastries, small sandwiches, and other finger food on practically every table surface in the room. Soon, the house was buzzing from every corner with voices of more than twenty women, or so it seemed to Emma. Just as fast as she refilled one platter from the kitchen, another one was empty and needed attention. The crowd then began to spill over into the hall and the kitchen as they made their way to the coffee and sodas on the kitchen table.

Reba Longford whispered to Sharon Taylor, "See that young girl with the apron on? You'll never guess who she is. Remember Marcia? Married Joshua Parker? That's their daughter. Looks just like Marcia, doesn't she?"

"I remember seeing her in the Rucker's store a while back," Sharon answered. "She looks different."

"Well, she's kinda' dressed, ah, well ah, better - you know."

"Yeah, cleaner looking," Sharon answered.

"You're right, and I don't know, maybe even - oh, look! Here's Flora's nephew coming in. Isn't he adorable?"

"Flora's nephew? I didn't know she had any."

"Actually, he's Tom's nephew," said Reba.

"Funny, he doesn't look anything like Tom. So handsome!"

Both women snickered, then stopped suddenly. Hugh and Emma were talking in whispers on the other side of the room. After a few moments, they both left.

Reba and Sharon shot nervous glances at one another, neither saying what thoughts were taking form in their minds.

In the kitchen, Emma asked Hugh, "Where you been? I thought you said you was coming right back."

"I did, too. But Lonnie asked me to do him a favor and stay with Uncle Tom while he ran an errand. At first, I said 'no', but then he convinced me."

"How?"

"Five bucks."

"Five dollars? He must like that girl a lot!"

"Probably. He still wasn't back when I left. Uncle Tom told me to come on back to the house. Said he'd rather handle the store by himself."

"That's odd."

"Not really. I had to ask him where everything was, so I couldn't help anybody much. And I dropped some eggs on the floor right in front of some old lady. Got all over her shoes. I thought Uncle Tom was going to swallow his tongue! Kept saying something about why he didn't just sell the damn store and get the hell out of town. He started ranting and carrying on so badly I just said it might be better if I left, and he agreed. I cleaned up the eggs before I left." He ended his story with a chuckle.

"Who was the old lady?"

"Lucy, somebody … she kept clicking her false teeth. Must not fit good."

"Lucy Tames! She's always coming in complaining! She brought back a whole chicken the other day. Said she bought it just the day before, and now it was spoiled. I recognize the wrapper on it. She'd had it for two weeks! Mr. Rucker believed her and made me and Lonnie go through all the chickens and smell each one like a couple of dogs. Lonnie griped and moaned the whole time. I said it was better than sweeping. Mr. Rucker came over and said we was doing it wrong."

"Smelling chickens wrong? How can you do that wrong?"

"Mr. Rucker says, 'See, this is how you do it!' and he stuck his nose right up one ol' chicken's butt and took a big snort. He musta' sucked up some juice or something 'cause he started chokin' and hackin' like I don't know what. And he had little drops of chicken stuff hanging off his nose like a booger, and then he started sneezing. Well, he sneezed so hard he knocked over the whole tub of chickens we had been smelling, and they scattered all over the floor. So, we had to stop everything and mop the floor, and Lonnie stepped on a blob of chicken fat and slipped down and—"

Flora's voice gently pierced the room, "Emma," she said quietly. "We're trying to have our meeting in the library. Your voices are carrying all through the house. I need you to come in here, pick up the cups and dishes, and put them in the sink."

Emma and Hugh managed to stop laughing, and both walked quietly around the edge of the group of ladies, picking up silverware and plates. Eyes, not heads, moved carefully around the room, following the two teenagers as they silently performed their task. Some of the ladies were still drinking coffee, so their cups could wait until later.

With nothing left to clear, the two of them silently set about washing what they had brought to the sink. Emma finally broke the silence.

"So what was you two fighting about?"

"Who?"

"You and whoever. You still ain't told me who, so I thought I'd ask what it was about."

"Just stopping a rumor."

"Rumor about who? Go ahead, I won't tell nobody!"

"I said NO!"

Flora's voice came from the door again, "Emma, I think that's all for today. There's so little left; I'm sure we can get it. Thank you so much for your time today."

"Yes, ma'am. I'll be going in a second."

Hugh took his aunt's interruption as an opportunity to duck out of the kitchen and down the hall. Emma followed a few seconds later and noticed the bathroom door shut tightly. It never would stay shut unless someone was in it with the door locked. Maybe he went towards his room, she thought. Hugh's bedroom door stood open, and he was not to be seen. Walking past the bathroom, she stopped and started to knock, but the sound of voices approaching the hallway changed her mind. Emma quietly stepped into the library and gathered her things from the small closet that had become her little private storage area. On her way out, some of the women nodded goodbye to her, but none spoke.

Hugh returned to the kitchen and crossed paths with Flora.

"Where's Emma?"

"She left just a moment ago. Come on into the library. Everyone's leaving, and some of them wanted to meet you."

Hugh followed her into the crowded room, trying to look out the window and be polite at the same time. His distraction was not lost on Sharon and Reba.

"If I was a young man and had my eye in the direction I think he does, I'd be looking for a reason to duck out of here," Sharon said under her breath.

"Flora should know a young fella like that doesn't want to mix with a hen party like this," Ruth answered.

Both women, having raised sons, spoke from experience. In about three minutes, they overheard Hugh talking to Flora.

"The keys? Are you going somewhere?"

"I just need the car keys to run an errand; won't be long. Maybe I'll stop by the store and see how Uncle Tom is doing."

Flora was extending her hand with the keys in it, then asked, "What errand do you need to run?"

"Flora, what a wonderful way you always have with making people feel right at home in your house!" Sharon blurted out. "And these fine young people. Don't we all worry so much when they start to drive? But I'll bet you've been driving for some time now, haven't you, Hugh?"

"Yes, ma'am. A few years now." Hugh cleverly used Sharon's interjection to gently pluck the keys from Flora's hand in full view of everyone, making it hard for Flora to voice an objection.

"I won't be long," he said.

Hugh pulled out of the driveway and, within two minutes, saw Emma walking up ahead. He pulled up next to her and called out.

"This time, I'm giving you a real ride home, and no one's watching."

Emma kept walking and just looked at the car slowly rolling beside her.

"Emma?"

"What?"

"You gonna' get in?"

"Who was you fighting with?"

"Get in first. Then we'll see about it."

"No, I ain't gettin' in no car with someone who won't tell me stuff like I asked."

"Okay, I had a fight with Lonnie."

Emma stopped abruptly. "Lonnie? Ain't nobody ever whupped Lonnie! I seen him in a lot of fights behind the schoolhouse, and nobody ain't never whupped him!"

"I never said I WHUPPED anybody."

"So, he done you?"

"No, it was about even. He might have a black eye by tomorrow."

"All right. Now, what was it about?"

"Get in, and I'll tell you."

Emma frowned, then smiled and hurried around to the passenger door.

"I thought you and Lonnie got along okay."

"We do. At least, we do now."

"So, what was ya'll bustin' each other's butt about?"

"Nothin'."

"Hugh, you promised to tell me!"

"I promised to take you home is all I promised. So, where do you live?"

At about forty miles per hour, Emma grabbed the door handle and started to twist.

"Alright, alright! I'll tell you! It was you. It was all about you."

Emma stared at him in amazement.

"Someone told Uncle Tom stuff about you and me, and I found out it was Lonnie who said it, and we got into a fight. It's that simple."

After a few moments, Emma finally found her voice. "Stuff? What do you mean, stuff? You and me?"

"Well, you know what I mean."

"No, I don't."

"This is the way to your house, isn't it?"

"Yeah, and don't change the subject. I don't know what you mean by 'stuff'."

"Like you and I were a couple."

"Couple of what?"

Hugh was surprised at Emma's lack of understanding about such a simple thing. He said, "Look, think about Lonnie and what's her name, Patricia."

"What about 'em? You ain't making no sense."

Hugh just glanced at her and kept driving. Emma sat looking at him, confused. After about half a minute, her expression suddenly started to change. She blushed scarlet and covered her face.

"Figured it out, huh?" Hugh asked.

"I can't believe this. Lonnie … he ain't never paid no attention to me, and now … well, just what did he say?"

"Emma, when guys poke fun at each other, they can be kinda' cruel. He was just teasing."

"Yeah, teasing bad enough to make you want to whup his butt! Hugh, what did he say?"

"I don't really know what he said, but he said it behind my back, and that's what got me mad."

"Well, who'd he say it to?"

"Uncle Tom."

"Oh, Lord. Yore Uncle Tom's a hard man to work for. I'm just glad I'm doin' more for Miss Flora at the house. So, what did Mr. Tom say that Lonnie said?"

"Emma, I'm not really sure. Uncle Tom just has this fear that you and I might—well, I don't know. I guess he's afraid I'll pack you up in my luggage and take you back to Houston or something. Emma, your house is out this way, isn't it?"

"You passed it already. We was talkin'."

"Passed it? I didn't see anything back there. Nothing but –"

"Like I said, you passed it already. Turn around."

Hugh stopped the car and threw it into reverse. A short distance later, they were stopped near Emma's house, where a large oak tree kept the car partly hidden. From this vantage point, they could see her father asleep on the front porch. Hugh was speechless. The sagging tin roof had large patches of rust. All the wood siding was dark grey with age. The porch was the same color except for one new board, which extended from the steps to the front door. One window on the side was broken and patched over with cardboard.

"I didn't think anyone lived there. I honestly didn't know."

"Didn't know what? That me and Papa live like this? I never knew nothin' else since Mama died. That was so long ago I barely remember what she looked like. The house needs fixin', but it's been so long like this, I guess we just got used to it. Look, I better go before he wakes up."

"Emma, wait. Talk with me for a minute. No one should be ashamed of where they live."

"Did I say I was ashamed?"

"You didn't have to."

"How you know what I'm thinking? Look, I know where you come from. I know all about your rich family in the oil business.

Ain't it easy for you to say how other people should feel? You ain't got no idea! None!"

"I never told you about my family. How'd you know?"

Emma started to answer, stopped, then continued. "Lonnie told me." She clenched her fists. "Yeah, go ahead and say it. Now you're mad at *me* for talking about you behind your back. But it wasn't like you said! It wasn't no teasin' stuff he was saying."

"So, tell me. What else has Lonnie said that I need to know about?"

Emma clasped her hands and just looked at the floorboard. She felt her composure slipping.

"I just want to get through school so I can git outa' here!" She was almost shouting as tears welled up, "I didn't know how poor we was until a couple of years ago. I guess I really didn't notice people's clothes and houses and stuff like that. Most folks got neighbors, too. We ain't got nothin'. I got nothin'. I can't do nothin'. All I can do is take care of him!" She pointed toward her father, who hadn't stirred in his slumber on the porch. "He's had chances to move, but now it's too late." She tried to stop the tears, but the dam holding them back had broken.

After a minute, she gave a long sniff and quietly opened the car door, "I gotta' go. Hugh, I'm sorry you had to see this. I never could decide if you should. But now you know." Emma started to swing one leg out of the car when Hugh touched her arm. She turned and saw that he was leaning toward her. Slowly, she leaned to meet him, then stopped. Their eyes met, and their lips touched. They embraced in a single thought for a brief moment, but Emma suddenly leaned back. "This ain't right. I don't know why. But something ain't right." She got out.

Once out of the car, a few steps, she came back and asked, "Hugh, what do you think of me? Am I some kind of white trash?"

Now, it was Hugh's turn to be speechless.

"Lonnie said something the other day when you first got here. He said I was just Miss Flora's little white … well, you know. It was; he was just sayin' … I'm not even sure what I'm saying! Hugh, just forget everything you seen here. Forget everything I said. Just forget about me. I'm not yore little girlfriend or anything like that. You goin' to be leaving soon, and all this won't matter no more. Just go on back to Texas, and we'll all be fine here!"

Emma turned and quickly walked the distance to the house. Hugh sat stunned at the strength of her words. He thought, *Why didn't I say anything? Why hadn't I offered some consolation, something besides a stupid kiss? What good would that do? Did I think a kiss from me was that important?*

He was about to put the car into gear when he saw the old man begin to move in his chair. Hugh slowly backed up the car to make sure he remained hidden. Peering through the tall grass, he saw Joshua go inside. Once he was inside, Hugh eased the car into first gear and slowly rolled past the house and on back to Kisatchie. His first stop would be the store. He had to speak to Lonnie again.

Chapter 9

Hugh pulled up to the store with a spew of gravel as the car came to a sudden stop. As he entered the store, he tried to act calm to hide his thoughts. Mr. Rucker was helping several shoppers.

Between customers, Hugh asked, "Where's Lonnie?"

"Went home. Aunt Flora called looking for you. You think you can help me? Without any more accidents? Give your Aunt Flora a call first and tell her where you are."

Hugh was pleased to see that Uncle Tom was actually smiling. A volume of business always puts him in a good mood. One never heard Tom Rucker mention selling the store on days like today.

The rest of the afternoon went by quickly. Hugh managed to stop dwelling on Lonnie and twice found himself wondering how his folks were doing. Really, he wondered *what* they were doing. They always came back from these trips abroad with wild tales about faraway places, while each time religiously emphasizing that it was a business trip. He had been promised a trip with them so many times that he was tired of asking. They really must be thinking about him, though, because they did manage to bring him something upon every return. On one trip to Spain, they went to a sword factory in Seville and brought back some kind of blade used in bullfights. On another trip to Spain, they went to Pamplona in the first week of July and watched the running of the bulls. From a gift shop there, they brought him a hat, apparently an accurate replica of one Ernest Hemingway wore. Where were they now? Germany? This time, it'll probably be some goofy-looking short leather pants to wear—but only around the house. Spain? Germany? What's that got to do with Texas oil?

About closing time, Tom told Hugh to head on home, and he would catch up with him later. Aunt Flora was busy in the kitchen as usual.

"There you are. I wondered where you went!" she said.

"Oh, I needed something out of my school locker. Then I stopped by the store on the way home." He tried to look truthful.

"What time did you get to the store?"

Hugh shrugged, "Uh, not long after I left."

"Go anywhere else?"

"Well, yes, ma'am. I saw Emma walking home, and I gave her a ride."

She crossed her arms and said, "Hmm. I see. So, you saw where she lives."

"Yes, ma'am."

"So, what did you think?"

He pondered for a moment and spoke without looking at her directly. "Well, it's a shame what happened to her family. I mean, I know her dad has a bad reputation, but none of what I saw today is her fault."

"Yes, that's right. And none of us, especially you, are to blame for the conditions there, either. It was her father's choice to be the monster he is - or was, I mean. Her mother just threw herself to the dogs when she married him, and Emma is the sad result of it all. That's just the way it is. I have tried to give her the benefit of seeing us and our manner of living so she can at least have an example to follow."

"To follow? When? When is she going to have the chance to change anything? From what I hear, all the changes she's gone through have depended on other people to make them happen. They still have no hot water in the house. No plumbing. No money to speak of."

"That's her father's fault. He drinks away what little they have."

"So, what's she supposed to do about it? She's sixteen, almost seventeen. Her reputation at school is set in stone, not because of what she is, but because of what people remember. God, I just feel sorry for her!"

Flora's response was immediate. "Hugh, I appreciate your compassion, as I'm sure God does as well. But could you be a little less casual with the use of His name? I know you're not taking it in vain, but it just seems a little careless. I know your mother would agree with me."

"Yes, ma'am." *My mother is the one I learned it from*, he thought, smiling to himself.

"And as my father would always say to us, 'Be careful when you feel sorry for someone of the opposite gender. You might feel sorry enough to marry them.' And falling in love with someone out of pity is a tragedy in itself."

He looked at her with eyes wide open. "Aunt Flora! You're way ahead of me. You've already got me married to someone I really don't know that well." While he silently hoped she believed what he was saying, his thoughts were in another direction.

Flora interrupted his pondering, "Oh, by the way. Ellis Carmichael called. He and Scott Turner are going to Alexandria to the movie tonight. They wanted to know if you would like to come along. I told them you probably would but that you would call them. You didn't mind my saying that, did you?"

"No, of course not. Sounds like fun." He started toward the phone. "Let me call him now before it gets too late."

"That's fine. Just remember, you go exactly where you say you're going and nowhere else."

"Of course. Wouldn't think of it." He ended with one of his charming smiles. He knew what Aunt Flora liked.

From the phone call, he learned that Ellis was driving and was just about to leave to pick up Scott. Hugh gulped down some supper and was heading out the door when Tom came walking in. Ellis' family car, a brand-new Ford, powder blue, was sitting in front of the house with the motor running. Ellis and Scott were singing to something on the radio.

"Where's he off to?" Tom asked Flora.

"Oh, his friends called. They have plans to go to the movie show in Alexandria, and they invited him. He's so popular and did it so quickly. Everybody likes him. Reminds me of Todd."

At the sound of their son's name, Tom's expression immediately changed. He walked into the living room a few steps and turned to face his wife. His hands made a downward chopping motion.

"Damn it, don't do that to me, Flora," he whispered. "Don't blindside me like that! You know what that does to me every time you talk about him so easily like - like he lives next door!"

"I'm sorry, Tom. I guess Todd was on my mind when we had to fix up his room for Hugh. Every time he walks in and out of that room, I can't help but remember when Todd was here."

"Tom, I'm really sorry." She put her hand on his shoulder. "But I tell you this each time it comes up. Todd did exist. He did walk on this earth for eighteen years. He did affect the lives of so many people, especially you and me. He's in our memories, so please don't act like he never was here."

Tom wiped his eyes and said, "You put him on the same plane as Hugh. He can't be replaced, Flora. Don't even try! Not with Hugh, not with anyone."

For a moment, she felt her husband's pain and knew she had brought it to the surface. She reached out and carefully took him in her arms. "I'm sorry. I know you miss him. I do, too. But we just can't be on the verge of mourning all the time."

"I'm not mourning. He's gone. I've never tried to ignore that fact. Just don't try to replace him. And give me some warning if you're going to talk about him."

Tom kissed his wife gently and went into the bedroom.

The three moviegoers were on Highway 165 to Alexandria. Ellis was cruising at a speed far above the legal limit. No one knew exactly how fast he was going because he had stopped just outside of town and disconnected the speedometer cable. The last time they had taken the car, Ellis' father had scolded him soundly the next day for putting so many miles on it. He and Scott were in the front seat, reliving an episode from the day before. Hugh sat in the back.

"Who are you guys talking about? Hugh asked from the back.

"George. George Towers. He's Beverly's brother. Remember her?" Ellis said, looking back at Hugh.

"Hey, look where you're going!!" Scott yelled.

Ellis swerved the car just in time to miss a head-on with an oncoming truck.

"He gets like this," Scott said with a big laugh. "It'll get better as the evening goes on."

"Did you tell him what we do?" Scott asked.

"No, I didn't have a chance to," Ellis answered. "You tell him, I gotta' drive."

Scott turned around in the seat to face the bewildered Hugh. "See, I got this fake ID, right? Well, I've only had to use it once. But we found this place on Robert's Avenue that will sell to anybody. This last year, I seemed to have, well, matured a little." He punched Ellis, and they both laughed. Ellis nudged the gas a little more.

"Hey, what's the hurry, Ellis?" Hugh asked.

"Let me finish," Scott said. "That's part of the plan. See, we hurry up and get to the movie before the last feature is over, and we see the ending. Then, we see the beginning of the next feature, and we leave."

"Leave?"

"Yeah, if anyone asks about the movie, we tell them about the beginning and how it ends, and that's all they care about. As far as they're concerned, we went to the movie. That gives us lots of spare time."

"For what?"

The two in the front seat glanced at each other. Scott asked, "Hey, is all of Texas dry? Boy, what do you guys do on Saturday night? C'mon. What kind of beer do you like?"

Hugh swallowed hard. "I guess I like most any kind. But I'm not really in the mood for a beer tonight. I didn't know that's what we were doing."

Scott turned again and gave him a condescending look.

"Well, okay. Maybe just one."

The movie was a western with some actors Hugh had never heard of. They stayed in the theater no more than forty-five minutes since one feature ended, and another started immediately after. The trip to the liquor store was easy. Ellis drove, dropped Scott off, and made the block. Scott was just coming out when the car pulled up to the curb.

"Now we go to the levee," Ellis said. "We got just the place. No one knows about this place."

"That's what you said the last time, dumb shit," Scott interjected with a bounce on the seat.

"Where are we going?" Hugh asked.

Ellis explained, "We found a couple of places on the Red River levee that nobody ever checks. We could drink and run naked in the broad moon light, and no one would bother us. We'll be sober by the time we get home."

"Works out great," Scott announced. I got three six-packs in here."

Ellis bounced in the seat. "Three? Where in the hell did you get the money for three?"

"I got my ways. Don't worry. Besides, we got three in the car, so we needed three six-packs."

"Hey, wait a minute. I can't drink a whole six-pack," Hugh explained.

Ellis howled out the car window, "All the better for us! AHOOOO!!!"

Scott turned around to Hugh and said, "Isn't this great? He's already wound up, and we haven't even started!"

The car turned off onto a dirt road that followed the crest of the levee for about a mile. A gate appeared, which Scott quickly opened and closed after the car passed through. Both boys in the front seat had opened their first beer and were guzzling like their lives depended on it. Hugh held his and nursed it along slowly. Another half mile and the river turned east, putting the gate and the main highway out of sight and out of earshot. Ellis brought the car to a stop, hopped out, and threw his first empty high up in the air. Scott and Hugh were looking for a place to sit on the grass. They stacked the three six-packs in front of Hugh.

"Gimme' another one," Scott asked while he fumbled in the dark.

"Where are they?" Ellis said.

"Oh, there they are. Reach over there and hand a couple of 'em to me, Texas. Did you finish yours?"

"Uh, yeah. Sure. Didn't you see me throw mine away?"

In the twilight, Hugh had found a varmint hole hidden in the grass on the levee where he sat. The others didn't notice that as the evening progressed, the hole filled up with beer.

"Scott," Ellis said. "You bring any cigarettes?"

"Got 'em."

"Gimme' one. Gotta' match?"

"Sure."

Ellis took the pack of cigarettes and started walking off in the dark.

"Where you going?" asked Scott.

"I gotta' piss."

"Already? Hey! Don't piss on my cigarettes!" Scott looked at Hugh and said, "He's crazy when he's drunk. He'll probably go out there and try to piss while he's lighting a cigarette and end up settin' his pecker on fire! Hey, Texas! You ain't said much tonight! Havin' a good time?"

"Oh, yeah. Uh, great!"

"That's good. We'll do it again," he clapped his hand on Hugh's shoulder. "You know, you're okay. Even if you do wear them silly boots to school!"

The beer supply dwindled rapidly.

Watching the time, Hugh said he thought it was about time to go. The other two could barely stand.

Scott looked at Ellis and said, "You ain't drivin'. I am."

"Naw, y'not. I can drive."

"Gimme the keys."

"Kiss my ass. Git in the goddamn car before we… before it's too late."

"Too late for what?"

"I dunno. Too late to … hey, we didn't find any pussy this time! I just remembered!"

"No pussy by the riverside! But wait, we didn't find any the last time either. Levee just ain't what it used to be, huh?"

Both boys were having trouble standing. Hugh noticed that they both were looking at him, but neither appeared to be focused on anything.

Ellis said slowly, "No, we didn't find none because last time you was sicker than shit, crawlin' around on your hands and knees talkin' about your daddy's car."

"Huh?"

"Remember? You 'uz going around saying, 'Buick, Buick.' Only you said it with a little more gurgle."

Both boys fell back, laughing hysterically. Hugh watched the spectacle that he identified with too closely. Earlier that summer, Southern Comfort had been his downfall. He'd sworn an oath to himself it would be the last time. Thankfully, he had planned to spend that night with one of his drinking buddies, the father of whom was exceedingly understanding and had him at least looking halfway refreshed by the next morning before he went home. His parents never knew. But tonight, he knew there was no way either of these two were driving thirty miles back to Kisatchie. It wasn't a matter of ethics or legal principle since neither one of them could find the car, let alone the steering wheel. He dug into Ellis' pocket and had the keys before Ellis knew what happened. After pouring both of them into the back seat, he turned the car around and headed home. When they came to the gate, he stopped the car, turned off the engine, opened the gate with the keys in his hand, drove through, and repeated the steps on the other side to close the gate. Halfway through the process, he had to put Scott back in the car after he hopped out yelling, "Hi, Mom! We're home!"

"Scott, you dumb shit!" Ellis yelled. "We're still on the levee. Git your ass back in the damn car!"

"You guys open your windows back there," Hugh called back to them. "The fresh air will help you sober up."

"Who's he think he is?" Ellis slurred. "This is my car! I'll open my windows only if I want to!"

"Ellis!" hollered Scott. "Don't talk like that about our driver up there! Hey boy! Take us home! Ellis, shut up and open your damn window!"

Traffic was light on the way home. The first few miles, Scott hung out the window and yelled at the cars going by. He threw a couple of empty beer bottles at passing road signs. Then he wanted to go full face into the wind with his mouth open. He was having great fun until a bug flew into his mouth. The next ten minutes were spent listening to Scott gag in the back seat and Ellis telling him to shut up because he was making everybody else sick listening to him. As they approached the edge of town, both were beginning to act relatively sober.

Ellis spoke from the back, "Hey, Hugh. You done good driving for us like this. I don't know how you did it. How many beers did you have?"

"I don't really remember. I probably didn't have as much as you guys did."

"Well, whatever it was, thanks. So, listen, you better let me drive now. If anyone sees us in this car before we get home, they better see me driving it. Why don't you pull up here and switch with me?"

"You sure?"

"No problem."

Hugh pulled over on the dark highway and got out. He passed Ellis in front of the car and climbed into the back seat. That was when he realized that Scott had climbed over into the front seat. The two in the front seat spoke quietly to each other while Ellis put the car in gear.

"What's that?" Hugh asked from the back.

"Nothin'," came the reply.

Within minutes, it was clear to Hugh that they weren't going straight home.

"Hey, where are we going?"

"One last stop," said Scott.

Quickly, Hugh recognized the pock-marked road to Pittman. The two in the front were starting a deep-throated giggle.

"Really, where are we going?"

"Almost there," said Ellis. "Wanna see your girlfriend? Emma's place coming up. All right, on the count of three … one, two, three— HEY, EMMA!!!!" The two boys in the front seat yelled as they sped by the Parker house.

"What the hell are you doing?"

"Wait. It gets better. If her old man's awake, it'll be great!"

A few yards later, Ellis turned the car around quickly and headed back past the house again. This time, he slowed down and stopped.

"Hey, Emma!" Scott hollered loudly out the passenger window. "We got your honey out here! He's in the back seat, and he's just bustin' his pants to see you!"

Hugh reached up and grabbed Scott's shoulder. "Damn it! You didn't tell me anything about this. What do you think you're doing? Ellis, get going!"

Ellis drawled out slowly, "Naw, not 'til she comes out. She always does - comes out fightin' mad."

"I can't believe this!"

Scott pried Hugh's grip off his shoulder and said, "Yeah, she comes out, then her old man does. That's the fun part. He's usually so drunk he can't see straight."

"Wait, here comes somebody, 'round the corner of the house. Look over there!"

A flashlight stabbed the darkness and flashed full on Hugh's face in the back seat. The light blinded him as a huge voice bellowed out, "Whut you boys doing here trying to scare these folks? G'won now! Git! Don't make me mad!" The voice seemed out of place.

In the darkness, Hugh heard Emma's voice speaking softly, "Who's that in the back seat? Shine it over there."

The light stabbed Hugh's eyes again, and he ducked down in the seat.

The huge voice spoke again. "You heard me now. You better git!"

The tone of the huge voice changed abruptly. The three in the car could hear it distinctly. It seemed to be directed toward someone else, someone in the shadows of the house. "Mr. Josh, we takin' care of it. Mr. Josh - Mr. Josh, you don't need to be out here. Emma, git him back inside. Emma, watch him—watch him! He's got his shotgun!"

BOOM! The night air exploded. BOOM! Shotgun pellets from both barrels sprayed the side of the new car. "Ellis, drive! Get us outta here!" Scott was yelling.

Ellis floored the Ford and pulled up a minute later in the glow of the first streetlight they came to. All three got out to inspect the car.

"You idiots!" Hugh screamed. "You almost got us killed back there! How many times have you done this? How many times do you think you could do this without something like this happening?"

"Hey, man! Look at my dad's car!" Ellis moaned. "Look what he did!"

"What are you going to tell them?" Scott asked.

"I dunno. Aw SHIT! Look at it! I gotta think. Help me think, guys. What am I gonna say?"

"We could tell 'em it happened in Alexandria," Scott suggested.

"No, that won't work. They'll call the police and all that stuff! What a bunch of CRAP!"

Scott tried again. "Maybe we could tell 'em it happened on the highway, just out in the middle of nowhere."

"Go ahead," said Hugh. "Next thing, the sheriff will be called about some madman shooting at cars in the dark. Then you got to come up with some details. Better get your stories straight."

"Hey, wait a minute! What's your story going to be?" Scott asked.

"I don't have much of a story. It must've happened after you dropped me off. And you dropped me off right here under this light!"

"Why would we drop you off here and not at home?"

"Beats me. My version is that you guys were planning something else tonight, so I asked you to drop me here. Don't worry about me. You got enough to worry about. I'll walk the rest of the way."

Hugh took a step back and thrusted his hands into his back pockets. The other two thought for a minute got back in the car, and sped away. Under the streetlight, the bugs were thick. The Louisiana night was still hot and muggy. In both directions, the road was dark. Clouds had rolled in off the Gulf and had hidden the moon completely. The only lights visible were peeking through the trees, lights from Emma's house. Without hesitating, he started back towards the Parker house.

About twenty yards away from the house, he stopped to think. He wasn't sure why he had come back there. He just knew there was something he had to do, and it was slowly coming into focus in his mind. The question was how to do it.

He crouched down behind a thicket and watched the house, thinking. A strange car was parked along the side yard. Had it been there before? Who was Emma talking to when the whole thing happened? As though driven by something invisible, Hugh felt himself rise up, half standing. Two silhouetted figures came through the door and onto the porch. Hugh couldn't hear what they were saying from his hiding place. He decided on a direct approach.

"Emma?" he said loud enough to be heard, so he thought. The two kept talking.

"Emma!" he said a little louder.

He saw the smaller of the two figures stop and turn in his direction.

"Who's out there?" The flashlight came on again and shone toward the road.

"No, I'm over here. I want to talk to Emma."

"You ain't talkin' to nobody," came the man's voice again. "Where are you? If I catch you, I'm gonna make yo' butt look like scrambled eggs."

Emma's voice came through the darkness, "Wait, I think it's Hugh. It sounds like him."

"Emma, it's me. It's Hugh. I just want to talk to you."

The flashlight beam found Hugh's hiding place, and the bushes trembled as though a bull elephant was rushing through them. A large hand grabbed Hugh from out of nowhere and half-carried, half-dragged him toward the house. The grip on his left upper arm felt like a gigantic vise, crushing every nerve, muscle, and vessel. He felt himself lifted just enough that only his right shoe touched the ground. It seemed to take an eternity to get there.

In the glow of the porch light, Hugh saw his captor was the largest black man he had ever seen. For a moment, he felt sheer panic.

"Put him down, Oscar. Don't hurt him," Emma's voice had a tremble to it.

"You was in the back seat, yeah! Miss Emma, who dis' be?"

"This is my friend, Hugh."

"Yo' friend?"

"Please, I can explain," said Hugh, trying to free his arm. The tingling sensation was getting worse.

"So, talk!" Oscar growled and gave him a shake. His arm was throbbing now. He hesitated, and Oscar started to shake him again.

"Emma, make him stop! My arm's hurt!"

"Talk and do it fast!" Oscar released him, and Emma remained silent.

Hugh rubbed his arm as he spoke. "I was invited into town with the other two. I didn't know what they had planned. I really didn't know. There was nothing I could do. They had me in the back seat! Emma, please believe me."

"Why should she believe you?" Oscar demanded. Emma still hadn't uttered a sound.

"Emma, please don't just stand there. I'm apologizing. Why else would I have come back here like this? I'm telling you, there was nothing I could do!"

"Where'd they go?" she asked.

"They went home."

"Why didn't you go with them?"

"All I could think of was to get as far away from them as I could. They let me out about a half mile back down the road."

"Who's out there?" a voice from in the house yelled out.

"Nobody, Papa. We're just talking. It's just me and Oscar. You go on back to bed." She waited a few seconds, then continued, "Hugh, do you know how lucky you are? He could have killed you!"

"Yeah, I know that. I just wanted to come back and explain."

Hugh took a step closer, and Emma turned on her heel and started back inside. "Oscar," she said over her shoulder, "Can you give him a ride home? He'll get lost in the dark, and he doesn't know south from north."

Oscar watched Emma as she went inside, then looked back at Hugh, "Boy, you go stand out yonder in the road where I can see you. I'll bring the car. Git over there, and don't you move."

The brakes of Oscar's old Plymouth made a soft musical tone on the graveled pavement. "Git in," he said.

Nothing was said for the first minute. Hugh finally broke the silence, "I'm really sorry about all this."

"You don't know how sorry it could'a been."

"Well, I appreciate your understanding and your help with the ride and all."

"You welcome. Something you gotta know. Joshua Parker done killed two men back in the day. Nobody done nothing about it 'cause he worked for Whitmyer back then. Nobody went to the law. They most likely needed killin', but anyways, he done it. Sometimes, he thinks he back in them days. Yeah, you lucky. Me and Miss Emma, we hid that shotgun from him a while back, and looks like he found it. Didn't know 'til tonight that he had it. Them other two boys okay?"

"Yessir, they're fine. Just scared."

Oscar chuckled, "I think you the one scared. No white boy ever said 'sir' to me."

"May I call you Oscar?"

"My name."

"Oscar, could you let me off just before the house? I don't want anyone in the house to see this car with me in it. Wait, I'm sorry. That sounded awful. What I mean is, I'm going to tell Uncle Tom and Aunt Flora that I walked home after I got dropped off. You understand?"

"You gonna lie to them folks is what you sayin'. What if they ask me anything?"

"Why would they ask you anything?"

"Something to think about. Jus' never know."

Hugh thought for a second. "So, why were you at Emma's house tonight? If you don't mind my asking."

"I don't care. I been taking care of that family for a long time. Once in a while, Mr. Josh gets a little drunk and then gets in a bad way. Emma runs out the house while he tears up the place. She comes to my house, and we go back a little later and cleans it up. Tonight weren't too bad. Never know what gonna' set him off, though. You and yo' friends come right into the middle of it. Bad timin' for you. Yeah, you's lucky."

Hugh had been so busy listening he hadn't realized the car was slowing down. Oscar had now come to a full stop.

"House's right yonder through them trees. You be careful, hear?"

"Thanks," Hugh said. Before he shut the door, he reached inside and offered his hand to Oscar. A huge hand gently grasped his and shook once.

The Rucker house was a picture of contentment when Hugh walked in. Uncle Tom was reading, and Aunt Flora had a basket of knitting. They both looked up when Hugh came in.

"How was the movie?" she asked.

"Oh, great! Good western."

"Wonderful. Ellis and Scott are such nice boys."

Hugh tried to act nonchalant, "Uncle Tom, what're you reading?"

Tom Rucker just held the book up for Hugh to see the cover.

"There's a whole bookcase like it in the library," said Aunt Flora.

"Good idea. I think I'll get one and go to bed and read."

"Is it that late?" Tom finally asked.

"No, I just feel like reading. I'll see you in the morning."

"Good night," Flora and Tom said almost in unison.

Chapter 10

The next day, the Ruckers went to church as they did every Sunday, almost without exception. When the service was over, Hugh bumped into Scott on the way out.

"How are you feeling?" Hugh asked.

"What do you care?" Scott jabbed back. His eyes looked a bit blood-shot.

"Hey, I was just asking. Have you talked to Ellis?"

"I hadn't seen him. Anyone asked you any questions yet?"

"No. Anyone—like who?" Hugh looked puzzled.

"The sheriff or State Police. You know, those kinds of folks."

"I don't get it. Why would they ask me anything?" He glanced around to see who might be listening.

"Well, I and Ellis talked about it last night. We weren't sure if you'd say anything to the Ruckers. You know, we should have given you a ride so you wouldn't be so late getting home. Being late always brings up questions."

"I got home on time. Don't worry."

Scott looked at him intently, "You did? How?"

"Don't worry. I managed. Tell Ellis not to worry. Nobody has asked me anything. I'm not going to say anything different from what I told you last night. It must have happened after you dropped me off."

The parking lot slowly emptied as churchgoers headed home. Hugh sat in the back seat, listening to Tom and Flora talk about whatever came to mind as they drove home. It was a lazy Sunday. The summer heat was finally starting to mellow, and the Autumn crispness was just a few short weeks away. That meant home to Houston when his parents would return. As they rounded the last turn to the house, Hugh caught a fleeting glimpse of a figure in the woods near the house. He saw it, and then it disappeared. Neither Tom nor Flora said anything, so he assumed they hadn't noticed.

Turning around in his seat, Hugh looked through the back window and saw a face, a familiar face, peering over the azaleas that bordered the Rucker's property.

They entered the house, and Hugh went to his room and changed clothes. The Ruckers always had a late lunch on Sunday, so he had time to spare. The woods beside and behind the house had become familiar to him, and neither Tom nor Flora found it unusual when he said he was going for a walk and would be back in a couple of hours.

As he left the house and started on the trail through the pines, he knew she would be watching. A few feet into the shadows, Emma peeked from behind a tree.

"I saw you from the car."

"I know. I figured you did. You turned around and looked."

"Look about last night. I didn't know what those guys were going to do."

"I know. And I didn't come to talk about them. I already know what kinda' of jerks they are. Their mamas probably think they're little darlings." She brushed her hair back as she talked.

"Probably. Aunt Flora thinks so."

"I just wanted you to know I don't hate you for what happened. Last night was a bad one for Papa, and you was just part of it. Bad timing, I guess."

"Oscar told me. Does your dad ever hurt you when he gets like that?"

"No, not yet. I don't guess he would. But I never know. It's always just best to get out of the house when he's mad."

They walked further into the woods. The shadows moved with the breeze.

"Was he like this before your mother died?"

"I don't remember."

"How old were you when she died?"

"Nine, ten, something like that. I'm not sure anymore. I just remember she liked to sing," Emma looked off in the distance.

"Did she have a favorite song?"

"I only remember one." She caught a mischievous look in his eyes. "No, I'm not gonna' sing it!"

"Oh, come on …"

"No, you'll just laugh. I always just sing to myself."

Hugh plopped himself on the ground and said, "Well, I'll just sit here until you sing to me."

Emma looked at him hard and pursed her lips, "Promise not to laugh?" She cleared her throat and began:

> *"Red sails in the sunset,*
> *way out on the sea.*
> *Oh, carry my loved one,*
> *home safely to me."*

"That's all I remember," she folded her hands on her face and blushed.

Hugh simply sat there on the ground with a look of marvel on his face, "My God, a singing artist! Do you do anything else?"

Hugh stood, and they walked in silence for a minute or two, listening to the trees whisper in the breeze.

"Tell me more about your pictures, the stuff you draw."

"What about 'em?"

"You're really good. You ought to work on it more. I'll bet you could sell some for a decent price."

"You said that the other day. You really think so?"

"Absolutely. You just need someone to make the connections for you. Why don't you give some of them to me and I'll take them home. My mother knows some folks who might be interested."

Emma was glowing again. By now, they had walked to a secluded spot off the trail. Emma sat down cross-legged on a thick mat of pine straw, looked up at the clouds, then turned to him and asked, "Why can't you just move here?"

Hugh stood looking down at her. Her eyes were the bluest he had ever seen. He had noticed the dress she wore hugged her figure just so slightly, just enough to suggest what did lie beneath. As she talked, her breasts barely rose and fell with each breath. She leaned forward with her elbows on her knees and propped her chin up. Every move she made was suddenly hypnotic to Hugh. He had seen girls try to tease boys with their body language or the way they made their clothes fit. Emma did none of these things. It was just her natural innocence that was so beautiful. A small ant crawled onto the calf of her leg. She casually swept it off with one hand, causing the hem of her dress to flutter and land on her thigh, leaving her knee exposed. She didn't seem to notice or care.

"Maybe I could move somewhere else and sell pictures. Maybe I ought to go to New York. I could get on a plane at Kisatchie International Airport and fly to New York!" She fell back laughing.

"You should try looking in the mirror when you draw," Hugh said.

"Huh?"

"Self-portrait. You'd look good in it. Ever tried it?"

"Naw! C'mon Hugh! Who'd want to look at it?"

"I would. I'm enjoying just looking at you right now. I wish I had a picture to take home with me."

"Hugh! Stop teasin' me. You seen where I come from! Who'd want to look at me?"

Hugh sat down beside her, close enough that their arms and shoulders touched. She shifted toward him a fraction, and one knee nudged Hugh's leg.

"I had a dream about you the other night," she said.

"Yeah? What was it about?"

"You and me. We were walking down some old road, going somewhere. You had your arm around me, and you were ready to kiss me, and I woke up."

"You mean like this?" He kissed her ever so lightly on her lips. Then again, more intensely.

She paused and took a deep breath. "Hugh, what am I gonna' do after you leave?" she asked. "You really are the best friend I've ever had."

Hugh slowly reached out and took her hand. She clasped it quickly and squeezed. The two of them sat for several minutes, just staring at the ground. While still in a silent daze, she brought his hand to her lips and held it there. He leaned closer, still not making eye contact. She took his whole arm and hugged it to her like she would a favorite doll. Hugh felt his arm cradled between her breasts and saw the whole world begin to kaleidoscope in front of him. The woods were suddenly full of smells and sounds he had never noticed before. A cardinal hopped in a tree a few feet away. It was the brightest red he had ever seen. The wind gently spoke in the huge pines around them. There was no sound of a car engine or the voice of another person. The entire world had departed and left them alone, just the two of them beneath this canopy of trees with the ferns standing guard. Hugh took his free hand and reached across to her clasped hands. He freed the arm she clung to and wrapped it around her shoulders. In his embrace, Emma leaned her head into his shoulder, then looked up at him. Both were breathing faster. Emma started to say something, but Hugh stopped her. He leaned down, and their lips met again, softly at first, then as if some secret language had been there all along, the silent words of their eyes and lips pulled them together as sure as a blossom seeks sunlight. Both were breathing in short gasps, and their mouths parted for a moment while they breathed deeply. He pulled her to him again, and they kissed and embraced completely.

"I can't let you go back," she said.

"I'll have to," he said. "But we don't have to talk about it now. I've still got a couple of weeks left."

"I can't stop thinkin' about it, Hugh. I never felt like this about nobody before. It's like I'm goin' crazy or something."

"I know. I'm thinking the same way."

They both laid back silently with their arms around each other. For a full minute, neither said a word.

Finally, Hugh asked, "You're quiet. What are you thinking?"

"I'm just remembering the first time I saw you. You was in the store and I was going out the back. I barely caught a quick look at you. I didn't think nothing of it then. Then I seen you when you come in the house and scared me to death. Remember that?"

"I remember."

"But before that, I think I seen you and —"

"What?"

"Oh, nothing. I was just trying to recollect .... Hugh! You like to swim?"

"What? Well, yes. Why?"

She raised up on one elbow and looked at him directly. "I thought so."

"That's an odd question. Why do you ask?"

"Well, I just thought that, you know, after last night; I mean, I figure you went with the other two just to be friendly."

"Sorry, you've lost me." He dropped his embrace and leaned back.

"Well, I was wondering if you really like to swim, or did you go swimmin' with them guys a while back just to be friendly."

"No, I like to swim. I was … wait, how did you know I went swimming with them?"

"Hugh, you still don't have no sense of direction. That pond is right behind my house. I was headed there myself when I heard you."

"You—heard us?"

"Yeah. At first, that is."

"Okay," Hugh said slowly. "And then?"

"Oh, I seen ya'll git in the water."

Hugh had a look of astonishment on his face. "You watched us?"

She started talking faster. "Well, I ain't never seen a bunch of guys without no clothes on before, so I figured it wasn't no harm. Was it?"

Hugh laughed quietly. "You did that? I can't believe this."

"Well, a girl's got to learn somehow, don't you think?"

The two looked at each other cautiously and then laughed.

A few seconds passed then Hugh asked, "So what did you think?"

"About what?"

"Don't make me say it! About what you saw!"

"Oh, that. Well, I dunno. What was I supposed to think?"

"Okay, we're going to talk around the subject. I'll ask this way: Did you stick around, or did you leave immediately?"

"Well, I had to make sure I didn't miss anything." She ended with a giggle.

"Anything like what?"

"Like, you know, what it's for - or something like that."

"What's what for?"

"Hugh, you ain't making this easy! Now I'm just sorry I told you." She felt herself beginning to blush.

Hugh laughed, "No, you're not. You've been dying to ask somebody about this, and now you have. Remember, I'm your best friend."

"So, why do I feel funny asking you?"

"I guess I would, too."

"I seen baby boys before, but I just never seen full-grow'd men like that. I just—I just never had."

"So you never told me what you thought," he said.

"It wasn't what I thought. It was what I was feeling. Never happened before."

"What was it like?"

"It was kinda' like all the blood was running up to my head, then back down again. Sorta' like that, but only a little, I guess. But it wasn't nothing like -"

"Nothing like what?"

"Like what I felt just a couple a minutes ago. With you. It was the same, only a whole lot more. Is that okay? I mean, it ain't wrong, is it?"

"Uh, yeah. Sure, it's perfectly normal. I suppose everyone gets that way once in a while."

Emma lapsed back into silence. Hugh stared at her inquisitively.

"What's wrong?"

"Well, you done a good job getting me to laugh and think about something else, but my mind keeps going back to how much I'm going to miss you."

She reached up and kissed him long and hard. They moved away from the tree and leaned back on the pine needles. Hugh stretched out on his back and was about to sit back up when she placed her hand softly on his face, and he lay back down. Slowly, she kissed him again. She felt his hands on her hips. The hem of her dress came up with his fingers. She clutched his shoulders and rolled back, pulling him with her. Clumsily, they fumbled with their clothes. A blue jay shrieked in the tree above them, which caused them both to gasp and look around.

"Hugh, I ain't never done this before."

"Me, neither."

"I'm not even sure what it is I'm doin'. I just know I can't stop."

"Yeah, I know."

Roaming hands seemed to find a home, and the whole world became warm and moist. His entrance was awkward.

Emma inhaled sharply through her teeth.

It was over quickly, too quickly, like a dream with the promise of something, but the dream ended because the whole world was watching.

Hugh sat up and looked around. The forest suddenly seemed to have a million eyes. Emma rolled away from him into a fetal position and covered her face.

Seconds, then a minute, went by, and neither spoke a word.

"Emma, my knees feel like jelly," he finally said. "I don't think I could stand up if I had to. You okay?"

"I think I'm bleeding a little."

"Oh, jeez! God, I'm sorry. Emma, I didn't mean to hurt you. Here, let me - well, I got a handkerchief. Here!"

Emma took it, rolled away from him, and accomplished what she could.

"You said you've never done this before," she asked.

"I haven't."

"Then how do you know so much about it? You seemed to know what to do."

"I just do. Emma, it's no secret. You're acting like you don't know what just happened."

She studied his face carefully. "Hugh, you done broke out in a sweat. You okay?"

"It was a mistake. A stupid mistake. I should have never done this. I didn't lie to you. I've never done this before, but I knew better. I should have known."

"What's wrong with it?"

Hugh propped up on his elbows and shook his head.

"I asked you what's wrong with it. Why was it a mistake?"

Hugh searched for words. "It just is. Don't tell anybody about this." He tried to secretly glance at his watch.

"I know," she said. "You gotta' go. Git up and turn around. You got leaves and pine needles all over the back of your shirt. Seems like every time I see you, you got a problem with a dirty shirt. And your buttons are undone."

"Yeah." He uttered a weak laugh.

They were both now on their feet. Emma was helping him button his shirt. She gave him a long, hard look.

"What?"

"I love you, Hugh."

They both stepped closer, looked at each other for a moment, and had one final, long kiss.

"I'll see you tomorrow at school," he said. "I don't care who sees us together."

"Me neither."

Hugh gathered as much of his composure as possible and walked back into the house as though he had been on a long hike. Uncle Tom and Aunt Flora were sitting in the kitchen, both with anxious looks on their faces. Tom was the first to speak.

"Hugh, we need to ask you something."

Chapter 11

Hugh felt his heartbeat quicken. "Yessir, what's that? Uh, I was just walking out back, that's all. Beautiful day, huh?" The words almost croaked out, and he hoped they wouldn't notice.

"Listen to my question," Tom said gently. "You got home about ten last night, wasn't it?" The question seemed to blindside him, coming from nowhere.

"I guess so. Yessir, that's right, about ten," he said with a look of puzzlement.

Flora spoke up, "Do you know anything about damage to the Carmichael's car last night?"

"Damage? What kind of damage?"

"Ellis says someone shot at you fellows."

Hugh paused a moment. "Shot at us? No," he said thoughtfully. "I would have remembered that! Must have happened after they dropped me off." His excuse sounded a bit premature.

"Ellis told the sheriff he dropped you off at nine-thirty. At first, he said you weren't with him. Then, he changed his story and distinctly said you were with them when it happened."

Hugh was silent.

Uncle Tom spoke with a slow tone that Hugh had never heard from his uncle. "I have two questions to start off with, Hugh. What was your involvement with this 'damage' to Carmichael's new car, and where were you from nine-thirty until ten?"

Hugh sat down and remained silent. He was looking at the floor, but his eyes darted from side to side. He started to speak but uttered not a sound.

Finally, he said in a hushed tone, "I don't know what to say."

"We don't either," said Flora.

"I didn't do anything wrong."

"Tell us about it," Tom said.

Hugh thought for a moment, trying to regain his composure. "It was dark, and I asked them to stop and let me out."

"Why didn't you want them to bring you home?"

He tried to answer calmly, "Well, on our way back from the movies, Scott and Ellis started yelling out the window at cars and houses, and I just didn't want to be around them if they got into trouble."

"So, you walked home?"

"That's right."

"From where? Where did they let you out?"

"I'm not sure. It was dark. I don't know my way around town very well."

"So, you were in town?"

"Maybe. Maybe just outside of town. There was a streetlight. That's all I can remember."

"That's it?"

Hugh simply nodded. Flora and Tom sat like a pair of sphinxes, waiting to hear more. Hugh's eyes rose to meet their stare. All three simply sat.

Finally, Tom said, "You may as well know the deputy sheriff is on his way here. He's going to ask the same questions. The silent treatment won't work on him."

Flora added, "If you did nothing wrong and somebody shot at the car, what are you holding back?"

"Wouldn't it be easier to just fix the car?" he asked.

"Easier than what?" Flora countered.

"Easier than all this. All these questions."

"Hugh, where were you when it happened?" Flora pleaded.

"Who shot at you?" Tom demanded in a firmer tone. "That deputy is on his way, and you better start answering some questions."

"I don't know who shot at us—at them. I wasn't with them."

"How did you get home? Walk?"

"I got a ride."

"You just said you walked."

"A ride with who?" asked Flora.

"Some colored man."

Both Tom and Flora sat up a little straighter. "Who was he?" They both seemed to speak in harmony.

"Like I said, it was—"

"We know; it was dark!" Tom was trying hard not to explode.

"You don't know where you were or who took you home, all because it was too damn dark!"

The three-way stare resumed. After a minute, Flora tried another approach, "So, how was your walk in the woods?"

Hugh looked stunned at the sudden change of subject. He hoped his look of shock didn't show.

"You were gone a long time. You have grown to love those woods back there, haven't you?"

Hugh realized he was holding his breath. He let it out and said, "Yes ma'am. Real peaceful."

"Not a soul to bother you, huh?"

Hugh just shook his head.

Flora continued speaking softly, "Yes, Emma was telling me the same thing the other day. She comes to the house by that way on occasion."

"Um, Aunt Flora, there's something you ought to know. Those boys aren't what you think they are," Hugh suddenly said with conviction.

"Which boys? Oh, you mean Scott and Ellis?"

Hugh had just started to say something when the phone rang. Flora answered.

"Yes, this is she. Yes, deputy. Yes, he was told you were … oh, you're not. I see. I see. My, how interesting. Well, yes, good citizens do come in all varieties. Thank you for calling."

She hung up, walked over to Hugh, and gave him a huge hug.

"Tom, this poor boy has been going through agony trying to protect his friends!"

Hugh held his breath again. He looked up at Flora cautiously.

"What happened? Who was that on the phone?" Tom asked.

"That was the deputy. He said they had a phone call from—what's his name? Oscar - Oscar Carter. He called to report hearing gunshots last night over by the railroad crossing near Church Road. That's over towards Pittman Mill, isn't it?"

"No, more to the east," Tom said. "Remember, the road forks by the old church. One goes to the mill, and the other one is called Church Road. The mill road goes to, uh, to Emma's house."

Hugh saw his opening. "Who heard the shots?"

"Oscar Carter, so the deputy said."

"Big guy? Big colored guy? Drives an old Plymouth?"

"I think that's what he drives," said Tom.

"That's who picked me up! How 'bout that?" Hugh was seeing a path to a clear conscience.

"Hugh, you were lucky. That could have been anybody!"

"So, this Church Road, does it have a streetlight?"

"Yeah, I think so," said Tom.

"That must be where they let me off! Oscar gave me a ride right after that! Isn't it great when things start falling into place?" He hoped they would believe his broad grin.

Tom started talking faster. "So, you were going to tell us something about Scott and Ellis. And I still want to know why they would say you were with them when you weren't."

"Well, they aren't the angels you think they are, but they mustn't know I told you this."

"What kind of beer do they like?" Flora asked softly with one eyebrow raised.

Hugh turned his head quickly at Flora's words. "Jax," was all he could say.

Tom began rubbing his chin. "Jax, huh? And you?"

"I don't much like it, Uncle Tom. I swear. I took a couple of sips just to go along, and they did most of the drinking. I drove them home from the levee outside of Alexandria and switched back at the edge of town."

"Switched, you mean let Ellis drive? Why?"

"Well, he was a little more sober by then, and he didn't want me driving through town."

"Who bought the beer?"

"Scott did." He turned and asked, "Aunt Flora, how did you know about the beer?"

"Ellis' daddy found an empty under the seat. Hugh, why are you protecting them?"

Hugh's voice became almost pleading. "Because I know you're good friends with their families, and I just wouldn't want to be the one to tell you."

She looked at her nephew skeptically. "So, why did they insist that you were with them when the shooting occurred?"

"I dunno. I really don't know."

"I do," said Flora. "They probably wanted someone to share the blame with. They both changed their story so many times with the deputy that he can't believe anything they say. He's not even coming over here to ask you questions tonight! He said he's had enough for one day."

"I'm sorry I lied to you, Aunt Flora. I just didn't want to get mixed up in it any further."

Tom and Flora both looked at Hugh, knowing they had no choice but to believe him.

"So, who's hungry?" asked Tom.

All three stood, and Hugh said, "I need some air first. May I go outside for a little bit?"

"Sure, it'll keep," she said. "Go for a walk. Go enjoy the woods again."

The next day, before classes started, Hugh saw Emma getting off her bus. As usual, she was the last one off. Her hair was pulled back and tied, and her walk was brisk. At the sight of Hugh, her eyes brightened. She looked carefully at him as she approached.

"Morning," she said, still looking at him carefully.

"You smell good."

"Thanks," she said with a timid tone. "You look tired."

"Long night."

"Me, too. I thought about you all night." Despite two books cradled in front of her, she walked with her arms brushed up against him. She felt a slight and familiar tingle when they touched.

"I thought about you, too. But Aunt Flora and Uncle Tom had other things for me to think about."

"What?"

"Ellis Carmichael's dad called the sheriff about the shotgun damage to his car. That was a new car. Ellis and Scott told 'em two different stories, and I told the Rucker's I wasn't even with them when it happened."

"You lied?"

"I had to. I told both Ellis and Scott that's what I was going to say so they would let me find my way home. I figured they could make up their own excuses. I just wanted them to leave me out of it."

"So, what happened? How come you're still worried? You didn't do anything. I'll even tell 'em how you come back to the house and —"

"No! Let's not complicate things with that."

"Sounds to me like tellin' the truth would be easier than what you're doin'."

"Emma, I don't want them to drag you into this. I just want it to be over. I'm leaving soon, anyway."

Emma stopped walking and looked soulfully at him. He turned and took two steps back to where she had stopped.

"I'm sorry. I didn't mean to say that. When the time comes, I will have to leave, and when I do, it'll all be over. They won't bother me if I'm in Houston."

"So, you're in a hurry to leave. That's nice to know."

"Not because of you! No! Just so this other thing will be over."

"Why don't you just tell them exactly what happened? You weren't driving, you didn't really know these guys that well, and you didn't know what they was up to."

"They'll never believe that. Besides, I don't want to get your dad in trouble. And another thing, Oscar has already told the sheriff that he heard gunshots that night. And he said they were coming from a place somewhere not even close to your house. Now they think there's some madman out there shooting at cars."

"Oscar," she said. "Still taking care of me and Papa. What'd he say to you on the way home?"

"Not much. Just told me a little about your dad. That's all."

They both said nothing for a full minute.

Finally, Hugh spoke. "So, how are you? I mean, after yesterday."

"Hugh," she said. "I gotta' ask you something. Why did you act like something was wrong after we did that, you know, whatever you call it?"

Hugh looked at her cautiously. "You ARE kidding, aren't you?" he said. Emma's quizzical look was convincing. Of what, he wasn't sure. "Look," he continued. "Either you're really telling me we have nothing to worry about, or you really don't have any idea what happened."

"Hugh, I told you I never done that kinda' thing before, and I meant it. Now, what's the problem?"

"Emma, you don't have to DO it to understand what can happen! Let me put it this way. It's for married folks. And you know how it is with them. Even THEY don't know when it's going to work!"

Emma thought for several seconds. "Did it work yesterday?" she asked with a serious look.

"Emma! I can't believe this conversation."

"Hugh, you don't have to get mad about it!" They kept walking slowly. Moments later, she said, "So, pretty soon, you'll be back home, huh?"

His eyes were shifting nervously. "Yeah."

"Kin you write to me?"

"Yeah."

She walked a step closer to him. "So, it's about married people? Hugh, I like the way that sounds."

"Emma, I gotta' go to college. I gotta' find a job. I got lots of things to do before I get married. You understand that?"

"So, why did we do it?"

Hugh was struggling for an answer when Ellis and Scott came around the corner, talking in whispers. All four stopped talking abruptly at the sight of each other. Hugh broke the silence.

"I need to tell you guys something."

"Forget it, fella'," said Scott.

"You might find this important," Hugh answered.

"Yeah," Ellis retorted. "We can see what side you're on. Didn't know you two were on such close terms. I shoulda' known."

Emma piped up and said, "For a couple of smart guys, you can really act stupid sometimes. Did you really think you could get away with what ya' done? And now, Hugh has something to tell you that might help, and you don't want to hear it. Real smart!"

"What's she talking about?" asked Scott.

"C'mon Hugh. Let's go. These two ain't worth helpin'."

"No, wait. Really. What is it?" Ellis asked again.

Hugh gave Emma a look that begged for her approval. She relented and let go of his arm.

Hugh spoke directly to Ellis. "It has to do with Oscar Carter. You know him?"

"Oscar. Oscar Carter—he's that big guy—yeah, I know him. What the hell has he got to do with this?"

"He was the one with the flashlight." Hugh stopped for a moment to let it sink in.

"So?"

"He told the sheriff he heard gunshots from somewhere around—what did he say—Church Road? Yeah, something like that. From what I know, that's nowhere near Emma's house."

"So, what's the big favor he did for us?"

"It means no one shot at you from Emma's house."

"Great! That lets her old man off the hook! We still gotta' explain where we were when it happened."

Emma took a step forward and spoke. "Look. I ain't the smartest person in the world. But even I can figure out what you need to do. You want to hear this?"

Ellis and Scott leaned forward. After a moment of silent telepathy between them, they both nodded in agreement.

"Okay. Does your folks know you was out drinking?" she asked.

One boy nodded, the other shook his head. Emma rolled her eyes.

"Well, I told them we had a beer," Ellis said.

Hugh raised an eyebrow.

"Shit, why NOT tell 'em that? They only found one bottle in the car!"

"Okay," Emma continued. "You went to the show, got a beer, drove through town, dropped Hugh off, and went over by Church Road, and that's where somebody shot at you."

"Hey, how'd you know we went to the show?" Scott asked.

"And how'd you know we dropped him off?" Ellis asked.

"I told her," said Hugh.

"Why'd you tell her all that?" Scott asked, pointing to Emma. "And when did you have a chance to tell her?"

Emma started to answer, but Hugh interrupted. "That's none of your business. The key to this is that Emma knows the whole story. She didn't start it; you guys did. Look, I'm going to be gone, but you're staying. I'd be nice to her if I were you."

"Nice, hell. I'll just stay out of her way like I always do. Who'd believe her, anyway?" Ellis snorted.

Hugh half-turned to leave, then looked back at them. "But you must admit, her version of the story sounds believable unless you really want to stir up something. C'mon, Emma. We don't want to be late."

Ellis and Scott left in another direction. Scott was mumbling, "I still don't get it. It was her old man who shot at us. We didn't do nothin' wrong."

The deputy talked to Ellis and Scott again that evening. They used Emma's home-spun account of the night in question, and it was taken as gospel, but only after severe skepticism from the boys' fathers and the deputy. All seemed to be quiet after that.

Hugh and Emma had to be satisfied with seeing each other only during school. Emma's working arrangement with Flora included only weekends during the school year. That is, except for the next Friday when the water at school had to be turned off due to an unexpected plumbing problem. School was dismissed at noon, and the buses poured into the school yard at 11:30 that morning to load up and take everyone home. Emma and Hugh decided to walk to the store from school. She had no real reason to go home, and Hugh had only one week left. They both knew they couldn't hang around the store long, not under Tom Rucker's watchful eye, but the casual stroll was time together and best done at a slow pace.

"You gonna' write to me from Houston?"

"Sure."

"I am really gonna' miss you." She looked at him wistfully.

He took a deep breath and exhaled slowly. "I'll be back."

"When?"

He shrugged and said, "I don't know. Whenever I can. Mom and Dad do a lot of traveling, so you never know."

"They come here a lot?"

"Well, not so far, but I can work on them." He finished with a slight smirk on his face.

"You got lots of friends in Houston?"

"Sure."

"Any of them girls?"

"Well, yeah. Half the world's made up of girls. I don't avoid them."

"Any of them special?"

He looked off into the distance as they continued to walk. "I've got some good friends that are girls, yeah."

"I mean really special."

Hugh stopped and turned toward her. "Emma, don't do this. Look, what we had together was wonderful. I've never felt so close to anyone before. I'll never forget you. But we're too young to be thinking about anything permanent. It's just too —"

"I wasn't thinkin' about anything permanent. I was just thinkin' that I didn't want you to go. It ain't fair. You the first boy I ever loved, and I get to have you only for a little while." She swallowed hard. "Makes my stomach hurt."

They stopped at the corner of the store, out of sight of the front entrance. Hugh glanced around and saw no one on the road nor anywhere afoot. Looking back at Emma, he focused on the blue in her eyes and saw a slight shimmer of liquid. He held her face in his fingertips and kissed her lips ever so lightly. A noise from the nearby gas station invaded their privacy.

"I better go," he said.

Emma could only watch him turn and go.

Hugh walked into the store and heard men's laughter from a back corner. Must be a busy day, he thought. Woodrow Spears and two of his buddies were having a lively discussion about something while consuming sodas and candy bars. Hugh thought nothing of it when the group casually glanced over to see him walk behind the counter and speak to Lonnie. Hugh and Lonnie had finally developed a mutual respect since their encounter and their other differences. Hugh was explaining the water problem at school to Lonnie when the front door jingled again. Emma, looking for Tom, had entered the store and was timidly standing back, watching all the activity and waiting for her chance to ask Lonnie where Tom was. Woodrow said something quietly to his group of friends, then looked over at Emma.

"Hey, Emma!" he yelled out across the store. C'mere, I wanna' ask you something."

Emma folded her arms and assumed a disgusted look.

"Emma, I want to show you something! C'mere!" The others began to snicker. Seeing that she wasn't going to move, he started slowly ambling toward her. Hugh stood quietly watching.

"Woodrow, get away from me."

"Hey, I'm not planning on doin' nothin'. Least, I don't think so." He turned and grinned at his friends.

"How's that papa of yours? He still mean as a snake? I hear he's too drunk to do much damage to anyone these days. Maybe we ought to pay him a visit and talk over some old times."

"I thought you wanted to show her something," said a voice from behind him.

Slowly, Woodrow turned to see Hugh still standing behind the counter.

"You say something?"

"Yeah."

"You want to try that again?"

Hugh scratched his ear and said, "You heard me the first time. Leave Emma alone."

Emma began to look truly alarmed. Lonnie saw her start to step in between the two of them and gave her a subtle wave-off that none of the others saw. Puzzled, she stepped back and watched the encounter developing.

Woodrow sensed a challenge and could not, in good conscience, ignore it.

"You talking to me, boy?"

"I don't plan on making it a habit, but at the moment, yeah, I'm talking to you."

"I'm tending to a little business here, so why don't you just go piss in the wind somewhere. I'll get to you later."

"If you take one more step in her direction, your trip's going to be cut a little short."

Despite his swaggering, Woodrow could not conceal a hint of shock at Hugh's words. He turned and took a step toward Hugh.

"Glad to see you know how to comply," Hugh said.

"Comply? Lonnie, who is this?"

"You don't really want to know, Woody. If I were you, I wouldn't start anything."

"Lonnie, you want a piece of this, too?" Woodrow said, rubbing his palms together.

"Oh, I'm not going to do a thing," said Lonnie. "I won't have to."

Woodrow gave a look of comical amusement and said, "Well, if you're not looking for anything, I sure ain't worried about this candy-ass! Where you from, boy? Some little girls' school?"

He turned again to Emma and started walking toward her with a strong stride. About ten feet away, Emma pointed at something behind him that made him turn around and look. Off balance, Hugh caught him on the point of his shoulder with the butt of his hand, almost knocking him over.

Woodrow's face turned to scarlet, and he immediately swung a roundhouse left, which Hugh easily stepped away from. Before he could cock his right hand, Hugh peppered him with left and right jabs that sent him backward and upended into a bin of potatoes. Hugh stepped back and let him extract himself from the tubers, after which Woodrow proceeded to swing wildly as Hugh stood with hands at his side, deftly dodging and ducking with ballet smoothness. By now, they were toward the rear of the store and partially hidden from any view of the front door. Lonnie and Emma saw the two go behind a set of shelves and then saw the shelves shudder as a single smacking sound welled up from the small battleground. The sound of cans rattling across the floor followed. Moments later, Hugh calmly walked out into view. He stopped and leaned against the counter. In a few seconds, Tom Rucker came stepping in the front door. He was walking briskly, taking full strides, rubbing his hands together. All eyes nervously turned toward him.

"Hugh. Good! I was wondering where you might turn up. I heard they shut the school down early today." He hesitated for a moment and realized that Emma had stepped out from behind a glass display case and was standing next to him. Slowly, he said, "I thought maybe we could get some fishing in before dark. Emma, did you want something?"

"Yessir, but it can wait."

Just as Tom was about to say something else, a moaning noise stirred from the back of the store. Woodrow, holding his hand over his nose and mouth, emerged with his friends supporting him and headed for the front door.

"You gentlemen come back any time, you hear?" Tom said happily. He innocently turned his attention back to Hugh.

Lonnie had walked to the front and held the door open for Woody and his buddies. As they passed by, he said quietly, "Ice. Use lots of ice. I'll be glad to sell you some."

Hugh said, "Actually, Uncle Tom, Emma, and I are going to the house for some lunch. I haven't really decided what I want to do with the rest of my day. You want to join us?"

Lonnie let out a muffled laugh and pretended to be busy with something in a lower cabinet. Tom said nothing.

Hugh continued, "Well if you change your mind, we'll be talking to Aunt Flora."

Lunch went well. With Flora's permission, Hugh drove Emma home. He was back before Tom ever knew he had left the house.

The next day was Saturday, and Emma came to the house, as usual. Tom made sure Hugh was up early and busy at the store before she got there. At the end of the day, they had only a chance to briefly say 'Hi' as she came in the back as usual. Tom immediately sent him off on an errand to the other side of town. Sunday, the Ruckers all went to Alexandria after church to have dinner and a movie.

Just a few more days, Tom thought to himself.

Monday morning came, and Hugh was waiting at the school for Emma's bus as usual. From behind him, Hugh heard someone call his name. He turned and saw Scott motioning him to come closer.

"I got something to tell you." Scott's voice had a tone of concern.

"You actually speaking to me?"

Scott looked around and stepped closer. "Well, look … forget all that stuff. Ellis has a real problem with something else, and he's trying to cover his butt somehow. Where were you last weekend, last Saturday?"

"I went out with you guys. The river levee?"

"Wait, lemme' think. Naw, the Saturday before that. Where were you then?"

"I don't really remember. Why?"

"Can you say that me and Ellis was with you that night?" His voice was now just above a whisper.

Hugh looked off with a distant stare. He finally looked back at Scott in silence.

Scott continued, "Okay, I'll tell you what the deal is. Ellis found this little honey over in Tioga, that's the next town up the road. She really likes Ellis, and she's been handing out whatever he wants. He's been gettin' it every weekend for just over a month now, except the Saturday you went with us. So, a few days ago, he found this red spot on his pecker, and it started gettin' bigger. The spot, I mean, not his, well, you know. So, he goes in to see the school nurse the next morning, and the doctor is there, but he's just getting ready to leave. So, Ellis tells him what the problem is, and the doc just tells the nurse something and takes off." Scott hesitated to see if Hugh was listening. "So, it's like this; the nurse pulls out this big-ass needle and draws blood from him and says the doctor will be back in the afternoon. So, Ellis comes back in the afternoon, and the doctor sees him. He shuts the door and tells Ellis to show him."

"Show him what?"

"His pecker, dummy! So, he shows it to him, and the doc wants to see his hands. He asks Ellis if he's been in the woods lately. Ellis can't remember. So, he asks him if he's had his fly open in the woods. By now, Ellis is gettin' real scared. He ain't got a clue what this doc is talking about. So, the doc says he's got poison ivy on his hands, and somehow, he got it on his pecker. So, he ain't got no sex disease or nothing. He and the doc have a good laugh, and then Ellis got to thinking about when the three of us went to the levee. Remember he had to take a piss? He told me later he slipped down walking in the dark, and there were some low bushes he stumbled over."

"I'm surprised he remembered it. But what's the problem?"

"Yeah. Well, the blood sample had already been sent to the lab."

"And it came back already?"

"No, man! The bill! The lab sent a bill to his home address! His mom opened it and started asking questions. He don't want his mama to even suspect he's got somethin' going on in Tioga."

"You're kidding. This is too much! And now he wants me to lie about where I was? On what night? Hey, I don't remember where I was! Why does he have to drag everyone else into his story when he needs to get out of a jam?" Hugh was trying hard not to laugh but with little success.

"I'll tell you why you're gonna' help. Because now, he starts singing like a canary, and his folks know all about the night with the beer, us on the levee, and he went ahead and told them about buzzin' Emma's house. They know about Emma's old man and the shotgun."

Neither of them realized that Emma had disembarked from her bus and, while walking toward them, had heard the last part of Scott's epistle of gloom.

"What about my papa?"

"They know," Scott spat at Emma. Ellis' folks know it was your old man who shot at us."

Hugh interrupted, "Hey, wait a minute. Ellis doesn't give a damn about her father. He just wants to cover up what he's got going in Tioga."

"Not so loud," Scott pleaded. "No one, and I mean no one else, knows about that."

"About what?" Emma interjected.

"None of your business," Scott said.

"If it affects her father, it is her business," Hugh said.

"What he's got in Tioga has nothin' to do with that old man."

"What are you talking about?" Emma pleaded.

"It's got everything to do with her dad. Every part of this. The girl in Tioga, harassing Emma and her dad, the trip to the levee, and the shotgun damage … it's all connected because Ellis is doing the connecting. And you're right in there with him, aren't you?"

Scott was adamant. "Hey, look! We've got the whole story worked out. We just need you to say—"

Hugh grabbed Scott by the shirt, pinned him hard against the gymnasium wall, and yelled, "Give me one good reason why I should help either one of you?" Hearing nothing, Hugh released him and ran to catch up with Emma, who obviously had no plans to attend class that day.

"Where're you going?" he said, slightly out of breath.

"I gotta' find Papa. I think he has some work with Mr. Tulley at the gas station today."

"Gas station. Next to the store?"

"Yeah." Emma was now walking at a brisk pace and breathing a little harder.

They reached the edge of the school yard and turned towards town.

"What's going to happen?" Hugh asked, trying to keep up with her.

"I don't know. I just know that there's a lot of folks in this town who would like to see Papa punished for a lot of things. Maybe he deserves it, but that was a long time ago, and he's an old man now." She looked at Hugh without slowing down. "You will help me find him, won't you?"

"I never met the man. don't know what he looks like, but I'll help." That was when Hugh saw a slightly hunched figure out on the main road coming from the direction of Pittman. "Is that him?"

Chapter 12

"Papa! Somethin's happened! Papa, stop and listen to me!" Emma hurried toward her father in long strides.

Hugh didn't move. He had never had a close look at Emma's father. The man she was talking to could have been on a poster for the Salvation Army. His hairline was beginning to recede, and what was left had started to thin. It was silver-grey, uncombed, wet with perspiration, and hung almost to his shoulders. On the sides of his face, Hugh couldn't readily distinguish where the hairline stopped and the beard continued. His face, what part was visible, was a network of thin blood vessels in a background of ruddy complexion. A serpentine, contracted scar adorned the temple on one side of his head. On the same side, his ear seemed twisted and deformed. There was a thin film of black grime on his hands, giving them the look of machinery parts rather than human appendages. At first, the man looked perplexed, then he grimaced as he listened to Emma. The more she told him, the more Hugh could see his expression change, even at a distance. The grimace became a sneer, like that of a cornered animal. His face was slowly contorted while his eyes flashed and darted, menacing eyes. In less than a minute, the tired vagabond figure had changed into a walking cauldron of fury wanting to kill something.

Hugh couldn't hear her words, but Emma's gestures as she spoke were becoming more desperate, pleading. The old man tried to leave and dismissed her with a wave of his hand, but she stood her ground and blocked his path, still trying to talk. One shove from him and she was almost knocked off her feet. Hugh could stand no more and came closer.

Joshua saw Hugh and bellowed, "What does this piss-ant want?"

"Mr. Parker, I want to help. But you can't be pushing Emma like that."

"Get outa' my way!" With both hands, he exploded and grabbed Hugh like a rag doll and tossed him backward. He took a step toward the boy with his fists clinched.

"Papa! Don't hurt him! He's a friend!"

So focused were the three of them that none heard the sheriff's patrol car quietly roll to a stop about fifty feet away. The young deputy gave the siren one short blast and stepped out of the car.

"Joshua Parker?"

"Get outa' here, kid! Mind your own business!"

"Joshua Parker, I have a warrant for your arrest."

"Stick it up your ass!"

Emma pleaded once more. "Papa, listen to him! This is what I been trying to tell you!"

Joshua roared, "Arrest for what?"

"Assault with a deadly weapon. Don't make this harder than it has to be, Mr. Parker."

Joshua walked towards the deputy, then charged the last few steps like a bull. He clenched his teeth in pain as he felt the deputy's baton across his shoulders. The old man stumbled and tried to catch his balance, and the young officer expertly pushed him to the ground. Before anyone could react, Joshua felt handcuffs on his wrists and the deputy's knee in his back.

"Get off'n me, you little prick! I said get off!"

"Don't you hurt him!" Emma yelled.

"Don't worry, I won't. Mr. Parker, are you coming quietly with me?"

Joshua kicked his legs into empty air. His hair hung down in his face, mixed with sweat and gravel.

"Please, let me talk to him," Emma begged.

The deputy thought for a second and motioned for her to come closer. She knelt beside her father's face and spoke to him in whispered sobs.

"Papa, please don't fight this. It ain't your fault. We'll tell everybody how it happened. Papa, listen to me!"

Joshua was now fighting to catch his breath. Hugh had been standing like a statue, horrified at the deputy's tactics in apprehending such an old person, then remembered the old man's strength from moments ago. Joshua slowly got up, keeping his head ducked down. Several cars had stopped along the main road to watch the spectacle.

Emma was horrified. Amidst her tears and pleading, she turned toward the cars and screamed, "All of ya'll git outa' here! Stop looking at him like that! He didn't do nothin'! He didn't do nothin'!" She began picking up handfuls of gravel and throwing them at the onlookers. "Go away!" she wailed.

"Got her daddy's temper, that's for sure," someone said.

Hugh tried to console her, but she pulled away. He then walked quickly to the patrol car and spoke to the deputy, who was now behind the wheel.

"Where will you take him?" he asked through the driver's window.

The deputy spoke through a toothy grin. "Colfax. Got a private room all ready and waiting for him."

"Due process, right? Look, my name is Hugh Giles. I'm staying at the Rucker's house. They own that store over there. I can explain everything to whoever wants to listen."

The deputy's grin disappeared, and he drove away.

Emma was left on her knees sobbing in the middle of the road, watching the patrol car turn the corner, cross the tracks, and disappear. The crowd was beginning to disperse.

"I got to git to Colfax," she said.

"Wait. Let's think this out. What's the best thing we can do to help?"

"Hugh, we don't know what they'll do to him in that jail! He's got enemies everywhere! We got to go to Colfax!"

"Emma, just wait. Let me go get Uncle Tom."

"Uncle Tom? Uncle Tom? Is that all you kin think of?" she yelled as he ran toward the store.

What seemed only moments later, Hugh emerged with Lonnie and Tom. Emma was nowhere to be seen. In the distance, a car was crossing the railroad tracks on the road leaving town.

Tom said, "Hugh, I don't have time for this. I told you from the day you started chasing around after that little urchin that it would come to trouble. You're noble for trying to help, but now look! She's gone! Wouldn't even listen to you, of all people. You have no idea where she is. She obviously doesn't want your help."

Hugh skipped school that day. About three hours later, another deputy came to the Rucker house. A young woman in civilian street clothes followed him to the door. Hugh and Flora were sitting in the swing on the front porch.

"You Hugh Giles?" he said through the screen.

Hugh immediately sat up straight, "Yessir."

"Mind if I come in and talk to you?"

He looked first at his aunt, who nodded, then said, "Sure, come on in."

The deputy pulled up a porch rocker for the woman and one for himself.

"I looked for you at the school. They said you might be here." He pointed to the woman who came with him. "This here is Melba. She's a court recorder. We'd like to take your statement about what happened the night ya'll got shot at."

"My statement?"

"Well, with you leaving to go back to Houston and all, it might be easier this way."

"How did you know I was leaving?"

"I just know what the judge told me, and I don't know who told him. Can you do this?"

"So, what if I don't? It probably won't do any good."

"Then we'll get a court order that will bring you back from Texas. It'll be super complicated and expensive to do that. Judge Allentrot, he don't like complications like that. He likes to keep things simple. The more complicated it gets, the more he takes it out on the defendant. Understand?"

"So, my giving you a statement today will make it easier for Mr. Parker."

"Right."

"So, why isn't she writing all this down?"

The deputy cleared his throat. "Look, she is here to take your statement. You gonna' do it?"

"Yeah, sure. Where do you want me to start?"

At supper that night, no one had an appetite. Flora, Hugh, and Tom sat at the table in silence, picking at their food.

Hugh finally sat up and said in a decisive tone, "I never planned to get this involved with Emma. I didn't know a thing about her when I came here. She just seemed cute and … she was, well, she kinda' grew on me."

Tom tried to sound pontifical. "That's good to hear. Well, you see what curiosity with other people's lives gets you into."

"At least you admit she was human and had a life," said Flora.

"My dear, we live on a different plane than she does."

"We didn't before her mother died. And now she's out there somewhere, trying to do God knows what, and none of us are budging to help."

"I never said I gave up on her," said Hugh with a note of irritation.

Flora rose from the table and walked toward the phone.

"What are you doing now?" Tom asked her.

"I'm calling Lavenia. Maybe she's at her house."

Tom and Hugh sat in silence while Flora called the Carter house. In less than a minute, she had finished and hung up.

"They haven't seen her. Oscar's going over to the Parker house to see if she simply went home. She could've done that, you know. We never did stop to think of such an easy answer."

Lightning flashed far off in the distance and caused a flicker through the windows. The slow, muffled rumble of thunder arrived almost a minute later. For the next quarter hour, they all sat waiting. Tom flipped through a magazine while Flora tried to knit. Hugh was about to offer to drive to Colfax when they all heard a car pull up at the front of the house. A loud knock at the front porch screen door came within seconds later.

"Mr. Rucker!" a strong voice called out. "Mr. Rucker!"

Tom got up from his chair and said, "It's Oscar. Heaven's sake! I wonder what he wants."

Oscar stood on the front steps and started talking before the trio could get to the porch.

"Somethin' bad wrong! Somethin' real bad. They done tore up Mr. Joshua's house and broke out all the windows."

"Who?" asked Flora.

"I don't know, ma'am. But they's somebody awful glad to see him in jail."

"What about Emma?" Hugh asked.

"She weren't there. I don't know where that child is. I sho' gettin' worried."

"Well, that does it for me," Flora said. "I'm going to Colfax. We'll find Emma."

Oscar wrung his hands and said slowly, "Everybody knows where they took him. Ma'am, if she went there, she woulda' gone to the jail, huh?"

"Exactly."

"So, why don't we call the jail and see if they know where she is. Maybe they seen her."

Hugh said, "Oscar, it's good to see somebody around here is thinking." Hugh retreated to the living room and reached for the phone.

Tom yelled from the porch, "Hugh, that's long distance!"

"Oh, shut up, Tom!" Flora shouted. "Here, Hugh. I'll make the call."

In less than three minutes, Flora had determined that Emma had indeed gone to Colfax and had tried to see her father and was refused entrance. The voice on the other end had said that Emma had stayed around for about an hour, then disappeared.

"So, she's in Colfax," Flora said with a note of concern.

"Or is she on the way back home?" said Hugh.

"We could go look for her," said Oscar. "We could go in my car."

"Oscar, you're very generous. I think our car will get us there quicker." She glared at her husband, who said nothing. "Tom, we're going to Colfax. I'm sure you'll want to stay here and read or take a nap!"

It took a half hour to reach Colfax. The distant thunder was getting closer. Hugh and Flora sped along the highway with Oscar in the back seat. He sat in the middle and leaned forward to listen.

"I'm glad you're coming with us, Oscar," Flora said. "I don't know where the jail is. You know your way around Colfax, don't you?"

"Yes'm. Grow'd up there. Turn left up there, ma'am."

Large raindrops began to hit the windshield.

"How soon do you think he'll be out on bail?" Hugh asked.

"That goes by how much the bail be and when somebody gonna' pay for it," Oscar said.

"You know about this stuff, Oscar?" Hugh asked.

"Seem like yest'day. Yessir, jus' the other day."

"You were in jail?" Hugh asked.

Oscar only nodded.

"When?"

"Long time ago, right before I went to work for Mr. Joshua, he gave me my first real good job. That's why I do everything I can for him. My family woulda' starve if it weren't fo' Mr. Joshua."

"What part of town is this, Oscar?" Flora asked.

"We almost there. Don't worry. My kids' school is on the next block. See that building up there with all the lights? On the right. That's it."

The raindrops were getting steadily heavier and more rapid. Flora parked the car across the street, and the three of them hurried through the front door of the Grant Parish jail. Behind a desk was a duty officer.

"He'p ya' ma'am?" he said.

"Are you holding Joshua Parker here?"

"Lemme' see," he picked up a piece of paper on the desk. "Yes'm, he's here. Who's calling?"

"We're friends. We'd like to see him."

"Well, it's getting kinda' late, you know."

"We drove a good distance to get here."

"You probably did. But it takes a while to get in and a while to come out, you know."

"What do you mean, 'a while'?"

Oscar spoke up softly, "He mean, dey gotta' search you before you go in."

Flora looked at Oscar, not comprehending what he meant, then seeing him raise his eyebrows, suddenly understood fully.

"Officer, we just want to speak to the man briefly. Couldn't you just let us in for a second?"

"We got our rules, ma'am."

"But you don't want to take all your time searching someone like me. Why don't you just walk back there with me, and you can see I'm not trying to sneak anything illegal to him. I just want to reassure him, that's all."

"I don't know," the man said slowly. "I'm sure you mean well, but I could get in trouble for this."

"Oh, we're not going to tell anyone," she said with a soft smile.

The officer looked at his watch and thought for a moment. "You know, the boss won't be here for another thirty minutes. You two; sit here. Ma'am, you come with me. You got exactly five minutes before I start gettin' nervous. After that, my butt's in a sling."

Oscar and Hugh found chairs next to a soda machine. The floor was gritty and scuffed. Flora followed the officer through a heavy door that shut with a solid thud after they passed through.

"Oscar, what do you think they'll do to him?"

"Old man like that? Don't matter. If it's a year, it may as well be fifty years. He won't be coming out."

"So, what happens to Emma?"

"Dat's what I be wondering. She got to make a livin'. Where she gon' go?"

"How bad was the house damaged?"

Oscar was deep in thought. "Nuthin' can't be fixed. It's just that without her pa there, people gonna' - well, you seen what happened the other night."

"But Oscar, that's his defense. He was protecting his home, and you're a witness."

Oscar's eyes opened wide. "Me? Who gonna' listen to me? Who you kiddin'?"

"Oscar, I've heard about you. People have relied on you for so many things. Don't sell yourself short. You're a good character witness."

Oscar shifted uneasily in his chair. "Ain't never had nobody call me to talk in no courthouse."

"Oscar, it's not hard. You just tell the truth. Like you always have."

"I done lied once already."

"How? About what?"

"About dem' gunshots I heard. I didn't hear no gunshots on Church Road. But I told the deputy I did."

"Oscar, for all you know, there were gunshots over there. Think hard. There probably were, right? Way off in the distance! Probably no one else heard them! Besides, they're not going to ask you about that. If they do, stick to your story! Who's going to prove you wrong?"

"What you sayin'?" Oscar was sitting up straight now.

"Who's going to say you DIDN'T hear gunshots way off in the distance? You never said the gunshots you heard were the ones that hit Carmichael's car. Once they get that question out of the way, you can go ahead and tell them about all the times folks have driven by Emma's house trying to rattle them. How many times did it happen?"

"Hard to say. For a while, it was most every weekend. Ask Miss Emma."

Emma's plight suddenly came back to Hugh's thoughts. How long had Flora been in there with Joshua? The rain outside was now coming down in sheets.

"Oscar, we've got to find Emma."

"I know some folks I can ask."

"Who?"

"Some of 'em pass right through here, 'especially on Saturday night. We can drive through some neighborhoods. I used to go to school around here. My kids go there now." It was the only school in the Parish for kids like Oscar's. He glanced up. "Look, here comes Miss Flora."

Flora came through the heavy door and turned to thank the young man who had let her in. She looked at Oscar and Hugh and motioned toward the outside door. The rain had suddenly stopped as quickly as it had started.

"I have never been in a place like that before! Those poor men."

"Did you see Joshua?" Hugh asked.

"Yes. He's okay. Very subdued. He didn't say much; just sat there. The only time he really said anything was when I asked him if he knew where Emma was. He said he didn't know, and he's worried about her."

"Oscar says he might know some people to ask," Hugh said.

"People like who?"

"People I know. We got to drive there, though."

"All right. Get in the car, and let's go."

"Miss Flora, this ain't gon' sound right, but we need to drive through my kinda' neighborhood."

"Yes, I assumed that to be the case. I'm not worried."

"Ma'am, people ain't gonna' talk if they think this be your car. I think you and the boy here best sit in the back and let me drive."

Flora looked perplexed.

"He's right, Aunt Flora. It's got to look like Oscar wants to be here. That won't happen with him in the back seat. That would look like you just dragged him along. Let Oscar drive and do the talking."

Reluctantly, she handed him the keys.

In less than two minutes, they were driving through parts of town with dark stretches between streetlights. Silhouettes moved in and out of the shadows along the street and between buildings. Softly, Oscar spoke to one of them, or more like, he made an unintelligible sound almost under his breath, and it turned toward him.

A few steps closer, Oscar asked quietly, "You seen a white girl around here? She's 'bout sixteen, blond hair, probably looks lost?"

"Maybe," it answered. "Stay put."

The figured left and came back seconds later with a man closer to Oscar's age. They both spoke in hushed tones.

"You looking for a white girl? How come?"

Flora leaned forward in the back seat and inhaled to speak, but Oscar quickly shushed her with an upheld hand. It was as though he had eyes in the back of his head. The older man and the shadowy figure both took a step back at the sight of a white face in the car.

"It's okay," Oscar told them. "They lost somebody, and I'm just tryin' to help."

"Why you lookin' in this neighborhood?"

"Her daddy is in jail. She is trying to see him, we guess. Jail jus' right over there, so we look here."

"Go 'round the block - real slow. Be back here in five minutes."

Oscar nodded and put the car in gear. The rain had resumed in a slow drizzle. No one said a word until they turned the corner, then

Flora spoke from the back seat. "What are we doing? Who was that?"

"Friend of mine. I had to lay him off at the mill long time ago, but I found him a job here. He only missed two days work. We he'p each other."

Hugh asked, "But does he know where Emma is?"

"He checkin'."

The car splashed through some puddles as Oscar slowly took another corner and found themselves at the back of the jail. Garbage cans lay battered and empty, scattered along the sidewalk. A scrawny cat peeked out from behind one.

Oscar pointed up ahead and said, "Hardest whuppin' I ever got was on account o' three white boys on dat corner, back when I was about yo' age, Hugh."

"Why?"

"It don't matter now. Dey said somethin'; I said somethin'. You know how it is."

"Did you get hurt bad?"

"No, not bad at all. I jus' finally took out running when I seen they was pickin' up pipes and sticks."

"But you said it was your hardest, uh, whuppin'."

Oscar started to chuckle. "Yessuh, from my daddy when he found out!"

Oscar snickered for another second, then suddenly became quiet. "Look yonder. There she is."

Up ahead and to the right, a bedraggled, wet figure walked slowly along the street with a stumbling gait, her arms folded tightly in front of her. At the sound of the car, she ducked out of the headlight beam and stood behind some oleander bushes. The car stopped even with her, and she took a step further back into the shadows. Oscar quickly opened the driver's door, stepped out, and called to her.

"Miss Emma!"

Emma emerged from the bushes an inch at a time. She saw the car with someone standing on the opposite side. Then the passenger door opened, and Flora stepped out, followed by Hugh. Despite the warm evening, Emma approached the car shivering. Flora closed the distance to reach Emma, and she saw a blank look on the girl's face.

"They wouldn't let me in to see him," she mumbled.

"We know, dear. We called, and they said you had been to the jail."

She peered at Flora for several seconds with a puzzled look. "I just didn't know what to do."

"How did you get here?" Flora asked.

"A man and a woman stopped and picked me up. They took me to the edge of Kisatchie and made me get out. A man came along later and brung me here."

"You hitch-hiked here?" Hugh asked, astonished.

She turned and looked at Hugh, "You! You just stood there while that man knocked Papa down and almost stood on him! All you could think to do was to run and get your uncle! You wouldn't do anything!"

"Emma, I couldn't! I'd be in jail, too!"

She stepped toward him with clinched fists and began pounding on his shoulders. Her wet hair showered Hugh with droplets of water. "You didn't help at all! You just stood there!" she screamed.

The shadows began to move. Oscar glanced around and said quickly, "We got to get outa' here. Hugh, git her in the car right now!"

Flora held the door open with the seat back leaned forward. Hugh wrapped his arms around Emma and struggled toward the car with her. With Flora's help, they managed to get her inside the door. She was now screaming at all three of them. Hugh let go and endured her flailing fists, grabbed her arm with one hand, slid the other under her legs, and heaved her across the seat. Flora turned to get in the back seat with her, but Hugh was already half-way in. He sat down next to Emma and grabbed her wrists.

"Miss Flora, git in de' car!" Oscar yelled.

As soon as Flora's door shut, Oscar stepped on the gas and headed for the edge of town, but not by the way they had come earlier. Within what seemed like only moments, they were on a dark country road that Flora was unfamiliar with. He pulled the car over and stopped. Emma was growing weary but was still struggling with Hugh in the back seat.

"Oscar, where are we?" Flora asked anxiously.

"Don't worry, we'll be goin' home in just a second. Hugh, let go of her."

Hugh held on to Emma for another second and looked perplexed at Oscar. Understanding, he released his grip, and she promptly slapped him so hard it made his ears ring and his face tingle.

"EMMA!" Oscar shouted.

All three in the car jerked their heads toward Oscar.

"Emma," he said softly. "Yo' daddy's okay." He gave her a moment to comprehend. His voice was suddenly smooth and gentle. "We seen him. Well, Miss Flora did. Tell her, Miss Flora."

Flora spoke softly from the front seat. "Emma, I went in to see your father. He's fine. He's worried about you, though."

It took several seconds for her to comprehend Flora's words. She looked at all three of her rescuers one by one and began crying quietly.

"Now what?" Hugh said, astonished.

"I think she's just relieved, Hugh," said Flora. She handed Emma her handkerchief. "You must be starving."

Emma nodded and said, "I need to pee. Oscar, let me out for a minute."

Oscar opened the car door, but because of his size, he had to get out of the car to allow the seat back to fold forward. Emma slipped out of the car and disappeared into the dark woods. Moments later, she returned and silently climbed back in. Oscar turned the car around and headed back into Colfax.

"So, why did you take this road, Oscar?" Flora inquired.

"Miss Flora, the road to Kisatchie is clean on the other side of this town. I had to get her to quiet down first. What would it look like to see a colored man my age driving through the middle of Colfax wid' a screamin' white girl in the back seat?"

"Yes, I see your point, Oscar. I certainly do thank you for your help tonight." Flora turned to speak to Emma and saw Hugh put one finger to his lips. Emma had buried her face in Hugh's shoulder and fallen asleep.

She woke to the sound of the car going over railroad tracks. Soon, the lights of the Rucker house came into view. On the way home, Flora had begun to realize that she couldn't just drop her off somewhere. It was not only because of her state of mind, but she was truly alone. Even if her father was a drunk, at least he had been there. She also remembered Oscar's description of the damage done to Emma's house.

Tom had seen the car lights coming and was at the gate to meet them.

"Flora! I was really beginning to worry! Oh, I see you found her. Well, better be getting her home. You all look tired. I'll drive her."

"Thomas, you wait a minute! Don't be so quick!"

Looking over Flora's shoulder, Tom saw Hugh standing very close to Emma, his hand gently cupped under her elbow. "Flora, come over here. We need to talk." The two of them stepped away from the other three.

"Tom, listen to me —"

"No, you listen to me! Do you realize what you've done running off to another town with a colored man looking for that trashy girl, her daddy in jail, and you dragged Hugh along? Do you know what that looks like? Do you realize what could have happened?"

"Thomas! Keep your voice down!" she hissed. "When people need help, we don't worry about how it looks. We just —"

"Until later! I guarantee that sooner or later, we - no - YOU will regret having done all this. Flora, this is how it is with her kind.

They're in and out of trouble all the time. Her daddy drinks, and, for all I know, she probably does, too."

Hugh stepped over to where Tom and Flora were talking. They both stopped and looked at him. At the same time, they heard two car doors shut.

"Don't worry. Oscar's taking her home," he said. The old Plymouth's engine coughed into life.

"To her house, of course," said Tom.

"No, to his," Hugh said.

"You see?" Tom exclaimed. "Everything to its own level." Tom waited for a moment before continuing. "Hugh, your dad called. They came home a couple of days sooner than expected. So, we'll get you on the train, say, tomorrow afternoon? If not, then the next morning. How's that?"

Flora looked at Tom with pure contempt. "Couldn't wait to get him here. Now you can't wait to get him home!"

"Flora, I didn't ask them to come home early."

Hugh walked ahead and into the house. Tom and Flora continued their discussion up the front walk and onto the living room.

"Tom, could you try to be a little more sensitive in front of the boy? I mean, after the evening we've been through? It meant a lot to him and to all of us. Well, maybe not to you, but you really should have come to help us. You can't tell me you haven't grown the least bit attached to that poor girl. She's got so much potential. I can't help but love her. And Hugh, well, he thinks the world of her."

"I know. That what scares me. He's not old enough to make those kinds of judgments."

Hugh appeared from the hallway. "She knows I'm leaving, Uncle Tom. She just doesn't know it might be tomorrow. It wouldn't be fair to leave without telling her."

"Hugh, you don't owe her a thing! Go back to Houston! Get back with your friends! Find another girl. There's plenty out there!"

Flora calmly walked past Tom and whispered something to Hugh. He pulled his attention away from Tom for a moment to realize what Flora had said, then looked back at his uncle. "Okay, Uncle Tom. Whatever you say."

Tom looked suspiciously at his wife, who was disappearing into the kitchen.

The evening came, and Tom fell asleep with a book across his nose. Flora walked quietly into the hallway and picked up the phone. She spoke with her hand shielding her mouth and, after less than a minute, hung up.

The next day, Flora volunteered to take Hugh to the school building before class to clean out his locker. She dropped him off at the front entrance and proceeded to find a parking spot near Alton MacArthur's office. Hugh waited and watched school buses arrive one by one. He knew which one to look for because Emma was standing at the front by the driver, waiting to be the first one off. She saw him before the bus stopped, and the driver had to tell her to stay clear of the door. As soon as it opened, she flew out and leaped into Hugh's arms. The two stood there in silent embrace as the rest of the bus emptied out, walking around them like waters in a stream flowing around a rock. When the crowd finally cleared, he lifted his head off her shoulder and looked at her.

"You really don't know how much I'm going to miss you," he said.

"You said you'd write. You said you'd come back. You will, right?"

"You don't know how bad I want to."

"I love you, Hugh. I've never known anyone else like you." She held his face in her hands. "Do you love me?" she asked.

"The time has to be right, Emma. We both still have so much to do."

She studied his face. "I asked you if you loved me."

Hugh looked at her for several seconds. "Yes, I do."

She clutched him tightly and said, "Then I don't care how long I have to wait. I'm going to see you again, and the time will be right."

They stood with their foreheads touching as though thoughts and images flowed between them. Emma's fingertips moved over the buttons on his shirt. No words were spoken, but the messages were clear.

"Your shirt button's undone," she said softly.

"You got this thing for noticing buttons, don't you?" he said.

She tried to smile, "I do remember mama used to call me button."

"Button," he said. "I like that. It suits you."

A polite beep from Flora's car horn brought them back to reality. One last kiss and Emma went to class. Hugh walked down to his locker and cleaned it out.

Flora said nothing until they were almost home. "Hugh," she said. "Just be sure. The rest of your life is a long time. You're so young, and you really don't know this girl that well. And you haven't been here all that long, either. Maybe this is your first love. This is the one you'll always remember, no matter who you finally settle for. You'll always have a warm spot in your heart for her. You're going to be fine, and so will she. I'll see to it."

Hugh shifted in his seat. "You're right. She's special. We just enjoy being together so much."

"That's true. And right now, that's all you can see - the good part. When you've been with someone for a while, you find other things about that person you didn't see before. Things you didn't want to see."

"Aunt Flora, what are you talking about?"

"Hugh, you both come from different worlds. You grew up in wealth and opulence. Look at her. Hear how she talks. What do you have in common? Could you bring her into your life?"

"So, why have you waited until now to tell me all this? You saw we were getting involved. In fact, you called Lavenia last night to make sure that Emma and I would see each other this morning."

"Well, regardless of what you may think of my opinions, I do recognize that this is important to you. I'm saying this as a favor from me to you, that's all. Like I said, it's your first love. It's a learning process. What better place to do it than in an innocent little town like Kisatchie."

Hugh almost choked when he heard her last statement. Finally, he said very firmly, "So, this is an innocent little town, and I'm using Emma to do some of my growing up. Ask Emma how innocent it is."

"Hugh, I don't believe I've ever heard such harsh tones from you. I'm a little surprised! Why, this is a wonderful little town!"

The rest of the morning was a blur of packing and closure. Hugh had said goodbye to a few close friends at school that morning. It didn't take long to be ready; then, simply a matter of waiting. He paced the floor, reading a magazine of Uncle Tom's. Flora asked him if he would like to go to the store to pass the time, and he didn't. He would spend enough time in the car with Tom on the way to the train station. Finally, something occurred to him. He walked into the kitchen and sat at the table, watching Flora put away dishes.

"Aunt Flora, how do I stay in touch with Emma? I never thought to ask her for an address, and I never gave her mine."

"Well, you can certainly write to her care of general delivery in Kisatchie. Or you could write to her in care of our box number. I'll see to it that she gets it. Here, let me write it down for you. But you must write first. It wouldn't be proper for her to write to you first."

"Aunt Flora, sometimes I think I don't want to go back. Mom and Dad are always tied up with something else or going somewhere. I spend more time with the housekeepers than I do with them."

"Hugh, did you say you wanted to go to college?"

"Sure."

"Where?"

"Texas Tech, Texas A&M, maybe Rice, I'm not sure."

"To do what?"

"Not sure about that, either. Maybe law school. I've been thinking about writing for a living, though. You know, maybe journalism. Or engineering!" He tried hard to sound positive.

"And have your school counselors set you up with all the right classes to help you get in? That's a wide range of ambitions."

"Yes'm, they've helped me some." He paused and looked at her. "Okay, I'm not sure yet."

"You've seen this little school we have here. You want to go from here to some big college in Texas?"

"There's colleges in Louisiana—"

"Yes, but what do you know about them? You've already put in a lot of time and effort to plan your future. Hugh, you're a senior. It's a little late to change your game plan now. Look, I know what you're thinking. I was seventeen once, too. You and Emma both have so much growing up to do before—"

"Before what?"

"Hugh, things can change right before your eyes. If you stayed here, you and Emma have no guarantee that you won't hate each other by the end of the year. Stay in touch with her. Get some more years under your belt and think it through again. Look, why don't I call Tom and see if he wants to go to Alexandria early? You can go have lunch together and talk before the train leaves. He really does enjoy your company."

Hugh slouched in his chair and played with the saltshaker. He finally got up and retrieved his bags from his room while Flora called Tom. As luck would have it, Tom thought it was a great idea to leave a little early. *Great*, thought Hugh. *More time for lectures and sermons.*

Tom and Hugh had just pulled out of the driveway when the phone rang. It was Tom's sister calling from Houston. Her voice was caustic, as always.

"So glad to hear you're back. Last night? Oh, nothing much; we were just doing a little good deed for someone. Oh well, you know how your brother can exaggerate sometimes. Yes, Hugh behaved magnificently, as we expected. Perfect gentleman. You know, it's been years since we saw him last. He's such a nice young man. Talk to him? Why, he just left with Tom - to go to the train station. Yes, to come home. Isn't that what you said last night to Tom? Lots of time? Oh, I see." Flora paused. "We thought you wanted him home right away." Another pause. "Oh, you're not at home? I guess Tom misunderstood. Well, will there be someone at the house? Who will pick him up at the Houston station? I see. Yes, I know you have a house staff. So, you're off again for a few more days? I see. Yes, these things do happen. Well, thanks again for letting him stay with us. Sure, any time."

She went into the kitchen and poured a glass of wine from the bottle hidden in the back of the pantry.

Chapter 13

Joshua was arraigned before Judge Allentrot in a courtroom almost empty except for the judge, the bailiff, and a court recorder. His leg irons and footsteps echoed on the hard floor when he slowly entered the room. He was still wearing the same filthy clothes as the day he had been arrested. The bib of the overalls was stained with some unknown substance. A court date was scheduled for six weeks later, with bail set at $5,000.

"Mr. Parker, would you like to call someone?" the bailiff offered.

"Why would I want to call someone?" he asked.

"Your bail has been set. Someone needs to pay it."

"Why?"

"So you can go home and wait for your trial."

"How much?"

"Five thousand dollars. A bail bondsman could loan you the money."

"I don't borrow from nobody no more. Who'd come git me anyway? I don't own a car. Nobody wants me outa' here. I may as well stay where I am. How much longer did he say?"

"Six weeks. That's a long time, Mr. Parker. You sure you want to do it this way?"

Joshua pondered for a few seconds, staring at the far corner of the room. "Maybe I could call my daughter," he said absently.

"There's a phone right over there."

Joshua shuffled in short steps over to the telephone. The chains on his legs made a rasping sound on the cold, shiny floor. He picked up the phone and then looked around at the empty vastness of the courtroom.

"Now what's wrong?" the bailiff asked.

"I don't know why I'm doing this. We don't have a phone, and I don't know who else to call."

"What's the matter?" asked the judge, who had almost left the room.

"He doesn't know who to call," said the bailiff.

Joshua growled, "I can speak for myself, sonny boy!"

The judge peered over his glasses. "Maybe we should reconsider the bail amount, Mr. Parker. You don't seem too cooperative."

"Judge, you could set it at five dollars, and no one would come to get me out."

"That's not the amount I had in mind."

A door creaked open, and a court employee stepped in quietly. She had a stack of documents in her arms and whispered something to the judge.

"Mr. Parker, I've got a full day before me. Make the call, or don't make the call. Either way, hurry up and get out of my courtroom."

Joshua's hair hung down in his face as he leaned over the table where the phone sat. "Nobody, nobody," he mumbled and shook his head. A correctional officer tapped him on the shoulder and motioned toward the door. Joshua turned and walked in the direction he was pointed. Halfway to the exit, he fell to his knees and stretched his manacled arms on the floor in front of him. Like a trapped, dying animal, he uttered a loud bellow that almost sounded like 'Marcia!' but no one was sure. The few folks left in the courtroom stopped at the sound of his voice and held their breath. Held it and let it out when he quietly rose and slowly resumed walking.

The next day, Emma asked Flora if there was any way to get in touch with her father. Flora called the jail and was told Joshua could not take any calls. His bail was never mentioned.

Oscar refused to think of Emma going back home to an empty house. However, he did take her back there and, with his son's help on weekends, put new locks on all the doors as well as started repairing the windows. Each day, bit by bit, Emma began cleaning up the house in anticipation of the day her father would come home.

Saturday morning, four days later, Flora met Emma at the front door of the Rucker house and handed her an envelope. Her blank expression changed to one of faint interest, then bursting with delight. It was postmarked from Houston, Texas. Emma's hands shook as she carefully turned it to look at all sides as though she had never seen one before.

"What's the matter?" Flora said.

"I just never got no letter before."

"Go on and open it," Flora said. "It's yours."

"I know. He said he'd write to me." She couldn't stop smiling.

Emma opened the sealed flap, being careful not to tear the paper. Flora left her sitting on the steps to read it:

Dear Emma,

Right now, I'm on the train just outside of Lake Charles. I thought this was an express train, but I guess it's not. We've stopped at every little town south of Alexandria. I never knew there were so many. I made a new friend on the train. Her name was Annie. We talked for a long time, and I told her about you. She was really nice. I especially liked the part when she told me about her grandson, who was about my age. You didn't think I'd already found another girl, did you?

I really miss you, Emma. How is your dad? I worry about him being in jail. Will he behave if he doesn't have anything to drink? I hope they don't keep him there very long.

Are you still drawing? I plan to ask my mother about some art dealers in Houston. Remember? I told you I would. Annie thinks you ought to go to New Orleans and sell pictures in Jackson Square. I've never been there, but I've seen postcards of it. Annie says there are lots of beautiful old buildings and friendly people who speak with a funny accent. People from all over

the world come there on ships to do business. Well,
it's fun to dream about, anyway.
We have to make plans to get together again real
soon. I think we're pulling into another small town.
Take of yourself. I miss you. You're still my button
girl.
Love,
Puddin' Man.

Emma sat there, half smiling, half crying. She turned back to the beginning and read it again. After the third time through it, she realized a pair of feet were standing beside her. She looked up at Flora with a smile and moist eyes that almost brought Flora to tears as well. Silently, she reached her hand down to Emma, who took it and walked inside with her.

"I know I'll see him again," she said.

"Well, you won't if you don't write back to him."

"Oh, I'm gonna'. Yes ma'am! Kin I do it right now?"

"Yes, but I need your help moving some furniture first then I'll give you all the time you need."

Flora had never seen furniture picked up and moved so fast. Despite her fears, though, nothing was scratched or dropped. With each piece, she noticed a look from Emma that wondered if they were finished. Finally, Flora said she was satisfied, if for no other reason than to not feel rushed.

"Use the old desk in the library," she told Emma. "There's some writing materials in the drawer."

Flora left her alone in the big empty room and came back five minutes later. Emma had not written a single word.

"How's it going?" Flora asked.

"I don't know what to say," she said in a low tone.

"Well, just pretend he's here, and you're talking to him. What would you talk about? Ask him questions about Houston. Mention things he said in his letter to you. There's lots of things you can talk about."

Emma's mouth parted in a smile. Her eyes sparkled. "He said something about going to New Orleans to sell my pictures. Yeah, that's good. I'll ask him about that."

"Emma, have you ever written a letter before?"

She looked at the blank page as she answered. "No, ma'am. I never had nobody to write to."

"You go ahead, then. You'll think of something."

She sat for another ten minutes and tried to start. Flora quietly peeked back into the library and saw several pages wadded up on the floor. It was nice stationery, and Flora hoped that Emma would soon get a grasp on her thoughts. She finally seemed to settle on something:

> *Dear Hugh,*
>
> *Today, I got your letter. It was nice. I like the part about New Orleans. When do you want to go? I think about you all the time. I hope you think about me. Miss Flora is letting me use her stashunery to write on. I drew another picture yesterday. I am staying with Oscar and Lavenia until Papa gets home. We don't know when he will come home. We tried to call him. Hugh, I miss you. Please hurry back and see me. I love you.*
>
> *Love,*
>
> *Button Girl*

She read it and shook her head. Would Hugh really know how she felt? Did the words say anything? She hoped he could see the page and still remember, across the miles, what she looked like and understand how she longed to see him. She thought about showing it to Flora, then changed her mind. Folding the letter into an envelope, she walked into the kitchen with it.

"Miss Flora, kin you help me put Hugh's address on here? I think I know how, but I don't want to mess it up."

Flora patiently helped Emma and then told her where to find a stamp.

"On your way home, you can stick this in the mail slot at the post office. Now, we've got work to do."

Emma hummed as she worked the rest of the day. That afternoon, she stopped to mail the letter and started walking to Oscar's house, but at the last instant, she took a quick turn toward her own house. In minutes, she was looking at the front door and realized she didn't have a key to get in. The new windowpanes were still intact. Apparently, Oscar had replaced a few more boards on the front porch. Walking around to the back, she stood motionless, trying to picture the yard as her mother had seen it. Each huge oak had a wide flower bed around it. One tree still had a large climbing Jasmine that reached halfway up the full height of the trunk and was covered in white blooms. Once, there had been a bench just wide enough for two people in the far corner of the yard with a trellis of bougainvillea on either side, but it had disappeared years ago. The flagstone path leading to it remained like an unfinished painting. Hedges and shrubs had divided the yard into smaller venues, like rooms in the outdoors. Each section once had colors and plants arranged to make a carefully planned architecture with personality and secrets all its own. Now, everything lay withered and rotting. A garden plow with a broken handle was the most recognizable item in the backyard. Everything else was rusted metal or rotted wood, something or other from Joshua's days when he used to drag home anything of an interesting attraction. By the next day, he would have forgotten why he brought it there. Everything in the backyard lay where it was last touched, as though silently awaiting further instructions. A portion of a fence remained between the yard and the collapsed barn. The barn appeared as though the slightest breeze could make it disappear like dried leaves. Gazing at the tired wreckage, Emma wondered what New Orleans looked like. Next week, she told herself, she would look up something about New

Orleans in the school library. Jackson Square, he had said. Yes, and ships.

The next morning was Sunday, and all the Carters, except Oscar, had put on their finest clothes and were being lined up for inspection before going to church. Oscar sat in his big chair with bare feet, wearing trousers and an undershirt until Lavenia made him put on something else. Earl's job was to keep everyone in one general area until all could be made ready to pile into the car.

Emma's thoughts were colliding in a bittersweet conflict like fingernails on a blackboard. Each time she felt a glimmer of hope over the letter from Hugh, she felt a twinge of guilt for not thinking about her father.

Lavenia was barking orders, "Earl, make them kids set still. Don't let none of them go out 'n the yard." Something caught her eye. "Gloria's shoe's untied. Somebody fix it." Emma obliged.

"You comin' with us?" the child asked Emma.

"No, I better stay here. I don't think there's room in your car."

"Sho' there is!" said Lavenia.

"I really got nuthin' to wear. Ya'll look so nice. Go on ahead. I'm okay here."

"What about that dress you done wore las' Friday?" asked Oscar. "That looked nice, I think."

"Look who talking 'bout going to church," Lavenia scolded. "Man ain't been in years. Emma, c'mon. We got time. Go change."

"I ain't never been to church before," she admitted.

All in the house stopped and looked at her. "Yo' mama never took you?" asked Earl.

"I don't remember."

"Her mama was too sick to take her," said Lavenia. "And I know Mr. Joshua weren't goin' do it."

"Well, maybe I could," Emma said.

Suddenly, everyone in the house wanted to help her get ready, "You kids sit still!" Lavenia barked again. "Go ahead, Emma. We waitin'."

Emma disappeared and emerged less than five minutes later in a simple cotton dress Flora had given her. Everyone crowded toward the door while Oscar stood by and watched the parade.

"Hope you can put up with Lavenia's driving," Oscar chuckled as he went back inside.

"I kin drive as good as any man," Lavenia muttered once she was in the car. "Been doing it every Sunday for Lawd knows how long." She sat on the edge of the seat and hugged the steering wheel. It was almost touching her chin.

The church was ten miles away, and it took Lavenia twenty minutes on an unobstructed road to get there. Emma knew there were other colored folks in the area, but she had never seen so many gathered in one place. The day was beautiful, with blue sky and puffy clouds. The old church was tired-looking and seemed to sag in the middle, but it stood proudly overlooking a gentle slope, keeping watch over the comings and goings of at least three generations, maybe more. Behind it was a large cemetery. Gentle laughter rolled across the front yard of the church as friends greeted one another. No one seemed to notice the family with one white girl in the back pew. Emma listened intently to the sermon, which was spiced with a joyous 'amen!' from the gathering after almost every sentence from the pulpit. The preacher spoke of the meek, the poor, the downtrodden. Emma heard him proclaim judgment day was coming soon when they would be comforted, inherit the earth, and the gates of heaven shall be opened, to which most of the congregation shouted, "Amen, Brother Jacob! Hallelujah!" In the middle of the sermon, the preacher began adding some musical character to his words. As though on a hair trigger, the choir made a spontaneous start, and the congregation joined in. Before the song was finished, the preacher resumed his sermon in a loud speaking voice amidst the singing of the choir and the people. Everyone was of one harmonious accord with more finale than the high point of a Broadway musical. The mixture of a fiery sermon and a church full of singing souls clapping their hands in rhythm became so intense it almost brought tears to Emma's eyes. At the height of it all, it sounded as though millions of thoughts were given disjointed utterances as fast and as loud as human voices could manage, clear diction not being of any concern. She had never seen so many people so happy in one place at one time. When it was over, there were handshakes, hugs, shoulder pats, and smiles all around. All the Carter children wanted to hug Emma. Something joyous was being celebrated, but she didn't have the slightest idea as to what it was.

On the way home, Emma couldn't stop asking questions, "So, what did he mean by glorify?"

"We gonna' glorify God," Lavenia said flatly.

"How you do that?"

"We done it. Right there, today. You heard it. Then we gonna' go out and do what's right and meet our maker on judgment day. Holy Ghost gonna' guide us," Lavenia said.

"But, when it got the loudest, I couldn't understand what any of them was sayin'", Emma said.

"Right. That's the Holy Ghost talkin'."

"Does the Holy Ghost ever talk to you at home?"

"Why, sure. Happens all the time."

Emma looked puzzled, "I been knowing you folks all my life, and today is the only time I ever seen something like this."

Lavenia shifted in her seat. "You see, it's what happens when all the believers come together."

Emma could not hide her astonishment. "Well, whatever it was, it sure was fun. I'd like to do that again!"

The conversation continued until the edge of town. Lavenia had let Earl drive without Oscar's knowing it. Stopping, Earl switched places with his mother. "We goin' get him his driver's license next week, and Oscar goin' be one surprised man," Lavenia said.

"He won't be mad?" Emma asked.

"Oh honey, he's scared to death to teach these young'uns anything like driving. He afraid he might get blamed for something. Probably right, too."

Earl piped up, "Mama's been letting me drive every Sunday for the past two years."

Claire, one of the older kids, chimed in, "Yeah, ran off'n the road the first time. Daddy kept wonderin' how all the dirt got on the back bumper. Earl backed right into a ditch, trying to turn around."

"I did not!" Earl said.

"I remember that," said Gloria.

"You not old enough to remember that," Lavenia said.

"None of us is goin' to get any older if you don't watch the road, Mama."

"Watch yo' words when you talking to me, son."

"Yes, ma'am. Would you kindly stop talking and watch the road, please?"

Lavenia took a firmer grip on the wheel, "Humph! That's better," she said.

As they entered town, Emma asked, "Lavenia, could you drive past my house and let me go in for a minute? I need to get something."

The diversion was a short distance, and Emma was in and out within a minute. She sat back in the car with what looked like a large shopping bag on her lap.

"What's in there?" Claire asked.

"Ain't none of yore business, Claire," Lavenia scolded. "Shouldn't be askin' about somethin' what might be personal."

"Oh, that's okay. It's just some of my drawing stuff. I thought of some things I wanted to try."

At the Carter house, Sunday lunch was always around two in the afternoon. Emma sat in the kitchen listening to Lavenia, who refused any help with preparing the meal. She said too much help just got in her way. A fan perched on top of the refrigerator, oscillating slowly back and forth. The air was hot but moving, nonetheless. There was a faint smell of buttermilk. Emma sat in a corner with her sketch pad and chalk. One of the children walked by and gave a squeal of delight, pointing at the page Emma had just finished.

"What? What is it?" Lavenia asked with a look of alarm.

Emma turned the page around and showed Lavenia a picture of Earl in the church surrounded by a congregation of worshippers in various stages of animation. Some were dancing in the aisles, some were on their knees, some simply looking upward with their arms reaching to the heavens. The likeness of Earl was flawless.

"Would you look at that?" exclaimed Lavenia. "Honey, I heard you could do some of this stuff, but I never - well, it shouldn't surprise me none!"

Emma looked at her quizzically. "Why do you say that?"

"Oh, it's in the blood. You got that from yo' mama! She could draw anything. I used to sit and watch her for hours. You know, that was the one thing that would make Mr. Joshua sit down and smile, jus' looking at your mama's pictures. She know'd how to make things jus' jump off'n the page like they was alive. Like that one, you just done there."

"I guess I knew my mother did this. I wasn't sure."

"Why, yes! Don't you still have all them pictures she made?"

"I never seen a one of 'em. Papa got rid of most of her stuff."

"Oscar! Oscar! C'mere a minute."

Lavenia and Emma could hear Oscar's chair squeak as he leaned forward to stand up. The sound of him loudly clearing his throat as he walked slowly toward the kitchen was a clue that he had been asleep when Lavenia called him. She was used to it, though.

"Oscar, look what Emma done."

He took one look at it and said, "Better not let Mr. Josh see that."

Lavenia stopped her cooking and peered at Oscar. "Why you say that?"

"Emma, what happened the las' time he seen you drawing?" He looked at Emma with raised eyebrows.

"He got mad."

"Then what?"

"He got drunk."

"Uh-huh, that's right. When Miss Marcia died, he took and burned every one of her purty pictures. He don't want no reminders. I swear, the man still suffers. Misses his lady sumpin' bad."

"I guess that's why he doesn't want me to do this." Her thoughts became clouded and dark again as she pictured her father in a jail cell.

"Tha's it exactly," Oscar declared. Noticing the change on Emma's face, he tried to lighten her despair. He bent down and look carefully at the picture. "Okay, let's see what you got here. Hey, that's our man Earl! Hey, Earl! C'mere and look at this. There he is sittin' up there in that church with all the rest of them—"

"Careful, Oscar," Lavenia warned.

"I was goin' to say something nice. Don't worry." He looked at the picture closer. "Emma, honey, that's a good piece of work. Hey, Earl! Come look at this."

Earl came trotting into the kitchen with three of his younger siblings hanging onto him. He managed to free himself and took the picture in his hands. His eyes slowly opened wider.

"Do I really look like that?"

"How you know'd it was you?" his father said. "If it ain't you, who is it, then?"

"Man, that's somethin'!"

"You can have it, Earl," Emma said.

"Wow, thanks. Look, there's the choir up there in the back. You even put in the church windows. How long did this take to do?"

"She had it done a'fore I even know'd she was doin' it," Lavenia announced.

"Kin you do more?" he asked.

"How 'bout this?"

With quick strokes of her pencil, she sketched the corner of Carter's living room, complete with Oscar in his undershirt, sitting in his favorite chair. Lunch suddenly took low priority. Two hours later, she had drawn Lavenia and Oscar together and individual portraits of three of the children.

Earl spoke up. "Mama, I got an idea. You remember that bake sale we havin' at church next Saturday? Emma could go there and draw pictures of people while they just standing there. She could sell 'em right there."

"Wouldn't be right making money at God's house like that, though," Lavenia said.

"She could split it with the church," Earl suggested.

"Yeah, be nice for the church."

"Ain't ya'll forgetting something?" Oscar growled. "Nobody asked Emma if she wanted to do it."

All eyes turned to Emma, who just shook her head, "If Papa ever found out, he'd be so mad. Just like before."

"That's what I was tellin' ya'," said Oscar.

Earl carefully thought before he said anything further. Finally, he said, "Would you have to tell him? You could leave your stuff here instead of at your house. And if he never asked you, you wouldn't have to lie to him. And why would he even think to ask you? Anyway, for right now, he's still in jail, ain't he?"

"Earl!" Lavenia and Oscar both scolded him.

Emma found herself looking at two scowling parents and one smiling teenage boy.

"I don't know. I'll think about it."

Lavenia went back to her cooking. Oscar returned to his chair. After a few minutes, Emma asked, "Does the church need much money?"

"All churches need money."

"Then why don't people just give the church some money?"

"Where they gon' get it?"

"Same place they'd git it to buy pictures, I guess."

"What they do is they spends they money if'n they think they gettin' something back. They gon' buy pictures, or they gon' buy something else. Either way, they git something for they money; something they can see and hang on to."

Emma replied, "Well, maybe I could draw up some before the sale and do a few while I was there. Ain't nobody gon' buy 'em, though."

"You sure you want to do this? I mean, thinkin' about your papa and all that?"

"I know. But I been drawing at Miss Flora's, anyway. May as well keep on doin' it."

"Good. And only if'n it's what you want to do." She wiped her hands on her apron. "Ya'll c'mon and eat!"

For the next few days, Emma spent all her spare time drawing. She drew different views of the old church, as though she were standing right there looking at it. There were several scenes of old sawmills, three of the Carter's two dogs, and countless sketches of the Carter children playing. The day of the bake sale, she had twenty.

On an old picnic table, Emma's art was displayed, propped up by small scraps of wood, smooth stones, or anything available. They went for a dollar each and sold out within the first hour. Emma made several portraits during the sale using a music stand as an easel for her sketch pad. The name 'Emma P.' found its place in a lower corner of each one. Her hands moved with no wasted motion, and her eyes shifted up and down from the page to her subject. Onlookers crowded behind her to watch the face, and details suddenly materialized on the page. Several bakery items were left unsold. Emma went home holding seventeen dollars. Some paid her more than she had asked for.

The next day was Sunday, and Emma arrived at church with Lavenia and her troop. No one ignored Emma that day. Each member of the congregation felt the need to speak to her, to reach out and just touch her, to make eye contact. Recognition. Silent, loving words.

On the way home, Earl said with a laugh, "Leave it to a white girl to steal all the attention."

That night, she sat on the front steps and wrote another letter to Hugh using the light of the living room that spilled through the doorway and cast faint shadows on the front yard.

Dear Puddin,

Things are going pretty good here. I been staying with Lavenia and Oscar. I went to church with them the last two Sundays. I went to a bake sale and sold some of my pictures. I made seventeen dollars. Folks was nice. Papa is still in jail. His trial won't be much longer. I have not talked to him. He can't come to the phone. I don't know why. I hope they treat him okay. I feel so helpless about him. Will you write to me again? I miss you. School is okay. Folks talk about you a lot. You have lots of friends here. I can say hi for you if you want me to. The store is fine. Miss Flora stays gone most of the time when I'm at her house on Saturday. I'm on Lavenia's front porch. I have to go in now. The mosquitoes are starting to bother me. I love you.

Love,

Button.

Three more weeks went by, and Emma found herself at Flora's again. The pleasant Saturday routine was now like a different world.

"Mr. Rucker misses you at the store now that school has started again," Flora said. "Doesn't your father's trial date come up soon?"

"Yes, ma'am. Next Tuesday. I was wondering if maybe you could help me with something."

"In what way?"

"I need a ride to Colfax."

Flora clasped her hands behind her back. Her eyes darted around the room like they always did when she was thinking. She spoke with an air of caution. "Why, yes. I suppose we could do that. What time will it be?"

"I don't know. I jus' remember someone told me it would be next Tuesday."

"Yes, well - why don't we call? That would make sense. Uh, how are you doing at the - uh - Carter's house?"

"Oh, real good, Miss Flora. I been going to church with them and everything!"

Flora could not hold back the look of shock and astonishment. It was as though someone had used profanity in the middle of the Lord's Prayer.

Emma saw her expression change and asked, "What's wrong? Are you okay?"

"Yes, I guess I just wasn't expecting to hear that. Uh, well, so - what did you think of it? The church, I mean, the service. You know, I mean, what did they do?"

"Oh, it was so much fun! They was all clappin' and jumpin' around and singing … I never heard so many people who could sing so much! Everyone was just so happy and sayin' things like 'Amen!' and 'Praise the Lord!' and 'Hallelujah!' You know, stuff like that."

"Were they shouting?"

"You mean hollerin'? No, they wasn't doing that. It was kinda' loud, though."

"No, I said, shouting. Could you understand everything you were hearing?"

Emma thought before answering. "You know, I asked Lavenia about that, and she said something about the Holy Ghost."

"Yes, I know. It's called speaking in tongues. Some just simply call it shouting."

Emma looked at Flora with a quizzical look. She said slowly, "You mean all of them people was like - but - do you do that in your church?"

Flora's demeanor suddenly stiffened, "No, we worship in a more restrained manner."

"Oh, you got to come with me to Lavenia's church! They's just all these people dancin', and singing, and clappin' they hands … it's a lot of fun! I don't know much about God or nothin', but I hope you have that much fun at your church!"

Flora searched for words, then finally said, "Why don't we call and find out about your father's court time?"

Chapter 14

Houston, Texas

Hugh Giles had gone to sleep thinking about Emma. He woke up before anyone else in the family and was still thinking about her. The first stirrings of morning sent small, faint slivers of sunlight through his bedroom window curtains. Where was she at that moment? What was she thinking? Knowing her had been an extended journey of discovery in so many ways. The thought of her gave him a twinge of arousal that flipped in his mind to thoughts of guilt. She had been so generous with her understanding and forgiveness on so many fronts. Did she still feel that way?

Breakfast in the Giles house was organized chaos on a school day. He was an only child, but it seemed like a whole tribe was trying to launch their day and go separate ways. By the time he dressed and came into the kitchen, the housekeeper, Isabella Cortez, had breakfast on the table and was digging in the refrigerator to plan supper. Hugh often wondered when she had time to be in touch with her own family in Guatemala. But hard work and long hours were the price she paid for the political sanctuary in the bowels of the Giles empire. Her room was a loft above the three-car garage. A middle-aged woman with three grown children back home, Isabella often spent time listening and talking to Hugh, who had developed a strong comprehension of Spanish from her and a sense of confidentiality that was mutual.

"This girl, she wrote to you again?" Isabella asked Hugh as he gulped down breakfast.

"Um-huh," he mumbled with a mouthful.

Isabella sat across from him and was about to say something else when his mother's voice cut through the morning air like a buzzsaw.

"George, are you going to the downtown office today?" she yelled down the hallway toward the master bedroom. "George! Did you hear me? Oh, forget it!"

Rose Giles came into the kitchen like a Gulf Coast hurricane. In fact, that's how she presented herself in most places. Her first-morning victim was Isabella.

"Isabella, I told you I didn't any more French toast in this kitchen! How many times do I have to tell you!"

"Mom, wait a minute," Hugh interjected. "I told her that's what I wanted. If you're going to jump on anyone, jump on me," he tried to keep his voice sounding civil. "I think she makes good French toast."

"Well, she's made enough for a damn army! Are you going to eat all that?"

Hugh's father, George Giles, appeared and stepped into the conversation carefully. "Wow! French toast! Thanks, Isabella." He turned and winked first at Hugh, then Isabella. They both looked away to conceal their grins.

"What? Am I outnumbered in my own house?" Rose screeched. "Never mind! I'll eat at the club!" With that, she left with a huff. Breakfast at the club, followed by a few hours of gossip and slander, then a 3-martini lunch.

George Giles was the heir apparent to the Giles Oil empire. He had more money than God, but you would never know it by the way he acted. His father, Jerome Giles, started as a wildcat driller when his son was a child and spent much of the time away from home, leaving George to be raised by other family members. George's mother died from pneumonia when he was seven years old. Now, at a ripe age, Jerome was still the titular head of the company, but everyone reacted when he ordered something done.

With Rose safely gone, Isabella said, "Hugh, tell your papa about that girl you met."

Hugh looked nervously at his father then at Isabella. She suddenly realized her bad timing and covered her mouth with both hands. Her eyes glistened and she hurried from the room.

George stared at his son with a question on his face.

It started out as a brief, passing anecdote which started at the beginning of his visit with the Ruckers, but as Hugh began talking, he couldn't stop.

Thirty minutes later, he said, "And now, her dad is in jail for something that wasn't his fault," he concluded. But there was one detail in the telling that he left out.

"Let me talk to your Grandpa Jerome," was George's parting comment.

George was late for work and Hugh missed his first class.

Chapter 15

The courtroom was packed with people of all descriptions. Emma and Flora stood in the back, waiting for empty seats to appear. Three sheriff's deputies stood around the edge of the crowd. Near the front were several men in starched collars and ties. Their suit coats were draped over the backs of chairs, and ceiling fans whirled above.

"Are all these people here because of Papa?" Emma asked.

"I'm not sure," Flora said. "We'll just have to wait and see."

"When you called, did they say what time? I don't see Papa anywhere."

"They just told me that court for today started at ten in the morning."

"You ever been to a court before, Miss Flora?"

"No, I can't say that I have."

Another uniformed man walked into the room from a door behind the judge's bench, and all the men in front began straightening their ties and putting their coats on. The crowd noise seemed to diminish.

"All rise!"

The uniformed man was saying something else when Emma asked, "Is that the judge?"

"The Honorable Henry Thompson presiding!"

A low murmur flowed though the crowd upon hearing the judge's name. A man of early middle age walked in wearing a black robe, unbuttoned in the front. Heads began to turn as the judge quickly rearranged items on the bench in front of him before sitting. He then folded his hands in front of himself and briefly bowed his head. Perspiration glistened on his forehead when he looked up.

"Please be seated. My name is Judge Henry Thompson. I was asked to come here from LaSalle Parish due to a sudden illness on the part of Judge Barry Allentrot, whom I'm sure you all were expecting to see. Justice, however, really is blind and should be metered out in fair proportions no matter who is sitting on this bench. For those of you who fear the mind of a stranger sitting up here, I assure you I have no ax to grind with anyone in this town or this Parish. Although, I can't help but remember that when I was in high school, Colfax kept us from going to the regional finals in basketball."

The judge let out a small chuckle and looked around the room. No one else made a sound.

"Okay, it looks like you want to get down to business," the judge said. "Just remember, it's going to be a long day, and I don't appreciate the heat any more than you do. Bailiff, call the first case."

Emma and Flora looked at each other, and both mouthed the words, *'First case?'*

The first case was one of drunk and disorderly conduct on the part of three men from Dry Prong, a small town with a unique name from the other side of the Parish. The judge made a stab at humor once more.

"Dry Prong. Is that a town or a situation?" he said with a weak smile. "How do the defendants plead?"

With a guilty plea in hand, the prosecutor presented his facts crisply and with blunt candor. The public defender made a weak argument and just shook his head when he sat down. After some remarks, the three were sentenced to two weeks in the Parish jail.

The next three cases went by just as fast. It was approaching 11:30 when the judge turned to the bailiff.

"Can we get one more in before lunch?" he asked.

"Yes, Your Honor. Next one's quick."

"Very well, call it in."

The bailiff began with the usual docket and case number, which Emma and Flora almost ignored.

"The case of The People versus Joshua Parker. The charge is attempted assault with a deadly weapon and resisting arrest."

Flora and Emma's eyes shot up to the front of the room upon hearing Joshua's name. The room suddenly hushed of all background noise and allowed the rustle of leg chains to be heard, slowly dragging across the floor. Joshua entered with the appearance of a wild mountain man, his grey hair and beard looking like he had just stepped out of a whirlwind. Flora recognized the coveralls he wore as the same as the night she spoke to him in the jail. His clothes appeared unwashed. Joshua kept his eyes glued to the floor as he walked. The guard pulled out a chair and pointed to it. The chains caused a brief moment of imbalance as he tried to position himself to sit. Catching himself on the railing, he looked up for a moment, and Emma saw fear and pleading in his old eyes. There was no snarl of resentment on his face but rather defeat and submission. The bestial face was gone. Finally sitting, he kept his eyes glued to the table in front of him.

Emma whispered, "Miss Flora, he's lost weight. He looks awful." Her chin quivered when she spoke.

The judge looked at Joshua and then at the bailiff, "A quick one, you say? Why does this man look like a shipwreck in my courtroom? Sir, when was the last time you took a bath? Mr. Parker, would you look at me and answer my question?"

Joshua slowly raised his head and peered at the judge. His lips moved, but no sound came out.

"I'm sorry, Mr. Parker. I couldn't hear you."

"I don't know," he croaked.

"You don't know when you last had a bath?"

"I - I don't know why I'm here," he said and carefully turned his head a few degrees to each side.

"You are charged with a crime, Mr. Parker. Do you understand that?"

Joshua nodded and lifted one hand reluctantly. The judge looked at him and raised an eyebrow. "You have a question?"

"Why am I here?"

"I answered that, Mr. Parker. Who is the public defender in this case?"

The bailiff pointed to one of the starched collars in the front of the room. The judge looked over his glasses at the lawyer, "When were you given this case?"

"Your honor, I was informed of it at the end of the day yesterday."

"Yesterday. And I don't even know what your name is. Never mind introducing yourself just yet. You shouldn't have to. If you do things as we do in my home Parish, your name should be here on these papers somewhere. Therefore, you shall remain nameless until the bailiff can point out your signature on these documents."

The bailiff looked flushed and speechless as he shrugged open-mouthed. Judge Thompson was about to speak further when a voice came from the back of the room.

"Your Honor, with the court's permission —"

All eyes turned to see a young man hurrying up the aisle with a briefcase in hand and the back of his shirttail hanging out.

"I'm sorry, Your Honor. I got here as soon as I could. My train was delayed."

"Excuse me," said Judge Thompson. "Please don't let me interrupt whatever it is you're doing, but could you please tell me who you are?"

"I'm Mr. Parker's defense attorney. Again, I apologize for my tardiness. I really couldn't help it."

The judge looked perplexed. "Mr. Parker, did you know you had a defense attorney?"

Joshua gave the judge a blank look and shrugged.

"And you say your train was delayed? From where?"

"Houston, Your Honor. I traveled all night from Houston to get here. And for the record, I am licensed in the State of Louisiana."

"Why weren't we informed of this?" asked the judge.

The bailiff was about to answer when a woman entered the courtroom from a side door behind the bench and handed the judge a note.

"Never mind Mister, uh, Stockman. Your letter of announcement was just given to me. Mr. Stockman, it's almost noon. What do you say we continue after lunch?"

"Thank you, Your Honor. That would help immensely."

"Court is in recess until half past one."

The judge's gavel came down, and the bailiff called the room to its feet. Joshua barely lifted himself out of his chair.

The courtroom was instantly immersed in a wave of human voices. The judge left the room, and a guard put his hand on Joshua's shoulder. Emma saw the young lawyer shaking a finger at the guard and speaking angrily, although she couldn't hear what was said. Finally, the guard said something to both men, and they headed for a side door together. Emma pushed through the crowd, with Flora trying to follow. Before she could reach Joshua, he was out of the room, and a guard stood in front of the door.

Down the hall, Joshua and the new stranger were taken through a locked door of iron bars and into a large bathroom where there were sinks and a shower stall in one corner. A coarse curtain hung from the ceiling in front of the shower. The stranger turned on the hot water and then looked at Joshua.

"Mr. Parker, this may come as a surprise to you, but I am your attorney. My name is Eugene Stockman."

"Why are you here? Who sent you?"

"I can explain while you're getting cleaned up. Go ahead and get those clothes off." He turned to the man at the door. "Guard, take those restraints off and get this man something decent to wear. Something that fits!"

The guard just smiled and shifted his feet.

"Do I have to quote chapter and verse of Louisiana Statute to you, or do you not value your job that much?" He turned to Joshua, who was trying to unbuckle his clothing. "Or shall I send him into the courtroom like this?"

The guard suddenly took more interest and groped for words.

"Well, I can't leave him unguarded."

"Are you the only guard in the building? I don't think so." Stockman walked briskly to the door and brushed past the guard. He opened the door and shouted into the hallway, "Is there anyone with half a brain in this building!"

Three guards suddenly appeared.

"You three, come in here!"

The three unknowing men stepped into the bathroom, and Stockman continued his sermon to the first guard. "Now, I've got three to replace you. That make you feel important enough? I'm sure you know where the laundry room is around here. Find this man something decent to wear in Judge Thompson's courtroom! And bring a comb while you're at it!" Stockman closed the hall door after the man left but then opened it again. "On second thought, bring a barber, too!"

Joshua had stepped into the shower. Eugene pulled the curtain to give him some sense of privacy. Steam began to rise and fill the room. From beneath the curtain, he could see bruises and abrasions on the man's ankles.

"Who sent you?" Joshua asked again through the curtain.

"Let me start at the beginning, Mr. Parker. You have a daughter, right?"

Joshua jerked the curtain back immediately and looked at the young lawyer. Eugene was startled by the sudden malignant look in Joshua's eyes.

"My daughter? What's happened to Emma?"

"She's fine, Mr. Parker. Well, I guess she is. I don't really know. But the important thing is that a friend of your daughter comes from a family in Houston, and they asked me to come represent you. Apparently, there was concern that you might not get a fair shake, and it looks like their premonition was somewhat correct."

"Ain't nobody ever done me no favors. What's the catch?"

"No catch, Mr. Parker."

"What family in Houston?"

"Mr. and Mrs. Jerome Giles. They have a grandson named Hugh. They own controlling interest in several oil companies."

"Long as they ain't lumber folks."

Stockman paused, "Pardon?"

"Nothin'. You say his name's Hugh? I never heard of him."

"Well, he knows your daughter, and he knows all the details of the incident that brought you here."

"How'd he know that?"

"We'll get into that later. Let's just get you ready for today. This may take a long time, Mr. Parker."

The guard returned with a set of prison clothes and another man carrying a small satchel. The second man had a timid look about him.

"Is that the best you could do?" asked Stockman. "And who is this?"

"I'm the barber. I must say, my lunch was interrupted for this."

Without hesitation, the attorney pulled out a ten-dollar bill and stuffed it in the man's pocket.

"I'm not totally heartless," he said. "Even if I am a lawyer. He'll be finished in a minute, then Mr. Parker will tell you how he wants his hair cut." He looked at the guards and said, "Did anyone think to bring a chair, or do you folks normally get a haircut standing up?"

A few minutes later, Joshua was in clean prison garb and walking toward the door of the bathroom. His hair was parted and no longer covered his ears. The beard was gone. A thin line mustache remained. When they came back to the barred doors, Flora and Emma were waiting. Flora stood speechless at the metamorphosis of Joshua.

"Papa!" Emma yelled. It was all she could say. This was the first time in many years that she had seen her father look so dapper, even in prison-issue clothing. The two hugged as much as Joshua's chains would allow. The guard started to interrupt their silent embrace, but one look from Stockman, and he backed away.

"Sir, the judge will be in the courtroom soon," the guard finally said.

Before Joshua released Emma, he asked, "Honey, who in the hell is Hugh?"

"You never met him, Papa. But you will someday. I promise."

The group finally turned toward the courtroom door and entered. Everyone was seated, and the judge was in his chair.

"We were about to start without you, counselor. "Where is Mr. Parker?"

Joshua breached the doorway just as his name was spoken, "Right here, Judge."

Judge Thompson caught himself staring at Joshua as he walked in. The party all entered, and Joshua and his attorney seated themselves. Emma and Flora began looking again for an empty seat.

"May I ask, if you don't mind, who these two ladies are?" the judge inquired.

Joshua turned in his chair and said, "Well, that's my daughter, Emma, and the other lady is Flora Rucker. She's from Kisatchie. That's where I'm from."

The judge half rose from his chair. "You fellas in the first row. Do you have any involvement with this case? No? Well, I want two of you to get up and give these ladies a place to sit. Now!" He waited until Emma and Flora were in their new seats. Emma reached up and touched her father on the shoulder.

"So, Mr. Parker, you are charged with attempted assault with a deadly weapon and resisting arrest. How do you plead?"

Joshua shrugged and was about to say something when Eugene Stockman spoke up. "Your Honor, my client pleads 'not guilty' on the grounds of self-defense."

Judge Thompson looked at the bailiff again. "You would have had this one done before lunch, eh?"

Stockman continued, "And furthermore, my client and I wish to have the charges dismissed and file charges against the Parish for not allowing Mr. Parker his right to due process."

"Whoa, slow down. I just asked how your client pleads. We'll get to the rest later. He paused. "Okay, so it's later. What are the grounds for all the rest of what you just said?"

"First of all, I have sworn testimony from one Hugh Giles that he was in the car the night of the alleged assault and that Mr. Parker was deliberately provoked into thinking that his home and family were in danger. We submit that his actions under the circumstances were justified."

The judge was shuffling through the papers on the bench. He finally looked at the bailiff. "What testimony is he talking about?"

"Your Honor, I'm sure the bailiff knows nothing of the testimony, but I have a carbon copy of it right here with the signature of Hugh Giles, the deputy who took the statement, and the recorder. Apparently, the statement never made it to the files of this case."

"Who's the deputy? Bailiff, read that name and see if you recognize it."

The bailiff looked at the statement in Stockman's hands and said to the judge, "Yes, Your Honor. He's one of ours. I also know the recorder."

"Furthermore, your honor," Stockman continued, "I found out during our recess that Mr. Parker was denied all privileges normally afforded to prisoners in this facility, such as toilet facilities, phone access, regular meals, and so forth. He has been kept in metal restraints the whole time, even when behind bars. There are skin lesions on his ankles as evidence of what I am saying. I also found out that several of the correctional officers who mistreated Mr. Parker were from families that had been previously employed by Whitmyer Lumber years ago. Mr. Parker was required by company policy to inform them of their employment termination because the mill where they were working was in the process of closing. Mr. Parker fully admits to the harshness of the historical facts surrounding the closure of the Whitmyer mills, but he has committed no crime against the families of his jailers and should not have been denied fair treatment while incarcerated."

"I'll say it again, slow down," the judge admonished. "Let's get back to this self-defense business. We're talking about a criminal event here. How did this case get into a court schedule along with misdemeanors and traffic violations?" He looked now at the clerk of the court.

"We had an opening, and Judge Allentrot said to fit it in," the clerk said.

"I can see you did just that. Mr. Prosecutor, did you know about this sworn testimony from one, ah, Hugh Giles?"

"Your honor, we've been real busy and—"

"Answer the question and remember I can verify what you say."

"Yes, your honor. I was aware of the deposition of Mr. Giles."

"So, tell me, did any of YOUR family work for Whitmyer Lumber? Never mind. Don't answer that. Don't forget, I'm a lawyer, too. And I detest seeing my profession being used this way. Okay, who's got the mystery testimony from Hugh Giles?"

Joshua raised his hand.

"You have it?" the judge asked.

"No, sir. I just have a question." He turned to Emma and asked, "Emma, who in the hell is Hugh?"

The courtroom rippled with restrained laughter. The judge elected to let everyone enjoy the moment. But only for a moment.

Eugene Stockman looked across the room at the prosecutor's table, "After you, sir."

The prosecutor cleared his throat and pulled a sheet of crumpled paper from his collection. He started to read, and the judge interrupted.

"Let me see it," said the judge.

The prosecutor ambled up to the bench and handed the document to the bailiff.

"Mr. Stockman, let me see yours," the judge ordered.

Eugene complied and handed his to the bailiff.

After about two minutes of silence, while Judge Thompson read the two identical statements from Hugh, he said, "Both of you come up here."

Both attorneys approached the bench. The judge spoke quietly and slowly. "This case has been nothing but a piece of shit from the day Mr. Parker was arrested. His sixteen-year-old daughter lives alone; her father was not allowed to get in touch with her, she was not allowed to call and talk to him, no defense attorney was appointed—don't interrupt me! There's no defense attorney on file for Mr. Parker, regardless of the laid-back ways you do things around here. This case should have never come to trial in this court. There should have been a hearing in which all these details would have cleared up without bringing it to this point and cluttering up the schedule. Furthermore, if there had been a trial, it should have been a jury trial. Jury trials are expensive and time-consuming, but that's no reason to deny a man his right to due process, using your words, Mr. Stockman. I'm going to cite the deputy for not properly filing the testimony, the clerk for not following up on it as required, and the correctional staff for their inhumane treatment of a prisoner." He turned to the bailiff and said loudly, "Was social services ever notified of the fact that there was a minor living at home alone? I also want to see those other boys who were in the car with Hugh Giles when the incident happened. I want them here tomorrow. What a way to run a Parish!" He looked back at the two attorneys. "Now, get back to your seats."

Both attorneys walked back to their respective chairs. The prosecutor's shirt was drenched with perspiration. Eugene Stockman had a smooth smile.

"Will the defendant please rise?" the judge said. "Joshua Parker, in light of the total information regarding this case, I cannot place all of the blame on you for your actions. However, you did fail to exercise good judgment when you fired on the automobile containing a group of youthful agitators outside your home. That is the only wrongdoing you are guilty of. But your actions at the time of apprehension are understandable. For that, I sentence you to six weeks in the Parish jail, considering the time already served. And any remaining time is hereby suspended. Mr. Parker, you're free to go."

Emma jumped up from her chair and shouted, "Hallelujah!"

The courtroom erupted into both laughter and surprise. His teeth clenched, Joshua held out his wrists to the guard and jerked on his chains. The guard unlocked his hands and started to walk away. Joshua pulled him back by the sleeve and pointed down to show that his feet were still chained as well. The guard quickly worked the locks and backed away. Joshua turned and gave his daughter a warm hug, and the four of them walked out into the hallway.

Flora cornered a courthouse employee and asked, "Is there a phone somewhere I could use?" She was pointed toward a particular corner of the room. After a few brief words with the operator, she finally said, "Lavenia? This is Mrs. Rucker. We're bringing Mr. Parker home. Yes, he's fine. Could you take some sort of a covered dish over to their house? I don't know if there's any food in the house, and I'm sure they'll be hungry when we get them home. Thanks so much. Bye." She dialed the operator again and placed another call. One ring, two rings—"Tom, we're on our way home. I'm not sure if I overheard the judge correctly, but to be on the safe side, you better call the Carmichaels' and the Turners' and tell them to get Ellis and Scott out of town for a few days. At least until this judge goes back home. I'll explain later."

In the hallway, Joshua asked again, "Honey, who is Hugh?"

"I'll tell you in the car, Papa."

In Flora's car headed back to Kisatchie were Eugene Stockman in the front seat and Emma and Joshua in the back. Flora explained to Joshua who Hugh was and the circumstances of his visit.

"So, this guy, Hugh, has been writing to you?"

"Yessir," Emma said with a blush. "He's real nice."

"How come I never heard of him?"

"I guess you was under the weather a lot, Papa."

Joshua turned and looked out the window.

"Miss Flora," Emma said half-urgently. "Could you stop the car for a minute?"

Flora pulled over and let Emma out. She quickly walked around to the back of the car and vomited. In a few seconds, the nausea was over. She climbed back in and sat next to her father. Her eyes were a little moist from the retching.

"I'm fine," she said. "I never been in a court room before. Just got me a little nervous."

"Little late for that," said Eugene. "Excitement's all over. Mr. Parker, we'll file a motion to have this whole thing struck from your record. There is no reason you should have anything like this on public record."

"Public? Naw! Leave it! I want them sonsabitches to know who they're dealing with! Don't come around my house whoopin' and hollerin' in the middle of the night. They won't be doin' that no more! I'll give 'em another dose of what cures it!"

Flora and Eugene exchanged nervous glances in the front seat.

About halfway home, Flora asked Eugene, "Mr. Stockman, do you have plans to stay with us for a few days?"

"No, I just thought I'd find a place to spend the night and catch the next train out tomorrow. I saw that you do have a passenger run tomorrow out of Kisatchie. Am I pronouncing that town correctly?"

"Absolutely correct. In fact, near the train station, there is a boarding house that most likely will have a vacancy. It's nothing fancy, but it'll put you to sleep. Emma, I called Lavenia and asked her to bring something over for you and your dad for supper. She said she'd bring the rest of your things as well."

"The rest of what things?" Joshua asked.

"Papa, I been stayin' at Lavenia's while you was gone. I didn't think you'd mind. I was afraid to stay in the house by myself. Some folks came by and broke out a few windows, so Oscar and me, we fixed 'em and done a few other things to the house."

"Things like what?"

"We got new locks and new boards on the front porch. You know them two that was fallin' through? We fixed 'em."

"Sounds like Oscar and Lavenia are good friends," Eugene said.

"Yeah, best folks in town," Joshua said flatly.

Not far from town, Joshua asked, "Did I understand you right that I don't owe anyone for your services, Mr. Stockman?"

"Consider it a favor of the Giles family."

"So, what was that stuff you was tellin' the guard about Louisiana Statutes and all that?"

"That's called a calculated risk, Mr. Parker. I assumed the guards wouldn't know a thing about the details of Louisiana law, so I made them think I did."

"So, what you said to them was pure bullshit? Pardon me, Miss Flora."

"That's right. And it worked, too. Didn't it?"

"And what if'n it didn't?"

"Oh, that was just the beginning. I learned some time ago that when Jerome Giles says make something happen, you make it happen, one way or another."

"Sounds like some folks I used to work for."

Flora chimed in, "Well, you're almost home, Mr. Josh. Just around the corner."

"I thought you lived in town, Mr. Parker," Eugene said.

"You in it. This is town. Used to be. Ain't no more. Just me and Emma and the Carters."

"The Carters?"

"Yeah. Oscar and Lavenia. They're the ones Emma says she stayed with. Look yonder, there goes Lavenia's car right there."

"Probably dropping off your supper, like I asked her to," Flora said. Her car pulled to a stop in front of the house. "Here ya' are! Home safe again!" Flora sounded almost relieved the day was over.

Stockman and Flora had both stepped out of the car so the back-seat passengers could exit. He looked at the house in silence. "You live here - Ah! This is your house! Yes, well - here we are! Like you said, home again. What a quaint old house! Is this any, ah, particular style?"

Joshua extended his hand toward Eugene. "You've done enough for me today, young man. You don't have to act polite. Years ago, it was a beautiful house. It's a piece a' crap today. That's 'cause I can't keep it up. Let me give you some advice. Stay in that Giles company long as you want to, but don't let 'em keep you on 'cause of promises they make. Give 'em your best, but don't give 'em your soul, boy. Don't never give 'em that." He looked inside the car. "Miss Flora, you're an angel. Thanks for everything." He turned and walked to the house with his arm around Emma.

Before they reached the door, Emma said, "Papa, I don't ever remember you being so nice to people."

He laughed. "I can't remember the last time I was sober this long."

Chapter 16

The next day, Emma caught her usual bus to school. Everyone on the bus knew something had changed because, for the last few weeks, she had used a different bus stop, the one closest to Lavenia's house. Today, she was within sight of her own house when she boarded. She felt all eyes on her as she walked to a seat in the back. The road was a ribbon of washed-out potholes, and Emma's ride in the rear of the bus turned out to be gut-wrenching. As soon as she arrived at school, she made a quick path to the girls' restroom and vomited. Two younger girls standing by the row of sinks waited long enough to see something worth talking about, then left. As Emma walked back out into the covered walkway, she met Beverly Towers.

"Emma, Mr. MacArthur's looking for you. He said you were absent yesterday and was just wondering." Beverly stopped and waited for a response. "So, where were you?"

"In Colfax–at, uh, my papa's court thing. It was supposed to be a trial, but it turned out different. He's home now."

"They turned him loose?"

"Yeah. He'd been there six weeks already. I guess the judge thought it was long enough."

"Nobody has seen Ellis or Scott today. Have you?"

"No, I just got here."

"You look a little green. You feeling okay?"

"Yeah, I'm fine. Just a little pukey, that's all. Probably somethin' I ate. I'll get over it."

Emma walked to Alton MacArthur's office. He was standing outside the door watching the students on their way to morning classes.

"Hi, Emma. Got something for you. Mrs. Rucker said it came in the mail for you yesterday while you were in Colfax."

He handed her a letter from Hugh. "I heard your father is back home again. How is he?"

The sight of Hugh's letter grabbed her attention like a steel trap. She barely heard Mr. Mac's question.

"Emma? Your dad"?

"Oh, oh, He's fine. When we got home, he said he ain't been sober this long since he can remember." She turned to leave, then stopped. "You got any more work for him?" She was smiling so hard that her jaws hurt.

"Could be, could be. I'll send word to him. Have a nice day. I'm glad everything turned out good for you."

It was still several minutes before class started. Emma went into the empty classroom, sat at her desk, and began reading Hugh's letter. Her hands were shaking.

Dear Emma,

It was so good to hear from you in your last letter. I hope you get this one in time to know that my grandfather heard about the problem your father had and is sending one of his attorneys to represent him on his court day. It was a last-minute decision, so I hope he gets there on time. His name is Eugene Stockman, and he looks like he's only a teenager, but he's really a lot older. More like 29. Anyhow, my grandfather told him if things don't go right, that he is to call back to Houston, and we'll fix it. Grandpa knows so many people he can probably fix anything. So, who are you seeing these days? I mean, are you going out at all? I've been out a couple of times since I got back. Just with friends, that sort of thing. Actually, I wanted to tell you that we have a formal dance coming up in a couple of months. I don't know if you could make it, but if you can't, I understand. I can find someone to go with me. It wouldn't be like a real date, but I really don't want to miss the dance, and it's no fun going alone. Let me know if you can come.

Say hi to the Ruckers for me.
Love,
Puddin.
P.S. We can send someone from Houston to come get
you and take you back.

Emma felt her heart sinking. *Houston,* she thought. *Does he really think I can just jump up and go to Houston?* She felt a pit of despair creeping into her thoughts; it felt as though someone had died. Never before had she been so bewildered. Bewildered and alone. Tears welling up, she left her seat just as the first of the students were coming in. She ran to the girls' room, went into one of the stalls, and locked the door. Five minutes later, she came out of the enclosure feeling totally numb. Hearing the tardy bell, she started to leave but felt her stomach in her throat again. Quickly, she returned to the stall and wretched, but nothing came up.

After rinsing her mouth out, she hurried back to class where Miss Caslick, the aging history teacher, was watching Emma's late entry over the tops of her glasses.

"Emma, I saw your books on the desk. Where were you?"

"Sorry, ma'am. Got a little sick. I'm okay now."

Two hours later, Emma was walking past the main office when the school nurse called to her.

"Emma? Emma! I heard you weren't feeling well. Come let me take a look at you so I can earn my pay for the day."

"I don't want to be late for my next class."

"With me, you always have a good excuse. Come in, let's take a look."

A few minutes later, she left the nurse's office having no more information than she went in with and certainly feeling no better. At noon, however, she asked the nurse for an excuse to go home. The nurse released her, not knowing the girl had no transportation. That didn't matter to Emma. She couldn't concentrate on anything anyway and just needed to get away from everyone. Maybe the stomach ailment was a blessing. Shortly, she was at the crossroads between going to her house or Lavenia's. Without hesitation, she turned to the Carters' house and was there in less than five minutes. She sat on Lavenia's front porch steps, reading Hugh's letter again. Each time she read it, she felt a knife plunged into her chest with a dull jab. *This is really happening,* she thought. *He's gone back to his life in Houston, and I won't see him again. That's it. It's over.*

"Child, what are you doing here?" Lavenia's voice caused her to jump in fright, "Emma, what's wrong? You crying? What that daddy of yours done now?"

Emma couldn't speak. She just handed the letter to Lavenia, who looked at it, then turned it sideways, then upside down. She squinted and handed it back.

"My eyes is bad. What it say?"

"He wants to go out with another girl."

Hearing this for the first time in her own voice brought another flood of tears. Lavenia scowled, then put her arms around her shoulders and gently massaged with her fingertips.

"Some things you just got to cry about 'fore they gets any better. Go ahead. Lavenia ain't got nothin' else to do for a little while." The two of them sat on the front steps with Emma's face buried in Lavenia's neck, gently rocking back and forth. The tears finally subsided, and the older woman held her at arm's length. "Emma, I tried to tell you once before. He jes' a boy. He ain't no grown man yet. He got a lota' livin' and growin' to do 'fore he chooses hisself a woman. What happen, gonna' happen. If it ain't right, it ain't gonna' happen 'cause it ain't s'posed to. Now stop your worryin' and go find you another fella'. Lots of 'em out there!"

Emma's crying had diminished to an occasional involuntary sniffle. Lavenia offered her some cookies and milk.

"No, thanks. My stomach's too upset."

"Lawd, you really let this boy put you in such a fix."

She looked up and said, "No, it was like this yesterday and the day before."

Lavenia propped her elbows on her knees and thought for a moment. "Letter come today?"

"Yeah."

Lavenia looked up at the clouds. "Hmm. Anything else hurt?"

"No."

"So, what you do 'bout it during school? You miss any class?

"No, today's the first day I was sick during school."

"So, you ain't sick during school, but you been sick for three days. Now, what kinda' sense is that?"

"It's usually over by the time I get to school."

Lavenia thought for a moment, and her eyes widened. She waited to form her question, then asked, "Emma, you got that time of the month?"

Emma looked at her quizzically.

"Yo' period, you got it?"

"Yeah. Well, no. It's a little late. But it's always off. Sometimes late, sometimes early."

"How late this time?"

"About a month."

Lavenia's eyes widened even more. "Ever been that late before?"

"Don't think so."

Lavenia was trying to find the right way to continue her line of questions. She kept looking at Emma, then pulling her gaze away. Twice, she opened her mouth to speak and changed her mind.

"What?" Emma finally asked.

"Emma, you ever, you know, have a boyfriend?"

"What are you talking about?"

"I mean, a boyfriend, like a real close one?"

"Hugh's the only boyfriend I ever had." She was about to cry again when Lavenia stopped her.

"Hey, you can cry later. I got to ask you something. You and Hugh ever, you know, do something together?"

"I don't know what you mean!" She was still looking at the letter.

"Let me put it this way. Something private. Something you wouldn't want no one else to see."

Emma looked at her closely. "Like what?"

"Child, it done time for you to grow up! Lawd, Marcia - what I goin' tell her? This child ain't knowin' nothin'!"

"Then tell me! Tell me what you're talkin' about!"

Lavenia moved a few inches away from Emma and then turned to face her directly. "Emma, you know what I'm sayin' is private parts? Your private parts? You understand that much?"

Emma nodded.

"All right. Good! Maybe we gettin' somewhere. So, did he put his hands on you?"

Another nod.

"Where?"

Emma's eyes quickly glanced at her lap. A confession of the eyes.

"So, dat's it. Nothin' more. He just touched you."

Emma answered slowly. "Well, no. There was this, I mean, I guess I felt something."

"Somethin'? You guess you felt somethin'. With what? Your hand?"

"Well, no, inside."

"Inside what?"

"Inside me. It wasn't but for a second or two."

Lavenia sat looking stunned for a moment. She held her hands over her mouth and then buried her face.

"Lavenia, what's wrong? I didn't do anything wrong - it felt good to be with Hugh. I remember he acted worried about it later, but it didn't bother me none. So, I told him not to worry."

"Child, I got to ask you one more question. Now listen close to me," Lavenia leaned toward Emma with a furrowed brow. "Did he get in yo' pants? Did he put his seed in you?"

"His what?"

"You heard me. I ain't goin' say it again. There weren't nothin' sorta' strange after?"

Emma looked deep into Lavenia's face. Lavenia's words had not sunk in; she was more focused on Lavenia's tone of concern. If there was a clue as to what she was talking about, Emma didn't see it. More than once, she started to say something but didn't. It was as though her mouth knew what to say, but her mind wouldn't allow it. The mind finally gave way.

"I dunno'! Maybe, I guess so."

Lavenia had heard enough, "Lawd Jesus, child! You gonna' have a baby! I jes' know it!"

Emma was totally confused, "A baby! Why? How?"

"You gonna' have Hugh's baby! You and Hugh. You better git to writin' right now and tell that boy. He needs to know it."

Emma got up from the steps and stood in the middle of the yard, perplexed.

"I must be dreaming. This ain't really happening! Lavenia, are you sure?"

"Sho' sound like it to me."

Emma didn't know how to react. "But how will I know?"

"Go see somebody."

"Somebody? Who?"

"You know any doctors?"

Emma was wringing her hands. "No, but do I need to go right away?"

Lavenia gave her a concerned look. Her words came like a buzz saw. "Child, if you be pregnant, you gonna' know it for sho' in about another month. Things like–clothes get a little tight for you, a little big at the middle, then you gon' feel it move. Feel like a whole buncha' butterflies inside. Then, later on, clothes don't fit. You gon' need bigger ones. An' you be hungry all the time."

Lavenia's frown was contrasted by Emma's apparent, sudden, jubilant look. "Lavenia, this sounds so exciting. I kin write to Hugh again and tell him, and then he'll come here and —"

"Emma!" Lavenia was almost shouting. "Think about this! You married to him?"

Emma shook her head.

"You ever know'd any woman, any pregnant woman what weren't married?"

She shook her head again.

"Nobody? You never heard of …? Look, you just think everything gon' be rosy? You think that boy gon' just drive up here and marry you and take you back to Texas? He already lookin' at other girls!" She held up the letter. "What you think he gon' do? He gonna' high-tail it outta' yo' life quick as a scared rabbit! What I worried about is yo' papa."

Emma was shaking her head but smiling. "Papa? Why would you worry about him? He's —"

"He's gonna' kill that boy! You said Hugh was worried about something. Don't you understand? This is it! Lawd, didn't that boy ever hear 'bout them rubber things?"

"What things?"

"Never mind. It too late to talk on that now! Wait, where you going?"

"To find Papa," she shouted back as she was leaving the gate. "I gotta' tell 'em."

"Emma, wait! Don't go yet! Let's talk some more!" Lavenia could only wring her hands as she watched Emma trot down the street and turn the corner toward her house.

Within five minutes, Oscar's car came into sight and rolled to a slow stop in exactly the place where the car was always parked. Oscar turned in the driver's seat and planted both feet on the ground before standing up. He walked toward the house in a slow shuffle with one hand on his lower back. It didn't take Lavenia long to explain the situation.

Oscar took a deep breath and exhaled loudly, "And now she gone to tell her papa? Don't that girl have any sense? Which way did she go, towards home?"

Lavenia nodded and pointed.

"Well, he ain't there. I seen him walking to town a few minutes ago. He sho' looks different. C'mon inside. We need to talk about this."

Joshua had received a message that said that there was a day's work waiting for him at the school. The meadow behind the baseball diamond was tall in weeds and needed to be mowed. The school had a small tractor with a hay-mowing blade that could cut a wide swath of grass. He knew the tractor well. Only recently, however, did he notice how rusty it really was. He wondered how many other things he had missed before he sobered up. He was halfway through mowing when he heard the school bell ring and saw all the children spill out of classrooms and onto the schoolyard. Morning recess would be twenty minutes long. He stopped the tractor and watched the children as they separated into small groups and did whatever small children did. Within minutes, some had circles drawn in the sandy dirt, and several hot games of marbles were going full blast. Others raced for the swing sets and merry-go-round. Their little voices were shrill and excited. The morning sun was beginning to get higher, but the early fall weather had slowly moved toward November, and the days had an invigorating balm. Listening to the laughter of the children, he remembered his six weeks in jail, the confinement, the smell, the absolute lack of compassion. The memory momentarily crowded out the scene of the pristine angelic innocence he saw on the faces of the children. He thought about Marcia and Emma when she was a small child. What grand plans they had made for her. It seemed like only yesterday.

The voice of Alton MacArthur suddenly startled him. "Mr. Parker! I see you got my message. Thanks for coming. Didn't mean to slip up on you like that."

"That's okay, my hearing ain't what it used to be. Sawmill took it. Beautiful day, huh?"

"Yessir, it is. You look good, Joshua."

"Thank you, sir. I feel good, too. Maybe a little trip to the place done me some good."

"Well, we all hope that you'll continue to look and feel like, well …"

"You mean everyone hopes I stay sober, right?"

Alton smiled and replied, "Yes, that's coming right to the point. I think you still have a lot to offer this town, and we'd be happy to see you prosper."

"You got powerful words, Mr. Mac. You didn't live around here when I had stuff to do for the Whitmyers. There's still a lot of bad blood floatin' around. It won't be gone 'til lots of folks get old and die. They got to take their thinkin' to the grave. That's the only way it'll go away. 'Course, if they teach them kids to hate me, it'll carry on for another crop of young 'uns. Maybe they won't hate me as bad as they parents did. Naw, I'll just take whatever comes along and make the most of it. But you won't see me running for office or nothin'." His laughter turned into a raspy cough. He cleared his throat loudly and spit.

The principal was about to turn and go when he remembered something. "By the way, did anyone tell you that we sent Emma home sick this morning?"

"Sick? She don't look very sick to me. Yonder, she comin' right there!"

Emma was running at a slow trot, something she could do for hours. When she reached the tractor, she was barely out of breath.

"Emma, Mr. Mac says you went home sick this morning?"

"No, I'm fine now. I'm jes' so excited, I can't wait to tell you something."

Both men looked at her expectantly. Emma leaned over to Alton MacArthur and cupped her hand against his ear. His facial expression was cheerfully inquisitive, then suddenly turned to instant shock and disbelief. The effect was not lost on Joshua. He watched as Alton backed away and then looked back at Emma.

"What is it, Emma? Tell me, girl," he said gently.

Alton was nervously rubbing his chin.

"Papa," she said gleefully, "You gonna' be a granddaddy!"

The bell announcing the end of recess rang just as Emma was speaking.

"I'm sorry, I didn't quite catch that, honey. What did you say?" Joshua asked.

"Lavenia thinks I'm gonna' have a baby!"

Joshua's eyelids narrowed, and he slowly put one foot on the step to climb down from the tractor, "She thinks what?" He bellowed, "Girl, what the hell have you been doin'? Why would anyone even think you might be pregnant?" Joshua was off the tractor and walking slowly toward Emma. "Girl, we poor, but we ain't trash! Now, answer me, what have you been doing and with who?" He took his hat off and swatted at Emma, who quickly ducked and backed away. "Don't you run from me, girl! Stand still!"

Emma's feeling of rejoicing was suddenly shattered as she saw the full fury of her father, now sober, in his well-known demonic state.

Alton MacArthur tried to intervene. "Joshua, anyone can understand why you're upset, but you must control yourself. This is not the time to do anything rash!"

Joshua kept trying to reach and grab Emma, but Alton repeatedly stepped in front of him and blocked his path. "You stay outa' this! Emma, git yourself home right now. I'll take care of you as soon as I git there myself. Mr. Mac, git outa' my goddamn way! She's my daughter, and I'm gonna' give her the beatin' like I never give her before!"

Alton MacArthur stepped up close to Joshua. Their noses were almost touching. Joshua gave him a shove. Alton maintained his composure but managed to stay between the two. Joshua shoved him again and shouted, "Git your ass outa' my way!"

Alton turned slightly to Emma and said, "Emma, go to my office and stay there. Go now. Go to my office!"

"No, goddamn it! I told you to go home! Alton, damn you …"

Joshua unleashed a backhand that caught Alton MacArthur in the jaw like a sledgehammer. He stepped back to catch his balance and saw that Joshua was again reaching for the terrified girl, who was now running backward before turning and breaking into a dead sprint toward the school building.

Alton instantly cleared his head and pounded a right fist into Joshua's face just below the eye. The older man simply stood there and blinked. He tightened his jaw and drew back his right fist, but Alton's left jab was quick. It landed on the point of Joshua's chin, and his head snapped sideways. The effect took a moment, but Joshua finally stepped back, and his knees buckled.

Several high school boys and a handful of teachers were running out toward the scene. It was over before they got there. Alton helped Joshua to his feet and told the gathered crowd to go on back to class.

He spoke where the others could hear. "Mr. Parker, we'll walk to my office and have a talk. Just calm down; we'll work this out. You okay?"

Joshua didn't answer.

The two men arrived at Mr. Mac's office only to find it empty. He stopped several students who were walking by to ask if they had seen Emma. None had. He was worried and perplexed. Joshua grew more impatient as Alton tried to imagine what to do next. He couldn't keep her in school if she was pregnant, but he had nothing official to base it on. He couldn't ask Joshua Parker to stay in the office unless he decided to ask the Sheriff to intervene. But what of his own actions? He had raised his hand against a parent of one of his own students. The notion of self-defense was subject to much interpretation. But knowing the mind of Joshua Parker, he couldn't see himself being charged with anything. Joshua would settle differences his own way. He finally decided he would keep Joshua there in his office for as long as he could in hopes of cooling him down. The whereabouts of Emma were still a nagging worry.

"She can't have gone too far," Alton said out loud to himself.

"She probably went home like I told her to," Joshua proclaimed from the office chair. "So, why am I sittin' here? You callin' the law on me?"

"No, Joshua. I won't do that." His voice got stronger. "But I am going to stop by your house with someone of authority. And if I find you have harmed one hair on that girl's head, by God, I'll beat you to a bloody pulp and then have them put you under the jail!"

Joshua leaned forward and spoke slowly and deliberately, "You know, the one thing I been good at was making people think I was the devil. Yeah, I got a temper. I know that. And yeah, I been in some hard fights. Had to do some things I wouldn't want nobody doin' to me. But how many times you think I done beat that girl already? Every time I look at her, I see her mama. Could you see me raise a finger against Marcia's flesh and blood? I'd just as soon cut my own throat."

Alton studied Joshua for a moment and swallowed hard, "Go home," he said through clenched teeth, "Just remember what I said. Not one hair on her head. Or I swear I'll kill you!"

Joshua rose from the chair and put his hat back on with a hint of anguish in his eyes. He stopped at the doorway and looked back at Alton MacArthur. Without saying a word more, he turned and left.

He arrived at his house a few minutes later, his shirt soaked with perspiration. He walked through the living room, into the kitchen, and onto the back porch. "Emma!" he called out. "Emma, where are you?" He walked into the backyard to the edge of the woods. "Emma! It's okay! I'm not mad! Come on home!" A fussy blue jay fluttered in the tree above him and called out. He walked around the outside of the house, expecting to see her bouncing from behind a tree or skipping out of the woods with some treasure she had found. She really was a young woman, he thought. Where did the time go? Where was she?

He walked back into the house and looked in her room. Her room was immaculate. An idea came to his mind, and he hurried out of the house and down the road - towards the Carter house.

Oscar and Lavenia were in the front yard and saw him coming. They could see he was out of breath before he reached the gate. "Oscar, better put the dogs up. They'll eat him alive when they see him. I wonder what he wants."

Joshua arrived at the Carters' gate breathing hard and leaned against the post with his head down. Oscar had returned to his chair after putting the dogs in their pen. Neither he nor Lavenia rose to greet him. Joshua finally had enough wind to speak and said, "You know where Emma is?"

"Last time I seen her was a couple hours ago, and she was on her way to find you," Lavenia said.

"She found me," Oscar's breath was still somewhat labored. "Now she's disappeared."

Neither Oscar nor Lavenia said a word.

"You ain't seen her since then?" Oscar finally asked.

Joshua just shook his head.

"We wouldn't lie to you, Mr. Josh. We ain't seen her, and she sho' ain't here. Where'd you see her?"

Oscar sat on the ground outside the fence before answering, "At the school. She … she thinks she's pregnant. Lavenia, what did she tell you?"

Lavenia shot a glance at Oscar.

"Well, dammit, what did she say?"

Oscar's answer had a tone of resentment. "Mr. Josh, yo' daughter ain't no little girl no more. She got her own private life. What she told Lavenia, I ain't even heard yet. They talk together like women talk. Grow'd women. That's what Emma be now. I don't ask too much. What you got to know is this–Emma probably pregnant. She ought to be going to a doctor. Give her a couple mo' months, you gon' know for sure. She needs family right now. If that baby be real, then he on the way. Ain't no stopping that. I know this: Emma went lookin' to tell you her good news. Now you can't find her. What happened? What'd you do to her?"

"Goddamnit, everybody thinks I'm a child-beater or something! Yeah, I got upset, but she's seen that before."

"Yessuh, and she always come running here when she do see it," Lavenia interjected. "But she ain't here this time, Mr. Josh. And that got me worried. Real worried."

"Where should I look?"

"Mr. Josh, you go home and keep checkin' around the house. I'll drive around and see what I can learn. Lavenia, call Miss Flora and see if'n she be there."

Flora Rucker had just finished talking to Lavenia and was dialing the store. Her husband answered. "Tom, have you seen Emma? No? I just had a very disturbing phone call. She's ran off for some reason. I'll tell you about it when you come home for lunch."

Joshua had gone back home like Oscar had suggested. Until nightfall, he silently walked through every room, not sure if he was looking for Emma or just an explanation. He looked in her room one more time and saw that now her closet door was open. A few loose items of clothing lay on the floor. A feeling of loss and helplessness enveloped him, which he had felt only once before. His feet carried him to the front porch where every night sound, every chirp of crickets gave him hope that it was her footfall coming up the steps. He sat there until total darkness settled in, then he retired to the kitchen table where he had had so many wonderful, loving moments and conversations in years past. Finally, in his solitude, the words poured forth as in a prayer, Joshua Parker style.

"Marcia, I'm sorry. I didn't do it right. I really screwed things up this time. She was the last bit of you I had left, and now even that's gone. Tell me what to do. Please tell me what to do."

Exhausted, he slumped back in the chair and imagined the day they moved into the house. As he dozed, images of that day seemed to melt together. Marcia was standing at the front porch directing where pieces of furniture should go. Workmen from the mill were happy to oblige Joshua's call for volunteers to help unload and arrange Marcia's new household of goods, which had been delivered all in one shipment out of New Orleans. For them, it meant getting away from the mill and seeing how the Parkers lived. Marcia was marching through the living room and into the kitchen to show Joshua a framed picture. It would go on the largest of the walls with two smaller companion pictures on either side. As he imagined her standing there, radiant and happy, her words began to slur and go as if in slow motion. A pained look came over her face as she slowly clutched at her throat. Her face turned scarlet, then dark blue, and her eyes rolled back in her head. Joshua tried to reach out to her, but he couldn't move. A faint strand of light began to focus behind her as her feet came off the floor. She hung there while a gentle sway from side to side rocked her as if she were going to sleep. Joshua tried to scream, but no sound was uttered. Marcia's body then suddenly burst into flames as Joshua awoke with his head on the kitchen table. He raised up, flailing his arms and fighting off invisible invaders, then realized he was alone in the house. The name of Marcia, although only whispered from his lips, flowed forth inaudibly from the house into the night, heard only by the trees and the night creatures. It was then that he remembered where he had left that last bottle.

Chapter 17

The bus came to a stop in the damp autumn hours of morning as the sun appeared through the crowns of the pine trees. Two passengers boarded, one a man with a suitcase and a guitar. The other a bedraggled and exhausted young woman with only a large satchel of clothes, a sketch pad, and a box of assorted pencils and chalk. She had walked, hitchhiked, and pleaded her way to Colfax, where she knew she had once seen a bus station sign. Despite having not slept all night, she managed to stay awake, sitting on a rusting metal bench outside the small gas station that also doubled as a bus stop. The greyhound departed Colfax at 6:30 A.M. and headed for the outskirts of Kisatchie, where it would sit for fifteen minutes at another small gas station on the main highway. Emma was fast asleep in her seat, not knowing she had come right back to within three miles of her own home and her father before proceeding onto the southern stretch of US Highway 71. In her sleep, she dreamed of the mill pond, of Lavenia and her laughing face, of boys swimming, of seeing her father in the courtroom, of Hugh and the way he looked on the path that day in the woods. The bus stopped five more times in small, rural towns on its passage south. The last leg terminated in Baton Rouge, where she finally awoke and disembarked. She sat in the terminal surrounded by crowds of strangers, listening to their voices echo off the cold, hard walls of the station. In Colfax, a storekeeper had sold her the ticket to get this far. There was no storekeeper here. Lost in her thoughts, she noticed folks looking at a large sign posted high on a wall. Some just stood and looked. Others looked and then walked to a set of windows with bars where someone would take their money in exchange for a ticket. She left her seat and walked to gaze at the board with the rest of the crowd. She recognized the names of towns like Lafayette, Lake Charles, Thibodaux, and Ville Platte. Names on a board. She had seen them on a map and read about them somewhere. Two of them shouted out to her like vivid pictures in a book. One was Houston, and the other was New Orleans. She counted her money again and realized she had just enough to go to New Orleans with three dollars left over. Houston was beyond her meager funds. Everything around her seemed to be in a slow-motion dream world. People passed in front of her like phantoms, ghosts. Nothing seemed real. She was hungry. Wandering aimlessly, a telephone booth came into view. She picked up the receiver and dialed the operator.

"This is the operator. How may I help you?"

She spoke slowly. "I need to talk to Hugh Giles. That's H-U-G-H. He lives in Houston. I don't know the number, but could you look it up for me, please?"

"I'm sorry, this is not directory assistance. I'll connect you."

The phone made buzzing and popping noises. A voice materialized. "This is the Houston operator. What number, please?"

She rubbed her eyes and spoke, "I don't know the number, ma'am. I need someone to look it up."

"One moment, please. I'll try to connect you with someone who can help." Several seconds went by. Another voice. "This is the shift supervisor. How can I help you?"

Emma cleared her throat. Through the open door of the station, several large diesel engines started and emitted their low, almost guttural, roar into the station. The noise suddenly made it difficult to hear the voice on the phone. She tried to close the door of the phone booth, but the hinges were stuck. "I'm trying to reach Hugh Giles," she shouted over the background din. "I don't know his number, but he's real rich, and his daddy has an oil company. I gotta' talk to him."

"I'm sorry, miss. I need more information than that."

"I had his address, but I left it at Lavenia's. She lives near my papa, but they don't know where I'm at. I gotta' git to Houston, and Hugh doesn't know I'm trying to call him." Her voice was beginning to feel strained.

"Ma'am, I can't help you without more information."

She felt a slow panic rising as reality set in. "But I ain't GOT no more information! Hugh, he doesn't know about the baby, and my papa's mad, and I don't know where else to go, and I got to git hold of him."

"Ma'am, have you called the police?"

"I don't want the police, I want Hugh!" Her eyes burned, and her head was pounding.

"Ma'am, I'd like to help you, but I'm not sure what to do. There's lots of people named Hugh. Where are you right now?"

"I don't know," she sobbed. "I think I'm at the bus station in Baton Rouge."

"Are you from Baton Rouge?"

"No, I'm from Kisatchie. But really, I'm from a little town outside Kisatchie, only it ain't a town no more. It's just—my papa's there, and he's just—I don't know …" She took a deep breath and sobbed.

"Miss, I wish I could help you."

"You just keep trying to call Hugh for me. Tell him I'll be in New Orleans, at Jackson Square. Tell him I'll be there. Please tell him!"

"Ma'am, who is Hugh? Is he your husband? Ma'am? Are you still there? Hello?"

Thirty minutes later, a Baton Rouge policewoman walked through the bus terminal. Seeing nothing that caught her attention, she left.

In the rear of the bus, the engine emitted a constant, low-pitched, dull roar while the tires beat out a rhythm on the creases in the pavement. The ride was smooth except for a gentle sway as the driver kept the bus on the road. Traffic on the two-lane highway would sometimes cause the driver to brake and partially arouse Emma from her hypnotic trance. It was at these brief interludes that she saw from the window how flat South Louisiana was. Water seemed to be everywhere. It appeared that on every small high point of ground along the highway, there was a run-down honky-tonk with colored lights in the windows, a flat roof, and a white oyster shell parking lot. In the distance, she saw cotton fields, picked of their crop with only wispy white remnants clinging to dried leafless branches. After a summer of bearing fruit and holding it for the pickers and their machines, the fields now looked lifeless and barren. The rows whizzed by in a continuous mosaic that put her back to sleep. The pattern was interrupted by an endless bridge that seemed to be several miles long with thick swamp on either side. At each break in the green foliage, there was more water, much of it covered with a green film. She saw two men in a narrow boat pushing their way through the undergrowth with long poles. The inside of their boat was filled with silvery fish.

Storm clouds assembled to the south, conspiring somewhere over the Gulf of Mexico. Every small cloud in the sky seemed to grow on cue from the others, and the bus was soon pushing at a snail's pace through a blinding thunderstorm. Within twenty minutes, the rain stopped, and a blue sky emerged. The bus pulled into a large gas station with an adjoining general store and stopped to let passengers off. While the driver waited to take on more passengers, the smell of wet asphalt permeated the interior of the bus. A slight breeze swirled diesel exhaust to the front of the bus and into the door. The mixture of smells brought a wave of nausea to Emma's throat. As she made her way to the front to ask how long the delay would last, the door shut, the gears clashed, and the huge wheels turned back toward the highway. Emma swallowed hard. Her mouth tasted like old cheese, and her bladder felt like it was about to burst until she saw someone entering what looked like a toilet just two rows behind where she had been sitting. As soon as the small closet-like room was vacant, she went in, heaved several times to no avail, then sat down to relieve herself. Back in her seat, she tried to sleep again, but the scenery whizzing by her became less that of swamps and wilderness and more of houses, people, and civilization.

The bus pulled into a terminal and parked beside several other buses. Everywhere Emma looked, people milled about. She gathered up her belongings and walked to the front of her bus, where she saw the driver was standing alongside the coach, handing baggage to waiting passengers. He looked at her closely and asked for her ticket stub. She wasn't sure why he wanted it; all she had was in her hands.

Looking again at her ticket, he said, "Ma'am, this isn't your stop. This is Metairie. You better be getting back on. We'll be in New Orleans in less than an hour."

She croaked a raspy 'thank-you' and climbed back on. Her original seat was still empty, and she felt a twinge of security in going back to something, anything, that felt familiar. From the window, she saw swarms of people hurrying to places unknown, others just standing and waiting.

The bus door closed yet again, and she watched city blocks race past her. They crossed over canals and train tracks. It was there that she saw what appeared to be a single train car moving by itself, but unlike any train car she had ever seen. It was short and stubby looking and loaded with people, all standing. First, she saw one, then another. Then, they came to a wide street with several lanes of traffic going in both directions. Down the middle was a wide median with more tracks. Huge buildings stood tall on either side of her field of view. They seemed close enough to touch one another. She pressed her face against the glass to see the tops of some of them. A gigantic Walgreens Drug Store went by. Finally, the bus made a turn and began to slow down. The driver shifted gears, and the big diesel engine roared in a crescendo to a higher pitch, then diminished. The driver turned across the sidewalk into a wide driveway and pulled into an empty space under a tin roof.

Air brakes let out a piercing hiss, and the bus door popped open. The driver stood from his seat and said, "This is the end of the line, folks. Welcome to New Orleans. Claim your luggage beside the bus on the right side."

Before she could stand, everyone in front of her crowded into the aisle and slowly moved forward. A woman across the aisle was holding a sleeping baby and was trying to gather her belongings together. Emma made eye contact with her, and with some hesitation, held out her hands to hold the baby for the woman. Her gesture of kindness was met with cold disregard. The crowd shuffled toward the front, and Emma finally found herself standing in the parking lot of the bus terminal amidst human voices, thundering diesel engines, and the smell of exhaust fumes. She watched the crowd and followed them into the building, where the air had a stale, smoky smell. People were everywhere. This station was much bigger than the one in Baton Rouge. In this one room, there were probably more faces than in all of Kisatchie, unknown faces. She saw no signs guiding her to her next point of decision, no one telling her what came next. She suddenly realized she was ravenously hungry, but there was nothing that looked like a place to eat. The scene before her offered no welcome but stood like a reluctant host in a doorway with arms folded, being forced to grant her entry. She felt like an intruder, naked in a room full of strangers, but no one cared to notice. All her senses were on edge as turbulent gray skies peeked through the windows and robbed her of any feeling of belonging or warmth.

An empty spot on a bench became her focal point. She sat and counted her money again. Three dollars and some loose change. It felt like middle to late afternoon. Finally spotting a large clock on the wall, she saw it was 3:30. Her attention turned again to hunger pangs. She noticed that her hands were shaking ever so slightly. Nervous, or just hungry, she wasn't sure. By 4:00 P.M., she finally mustered up the courage to find someone who could direct her toward some food. She spoke to the first person walking by.

"Mister, 'scuse me. Is there a place to eat here?"

The man just drove his hands deeper into his pockets and walked faster. Another pulled his cap down and looked away. After several tries, she retreated to her seat, only to find it had been taken by an older woman with a hacking cough. Voices around her blurred together. All the faces began to look alike, and they were all looking at her. She distinctly heard laughing sounds swirling throughout the building, laughing sounds that penetrated and pulled at her insides like a thousand demons telling her that she was stupid, unwanted, ignorant, a joke in the eyes of the world. The voices followed her to the door but left her immediately as she stumbled outside onto the sidewalk. She pulled herself to the edge of the walk, sat with her back against the building, and sobbed amid the crowd that passed by her. Faces paused only long enough to glance down at her like a common object of curiosity and then walk on by. She tried to shut them out by burying her face in her hands. Something touched her on the shoulder. She uncovered her eyes and was startled to see an old man with a scruffy beard staring at her only inches away from her face. She inhaled suddenly but made no sound. The old man had bloodshot eyes and yellow teeth.

"You stay right there, missy. Brownie gonna' get some help," he said.

Emma stood and stepped back to lean against the building, clutching her satchel of clothing and her box of drawing materials. She sniffed loudly and wiped her nose across the back of her hand.

In less than a minute, a strong voice with a strange, clipped accent came very clearly from out of the crowd, "So, here you be wid' no handkerchief, just like Brownie say. Pity. You can't make much impression like dat."

Emma searched the crowd for the source of the voice, then heard it again. "Som'ding got you weepy, girl? You tell Mercedes about it."

Emma finally spotted a large-boned, buxom woman with a mulatto complexion walking toward her. She wore a scarf around her head tied in the back and another around her neck. The dress she wore was brightly decorated with floral designs and extended from her shoulders to below her knees. Hanging on one ear lobe was a large dangling earring. She had heavy makeup and a cigarette between her fingers. The woman's body looked young, but something about her looked old. Her face was without noticeable wrinkles, but her knuckles were gnarled and disfigured. She smiled as she approached Emma, and the disguised wrinkles on her face showed themselves. Her gaze was mesmerizing. She walked up to Emma and stood inches away from her.

"I knew you were coming today," she said. "What took you so goddamn long?"

Emma had suddenly forgotten her empty stomach and her fears of this strange place. She wanted to disappear into the brick wall she leaned against. "Who are you? How did you know I was coming?" she asked.

"Everyt'ing tell me! De' cards tell me. Bones, dey tell me. And last night, Orum, he tell me."

She looked around at the crowd and asked timidly, "Who's Orum?"

"Later, honey. We got to get you fixed up first. Where you stay? You eat yet? Come go wid' Mercedes. Everything be okay."

Before Emma realized what was happening, the woman had taken her gently by the hand and was trying to walk her away from the bus station.

"Wait, I'm not so sure about this."

"You wan' wait? We wait. You need some time? Tell Mercedes what you want."

The woman's hand felt warm and soft. With her thumb, she gently rubbed the back of Emma's hand. For some puzzling reason, Emma slowly felt oddly at ease with this strange woman. Her smooth voice with round tones and her warm smile seemed so genuine, like an opiate. Several minutes passed, and Emma finally decided that her options were limited, so she spoke to her mysterious friend.

"You talk kinda' different," Emma asked. "How come?"

"You from New Orleans? 'Course not. Me neither. I come here twenty years ago from the island. Ya know 'bout Haiti? You go dere?"

"You're from Haiti? Why'd you come here?"

"Orum. He come here—look for work down by the river. Orum my man."

"And Orum told you I was coming?"

"Yep. You hungry? We walk to the French Market. It 'bout a mile from here. Is okay for you?"

Still unsure, Emma gave a weak smile and nodded. "Where do you live?" she asked.

"I live here, maybe over yonder, maybe by de river, by de bus station, wherever I want."

"I meant where's your home?"

"I tol' you. My home Haiti. But I live here."

"Okay," Emma said slowly with some caution. "So, where do you sleep?"

"Lots o' places. Anywhere somebody got a roof and no lock on 'de door!" She finished with a raspy laugh.

The two continued down the street, hand in hand, oblivious to the passersby who turned to look curiously at them. The faint smell of fish gradually grew stronger until; finally, Emma could not hold back her question.

"So, where are we going?"

"I done tol' you—French Market. You smell 'dat? Lef' over fish from dis' morning. Get real ripe in 'de afternoon. Lots 'o fruit, too. Melon, banana, tomato - what you like, heh?"

"I just want something to eat. I eat better in the afternoon, anyway."

"Don' worry. We get."

Mercedes had finally released Emma's hand and was walking silently, a slight squint to her eyes. Finally, she stopped on a corner.

"Girl, you see dat alley over 'cross 'de street? Not over there, over yonder!" She pointed discreetly to Emma's left.

"I see it."

"Meet me over there. Now you go up to the man standing by his fruit stand, and you talk to him. You talk good to him. Make sure he listen good."

Emma was puzzled. "Why do I want to talk to him?"

"He gon' feed you, only he don' know it. You tell him you jus' got here. Tell him you got nowhere to stay, no food to eat, no daddy, no mamma, no money, no—"

"But I got some money. It ain't much, but—"

"Child, you hush up! Put that money away. Don' be lettin' nobody see you wid' money in dis' part o' town. You go talk to him like I tol' you. Don' pay no mind to me. Jus' meet me like I say." She pointed again to the alley.

Emma turned to get her orientation and to spot the meeting place Mercedes had pointed out. She looked back to ask something, and the woman was gone.

"Mercedes? Where are you? Mercedes?" Emma stepped off the curb and looked in every direction and saw nothing and no one.

After a moment of reconsidering her next move, she decided to follow her instructions. She crossed the street at a diagonal and approached the man at the fruit stand. She stood several feet away, saying nothing until the man realized he was being watched.

"He'p you, ma'am?"

"Well, I don't know. I'm new in town, and I don't know my way around very well."

"Tourist, huh? First time here, I bet."

"Well, yessir, first time. I got to get me a job somewhere. I'm really short on money, and I don't have a place to stay, and I'm awfully hungry."

"I thought you said you was a 'tourist!" the man said gruffly.

"No sir, you said that. I'm just new in town, and I'm really short on money and—"

"And looking for a handout. Why don't you try somewhere else? Look, you said you were short on money. That mean you got at least some cash?"

Emma pulled thirty-five cents from her dress pocket. "I spent almost all of it on a bus ticket. I was trying to get to Houston to see this boy that I know, but I didn't have enough to get there, so I come here, and I called the operator in Houston, and she's gonna' call Hugh for me, and he's gonna' meet me here, but first I gotta' find a job, and make some money so I kin have something to eat and a place to stay, 'cause —"

"Hold it, hold it, for Christ's sake. Gimme a nickel. Here's an apple."

A loud voice from the side interrupted them. "Maurice! Watch your stuff! Behind you! She's cleaning you out!"

The man whirled around and saw nothing. Emma was standing at a slightly different angle and looked where the other man was pointing. She thought she saw a fleeting shadow go around the corner, then realized that several pigeons were launching from the ground, startled by something.

The fruit man looked back at his helpful informant and shrugged. Emma took another nickel from her small stash and said, "Could you spare two apples?"

Bidding the man a friendly goodbye, and thanking him repeatedly, she walked slowly to the alley where Mercedes had told her to meet her. She stopped and looked. Then, thinking she had the wrong spot, was about to go back into the street when she heard a whispered sound from behind her.

"Hssst! Hssst! Hey, girl! Back here!"

Emma went back into the alley and saw a head peeking around the corner.

"Hurry up," she hissed. "Is no good here. I think he see me."

"Mercedes, what were you doing? Look at all that stuff! Did you steal that?"

"C'mon. Can't talk now. We gotta' move. Hurry!"

The older woman walked fast at a half-crouch, gathering up the front hem of her dress to make a pouch for her loot, while Emma did the best she could to keep up with her. About two minutes later, they were on a steep grassy slope looking at the widest river Emma had ever seen.

"Oh, man! Look at that! Must be a hun'erd miles across!"

"An' you say I talk funny? Sit, girl. Let's eat. Here, I got a knife. We peel some banana, some mango, some apple, hey - we gotta' fruit salad! Here, spread out this newspaper. Don' worry, it clean. Hey, you work pretty good, girl. Maybe we stay together a while, no?"

"Mercedes, I can't go 'round stealin' stuff."

"You steal? You? You didn' take nothing!"

"But I was helping you. Ain't that the same?"

"Eat some o' this stuff, and then tell me what you think."

With a look of resignation, Emma dove into the fruit. Several bites later, she admitted it was good.

"So, tell me again, how you know'd I was coming?"

"I tol' you, lots o' things."

"You said someone's name. You said Orum. Who's that?"

"Like I said, he my man."

"So, where is he?"

"Orum? He dead, girl. Been dead long time."

Emma looked perplexed, then almost laughed. "You said you talked to him!"

Mercedes nodded in agreement. "I go talk to him any time I want. He tol' me last night you comin'."

Emma stared at her new acquaintance. "You ain't serious, are you?"

Mercedes just nodded while she chewed.

Emma was totally absorbed in this new revelation. She shifted her posture, sat cross-legged, and declared, "Folks don't just talk to dead people. Mercedes, that can't be true. You're not telling me the whole story, just like you didn't tell me you was going to steal from that fruit stand."

"You not telling me everything, either."

"Like what?"

"Like why you come to New Orleans." Mercedes cocked her head and looked at Emma.

Emma was speechless for several moments. She rose to her feet and turned away to face the river. Mercedes walked around to face her and saw tears beginning to flow. Tears from sad, tired eyes.

"Tell me about it, girl."

"My name isn't girl, it's Emma. And I'm not telling you anything until you tell me how you knew I was coming."

"Emma, look right straight at Mercedes and listen to me. Orum told me! He say I gotta' watch after you 'til you don't need no more watchin'. What more I gon' tell you? No more to tell! Well, maybe one more ting. Hmmm—you say you eat better in the afternoon. Why 'dat?"

"I git sick in the mornings. Don't know why, just do."

"Sick in de' mornings, all alone in a big city, got no money - when de' baby come?"

"What baby? I don't know anything about no baby."

"What you want, boy? Maybe girl?"

"I said I don't know nothing about no baby! Now, leave me alone!"

"Fine, I just sit here and talk to Orum."

Emma stood and walked away a few steps. She turned and yelled, "Stop that! I don't want to hear nothing else about no baby or no dead people or ghosts -" Emma realized she was screaming at this gentle but crafty woman who had appeared out of nowhere and was the only person she knew within a few hundred miles.

After a few minutes of gazing out at the river, Emma began to feel the tightness in her neck unwind slightly. She saw that Mercedes was staring at her, more like through her, looking at something beyond infinity. Emma moved around to one side and noticed that

Mercedes' eyes never moved; she did not even blink. She tried looking in the same direction and saw only cars going over a long bridge that spanned the river. Still unsure about this strange woman, she decided to wait patiently. In a few minutes, Mercedes opened her mouth as though she was yawning. She blinked several times, then rubbed her face.

"You okay?" Emma asked.

Mercedes gave a hard shudder and said, "Yeah. Just fine. Orum says to tell you hi and that he's hoping for a boy."

Emma began to wring her hands and said, "I guess a boy would be okay."

"I knew it! I knew it! I knew it! You gonna' have a baby!" Mercedes was up and dancing, clapping her hands. "Man, this makes me happy like Mardi Gras. I feel like dancing! Girl, we know your secret now. And we gone make it happen."

"Sounds like you just trying to make a lucky guess. I still don't believe you talk to dead people."

Mercedes stopped long enough to grin and wink at Emma. "We see 'bout 'dat!"

Emma couldn't believe her ears. She was exhausted. The letter from Hugh, the encounter at the school, escaping to go home and pack, evading her father, the bus trip, and now this woman who dances on levees and talks to dead people—it was finally too much. Emma sank to the ground with a blank look on her face. Her focus was somewhere far away, in a safe place where no invaders could violate her life. She imagined trees and birds, Flora's front yard with the azaleas blooming, the wood-planked pathways through the woods behind her house, her favorite private spot beside a huge ancient oak tree where squirrels always came to busy themselves in the open where she could see them. She felt her mother's presence, and for a moment, the world was not such a bad place.

"Emma! Emma! Talk to me, child." Mercedes was imploring and shaking her arm."

Emma looked at her with tired, sunken eyes. "I've got to find Hugh. He's the daddy of my baby. He said someday we'd come to New Orleans, but I had to get away, and I don't know how to find him now."

Mercedes gazed off into the evening haze. "We find him. Marie gon' help. We find him."

"Who's Marie?"

"Friend of mine. Eat some more. We got some walkin' to do."

"Where are we going? I'm tired."

"Saint Louis Cemetery. We talk to Marie. C'mon. You eat while we walk."

Emma felt she had nothing to lose in following this strange woman from Haiti. After more city blocks than she could count, she began to doubt her judgment in tagging along.

"How much farther is it?" she asked.

"Almost there. Almost."

Minutes later, they stood before an open iron gate in a high brick wall. Streetlights were starting to wink on as the sun sank lower. Mercedes walked cautiously through the gate but with no hesitation about where she was going. They passed row after row of large stone structures with inscription on the front of each one. Mercedes hesitated and mumbled beside certain ones. Before pressing on from each one, she would reach out and touch it. Old friends, fond memories.

"What is this place?" Emma asked.

Mercedes spoke in quiet, almost reverend tones. "Saint Louis Cemetery. I tol' you where we was goin'."

"What are these things?" she asked quietly, pointing to a stone enclosure.

"Vaults. Tombs. What else? Dis' a cemetery, girl."

"You mean, they got dead people in them stone boxes?"

"Whole families in some of them. Can't bury underground in this city. Casket, 'dey float right to 'de top. Got to bury in tombs on top. Big family? Take out 'de old bones and bury somewhere else."

"They open these things?"

Mercedes stopped and turned to face her. "Girl, how you s'pose they get dem' old bones out?"

"I don't know. But I'm learnin' lots about dead people today, so I wonder about everything, I guess." She ended with a look of disbelief.

"You don't make fun of the dead. Not now. Not tonight. C'mon, Marie, right over here."

Mercedes finally stopped in front of a large vault that carried the name of *Marie Laveau*. On the ground were dozens of pieces of red brick chips and scuff marks all around the base of the tomb. At the top edge of the tomb was a faded area with a red hue and a poorly outlined border where the red brick dust blended with the gray granite. Mercedes picked up one of the chips and handed it to Emma.

"Put your foot by the edge, Emma. No, the other foot. Look, do it like dis'." She showed Emma how to place her right foot sideways against the base of the tomb. "Now, take this red chip and make three 'X' marks at the top d'ere. Yeah, now put your hand on top of those marks. Cover your eyes and rub your foot against the tomb. Tell Marie what you want."

Emma followed her instructions to the letter. She opened her eyes and stepped away from the tomb. Hearing a sound, she turned and saw a group of people waiting in line behind her.

"Come sit wid' me," Mercedes said. We wait for Marie to say somethin'. Let dem' tourists through."

The crowds passed by, some starring at the two odd-looking women sitting on a stone bench nearby. Some of them reached out and touched the tomb of Marie Laveau ever so lightly as though only to say they had touched it, but not firm enough to behave as though they believed any of what they had heard from the tour guide.

"Dat's right. You talk to Marie!" Mercedes said to the tourists in a loud voice. "She hear you!" One man chuckled quietly. "You wait, fella' " Mercedes said with a half laugh. "Marie just might come see you tonight. She a busy woman, you know. She make her gris-gris for you." The man's grin disappeared.

"You're crazy, woman. You know that?" the man said.

"Crazy, my ass," Mercedes mumbled under her breath.

"What are we waiting for, Mercedes?" Emma asked.

"A message, child. A message. It's coming now. Be quiet." Mercedes sat very still with her eyes closed, her lips barely moving as though repeating something she was hearing.

Emma was totally baffled and mystified by this woman who gave the full impression of talking to someone.

"Marie, we can't do that!" Mercedes said out loud. "That man evil! What he gon' do to us? Marie, come back! Marie!" She was gazing upward as though talking to someone looking out from an upper window in the sky.

Emma could restrain herself no longer. "Mercedes, who were you talking to? What were you doing?"

Mercedes took a long breath and said, "Emma, we got something hard to do. Marie—she know about your problem wid' dis' boy - what's his name?"

"Hugh. It's Hugh."

"Right. Marie, she say we got to find the right person to get in touch wid' him, uh, Mr. Hugh." Before she said any more, Mercedes stopped and collected her thoughts. "By the way, tell me, who's Marcia? She say to tell Button to be careful."

Emma felt like someone had slapped her face. She looked at the older woman in stark terror and disbelief. What had she said? This was all too much. She was beginning to feel the drain of a long day. It was as though demons had been attacking her all day. She slumped down on the ground beside Marie Laveau's tomb. Her eyes looked hollow, and dark circles beneath them were pronounced in the evening dusk.

"Mercedes, I can't do anything more tonight. I feel like falling asleep right here."

Mercedes uttered a deep laugh. "No, you not sleep here. Got a better place."

She led Emma through the cemetery to a much older, less visited part where the masonry was green with patina, the names obscured by centuries of weather. A few scraps of paper blew around in a gentle breeze. Emma saw an empty soup can and a bread wrapper. The farther they went into this corner of the graveyard, the more Emma saw signs of neglect but also of a human presence. The borders of the pathways were not neatly manicured as the more frequently visited areas. The grass was tall against some of the vaults. Whereas most of the cemetery was maintained to allow visitation with a sense of dignity, this area seemed to be forgotten. Gradually, she heard muffled voices. She was certain that Mercedes heard them, too, but it didn't seem to slow down the pace of this strange woman. Rounding a corner, several faces looked up from their places on the ground and gave Mercedes an acknowledging nod. Their eyes were all fixed on Emma, however. She noticed that each one had made a small personal area demarcated by a collection of earthly possessions: a deck of cards, a pack of cigarettes, a comb, perhaps a small bag of unknown contents. Each one had something different. As Emma stepped carefully among them, they each moved to the edge of their territory to make sure Emma saw where not to settle. Mercedes stopped and stood over one woman who seemed to have more than her share of real estate.

The woman looked up and moved all her things closer together to make more room. "I was saving it for you, Mercedes. Really, I was."

"Humph! Move your ass over," Mercedes growled. "Everyone, 'dis here is Emma. She just got into town, and she needs some help from me. We take care of Emma tomorrow. Anyone tryin' to give her the wrong kind of help tonight gonna' see some blood hit 'de ground. Everybody understand?"

No one spoke, but it was clear they all understood. Mercedes knelt and pulled up the front of her dress. From seemingly nowhere, she produced a pouch that had been hiding beneath the fullness of her clothing. Her waistline suddenly became much smaller. Emma watched in amazement as she produced two candy bars, a watch, a group of keys, some strange coins, four .22 caliber bullets, and a small derringer pistol. She seemed to have no compunction about spreading these out between the two of them as though they were ordinary trinkets most women would carry in a purse. The last item, however, was a small pouch with a drawstring. She kept it in her hand, never letting go of it nor discussing what was in it.

"Mercedes, who are these people? Where do they live?"

"They live here. At night, anyways." She looked around and asked the group, "Where's Hondo?"

"In jail," came the answer from somewhere in the back of the crowd.

"What happened?"

A man close by answered, "He was plugging tourists for nickels and shit, and this one woman said something to him, and he got mad. Took his hat off and slapped her with it - right in front of a cop that was standing across the street."

"What street was he on?" Mercedes asked.

Another man continued, "Poydras. He probably be out in a couple of days. I know he eats well while he's in the joint. Hondo don't miss nothin'."

"You all hear that?" Mercedes said to the whole group. "Stay off'n Poydras a couple of days. Folks be watching for stuff there."

Emma was still dumbfounded by the tribe-like atmosphere. She whispered, "Do they all know you?"

"You damn right, and they damn sure do what I tell 'em. I got things that make 'em humble."

Emma looked at Mercedes inquisitively.

"Later. I'll show you later."

"Mercedes, these folks got no family? No home?"

"Family right here. Home right here, too. I know what you thinking. You thinking family like you got. Each other, they got. Your mama know you here?"

"My mother died when I was little. My papa used to work for a sawmill, but it closed, and he stayed in town. I was going to high school up until a couple of days ago."

"Where?"

"Kisatchie, up in Grant Parish."

"Okay, so now you here. Seems like you got more you not told Mercedes."

"It's a long story."

"We got all night."

"I can't talk anymore. I'm so tired I can't even feel my bones."

"Is okay. Not tonight. Tomorrow, we got to find someone, and I don't mean your boy, Hugh. Come morning, we got ground to cover."

As she lay down, Emma stayed silent for a few seconds, then said quietly, "Mercedes, my mother's name was Marcia. She called me Button."

Mercedes looked at her with one eyebrow raised. She smiled and said, "Yeah, see? I tol' you."

Chapter 18

Emma tried to sleep, but for the first few hours, she lay with her eyes wide open, listening to the night sounds of a big city. The grass beneath her offered no cushion at all, and she began to yearn for her own bed, her own house, even for her father. Slowly, as she felt herself relax, something moved in the darkness just beyond her line of vision. Movement, then nothing. She saw a head raise up and look at her. Mercedes let out a soft snore, and the head went down. Exhaustion finally overtook her in the humid hours of the morning.

She awoke feeling stiff and clammy all over. Her clothes stuck to her skin as she slowly rose to her feet. Her mouth was dry and tasted like fermented mangos. She dug through her satchel for a toothbrush. Looking around, she saw that all the faces she had seen the evening before had disappeared. Mercedes was nowhere to be seen.

"You sleep good?" A familiar voice said from behind her.

Emma turned and saw Mercedes walking towards her.

"Where you gon' use that toothbrush? Got no water here!"

"I'll make do without water. What I really need is a place —"

"I know. We all gotta' shake the dew off the lily in the morning. You see everybody gone? Each got 'dey own place, each one. Nobody bothers nobody. Here, you go behind 'dat one over yonder. I watch for you. Nobody come. You got tissue paper in there?" She pointed to Emma's satchel.

"I didn't have time to think of everything."

"Well, you'll survive."

"Oh, it's no problem. I spent lots of time in the woods back home." The words hung in her throat. Ducking her head, she went where Mercedes had directed her. In a few seconds, she emerged, looking marginally refreshed.

"Get your things. We go talk to Carmen. Let's go."

Emma crossed her arms over her stomach. "Mercedes, you're not hungry? I'm starving!"

Mercedes answered quickly, "We find Carmen. We talk, and Carmen feed us. I know Carmen."

When they reached the gate of the cemetery, Mercedes stopped and slowly glanced around as though looking to see if the city skyline had changed overnight. Without looking directly at Emma, she said, "So, tell me about what all happened to you. I gotta know."

The walk took almost thirty minutes, which gave Emma ample time to talk about everything that had happened to her during the summer. Mercedes listened without comment. From the cemetery, they headed back in the direction of the French Market but then turned onto Royal Street before reaching the market. Three blocks further, a small alley appeared with a set of outside stairs just around the corner. The cobblestones were still damp from the night air. The two women walked up the creaking steps to a weathered wooden door. Emma's satchel was beginning to feel heavy. Mercedes knocked twice and waited. The door opened a few inches, and a thick-sounding voice oozed forth from the dark interior.

"What? It's early. Who's there?"

"It's Mercedes. I'm looking for Carmen."

"Wait a minute."

They stood for several minutes until the door opened again. This time, the same voice was quick and blunt. "Go back down to the front of the shop. Go inside and ask for Dora, and don't keep her waiting. She's got things to do."

They did as they were told and were led through the shop to a room in the back. A woman opened the door and closed it behind them. She appeared annoyed.

"You, Dora?" Mercedes asked. "I thought I knew all of Carmen's people."

"Why are you looking for Carmen?" she asked.

"Hey! You Dora or not?" Mercedes spat out. "We got no gripe wid' you unless you want give us one." She paused to let the words sink in. "So, where my friend, Carmen?"

The woman looked at both Emma and Mercedes with critical eyes. "Stay there," she said. "I'll call Carmen and ask if he can see you."

"Hey, lady. You tell Carmen we got a real problem here. You tell him like I say, or you and me gonna' mix it up right now. You understand? Where's your phone? I want to hear what you tell him!"

Emma listened intently and finally whispered to Mercedes, "Why are we doing all of this? It sounds dangerous."

Mercedes spoke in hushed tones, "Don't worry. We play a game. Carmen got like a fence around him. He got a fence of people, you know. Got to get through the fence to talk to him. Don't worry, we get it."

The woman finally hung up the phone and lit a cigarette. She turned and said, "Mr. Carlucci says for you two to wait here."

"You see?" Mercedes said. "Carmen, he be here soon."

"I didn't say that," the woman growled with a raspy cough. "I just said Mr. Carlucci wants you to wait here."

Emma and Mercedes sat in straight back chairs, staring at the woman who looked like her morning schedule had been rudely intruded upon. She looked to be middle-aged, but something made Emma think she was younger. As they waited, the woman brusquely excused herself and disappeared to another room. She reappeared with a small zipper bag and disappeared again into the restroom, but not before giving Emma and Mercedes a look of piercing daggers. In about a minute, she came out clutching the zipper bag so loosely that she almost dropped it. The look on her face was completely changed from one of hostility to a sleepy-eyed stupor.

The change in demeanor was not lost on Mercedes. She asked, "How many more like you around here?"

The woman slowly smiled and opened her arms in a shrug. It was then that Emma noticed the peculiar marks on her arms.

Mercedes also saw Emma's observation. "Don't ask. Not now. Later. We got to hold hands wid' the devil for a while."

Just as the woman was walking out, a handsome young man with cold, black, wavy hair stepped into the room. His shirt sleeves were rolled up and stretched tight over moderate-sized muscles. He held his hands out to Mercedes.

"My girl! How have you been?"

"Brock! You good lookin' kid! You still got a stiff one for Mercedes?"

The two hugged as Emma watched with a weak smile.

"Who's this?" he asked.

"This my new friend, Emma. She need some help from Mr. Carlucci, you know."

"Well, I'm here to take you there. Right this way, ladies."

The threesome emerged from the small dingy shop and walked a few steps to a stretch limousine parked with the motor running. Brock opened the door for Emma and held her hand as she stepped inside. The door closed, and she found herself alone in a spacious compartment. Within seconds, the two front doors opened, and Brock and Mercedes entered the front seat from opposite sides.

"Enjoy the ride," Mercedes said as the glass partition behind the driver slowly closed.

Emma was totally engrossed with the plush interior of the limousine. Never in her wildest dreams had she ever seen such opulence. It was like a room on wheels. Through the windows, she saw the same rows of buildings she had passed on the bus. The neighborhood gradually changed to homes with large front lawns and sculptured shrubs. Houses with immense windows and long driveways came into view. The limo pulled into a narrow, paved road flanked by brick pillars and a gate. A man in a uniform opened the gates and allowed them to drive past flowing fountains and enormous flower beds. When they finally stopped, Brock opened the door for her. Mercedes was standing out of the way, admiring the scenery and obviously waiting to see Emma's expression. Emerging from the limo and looking around, Emma was speechless. The lawn looked like gentle rolls of green velvet. The edges looked like someone had shaped them with a gigantic knife. A man in a black suit and bowtie stood in an open doorway and beckoned to them. Mercedes hesitated long enough to give Brock a big kiss.

With the butler's guidance, the two women were escorted through an expansive living room onto a veranda that adjoined a swimming pool and more gardens beyond. A small man sat at a table beneath an umbrella next to the pool. He rose to greet his visitors, and Emma noticed that his pants were too small for him. The cuffs were several inches above his ankles, and the waistline cut into his body like soft rubber. He had white curly hair, a broad smile, and gold inlay in most of his front teeth.

"Mercedes, I couldn't believe it when I heard you were looking for me! Oh, I hope you brought me another good tip like the last time. That one was a real long shot and went off at forty-to-one. I put a thousand on that tip you gave me! Lucky me!"

"Mr. Carlucci, you look younger than the last time I see you."

The two held out arms to each other and touched cheeks, first the right, then the left. The three then sat at the table, Carmen Carlucci and Mercedes seemingly as ease with the surroundings and Emma still aghast at what she was seeing.

"Mr. Carlucci, how is your father?"

Carlucci fluttered his hands over his head. "Ehh! He went back into the hospital last week. His ankles were swelling, and he was so certain he was going to die. I told him, I said, 'Pop, people don't die from swollen ankles.' He wouldn't speak to me for three days. So—Mercedes, today is a busy day for me, but I make time for you because you're my friend. What can I do for you?"

"It's this young lady here; you can help as a favor to me. I had a talk with you-know-who, and she told me to come to you."

"You still doing that voodoo crap? I thought you was smarter than that!"

"That voodoo crap got you forty-to-one odds in the fourth race last month! Remember that! Don't be talkin' down about Marie."

"Okay, I'm sorry. What does, uh, what's your name, sweetie?"

She looked up from the spot on the ground in front of her. "Emma. My name's Emma Parker."

Carlucci looked at her intently and spoke slowly. "Yeah, okay. What does Miss Parker need?"

"It's a long story, Mr. Carlucci. But what she needs is to find the daddy of her baby."

"Baby? I don't see no baby."

Emma interjected, "It ain't—it isn't born yet, Mr. Carmen."

Carmen Carlucci looked at Mercedes with a frown. "You bring me a young girl who got herself knocked up, and you want me to figure out who the daddy is?"

"No, that's not it at all. She know who the daddy is, but she having trouble getting word to him."

"So, who is he?"

"His name is Hugh Giles. From Houston. His daddy's an oil man."

Carmen Carlucci held up his hand, and both women remained silent. He looked at Emma, then at Mercedes, and back at Emma.

"Emma, sweetie, would you excuse us for a few minutes?" Carlucci asked.

Blushing, Emma silently agreed and walked around to the other side of the pool. As she waited, she looked over the spacious back yard. Finding another table, she sat and pulled out her sketch pad. Mercedes and Carmen continued their conversation.

"Hey, where'd you find this little hayseed? Why'd you hook up with her?"

"Look, I was at the bus station trying to make a living, and I see this girl sitting on the sidewalk, crying. She reminded me of *me* twenty years ago—okay, thirty years ago—and I stopped to help. Then I find out her boyfriend from some rich oil family, so I figured maybe we got a good angle somewhere, you know, to help her."

"You say the boy's name is Giles? Like in Giles' Oil? Holy shit!"

"I don't know about no oil companies, and all I know is what she told me. And also, this thing that Marie told me."

"God, here we go again with this voo —"

"You wait a minute! You listen to Mercedes! I don't never steer you wrong! Something good gon' come outta this. You see."

"Where's she gonna' live in the meantime? What can she do? I don't need any more girls right now."

"Not what I had in mind."

"So, what did you have in mind?"

Both look across the pool at Emma, who is intensely working on her sketch pad. A gardener walking behind her glanced at her work and stopped his task to see more of what she was doing.

"So, what's she doing now?" Carmen asked.

"I have no idea," Mercedes answered. "She had her satchel and that box when I found her. I never ask her what she got in the box."

By now, more of the staff had gathered around Emma to watch her miracle on paper unfold and take shape. Carmen and Mercedes made a wide circle around the group and approached quietly from behind her. On Emma's page was a pencil drawing of a cemetery with stone vaults, statues, and people around them. Some were lying on the ground, others on their knees. Some looked upward with arms raised. Others hung their heads. On each face was anguish, desperation, and fear of living another day. She tore that page off and began drawing the outline of a face. The eyes were slightly almond-shaped, the nose somewhat broad and strong. The cheekbones were high, giving the face an almost cat-like appearance. With the mouth, there came an inviting smile. The teeth were only partly exposed between full, wide lips. At the top, Emma's pencil went into a series of whirls that quickly created a scarf that encircled the hairline. A matching one appeared on the neck.

"Mercedes, that's you!" Carmen exclaimed. "I'll be goddamned! She drew that second picture in about—what—three, four minutes? Hey, this is some good-lookin' shit! Mercedes, did you know she could do this? I tell you, this girl's got class. I don't know where you come from, little lady, but we gonna' make the most outta' this."

Mercedes stood quietly, amazed, beside Carmen Carlucci, trying to act like a composed talent scout. She simply raised her eyebrows and gave him a tilted smile when he looked her way.

Carlucci's hands and arms were in constant motion as he spoke. "Okay, let me think. Where could we set her up? There's the shop on Royal and the one around the corner from it. What about—hey!" He whirled and snapped his fingers. "I know just the place! I got an empty storefront around from Pirates' Alley. Lots of artists hang around there. Lots of tourists with big bucks, too."

Emma finally looked up and asked, "What are ya'll talking about?"

"Emma," Carmen said with a note of jubilation. "I got a little place down in the Quarter where you can do as much of this as you want. Even got a little room off the back we can make into a bedroom. How many of these can you draw in one day? Never mind. It'll work." Carmen was becoming more animated as he talked. "This is going to be great. You'll even get to meet some of the people who work for me." By now, Carlucci was pacing in circles, rubbing his chin.

"Carmen, can I ask you something?" Mercedes wasn't smiling.

"What? Ask! Go ahead. Wait a minute. John! Hey John! Get one of the girls inside the house to fix her up with some clothes and shoes, you know, shit like that." Carmen was acting more excited.

"But, what about finding Hugh?" Emma asked.

Mercedes joined in with one hand on her hip. "Yeah, that's what we come here for."

Carlucci massaged his chin. "Okay, okay. I'll have my lawyer find out where this Giles Oil Company is, and we'll write to them.

We got, how long?" He gingerly reached out and patted Emma's tummy before she could back away. "Not even showing yet. We got lots of time to find your fella'. John! Tell the girls to think of a good maternity shop, too."

Emma was led away by a smiling, courteous woman in a maid's uniform. Carmen Carlucci was rubbing his hands together as his eyes darted around. Mercedes could tell he was thinking.

"Carmen, this girl—she don't know how to ask what in it for her. So, I ask. How much this gonna' cost her?"

"Nothing! That's what so great about it! She can have her little studio and a place to live. She can draw all day long and sell them for whatever the market will bear. Does she need anything else? Art supplies? Tell her to make a list."

"Okay, fine and good. But, right now, she lookin' for two things - breakfast and her boyfriend."

"She'll get 'em, she'll get 'em! Why didn't you tell me the kid ain't eaten yet? How 'bout you? Some scrambled eggs? Hash browns? Little ham?" With a simple nod, the word was passed into the house to make breakfast for Carmen's guests. "We do it better'n anything at Brennan's."

Brock had walked out of the house toward the pool. He was standing at a polite distance, waiting for an opportunity to interject.

"Mr. Carlucci," he said. "You wanted to see me?"

"Yeah, Brock. Go to the—sorry, you know Mercedes here, don't you?"

"Yessir. I brought her here, remember?"

Mercedes reached out and hooked two fingers into Brock's pants pocket and pulled him closer. The gesture wasn't lost on Carmen.

"Oh, yeah, that's right. Awright, you two, knock it off. Brock, tell Charlie to get some guys and go open up the little shop off Pirates' Alley. Remember the one? Clean it out like you was gonna' make an operating room out of it. Put a nice bed in the back room. Get some towels, washcloths, and shit like that, and put them in there. A set of sheets, too. And a pillow." He looked at Mercedes and said, "What else do we need?" Without waiting for an answer, he said, "And tell 'em to clean the goddamn mirror in the bathroom."

"Who's moving in?" Brock asked.

"That girl, Emma. The one you brought here with what's-her-name." He pointed to Mercedes with a grin.

"Don't worry, Mr. Carlucci. We'll fix it up real nice."

Mercedes waited until Brock walked away, then asked, "Okay, boss. What's the catch? You don't do nothin' like this for nothin'. There's somethin' in this for you, I know it."

"Hey, look, there's too many people around saying that Carlucci ain't a legitimate businessman and a good citizen."

"And this gon' fix it?"

Carmen Carlucci was becoming irritated. "Hey, you come to me for a favor. I give you more than what you ask for, and I get a ration of crap for it. She —"

"You haven't given her anything yet," Mercedes interjected with amazing clarity. "And one word from me, and she'll find answers elsewhere."

Carmen was caught in mid-thought by Mercedes' interruption. "You trying to scare me?" he said. "Me?"

"No, I'm just trying to find that thread of decency you keep talking about. The girl, she not stupid."

"Okay, you want me to charge her rent. Okay, a dollar a day!"

"Only Carmen Carlucci would charge by the day. Maybe you be thinking of one of your other businesses. I hear you got some that pay by the hour, ha!" Mercedes let go with her deep belly laugh that only a few select friends had heard. Carmen looked at her for a second and started to laugh along with her.

"Mercedes, you the only person in town who could tell me to go to hell, and I'd still love you. Okay, I'll charge her thirty-five a month."

"Hey, the price going up, no?"

"Okay, how about ten a week?"

"Wait a minute. We losing ground here! Look, what about five a week?"

"Done. I woulda' done it for nothing. Still can. Prices go up, prices go down."

"You still not tell Mercedes everything. But I find out what you up to. I find out."

Mercedes was about to say something more when she noticed a look of amazement on Carmen's face. She turned around to see what he was gazing at and saw Emma walking toward them, her hair still damp from a shower, wearing a gingham dress and new saddle oxfords. She had the innocent look of a newborn lamb. She could have been 'Dorothy' in *The Wizard of Oz*. Behind her, two women came carrying steaming platters of scrambled eggs, grits, sliced ham, a stack of French toast, and a pitcher of milk. Emma sat down and began shoveling food in as though she hadn't eaten in a year. She cleaned her plate and filled it again.

"Emma need one more thing," said Mercedes.

"What's that?"

"A doctor's appointment. We gonna' have us a fine baby!"

Emma was bent over her plate, chewing and looking back and forth between the two as they talked. She gulped down half a glass of milk so quickly that some spilled down the side of her mouth.

"When did you eat last, child?"

"Yesterday, with you. Remember that fruit stand thing?"

Carmen cocked one eye at Mercedes and smiled. Mercedes saw it and chose to ignore it.

"No, I mean before that. You only ate two apples, a banana, and one mango with me."

"Let's see, I had breakfast, went to school, came home and packed, hitchhiked to Colfax and caught the bus the next morning, came here, and met you—I'd say about two days."

"Wait," said Carmen. "You went home first? You got family?"

"My mama's dead, and my papa's drunk all the time. He's a good man, but I couldn't—" From behind the dinner napkin, she said with a muffled tone, "I hadn't thought about him all morning until just now. I hope he's okay. He don't know much about cookin'."

"So, why did you leave?" Mercedes asked.

"He found out I was going to have this baby, and he just—got mad, and then he —"

"He didn't hit you or nothin', did he?" Carmen demanded.

"No. I just couldn't stay around him no more. I just gotta' find Hugh. Excuse me."

Carmen and Mercedes, both surprised by Emma's sudden outburst of vocal energy, watched her walk toward the fence beyond the pool and wretch up all the breakfast she had just consumed.

"She eats better in the afternoon," Mercedes said flatly. "I told you she was pregnant."

Minutes later, Emma returned to the table and tried slowly to eat some more since there was still plenty left, and her stomach felt better. No one spoke while she ate. When she was finished, she wiped her mouth and looked at her two friends.

"Sorry about the mess over there on your pretty yard," she said. "I'll clean it up if you'll let me."

"Don't worry," Carmen said with a gentle smile. He spoke slowly. "It's done. Emma, we're going to make a comfortable room for you here for tonight. We'll move you into your new studio tomorrow. My secretary will have our family doctor come over this evening and have a look at you. Now, here's fifty dollars. It's just a loan. Pay me back within a couple of months." He caught a look from Mercedes. "That's interest-free."

"What's interest-free? Is that like credit at the grocery store?" she asked.

"Uh, yeah. Something like that."

"Wow, just like the grown-up folks back home."

Mercedes and Carmen look puzzled at each other.

"Anyway," Carmen continued, "After this month, on the first day of each month, you pay me uh, well, about forty-, no.... make it ten dollars. Ten dollars each month. That's your rent. Think you can make enough selling pictures to pay that?"

"I don't know. The only time I ever sold anything like this was at a church bake sale. I think the folks was buying stuff just to be nice."

A voice from behind them spoke up. It was Brock who had just heard about Emma's morning and had caught only the last part of the conversation.

"Mr. Carlucci, the guys are on their way to fix up the studio. It'll be clean and done by the end of the day. Maybe we should have Charlie round up some painters and let Emma tell them if she wants it repainted on the inside." He looked at his boss and shrugged. "It really needs it. I might also suggest that I take Emma around the French Quarter and show her what some of the other artists do and how much they get for their work. If she's new at this, we wouldn't want her to sell herself short."

Hearing this, Mercedes said with a shake of her finger, "Emma, just remember, Brock's MY boyfriend! Ha!"

Later that morning, Brock drove Mercedes and Emma back into town, dropping Mercedes off along the way. He continued with Emma to the French Quarter and parked in a hidden courtyard behind a wrought-iron gate among fountains and potted plants. They walked toward a large open area with a statue of a man on a horse. People were taking pictures of everything, especially of a large church nearby with a cluster of tall steeples.

"What's that big building there?"

"That's Saint Louis Cathedral, and this place where you're standing is Jackson Square."

Emma's face immediately showed desperation and hope at the same time. It was a though someone on death row had suddenly been given the remote possibility of a reprieve. She turned and turned, trying to take it all in. It was hard to hold back the tears.

"Did I say something wrong?" asked Brock.

"Oh, NO!" She sniffed loudly. "It's—it's just that Hugh said someday we'd come here together, and now I'm seeing it. He said it was so beautiful and it is! Oh, look! All the pigeons!"

The bells from the Cathedral spires suddenly drowned out any chance of speaking for the next few seconds. Before they could finish ringing, a tugboat answered the chimes from behind the levee. Emma didn't know which way to look. The smell of the river, the sounds of this part of the city—she was in a dream that was so real that for the first time since he had left, she felt like Hugh was standing right beside her.

Brock let Emma take as much time as she wanted to savor the moment. He had nothing else to do except look after her and be back for her doctor's appointment. He watched Emma's eyes drink in the surroundings, committing every detail to memory and fitting it into the image she had formed about this place. How can such a scene be so majestic and yet have such a precious, crucial piece missing? She felt her imagination had entered a world as old as the buildings, the smells, and the sounds that engulfed her. She was not the first, nor the last, to know what it was like to feel this place, have it talk to you, to tell you that you loved someone in such a perfect way that it had to be right and had to beautiful, and above all else, it just had to be.

Brock finally intervened, feeling that his time was running short. "You want to see your studio? It's just right over there." He pointed toward a corner of the square. "You can step out of your front door and be right here where we are now in less than a minute."

Emma couldn't speak, but her moist eyes and the look of anticipation told Brock all he needed to know. They walked in front of the Cabildo and turned the corner. She saw a two-story building with a covered balcony above, like so many others. The railing was ornate wrought iron. On the ground floor was a small door with shuttered windows on each side. Brock motioned Emma toward the door, and immediately, they were confronted by three men in white paint-spattered coveralls. Inside was a room so small Emma could cross it in four big steps. The interior walls were made of worn brick held together by old mortar that seemed to bleed sand that rubbed off with only a fingertip. The workmen had spread their drop cloths at the base of one of the brick walls.

"Ya'll gonna' paint?" she asked.

One of them answered, "What's it look like? Yeah, we're gonna' paint. You think we were gonna' piss on it or something? Who are you, anyway?"

Brock stepped forward and grabbed the man by the shirt collar, and slammed him against the wall. The man winced as Brock tightened his grip and pinched the skin underneath.

"Hey, watch it, man! Who in the hell are you two?"

"Who sent you here?" Brock asked, still pinning the man's neck against the wall.

"Charlie," he said with a raspy note of discomfort.

"That's right. And who do you think sent Charlie to get you?"

"Hey, I don't know. I just paint when someone tells me they need a job done. Long as the money's good, I take a job. Now, how 'bout lettin' go of me?"

The other two men had slowly walked around to Brock's blind side and were watching closely.

"Pal," Brock hissed, "Tell your friends to get out where I can see them, or your neck's going to be the next thing damaged around here." He rested his forearm across the man's throat and leaned gently against it, which brought on a spasm of coughing.

"Awright, awright! For God's sake, let go of me!"

Brock released the man and cocked his eyes toward the other two, who slowly backed away.

"The lady asked you a question."

The painter had to think for a minute to remember what Emma had asked. Finally, he answered, "Yeah, we're gonna' paint. That's what we do."

"You're going to paint the brick? That purty brick?"

The two unruffled men looked at each other at the sound of Emma's cornbread and biscuits accent.

"Answer the lady," Brock demanded. "Mr. Carlucci wants her to have her studio done the way she wants it. You can paint the back room and the bathroom if she wants it. Not this one."

Hearing the name of Brock's boss brought a firm look of recognition over all three painters.

"Hey, I just do what I'm told," said the first painter who was still craning his neck to get the kinks out. "Say, what about this other room over here? The door's locked."

"If it's locked, I guess it's for a reason."

Emma walked back into the back room and looked around at the bare walls and empty floor.

"Don't worry, Mr. Carlucci will have a nice new bed and dresser in here by tomorrow morning. You want a rug? Sure, you do. Let's go pick out one. I'll introduce you to some of your new neighbors along the way."

The painters watched as two left and turned the corner. Brock walked and stopped along the sidewalk while Emma peeked into every shop window they passed. She stopped at one and looked curiously at a riverboat drawing on display. The colors were stark and unnatural. A woman was in the back of the shop, seated in front of an easel, making bold sweeping strokes on the canvas. She looked over her glasses at Emma and put down her work. She walked over to the window and looked to see which drawing Emma was inspecting. Through the glass, she motioned them to come in, but Emma politely declined. Walking away, she leaned toward Brock.

"Did I see that price right? She wanted thirty-five dollars for that picture?"

"She's one of the premier artists of the French Quarter. You didn't like her work?"

Emma wrinkled her nose and said, "It don't look very real to me. You think I could get that kind of price for my stuff?"

"Never know. Try and find out. You ready for some lunch?"

Emma just nodded with a broad grin. Brock took her hand and led her to a narrow passageway that opened into a small courtyard. From a doorway, a man in a waistcoat approached them, called Brock by name, and showed them to a table without even asking what their seating preference was. He knew.

Emma promised to eat slowly and to keep it down at least until they could finish and leave.

"What's this place called?"

"This is The Court of Two Sisters. Been around here for a long time. It was the first place Mr. Carlucci brought me when I started working for him.

"One reason I brought you here is because this place was started by two sisters, one of whom was named Emma."

Emma's head never stopped turning, trying to see it all. "This is real nice. Hugh would like it," she said.

"Did you ever go anywhere outside of that small town of yours? I mean, you act like you've never seen a city before."

"I went to Colfax a couple of times. It ain't—isn't—near this big."

"How big is your town?"

"Well, there's me and Papa, there's Oscar and Lavenia, all their kids —"

Wait, wait … I get the point. Not very big, I take it."

"Naw, not like here. How many folks you got here? Couple a' hun'red, you think?"

Brock stopped his forkful of food in mid-air. "A few more than that, I believe."

They finished their meal, talked for a while, and simply left. The man who had seated them gave a polite nod.

Outside, a horse-drawn buggy passed slowly on the street. A grizzled old man with a top hat sat holding the reins and talking to two passengers. The swayback horse and the driver seemed to come from the same slice of time. Up ahead, about a half-block, a young boy was tap dancing on the sidewalk. An overturned hat with loose change lay in front of him. Brock tossed in a dollar, and the boy greeted him by name.

Brock was strolling slowly with his hands thrust into his back pockets. "Emma," he said in a serious tone, "The Quarter is a busy place. There's lots of fun and lots of money to be made. There's also things you don't want to get into."

"Things like what?"

"You'll know when you see them. If anyone strange asks you to do something or invites you to go somewhere, you check with me first. We're getting a phone hooked up in your studio. May take a week or so. You stay in touch with us. Tell us how business is going. Tell us if you get any unusual visitors."

"Unusual, how?"

"Okay, you know why you're here and who your friends are. Just be careful of anything outside of that for a while."

"Well, Okay. But Brock, what I really want to know is when are we going to look for Hugh?"

"We will, we will. He's in Houston, anyway. Didn't you say that he was?"

"Yeah, but—"

"Now, over here is a good place to hear some great jazz. You like jazz? That's okay. It kinda grows on you."

"Brock, how big is Houston?"

"I've never been there. I hear it's big, though. Hey! Here's a place where they might have a rug you like."

"I never had a rug before. Which side of town do you think he lives on?"

"Who?"

Emma just looked at Brock and cocked her head.

"Oh, that. Hell, I don't know. The north side's pretty ritzy, I hear."

Emma nodded but was busy looking up at the street signs. "How do you say these names? They're really weird!"

"You'll learn them. It takes practice. Let's cross over here. This is Royal Street. That one's easy. Lots of shops here."

"That one back there was Bourbon Street. That's a funny name. Kinda' like naming a street 'soda pop'." *Papa would like that one,* she thought.

Brock just pulled her a little closer. "Listen to me. You best stay off Bourbon Street for a while until you know your way around better. Especially at night." Brock knew he was probably twice her age, but he had the irresistible urge to put his arm around her shoulder as they walked. Hoping she felt relaxed, he did just that and felt no resistance from her.

"So, when do you think I'll hear from Hugh?"

Her question yanked Brock back into reality, so he gave her a quick squeeze and let go. "It depends on how much they want to answer the letter from Mr. Carlucci's lawyer."

"Hugh would want to answer it right away. He wrote to me before."

"Yeah, honey, but Hugh isn't going to be the first one to see this letter. It's going to take a while. You know, we can't just snap our fingers, and this Hugh character comes running!"

Emma stopped on the sidewalk and turned toward Brock. "He's not a character!"

Brock held his hands up in submission. "My fault. Bad choice of words." He let a minute go by. "Hey, you want to walk down by the river? I'll show you where the big river boats used to unload their cotton bales and—"

"You don't want to talk about him, do you? You don't want *me* to talk about him either, do you?"

"No, wait. I didn't say that. Look, I'm sorry. I guess I haven't been paying attention."

Her chin was trembling. She peered into his eyes for several seconds and finally spoke, almost in a whisper. "I'm not going to see him, am I? Why does this have to be so hard?"

"Emma, I didn't say you wouldn't find him. I'm just trying to tell you it's not going to be easy. But I don't get it. Why did you come to New Orleans?"

"I didn't have enough money to go to Houston. And I couldn't stay at home. Now, I feel so stupid."

"Now that you're here, what makes you think he'll come here looking?

"He would! As soon as he hears that I left town, he'd know I would come here. We talked about it!"

Brock reached out to her, and she pulled away.

"We said we'd help you find him. You said yourself he was in Houston. Nobody said he was coming here, did they? Think about it. Did he really say he would meet you here? Emma, how old is this guy? Still in high school, I'll bet." He gave his words time to sink in. "Yeah, I figured as much. Emma, he's got his family, and he lives over there in - Crap! What am I telling you all this for? This is none of my business." Brock looked around and then glanced at his watch. "C'mon, let's head back. We'll come back out tomorrow."

Emma had taken on a wild-eyed look. She kept backing away from him. "No! You're lying to me! I'm not leaving here! You're not going to help me; I just know it! I'll find him myself!"

She turned and ran back through the crowd. Brock tried to follow, but the mass of tourists closed around her like quicksand, heads turning only to see a young girl running frantically. A policeman bumped into Brock and looked him over closely. In a few seconds, Emma was nowhere to be seen.

Minutes later, Brock brought his car to a screeching halt outside the stone wall of St. Louis Cemetery. Jumping out, he quickly trotted toward the far back corner.

"Mercedes! Mercedes!"

A shaggy head peeked out from behind a vault.

"Hey, you! Where's Mercedes?"

The head disappeared. Brock tried to follow, but the figure had vanished. The afternoon sun was getting low and cast a glare in Brock's eyes. He kept on running.

"Mercedes!"

"What the hell is all the noise about?" came a voice from somewhere behind him. Brock stopped and whirled. Mercedes was leaning against a stone marker.

"God, I'm glad I found you. Mercedes, I lost her. She spooked on me. She just ran into the crowd, and I can't find her."

"What you want Mercedes to do?"

"Help me find her! God, Mr. Carlucci's going to kill me! You gotta' help me!"

"I gotta' what?"

"Okay, would you PLEASE help me find her? I'll buy you lunch for the next week - no, the next two weeks!"

"Sounds like a deal to me. C'mon, you tell me what happen on the way. Where your car?"

"You stupid shit! You dumb asshole!" Mercedes was yelling after hearing Brock's account of what happened. People on Canal Street turned their heads to see who was yelling as Brock's car sped along with the windows down. "You let her believe she was never going to see her boyfriend again?"

"I didn't actually say that! I was just trying to reason with her!"

"Did Carmen tell you to reason with her? Did he tell you to give her a sermon? Huh? He told you to take her downtown and show her stuff! Make her feel comfortable! Brock, she scared, for God's sake! She a runaway-pregnant-girl. Right now, she got ideas and things in her head hotter than moonshine gone jukin' her brain, then you go and try to be *reasonable*? God! What a dumb shit you are!"

All Brock could do was exhale loudly and step on the gas.

"What part of town did you two walk through?" Mercedes yelled over the roar of the car's glass pack mufflers.

"We started in Jackson Square, then Pirate's Alley, then down Chartres a couple of blocks, and we kinda' snaked our way over to somewhere on Dauphine."

"Well, what did she say?"

"What do you mean?"

"Give me some clues where she might be, stupid! What did she notice? What part did she like?"

"She did say something about her boyfriend and Jackson Square in the same sentence."

"That's where I'll start. You pull over here and wait."

"That's okay; I'll come help you look."

Mercedes gave him a look that would humble the Pope. "Okay. So, I sit here and wait."

Chapter 19

Brock could only sit, drumming his fingers on the steering wheel. At first, he was puzzled when Mercedes walked in the exact opposite direction than he had expected. Through the car's rear-view mirror, he saw her duck into an alley and come out about two minutes later, followed by two grizzly-looking ragtag figures. She disappeared again and reappeared with two more.

"Calling out your troops, aren't you?" Brock said to himself.

Mercedes and her posse finally made their way around the corner and were gone from view. The afternoon shadows were getting longer, and Mercedes knew the dark of evening was getting closer. There is a point of time in the early evening in the French Quarter when the nature of the crowd on the streets begins to change from shoppers and casual sightseers into those out to have a hard night of fun. Mercedes knew such time was approaching, and she knew it could be frightening to a naive country girl, especially one in Emma's present state of mind. If Emma only knew that yet another change happened in the Quarter at about midnight when the atmosphere changed from simply boisterous to dangerous, particularly if one walked down the wrong streets. Emma had no idea which ones were the wrong streets. She would probably be looking for solitude. How could she know that the safest place was among the crowd?

An hour later, Mercedes was really beginning to worry. There had been no sign of Emma and no rumors of her whereabouts. A hand tapped Mercedes on the shoulder. She turned and saw a small Mexican man in a stained shirt and ill-fitting pants looking at her.

"Hondo! I thought you were in jail! When did you get out?"

"About an hour ago. I hear you looking for some girl named Emma."

"You wouldn't know her, Hondo. She only got here yesterday. You were in the slammer."

"Hey, it don't take me long to catch up on things. You checked on Bourbon?"

"She wouldn't be there. Too many people."

"Some gal in a starchy-looking dress was at the corner of Bourbon and Toulouse a few minutes ago asking for directions to the bus station."

"Hondo, that might be her. Let's go."

The two of them were an unlikely-looking couple hurrying along side streets and alleys to the last place Emma had supposedly been seen. Mercedes stumbled into a trash can and sent the lid flying with a bang and a rattle. Hondo was about five foot four, weighed no more than one hundred ten pounds, and she was almost twice his size. When they reached Bourbon and Toulouse, the sidewalk had filled up with people, but no sign of Emma. Mercedes saw a stream of folks coming around a corner carrying Hurricane glasses from Pat O'Brian's club. Each was looking backward at something on the sidewalk behind them and around the corner, out of Mercedes' line of vision. Trusting her intuition, Mercedes hustled across the street and saw two men with slick hair bending down and talking to someone. A foot with a saddle oxford shoe stuck out into view, and she knew she had found her lost lamb. Emma was trying to get up, and the two men kept pushing her back to the concrete where she sat. Mercedes came on like a tank and bowled both men over into the street. They landed hard.

"What the hell—? Are you crazy, woman?"

The men got to their feet and started toward Mercedes but stopped suddenly when she pulled out a large whistle and blew an ear-piercing blast from it. Both men looked at each other and grinned, but it was all the time she needed. From under her skirt came the little derringer Emma had seen. She aimed it at one of the men, then the other. Hondo was dancing around like a busy mosquito.

"Emma, come with me!" She spoke loudly to the surrounding crowd, "We just gonna' back out of here, and everyone else gonna' stay put. Don't make me use this!"

The two men began to slowly spread out and approach Mercedes from both sides. "You got one shot, babe," one of them said. "I'll bet you've never even tried to shoot that thing." The look on Mercedes' face told the truth and turned to panic when she tried to thumb-cock the small gun, and the hammer was frozen with rust. The men relaxed a bit and began to swagger forward as Emma cowered behind her. A mocking, amused crowd began gathering to watch the spectacle.

"I'm telling you guys. You just asking for trouble!" She punched out another shrill screech from the whistle, and now the men were laughing. As they were about to play tag team with their two victims, a loud roar from a flathead V-8 and the blast of a car horn sent the crowd scattering. Brock exited his car and leveled the nearest assailant with one punch. He turned to the other, who had the good sense to turn and run.

"Get her in the car!"

Mercedes almost picked Emma up in the process of putting her in the back seat. The doors slammed, and Brock threw the car into reverse. The tires screeched for about half a block before he spun the wheel, and the car whirled around. The two women in the back bounced off both doors and the ceiling.

"My God, Brock! Slow down! We okay! Good God!"

Brock said nothing until he had turned onto Canal Street, where he pulled over and came to a stop. Then he turned and looked at Emma, who was completely consumed by raw panic. Brock was breathing hard.

"If you EVER take off like that again, I'll—" The look on Emma's face told him she was not hearing anything he said. Mercedes leaned forward and met him with cold eyes. Brock felt his anger melt away, and he reached out his hand and tried to gently touch Emma's arm. She withdrew quickly and reached for the door handle. Mercedes wrapped her arms around the girl and held her tight.

"Mercedes got you, honey. Ain't nobody gon' hurt my girl. No, sir!"

The three drove back to Carlucci's in silence.

Carmen Carlucci's house was set back almost fifty yards from the street. The sun was completely down, and small lights at ground level softly illuminated the edges of the long driveway. Brock could see his boss standing in the doorway, his apprehension like the radiant heat from a large fire, something which could be felt even at this distance. A familiar figure stood behind Carmen. Any time Carmen called Mario Puccini to the house, it was because some kind of plans were beginning to crystallize.

"Where the hell you been?" Carmen yelled from the doorway even before the car came to a full stop. He continued when Brock opened the driver's door. "I said, where in God's name have you been? I been worried sick about you! Hey! I'm talking to you!"

Brock rubbed his chin and walked slowly past Carmen without saying a word. Mercedes and Emma were still sitting in the car. Carmen stood with his hands on his hips, looking first at the back of Brock's head and then at the car. It was like his head was on a swivel.

Mario Puccini had taken a seat on a couch in the living room.

Carlucci came in waving his arms as usual. "Brock, you better come up with a goddamn answer really quick 'cause nobody ignores me when I'm talking! You know that!"

Brock took a long look at Carmen before answering. "Yessir, I know. I did something really dumb." He stopped and collected his thoughts for a second. "I tried to talk to her about her boyfriend, and she just went crazy on me. Took off like a wild rabbit, and we had a hell of a time trying to find her."

"What was she saying about the boyfriend?"

"She's determined to find him. I'd suggest that if we want to keep her on a leash, we better let her see that we're looking for this Hugh fellow, whoever he is. That's all she talks about."

"My God, the letter has already gone out! Make sure she knows that."

"Mr. Carlucci, right now, she doesn't trust a thing I say. Maybe if she heard you tell her—"

Carlucci was suddenly inches from Brock's face. He spoke decisively. "Brock, she is your responsibility from now on. If she doesn't trust you, then fix it so she does!" Mercedes and Emma were just coming through the door. He looked at the two of them, felt his own hostilities melt, then turned back to Brock and said, "Awright, I'll tell her this time. But you remember what I said. She's yours to deal with!" He paused and said, "Oh, excuse me. Mario, you remember Brock Montellio, don't you?"

The man on the couch gave a slight nod, but his face had no expression. Mario was about the same age as Brock and had grown up in Gretna on the other side of the river. His hair was combed to perfection.

Carmen turned to Emma. "Emma, honey, we was so worried about you! Listen, Brock tells me you was asking about Hugh. Okay, we got the address of his family's business, and we sent a telegram right after you left. If we ain't heard nothing back in a couple of days, we'll send another one. You okay, sweetie?"

"She's hungry," Mercedes said flatly.

"Brock, take these two ladies to the kitchen and get 'em something. Tell that new cook, what's her name? Shit, I'm gettin' forgetful! Anyway, tell her to fix whatever they want."

Mercedes and Emma had left the room, and Brock was about to follow when Mario Puccini spoke up. His voice was smooth. He could have sung tenor with no trouble. "Hey, Montellio, I heard you roughed up a couple of my boys tonight. They were just having a little fun, and you came on like John Wayne."

"Word travels fast. Were those guys working for you? I should have known. I can imagine what their side of the story was like."

"Hey, what's this?" Carmen demanded. "Brock, Mario and I have been business partners on a lot of things. We're about to wind up the plans on another one, and now I hear this?"

"Tell him," Brock said calmly. "Tell him what your 'boys' were doing when I bumped into them."

"How should I know? They didn't tell me no details," Mario said with a huff. "I don't ask my people to tell me what they do on their time off."

"You see that young lady who just came through here? They were trying to take a poke at her down in the Quarter. Yeah, they were having a good time. So good their pants almost didn't fit anymore. By the way, when it was all over, Emma lost the fifty bucks Mr. Carlucci gave her. You wouldn't happen to know where it might be?"

Carmen turned to Mario, his eyes blazing. He spoke to Brock without taking his eyes off Mario. "Brock, make sure everything is okay in the kitchen."

As soon as Brock was gone, Carmen walked over to Mario and slapped him across the face with a loud pop. Mario saw it coming and didn't move to fend it off, nor did his facial expression change. Carmen leaned over and spoke into Mario's face. "If you screw this up, I'll see to it that you stay on the other side of the river and never do business over here again. You won't be able to cross over for a damn quart of milk and a dozen eggs!"

Mario let a small grin show through. He tried to get up out of his chair, but Carmen stayed planted in his face. Finally, Mario held his hands up and said, "Okay, okay. I'll keep a better watch on things. You have my word. Look, I'll replace the fifty, okay?"

Carmen remained poised over him for a few more seconds, then stood and stepped back.

"But I gotta' ask you something," Mario said. "Why this girl? Look at the trouble she's already caused."

"Look, asshole. She cute, she's country, and she's pregnant. Motherhood, apple pie, and all that shit. It's a perfect picture. No one will suspect anything. I didn't plan it this way. She just sorta' showed up on my doorstep."

"And she's also very stupid, from what I've heard so far. How do you know she'll go along with it?"

"You think I'm going to tell her everything? We'll tell her what she wants to hear! And only what we want her to know! Where are your brains? You sittin' on 'em? No one will go looking in her little hole in the wall for the merchandise."

The men continued their discussion and lost track of time. Brock emerged quietly from the kitchen and sat across the room.

"How're they doing back there?" Carmen asked.

"They're fine. What you told her about the letter to Hugh's family really helped."

"Yeah, it went in the mail today. Should be there in a couple of days."

"I thought you said it was a telegram," Mario interjected.

"Oh, yeah. Telegram. Yeah, that's right. Say, listen, did she say if she was Roman Catholic or whatever? Never mind. I got Father George coming over in a few minutes. I called him earlier this afternoon while you two was getting lost in the Quarter. He's going to talk to her."

"About what?" Brock asked.

"How do I know? Just give her a blessing and stuff like that, you know. She's had a tough day, and I want her to know she's welcome here."

Mario rose from his seat and started for the door. "That's what I like about working with Carmen Carlucci," he said with a grin. "He does everything, first class."

Emma was still in the kitchen when Father George arrived. He was close to eighty and wore a hearing aid in one ear. Carmen directed him to the kitchen and motioned Mercedes to come out and give Emma and the priest some privacy.

They sat side by side at the table. The old priest waited for almost a minute before speaking. "Do you wish to talk about anything, child?"

"Yeah. What's that thing around your neck?"

"I mean, do you have anything that is troubling your soul?"

"No, not my soul. I sure do miss Hugh a lot. Hugh, he's my boyfriend. We're going to have a baby."

The old priest looked at her for a moment. "Have you confessed this sin to anyone?"

"Sin? What sin?"

"You said you were pregnant. How did this come to be? Do you not remember when the conception took place? The Holy Church can grant you absolution, but you first must confess what you've done."

"Well, I told Lavenia. Really, she told me. She's the one who figured out that I was going to have this baby. And I told Papa, and he got really mad. I didn't know he'd git mad like that, but I left home and come - came - here, so what else do you want to know?"

"Well, I think we're getting closer, but—"

"You said something about a church? Do ya'll shout in your church? That's what they do in Lavenia's church. Miss Flora says they don't do it in hers."

The priest looked at her blankly for a few seconds. "Would you want to take the sacraments tonight, child?" He reached into a pocket and produced a communion pyx, which he opened and placed on the kitchen table. From the same pocket came a pocket stole, which he put around his neck.

"What's that for?"

"Are you not familiar with this? When were you baptized, child?"

"When was I what?"

Carmen, Mercedes, and Brock were sitting silently in the living room when Father George came out with Emma behind him. He shook his head and looked a bit flustered.

"Everything okay, Father?" Carmen asked.

"Fine. She declined the sacrament. She, ah, told me she had already eaten. Carmen, I think you should enroll her in a catechism class right away. She has a lot to learn. I can recommend a school where a group of Sisters have done great things with troubled students. I must be getting back to the rectory now, Mr. Carlucci. I'm sure she's in good hands. Good evening, folks."

As he left, they all thanked Father George and stood on the front porch, watching his car leave by way of the long driveway. The two men went back inside, but Emma and Mercedes lingered outside. Mercedes found a seat in a large rocking chair and noticed that Emma's attention was preoccupied, looking out on the expanse of lawn in the darkness.

"You thinkin' about him, honey?"

Her voice was vacant and distant. "Sorta'. Mercedes, that man tried to tell me that Hugh and I had done something wrong. He said it was a sin. What does he mean by that? First, Hugh acted worried, then Lavenia got upset, then Papa gets mad, and now this man says—I just don't know anymore! Everybody talks about finding Hugh, but I don't see anybody doing anything. I just got a bad feelin'."

"Emma, all this is going to be worked out. It's just not as simple as you think it is. You awfully young to have so much on your mind."

"I just feel like I'm all by myself."

"C'mere, honey. You a big girl, but you not too big to sit on Mercedes' lap. We got to talk. Just sit here and close your eyes."

Emma did as she was told. Mercedes's voice suddenly had a soothing balm about it. Her words entered a hidden recess of Emma's mind and took root. Emma had never been held by another woman that she could remember. The arms that held her were strong but with a reassuring gentleness. Her lap and bosom were soft and enveloping. Emma felt like a child again. She curled her feet up under her and folded her arms close to herself. A teardrop fell from her face onto Mercedes' arm, and a silent sob went through her body. Mercedes suddenly felt her own heart tearing apart.

A cool breeze blew in from Lake Pontchartrain. Crickets chirped in the darkness. The older woman's voice was soft as velvet. "Emma, you don't worry none about your baby. It's gonna' have what every child oughta' have. Lots of good folks in this town, but right now, I got you. I got strong arms, and I got a heart with lots of room. We gonna' just sit here, and I'm gonna' hold you as long as you want me to. This is a beautiful place, this town. We gonna' show it all to you. Nobody's gonna' hurt you or your baby. You just sit there and listen to this squeaky old rocking chair and feel that cool, dark breeze coming outta' the live oaks over yonder. Sleep if you want. Just make sure you dream 'bout a place where nothing can hurt you 'cause that's where you are right now."

And dream she did.

The next morning, Emma woke totally refreshed, having slept until nine o'clock. She quickly got dressed and came out to find Brock sitting by the pool, finishing breakfast.

"Have some?" he asked.

Emma approached him cautiously. "I think I'll wait a while. In a couple more hours, I'm sure it'll stay down."

"Suit yourself. Have a seat."

Emma pulled a chair away from the table and sat. She wasn't quite sure what to say next. Brock tried to act casual.

"Where's Mercedes?" she asked.

"You didn't think she'd stay here, do you? That woman hasn't slept indoors in years. No, last night, after we put you to bed, I took her back downtown. She said she'd look in on you at the studio."

"I don't remember any of it now."

"You were tired. You'd had a big day. You look better this morning."

Emma rose from her seat. "Give me a couple of minutes, and I'll be ready to go."

"No hurry. We got all day. I'd like to help you get set up. I'm sure there's stuff you need."

"Yeah, sure. Brock, about yesterday—"

Brock just shook his head. "That was yesterday. Let's don't even think about it."

"But I need to think about it. Something that Mercedes said made me wonder what I would do if I don't see Hugh again?"

"Hey, the last time I tried to talk to you about him, you took off on me."

"I'm really sorry. I just—okay, maybe I grew up a little last night. Brock, I gotta know. What do mamas do when they don't have a husband?"

Brock pondered his answer. "Well, they work. They find a way to make a living, and they get on with their lives."

"What about the baby?"

"What about it?"

"Do they let you keep it?"

"Who do you mean, *they*?"

"I don't know. The doctors, the police, isn't there someone that—"

"Emma, this is going to be your baby to do with as you wish. You can raise him, uh, or her, or you can give the baby to someone else for adoption. You know, another family."

"Give it away?" Emma frowned and looked puzzled. "Well, can you give it away like that and then change your mind?"

"Ah, no. Usually not."

Emma felt a cold shiver when she heard Brock's answer. "So, I gotta' get a job, huh? All I know is housework."

"Don't sell yourself short, Emma. Tell you what, let's see what kind of art business you can start, and then we'll have our answer."

A short while later, the two were parked outside Emma's little studio. Carmen Carlucci had made use of his errand boys, gathering what he thought would be the supplies Emma would need. Brock had them all hidden in the trunk of his car. Emma's surprised look when she saw all of it was worth a million bucks to him. He couldn't help but see the difference in Emma since the night before. Bubbling with delight, she took out three easels, boxes of colored chalk, colored pencils, watercolors, oil paints, brushes, jars, rags, everything she needed from the spacious trunk.

"Brock, I never did anything with oil paints before. I've heard of them, and I seen some oil pictures, but I wouldn't know how to do it."

"Well, this is the place to learn. You got the natural talent. Just watch how others do it and play with it yourself. By the way, there's a good frame shop a few doors down. That's always good to have close by. You can sell pictures and send them business. In time, they'll do the same for you. Hey, look who's coming!"

Emma glanced up to see Mercedes and a band of her disciples across the street. Mercedes crossed over while the rest stayed behind.

"Hey, honey! You lookin' better today! I wanted to bring some of my friends along to see where your place was so they could send you some business. Is this guy behaving wid' you today?" She motioned toward Brock.

"Yep. Look at all this stuff Mr. Carlucci got for me yesterday! I can't think of a thing I need."

"How's the studio? How 'bout that back room? You got to live here, don't forget. Hey, you need a sign! Let people know you're here."

Both women slowly walked inside. The smell of fresh paint was still hanging in the air. Mercedes went to the bedroom and opened the only window to air it out. "Brock, make those guys put a screen on this window," Mercedes said. "The bedroom is kinda' small, but you won't be in there much during the day."

"Well, this is where the baby will be in a few months," Emma said. Brock and Mercedes shot a glance at one another.

"Yeah, you're right," Mercedes said slowly.

Brock held a finger to his lips where Mercedes could see and said, "Well, we're going to leave you to your business, Miss Emma. We'll come back to check on you after lunch. Oh, here's some more money to replace what you lost last night. You'll be okay for a while?"

Mercedes and Brock were about to leave when Mercedes stopped near the front door of the studio. "Brock, what's this? A closet?" She tried to turn the knob, but it wouldn't budge.

"I really don't know. Some of these old buildings have some strange things, like doors to nowhere. I have no idea where that goes. Probably just a closet. Looks like the door's been painted shut."

The two left, leaving Emma alone to sit and consider what to do next. If she was to begin making money, she better start producing something to sell soon, like today. She already had a small collection of work that just needed to be unrolled and unwrinkled somehow.

An hour later, a man and his wife looked in the door. They were wearing casual clothes, and each had a camera around their neck. By their accent, they weren't from New Orleans.

The man spoke first. "Miss, can you tell us where Audubon Park is? We seem to be a little turned around."

"I told you not to leave the map in the hotel, Roger," the wife whined. She was wearing sunglasses and chewing a very large wad of gum.

Emma replied, "I just got here myself. I don't really know where any of the parks are. Sorry, I can't he'p you."

"You visiting someone?" the man asked.

"Roger, that's none of our business. Leave the poor girl alone. She doesn't know where Audubon Park is. Let's go!"

"Hang on a sec. Miss, is this where you're moving in? I thought this block was all businesses along here. I'm a real estate investor, and I—I'm just naturally curious."

"Uh, this is my art studio. And I have a—well, you know, a bedroom in the back. But it's not mine. A friend is helping me out. I just rent it."

"You do art? I don't see any."

"Roger, c'mon!"

She smiled and said, "Well, when I said I was just got here, I meant like right now! I haven't had time to do any work yet. But come back tomorrow, and I'll have some then."

"Hey, great!" said the man as his wife pulled on his arm. "We're staying just a couple of blocks from here. We'll be back. By the way, what's the name of your studio?"

"I don't have a name for it yet," Emma said softly.

"Well, that's okay. What's your name?"

"Uh, my name is Emma."

"That's a good start. Work with that, and you'll come up with something."

Minutes later, there was a cardboard sign in the window that read, '*Emma's Art Studio.*' It was held in place with tape.

Emma worked through lunch and by mid-afternoon had at least a dozen charcoal sketches of people, buildings, ships, animals, anything her mind could conjure up. She was hard at work and didn't hear the footsteps at the door.

"Are you open for business, ma'am?"

Emma looked up and saw Mercedes standing in the doorway, pretending to be a shopper.

"See my sign? A man and his wife come by to look in, and he gave me the idea."

"How original," Mercedes said with no expression. "Couldn't you think of something else?"

"I like it. It tells people who I am and what I do."

She shook her head and said dryly, "Oh. Well, by all means, don't change it because of me."

Mercedes began looking at some of Emma's impromptu work. She was amazed at the minute detail this little country girl could include in her pictures. The faces seemed to jump off the page and speak. The last one reached out and grabbed her.

"My God, honey! I thought I was looking in a mirror! Is that me? Really? No kidding, may I take it over to the mirror in the back room?"

Emma nodded quickly and returned to her work. A few seconds later, Mercedes came out of the bedroom with a look of astonishment.

"It's one thing to draw this much detail, but how do you remember it so well? I mean, I wasn't even here when you did this."

"You just gotta' pay attention, Mercedes. There's stuff all around us that people don't see 'cause they not payin' attention."

"So wise for someone so young."

"You see the other pictures?"

"Yeah, I see them. We just got to get you some business in here. Who are these two people in this one?"

"That's Roger and his wife. They were looking for Audubon Park. I didn't know where it was."

"Aw, Emma—we got to take you there sometime. They got—"

"Mercedes," Emma interrupted. "Could you stay with me for the first couple of nights? I been trying not to think about it, but I can't help it. Brock told me there might be some bad things in the Quarter, and I didn't believe him. Then last night happened, and I'm just—"

"Emma, Mercedes will be here! Don't you never doubt that! You remember what I told you last night? We gonna' make this work."

Emma stopped her work and hugged Mercedes for several seconds. When she released her, Mercedes saw a look on her face that told no lies.

Emma learned one thing about New Orleans on that first night. The town never goes to sleep. The nights were still somewhat warm, and she was forced to open her one small window. Sounds of the street filtered in all night. Once she got up and saw Mercedes fast asleep on the floor of the studio, oblivious to the noise, *I guess I'll get used to it,* she thought.

The next day, Emma was up with the sun. She had started work in the studio, and Mercedes came out rubbing her eyes.

"You're going to spoil me, girl. Sleeping inside and takin' my time using a real bathroom again. Almost forgot what it felt like not to wonder who's coming in to chase me out."

Emma never looked up. "When do people start coming around?" she asked.

Mercedes was slow to answer. "About ten o'clock," she finally said. "When do you plan to open for business each day?"

"Whenever the others open," came the answer.

"Say, listen, don't let me disturb you, but I need to be going."

Emma realized she had been ignoring her friend. She stopped and hugged Mercedes again. "You'll be here again tonight, won't you? One more night, please? I'll be okay after that."

"One more, okay. I have to go tell some people where I was last night. They probably think I fell off a cliff somewhere."

"Say hi to Brock if you see him."

"Don't worry, something tells me he'll be by to check on you."

After Mercedes left, Emma returned to her work. Having lost track of time, she suddenly noticed the streets were filled with people, and two familiar faces were peering through the window. She raced to the door and propped it open. Roger and his wife stood smiling at the door, waiting to be invited in.

"Hi! Remember us?" she said.

"Come in, please. You can be my first customer ever. Did you find what you were looking for yesterday?"

"Well, we know where it is." said Roger. "What parts of New Orleans have you been in?"

"Well, I'm not sure. I've seen just parts of the French Quarter for now, but maybe—"

"Roger," his wife called. "Come look at this."

The man walked over to his wife and looked at the portrait of the two of them, both smiling and looking like typical tourists.

"Emma," she said. "How much do you want for this? It looks more like a black-and-white photo than a drawing. Is this what you typically do?"

"Yes, ma'am. I did these in a little hurry, but I can do better if I take my time. I just wanted to be ready to open."

"How much?" the woman asked.

Emma knew this was going to be a pivotal decision. She looked at the woman for several seconds, and as the woman was about to say something, Emma said calmly, "That one's ninety-five dollars." Roger swallowed hard and looked at his wife.

"You say you're new at this?" she asked.

"No, ma'am. I never said that. I've been doing this for a long time." Emma was amazed at the sound of her own words.

The wife looked at Emma closely and saw no room for negotiation.

"Done," Roger said. "Here's five twenties. Is there any tax with that?"

Emma didn't know what to answer. Finally, she said, "No, that's included." She handed the woman a five.

Roger and his wife thanked her very much and started to leave with their picture. Emma then thought of something. "Ma'am, you never told me what your name was."

"Emma, same as yours. Roger and Emma. From New York. Say, is there a frame shop around here?"

"Yes, ma'am. Down a few doors from here. I forget the name of it, but they do good work there. Real good. Everyone talks about how good it is. Yes, ma'am. Lots of people go there. Oh, tell them I sent you!"

They thanked Emma profusely, and as they left, she heard the wife say, "I thought she just moved here yesterday."

Emma was ecstatic. She ran into the bedroom, spread the cash on the bed, and examined the details of each crisp twenty-dollar bill.

Noise on the street caused her to turn and look. She gathered the money into a neat stack and found a safe place for it in her satchel.

The rest of the day was slow. She sold two more drawings for much less than she wanted. *Maybe the first one was just lucky*, she thought. Brock stopped by in the afternoon to see how she was doing.

"Brock, I made almost two hundred dollars today," she said excitedly when she saw him cross through the doorway.

"How much? Man, I haven't seen that much in a month!" He stopped and looked at her with a serious thought on his mind.

"What's wrong?" she asked.

"Nothing's wrong. You just shouldn't be here by yourself with that much cash around. You ever had a bank account?"

That afternoon, Brock convinced her to close up long enough to walk to the bank with him and open an account. She came out feeling like a professional businesswoman and was asking Brock all kinds of questions about banking.

"So, they pay me money to use my money, but I can come get it any time I want it?"

"Yep."

"But what if they done give it to someone else when I come to get it?"

"Then they give you someone else's. It doesn't matter, as long as it's the right amount."

"But what if everyone came at the same time and—"

"That's called a run on the bank, and you don't want to see that happen. But don't worry. That bank has lots of cash coming in and going out every day."

As they walked, Emma's studio came into view, and Emma reached for her keys. While he waited, Brock put his hand on the doorknob and turned. The door opened.

"I thought you locked this door."

"I did. I know I did."

"Let's check inside."

They both entered the small studio, Brock first, and in less than a minute, they determined that no one was there and nothing was missing.

"Brock, look at this." Emma pointed to the old mystery door near the front door. "It used to be painted shut. Now the paint's all cracked like it's been opened. What do you think happened?"

Brock tried to turn the door handle, but it was locked solid. The door did feel looser than the day before. "I don't know, Emma. I must admit, it does seem strange."

"Yeah. I know I locked the front door, and now this!"

"You know, we were talking a lot about your art and the money and going to the bank. I mean, maybe you meant to lock it and just forgot. And this other door; I don't know what's behind it, but you know, this entire city is built on a swamp, and things shift and settle all the time. Maybe that's what cracked the paint."

"Well, I'm going to keep an eye on it."

"I know you will, honey. You're getting to be a regular baptized citizen of New Orleans."

In Gretna, Mario Puccini picked up his house phone and dialed a number. He got an answer in two rings.

"Yeah, it's me. I want you to find out something. What's the going rate these days for a new baby?"

Chapter 20

Joshua Parker was up before the sun. He sat on the side of his bed in long underwear and rubbed his eyes. Things didn't focus too clearly at first, but he knew the world would be free of the cobwebs in a few minutes. The chill of the late fall was mild and barely penetrated the old house, but it made him shudder, nonetheless. His first step was to pull on coveralls and a denim jacket. Then he slipped on lace-up boots without tying them. He dragged his chamber pot out from under the bed, put the lid on it, and carefully headed for the back door. As every morning, his eyes moved toward the open bedroom door next to his, where he could see the empty but neatly made bed with the corner of the covers turned down, waiting.

The back steps were damp, and he grimaced slightly when he thought of the last time he took a spill going down to the yard. He stayed sore for days, and his clothes had smelled like the contents of the chamber pot. But at least he hadn't broken anything. Finished at the outhouse, he re-entered the kitchen and started a pot of coffee. The refrigerator wasn't empty, but not what he would call bountiful and overflowing. He had no trouble finding the bacon and eggs. Maybe he'd have sliced ham this morning instead of bacon. It had been kind of Mr. MacArthur to give him the custodial job at the school. The bottled spirits still beckoned to him, but he hadn't answered the call of the demon in two months. He was afraid the parents might object to the terms of his employment, but so far, no one had said a word. He'd been on the job eight weeks, and now he was even asked to help in the lunchroom. The older students would hush their conversations when he came near and continued in whispers after he passed by. But the younger children would wave and call to him when they saw him. He found himself looking forward to it. They called him Mr. Josh. The first day on the job, a delicate little girl had fallen on the walkway on her way to lunch.

Joshua hurried to kneel beside her and rubbed her skinned knee until the teacher in charge of the group arrived. Joshua's words brought her immediate comfort, and he implored the teacher to continue with the rest of the group. Tears dried, he held the child's hand and walked quickly to help catch up to her place in line. Ever mindful of parents' perceptions, Alton MacArthur saw the whole event and came to stand beside Joshua just as he released the child's hand and pointed her toward the door. *Her name's Brenda*, he had said to Mr. Mac. *She'll be fine. Just a little bump.* Joshua hooked his thumbs in his pockets and nodded approvingly of himself as he watched the children go inside.

That morning, he was mentally going over a list of tasks he would take care of that day at the school. However, he still had two hours before he had to be at work. His first priority, as he sat over his steaming coffee and the smell of the ham in the skillet, was something new for him. He pulled Marcia's bible down from where he was now keeping it on top of the refrigerator. This all started when he came across it two weeks ago, digging through an old box he found in a closet. She had bought it just a few months before she became ill and had spent hours each day turning pages. What he was originally looking for, he couldn't remember now, but it fell open at his feet, and Marcia's handwritten notes in the margin grabbed his heart like talons. That was the day, the first day, that Joshua had ever really prayed. It was as though he were someone else hearing Joshua Parker's words. All the fights, all the liquor, the hatred, and the betrayals became totally insignificant compared to the stark emptiness of that moment. Something from the past, maybe the walls of the house, which stood as silent witnesses, told him he had been at rock bottom and could go down no further, so he might as well turn around. He found one of Marcia's personal notes next to 1 Corinthians:13. The note read, 'Tell Josh about this one.' Apparently, she never got around to telling him. He found and read the words of the Apostle Paul to the Corinthians, words about love, and he recognized some of Marcia's favorite phrases. Now he knew where she got them. What else was there to learn about his dead wife? Surprising himself, he managed to make sense of chapter and verse and began reading each day. Some he couldn't understand, and he swallowed his pride and asked Alton MacArthur for help, but mentioned subtly that no one else need know about his question. That must have been the key because a few days after that, his job at the school seemed to expand to bring him in touch with the children. Alton MacArthur was a good man.

The coffee was good. The reading from the prophet Isaiah that morning didn't make sense, and the over-cooked sizzle of his breakfast on the stove suddenly caught his attention.

"Goddamn! Sorry," he said with a quick upward glance.

He cracked three eggs and had them on his plate quickly. Everything was gulped down in less than two minutes. He grabbed a piece of bread and wiped the egg yolk from the plate, then slurped down the last of his coffee. Quickly, he wiped off the stovetop and the table. All the dishes went into a pan of water to soak the rest of the day. He made sure the stove was turned off, then grabbed his jacket and hurried out the front door. The Home Economics room heater had not been working right for several days, and fixing it was almost beyond Joshua's abilities. A new part, suggested to him by Mr. Mac, had arrived, and Joshua was convinced he could make the repair. Usually, one day was largely like the next or like the one before. Today, however, was going to be long, he felt.

Amazingly, the heater repair turned out to be a five-minute job. The rest of his day was spent doing menial tasks, like unpacking new books, straightening up the locker rooms in the gymnasium, and fixing the lock on the maintenance shop door. At the end of the day, he crossed paths with Mr. MacArthur.

"Josh, you doing okay?"

"Yessir. Pretty light day today. I think I'll drain the oil from the tractor tomorrow. Won't be doin' any more mowing until spring comes. Don't like to see it set up all winter with old oil in it. Gets all gummy the first time you try to go and start it."

"You're doing a good job, Josh. I hope you can keep it up. The kids are really starting to like you."

"Well, I had my chance once to be something to look up to, but I guess I was feelin' too sorry for myself. Kids grow up, and you don't get no second chance. They leave and go—"

Alton could see the pain in his eyes. Unusual for Joshua Parker to show any pain, he thought.

After a moment of hesitation, Alton tried to change the subject. "I guess your idea about Halloween seemed to work pretty good this year. The school didn't have one broken window or a speck of graffiti anywhere on it. Everyone swears each year that it was kids from another school, but I don't know for sure. I talked to the sheriff, and they never can spare a full-time patrol just for the school. Remember how bad it was last year?"

"No sir, I don't guess I recall that. I wasn't paying much attention to nothing this time a year ago. Glad it turned out okay."

Less than three weeks before, Alton MacArthur had mentioned to Joshua how they had to be prepared for repairs to the school after each Halloween. After some thought, Joshua had offered a possible solution. To begin with, he spoke to some of the older boys after school one day as they waited for the second round of buses. First, two of them stopped to listen, and then the others followed suit when he said something that must have caught their attention. Within seconds, he had their thoughts captured. The old Joshua Parker charisma was still there.

That year, no ill fate came to the building during Halloween, and therefore, all high school boys were given an excused absence on the first day of deer season. The school board reluctantly approved the method, and Joshua got what he wanted: a set of newfound young friends.

"Now I got to think of something for the girls," said Alton. Joshua gave him a wink.

So, Joshua was making himself a hero and carving a niche that suited him very well. He eagerly looked forward to the days at work.

He came to work early and stayed late. But every evening, when his house came into sight until he dropped off to sleep, he was alone, a prisoner of his own guilt, thoughts, and memories. Sometimes, he spent his time on the back porch looking at the last glow of the sun well beneath the horizon. Other evenings, he walked the paths of the woods behind the house until it was almost too dark to see. His evening wanderings would sometimes take him to the old sawmill site, where he and Marcia had spent long evenings strolling around the mill pond where the water lilies bloomed. The aging mill was now a broken-down relic that simply stood as a decaying monument to something—Joshua didn't know what for sure. Maybe it was greed; perhaps it was just a passing era. It was as though the mill had a limited lease on Earth, and now the ground was consuming it, nourishing the tall weeds and young saplings that reached for the sky like young children craning their necks to watch a parade of clouds by day and stars by night. The mill once had a life, as did other things Joshua loved, and all that remained now was a rotting frame and his own stooped figure. Every evening, he went to bed expecting to die in his sleep, only to wake the next morning, eager to see the bright young faces at the schoolyard.

Chapter 21

Emma's unbridled personality, charm, and talent quickly became a magnet for tourists as well as for the local residents. When the weather was good, she enjoyed doing her work on the sidewalk outside her door, where people would stop and talk to her. It was her best marketing strategy, even if she hadn't intended it to be. But the weather was getting colder, even for New Orleans, as November had ended and December was slowly unfolding, one day at a time. Shortly after opening one morning, a familiar face came through the door.

"Good morning, good morning, good morning, my dearest Emma!" Carmen Carlucci was fulfilling his faithful Tuesday visit and always started off with the same greeting. Emma rose from her chair and gave him the same quick hug she always gave on Tuesday.

"I brought you some snapshots you can work on. This one is my friend Aaron. Great guy! Do anything for me! What do you think? Can you do something with these?" He handed her a group of photographs.

"What background does he want?" she asked.

"How about that one with the old house? You know, the plantation house with the tall columns and the big oak trees in front. You did one like that a couple of weeks ago."

"Sure. I can have this ready in about five days. I still got a bunch of others I haven't gotten to yet."

"No problem. Say, this is the best money-maker idea I ever heard of. Portraits from photos. That bunch you did for the Mennitos last week was terrific! I think your bayou background is the best, though."

"Mr. Carmen, could we hold off on any more for a while? I'm getting a little behind in my work, and I don't have anything to sell to folks that walk in."

Carmen looked closely at Emma. "You know, you do look a little tired. Maybe you need a day off. Tell you what. I'll tell Aaron that his pictures will be ready in two weeks. How's that?"

"Ah, that'll be fine, Mr. Carmen. But I'll have them done before that."

"I'm sure, but you won't be working on them tonight. The Carlucci family is having a Christmas party tonight, and we wouldn't be without our favorite French Quarter artist. Brock will come by to pick you up at about 7:30."

"Party? Gosh, I don't know. Will there be lots of people?"

"People? We don't do anything second class. The whole city will be there! Besides, you haven't been to the house in what, two, three weeks?"

"Is Mercedes coming?"

"Mercedes? She don't do parties. Hey, I gotta' go. See ya' tonight! Oh, I almost forgot. Here's the money for the last three you painted. Three hundred, right? Look at that; the dough just keeps rolling in for my girl!"

Christmas was indeed approaching, which boosted business tremendously. Emma had slowly developed a steady stream of customers, many from out of town. She insisted on staying open long hours while she sketched and painted well into the night after closing. Brock hadn't been by to see her in about a week. Mercedes came almost every day, though. Customers were sparse before 10:30 on any morning, so Mercedes usually stopped by around 8:00. Each day, she picked up the paper at the door even though Emma never ordered it. Mercedes told her that Carmen Carlucci probably thought he was doing her a favor by having it delivered. The newspaper headlines reminded everyone that it was Friday, the seventh day of December.

Emma had slept only a few hours the night before. Her eyes hurt, and she had awakened with a headache. Mercedes turned the page and folded the paper to a more manageable size. "Emma, you know what's important about today?"

Without looking up, she answered, "No, what?"

"Pearl Harbor Day, honey. Ever heard of that? Happened ten years ago today."

"I've heard of Pearl Harbor, but I can't remember why. Where is it?"

"Out in the Pacific. In Hawaii. Ring any bells?"

"Yeah, someone told me something about it. Can't think of who it was."

Mercedes spoke from behind the paper. "Pearl Harbor belongs to us, and the Japanese; they bombed it. Start of World War II."

Emma looked up from her painting and said, "Miss Flora told me about it. Her son died there. Must have been on December 7th."

"Probably was. They only attack it on one day. What brought that up between you and this Flora lady?"

"We were cleaning out his room, getting ready for—someone." Her voice trailed off.

Mercedes lowered the paper. "Huh? What's that? I wasn't listening too well."

Emma answered without looking at her. "Oh, we were just doing some housework, and she told me about him."

"Must have been sad."

"Yeah. His name was Todd. They didn't have any other kids. I wonder how the Ruckers are doing?"

"Call them and find out! You got a phone; Carmen pays the bills!"

"How do I get their number?"

"Just dial 'O' for the operator and tell them what you want. Tell them what town, what name, and what address. They'll get it for you."

"You mean they have, like, a book to look it up in?"

"Well, I guess they call the operator in whatever town you want, and they look it up."

"And then I can call that number?"

"Yep."

"I'm not sure about that."

"Why? I thought you wanted to know how they were doing?"

"Nobody knows where I'm at, and I don't want my papa to know 'cause he might come down here and—"

"And what? Honey, between me and Brock, we got this place covered. So many people keeping an eye on you, your papa wouldn't get within a city block of here without us knowing it. Call 'em if you want to! Call anybody you want!"

"I never used a phone long distance before."

"Well, you not going to learn sitting there. Pick it up and dial the operator."

"Okay, maybe when I'm finished here."

Mercedes rose and started toward the door. "You know, Brock said something the other day that made me think. You been at this for a bunch of weeks. You open seven days a week. Longer hours than anyone else in the Quarter. You making money hand over fist— got new maternity clothes, got money in the bank, got all kinds of new friends, but you not seen much of New Orleans at all! Honey, you working too hard! You need to relax and play a little. Got circles under the eyes. You gonna' make that baby born all nervous! What say we plan a day out once in a while? It's allowed, you know. When you work for your own self, you make your own rules, right?"

"Yeah, probably right. Carmen was by this morning. He invited me to a Christmas party at his house tonight."

"Oh, yeah! I heard about the parties at the Carlucci house. What you gon' wear?"

"I don't know. I just found out about it a few minutes ago. I'm not sure I want to go. All those people I won't know. I think I'd rather just get some sleep."

"Not go? You can't miss this. Carmen, he take care of you, don't worry. Brock probably be there, too. But Carmen gonna' have him busy running errands. But he be there. Hey, close up at lunch time. Go buy yerself something to wear. Girl, you got money!"

"Well, maybe."

"Okay, you think about it. I'll see you later. And don't forget what I said about the phone."

Emma counted to ten after Mercedes left and reached for the phone. She dialed the zero.

"This is the operator." An immediate flash of the Baton Rouge bus station came back to her. "Hello, this is the operator," the voice said again. "May I help you?"

"Uh, yes. I don't know how to do this, but I want to call someone, and I don't have his number."

"What city, please?"

Emma's heart thumped hard to think that this might actually work.

"Ma'am, are you there?"

"Uh, yeah—yes, I'm here. He lives in Houston."

"One moment."

Emma quickly went to the window and shut the curtains, then turned the sign on the door to 'closed'.

She listened as a series of operators answered across the state and into Texas. Her New Orleans operator was calm and patient. After a few minutes, she heard the voice say, "Go ahead, ma'am. I have the Houston operator on the line."

"Hello?"

"Yes, how can I help you?"

"I need to call someone, and I don't know his number. He lives in Houston."

"Yes?"

"Well, can you help me?"

The operator snapped, "Does this someone have a name?" The voice had a bite to it.

Her head was throbbing. "I'm sorry. I'm a little nervous doing this. His name is Hugh Giles. He lives with his parents."

"First name?"

"Like I said, Hugh."

"Ma'am, how old is Hugh? You said he lives with his parents? I doubt the phone would be listed in his name."

"He's seventeen."

"Sorry, It's probably under his parents' name. Do you have that?"

"No, I don't know his dad's name, but—"

"I'm afraid I can't help you, then."

"Operator, I'm sorry I'm makin' it hard, but I can't help it. It took me a long time to decide to do this. I never had a phone until a few weeks ago. I've never lived in Houston. This is my first long-distance call, and I need some help, really. Oh wait, I remember! His grandfather is Jerome Giles. Can you find that?"

"One moment, please." Emma shifted the phone to the other ear. "I'm sorry, that number is unlisted."

"You mean it's not there?"

"No, ma'am, it's here. I just can't give it out."

Emma began shaking her head in a panic. "What am I going to do?"

"Well, you've got to give me something to go on."

"I know. I don't know what else to tell you. He's Hugh Giles! I don't know what else to tell you!" Emma felt her chance slipping away.

"Well, I'm sorry. I can't do anything with what little you've given me, so—"

"No!" Emma screamed. "Please listen! I left home and came all the way down here to New Orleans because Papa was mad, and Hugh had to go away, and now the baby's coming, and Hugh doesn't know where I am, and I'm doing all that I can! So, don't tell me you can't help me!"

A knock came at the door.

She turned away from the phone and shrieked, "Read the sign! I'm closed!" Directing herself back to the operator, she screamed, "No! I'm not telling you I'm closed! I'm talking to someone who can't read a sign! Now start looking under Giles, any Giles! Give me every number in the book if you have to!"

What seemed like an eternity went by. Emma was exhausted by her own outburst and had a strange feeling of being someone else, someone she had never known.

A voice finally returned to the receiver. "This is the supervisor. What's the problem?"

"Ma'am, I'm really sorry. I didn't mean to yell like that. I just feel like I'm so far away, and no one will help me."

"Okay, you're looking for a number. Giles, right? Did you know there are about fifty numbers under the name of Giles? There's also several businesses under that name."

"His daddy works for an oil company."

"Giles oil?"

"I guess so, he never told me."

"Let's see. Here's the main number. Why don't you write it down, and then I'll connect you."

Emma's heart was in her throat as she heard the phone ring in Houston. A woman answered.

"Giles Oil, how may I help you?" There was a slight Hispanic accent in her voice.

"I'm trying to get in touch with Hugh Giles. Is this the right number?"

"Mr. Giles is in school today. He doesn't usually get calls on this number. May I take a message? I'll see that he gets it."

"Well, I'm a friend of his, and I'm just trying to get in touch with him."

"Yes, he's in school. May I say who called?"

Emma felt a small gasp escape from her own voice. It was as though Hugh was standing right beside her.

She stammered, "Ha … How can I get a message to him?"

"The home number is unlisted, but I know young Hugh. What a nice boy! I can give him your phone number."

"You know Hugh? How is he?" Her excitement was almost overwhelming.

"Hugh is fine, just fine. He came by my house last night. He's been dating my daughter for a few weeks. Lovely couple. I'm sorry, what is your name?"

Emma felt like she had fallen from a cliff. She sat in silence until the woman on the phone brought her back to reality.

"Ma'am, are you still there? Ma'am?"

"Uh, I'm sorry. I was thinking of something else; I—Yes, let me give you my number. My name is Emma Parker. I'm in New Orleans." She read the number off the dial of the phone.

"Oh, nice city. I was there once. Okay, I'll be glad to pass this along. By the way, my name is Rosa Dominguez."

"Thank you, Mrs. Dominguez. Oh, before you hang up, what is your daughter's name? You said she was going out with Hugh."

"Yes, I did. Her name is Angelina. Why do you ask?"

"I, uh, just wanted to know. So, thank you again. You'll tell him I called?"

"I'll see that he gets your message. So nice talking to you."

Emma held the phone close to her chest and squeezed her eyes tightly. The tears still seeped through.

Another knock came at the door. Ignoring it, Emma slowly walked to the bedroom and closed the door behind her. She lay on her bed staring at the ceiling. Should she try to call Lavenia? Or Flora? She suddenly felt very tired.

A tapping came from the window. She rose up and looked at the clock. It was almost eleven o' clock. Had she fallen asleep? The tapping continued. She rose and barely parted the curtains but saw no one. Leaving the bedroom and crossing the studio floor in her bare feet, she stepped out onto the sidewalk and peered around the corner. Brock's car was parked in front, but Brock was nowhere in sight. She felt groggy, and the sidewalk was cold.

Back inside, she opened the studio curtains and changed her sign to read 'open'. A few minutes later, Mercedes appeared.

"Hey, where were you? I was banging on the door, trying to get your attention."

Mercedes' entrance caught Emma in the middle of a yawn. "Yeah, I'm sorry. I was asleep. I heard you at the window, though. When I came out, you were gone, but I saw Brock's car."

"Wasn't me at the window. When did you hear it? What did it sound like?"

"You know, just tapping on the glass. It was about five minutes ago. I wonder who it was."

"Well, I got here almost an hour ago. I couldn't rouse you up, so I left. Looks like you could use a cup of coffee. What do you say we step out for a while? You buying?"

Emma didn't speak but gave Mercedes her answer by pulling on her coat and taking a scarf off the hanger. "Let's go," she said quietly.

"Better put some shoes on, girl."

As they walked slowly to the end of the block, Mercedes looked at her closely. "You okay? You're kinda' quiet. Maybe not completely awake yet, huh?"

"No, I just got lots to think about. Time is going by too fast, Mercedes. I don't know what things are going to be like in a few months."

"Hey, who does? But me and Brock take care of you, you know that. I don't know what you're worried about."

"I want to take care of myself. You folks are wonderful to do all these things for me, but I still haven't figured out why you're doing it."

"A lot of it be Carmen Carlucci's idea. Maybe he wants to spread his investments around. Maybe you're some sort of tax deduction or something. I don't know. I'm just glad he does it. I saw him just a while ago, in fact."

"Yeah - you know, I don't think I really want any coffee. Let's go back. I've had a couple of ideas I want to work on."

"Ideas?"

"Drawings … It's what I do, remember?" She gave Mercedes a big-eyed look.

"Yeah, sure. No problem. You seem to be feeling better. Want some company for a while?"

They both had turned and were halfway back to the studio when Mercedes stopped short and pulled Emma behind a parked car.

"What? What is it?"

"Look up there. At your studio. Front door's wide open. I know you locked it. I saw you lock it."

Emma peered over the car and saw nothing at first, then a man emerged carrying a suitcase. It seemed heavy from the way he carried it. She concentrated on watching the man and then realized that Mercedes had slipped to the other end of the parked car they were crouched behind. Emma tried to say something to her, but she held her hand up.

"I think there's two of them," she whispered loudly. "The other one's still inside."

At that moment, the other man came out carrying a large set of keys. He locked the door and followed the first man, who had stopped at a car a short distance away. The trunk of the car was open. They closed it, and both men got in the car and pulled out into the traffic. The car crept along the street straight toward Emma and Mercedes' hiding place. When they got close enough, Emma noticed a look of recognition on Mercedes' face.

"Those the same two who cornered you when you first came here. Remember that night? Me and my whistle?"

"Mario Puccini's guys?"

"That's them. I don't know their names, but I don't like the looks of this."

"Mercedes, we got to call the police. Maybe they were after me again. You think?"

"Let's go look first."

Emma fished out her keys as they both moved at a slow trot toward the door. She opened the lock, and Mercedes gently nudged her back. The door swung open slowly and nothing happened. Carefully, they entered, Mercedes first. Everything was just as they had left it. After a full minute of silence, Emma finally spoke.

"What is going on here? You know, this isn't the first time something like this has happened."

"I know. Once before."

"Well, I need to tell you something." Her face told Mercedes there was more to it. "In the last month, I thought I forgot to lock the door again. Maybe I really did lock it. Like, a couple of times."

"You mean you coulda' had visitors before and didn't tell me?"

"But like I said - I thought it was my fault. I wasn't going to go looking for you just to tell you I *thought* I left my door unlocked. You'd think I was kinda', I don't know - I just decided it wasn't anything."

"Did you tell Brock?"

"No."

"So, what do you think now?"

"I think this whole thing's crazy! Those two guys know where I live now, and I don't want to stay here!"

"I need to check something. Hang on a minute. I think it's time to check this mystery door." Mercedes pulled a small gadget from her dress pocket and fumbled for a moment with the front closet door. The lock gave way, and she opened the door an inch, then two."

"What do you see?" Emma asked.

"Too dark."

"Well, open it up!"

"Shush a minute, girl. There might be someone dead in there! You never know with these guys."

"Dead? In here?"

"No, I meant something - you know what I meant."

"Well, whatever you meant, the smell's getting worse."

"So, what did you find?" a voice behind them asked.

Both women gasped and whirled. Brock stood in the doorway. "What are you two snoops up to? How'd you get that door open?"

Emma pointed at Mercedes, who said carefully, "I got my ways."

"Okay, so we got it open. Let's see what's in there." He stepped forward and stuck his head inside. "Phew! Smells stale in here."

Brock disappeared through the door, and a light immediately flicked on. The two women carefully ventured in and saw only a small, empty room. The three of them walked around inspecting every corner, feeling the walls, shading their eyes from the glare of the bare hanging bulb. While Emma and Brock continued to look, Mercedes stopped abruptly at one point and cocked her ear toward the door they had just come through. She quietly stepped back to the door and spoke in a hushed tone to someone who had just entered the studio. Craning her neck to see, Emma caught a glance of Hondo just as Mercedes finished her conversation with him. Brock had not noticed the temporary distraction.

"Well, I don't guess there be anything here," Mercedes said quite positively.

"No, I think you're right," said Brock with a shrug.

"But -" Emma was about to interject and felt a concealed pinch on her arm from Mercedes.

"What's that?" Brock asked.

"Nothing," Emma answered. "Nothing."

"Hey, maybe now you can expand your studio. Look at all this extra space!"

They walked back out into the studio and stood for a moment, not sure what to say next. Then Brock exclaimed, "Oh, I almost forgot. What I came over for was to tell you we're getting you a new phone. That one you've got now has too much static on it. The last time you talked to Mr. Carlucci, he said he had a hard time hearing you."

"When will they do that? Emma asked.

"Probably today. Mr. Carlucci has a way with the phone company. By the way, he said he's concerned that you don't answer your phone when he calls. He tried a couple of times."

"It never rang," Emma said. In the whole time I've been here - oh wait, it did ring one time, and it was a wrong number."

Brock looked at the face of the dial and pulled a slip of paper out of his wallet. "No wonder, he said. "This number, the one on the phone, is the wrong number. Or maybe not, I don't know. Let me go to the pay phone across the street and call you. See if this one rings."

In about a minute, the phone rang. Emma picked it up.

"Hello? Brock?"

"Yeah. This number I've got in my wallet is the right one. I still don't know why Mr. Carlucci couldn't get it to ring. Maybe someone gave him the one on the phone dial. I got this one in my pocket from the phone company."

Brock quickly returned in a few seconds and found Mercedes and Emma looking at him blankly. "What?" he asked. "So, we got a wrong number. We'll fix it."

They both nodded and politely smiled. Feeling he had missed something, Brock hesitated, then clapped his hands together and said, "Hey, I got to be going. Let me know how the new phone works out."

As Brock started to leave, Mercedes put her arm on his shoulder and followed him to the door. She held it open for a moment and waved to him as he headed for his car. She closed the door quietly, then quickly turned to Emma and gripped her by the shoulders.

"Honey, we got to do something!"

"I know! I gave Rosa Dominguez the wrong number!"

"Who? What are you talking about?"

"Angelina's mother!"

"I don't know who or what you're talking about, but we got to get you out of here!"

"Move? Why?"

"I don't mean just move. I mean gone—like outa' town!"

"Mercedes, what are *you* talking about?"

"Did you see me talking to Hondo?"

"Yeah, I did."

"Well, he said that he saw Carmen Carlucci talking to those two earlier this morning."

"Which two?"

"The two guys that came in here! He knows them."

"He knows them? Brock beat the snot out of one of them, remember?"

"That was then. This is now. Carmen and Mario got something going on. Those guys work for Mario, and Mario does work for Carmen. Business is business. We just got to figure out what."

"Mercedes, I don't believe any of this. Mr. Carlucci wouldn't do anything to hurt me. He looks after me really good. I got more important things to worry about."

"Like what?"

"I got to call Rosa Dominguez back when I get the right number off that new phone."

"Who is this woman you're talking about?"

"She knows Hugh. She works for Giles Oil in Houston. She's going to give my number to Hugh."

"Look, honey, time to grow up. You need to learn something about men. You know, some men point it, and some men follow it. I think your Hugh done pointed it and then looked the other way."

"Pointed what? Mercedes, you don't make sense sometimes. You act like all men are bad. It's not true. Hugh's a good man."

"Okay, if that's what you want to think. Right now, we got other things to think about."

"And Brock has been just great to me."

"That's right. They taking real good care of you. That's because you make a good front for something. We just got to figure out what it is." Mercedes began to pace the floor and talk to herself. "Let's see, okay, don't hurry. We got time. What would they want in here?

By the way, when Brock walked in that mystery room yonder, did you see how quick he found the light switch - in a dark room?”

“Mercedes, I thought you knew Brock really well. I thought you two were good friends. I don’t understand.”

“Yeah, I know Brock. Like I know a lot of other people. I know enough to be careful. I gotta’ admit, he had me fooled. He comes around me; I just tell him what I know he wants to hear, same as I do with Carmen.”

They walked back into the mystery room and started looking closer. Silently, they looked carefully at every inch of wall for anything that might be another door or another clue. After several minutes, Emma said, “I don’t even know what I’m looking for.”

“Maybe something like this.” Mercedes pointed to a small white mound of something in the corner on the floor. She moistened her finger and lightly touched it. It was white and powdery. Carefully, she barely touched it to her tongue then spat. “Here, try this. Stick your tongue out.” She touched the white powder to Emma’s tongue quickly as though it was red hot. “Now spit it out. Feel that tingle?”

Mercedes walked back into the studio, with Emma following. The older woman was pacing the floor again, trying to think. She suddenly turned sharply and said, “Don’t ever forget that taste, girl. And stay as far away from it as you can! People get killed on account of that stuff!”

“What is it? I still don’t understand.”

“Of course you don’t! Where would you run into something like this in that little town of yours? It’s dope, honey. They must be bringing it into town and needing a place to hide it. I see how it all fits now. Who would suspect a little pregnant country girl with an art shop? And I’ll bet Carmen got it all set up, so Mario takes the blame if anyone gets caught. Carmen, you a real slick one!”

“Why would people get killed over it? What’s it for?”

“Folks get high on it, you know - like drunk, only different. Then they keep doin’ it, and then they can’t quit. Orum, my man, he got caught making a bad deal with some folks wanting to sell the stuff. They cut his throat. He died right there on the sidewalk."

The look of terror on Emma's face surprised even Mercedes. She stopped pacing and put her arm around Emma's shoulder. "I'm sorry if I scared you, honey. Didn't mean to, but you need to know what's going on around you. I remember the day Orum died like it was yesterday."

Mercedes sat in one of the two chairs in the studio. "Okay, we got to plan this right," she said. If they see you leaving, they gon' wonder about something. Okay. I got it. Here's what we gonna' do."

"No, wait. I want to talk to Brock first."

"Emma! You don't know what you doin'!"

"I know I trust Brock. If those guys were up to no good, then Brock's gonna' say something to Mr. Carlucci. That'll put a stop to it."

"Emma, you not making sense."

"It's perfectly plain to me. I'm not going anywhere. If something else happens, I'll think about it. Right now, I'm going to call Brock."

Emma called the Carlucci house and left word for Brock to call her. The rest of the day, she threw herself into her work until hunger pangs took control around mid-afternoon. As she walked two blocks to a small cafe where she ate, the spirit of the Christmas decorations in the French Quarter were almost overwhelming. The night before, she had ventured to the other side of Canal Street and found the Roosevelt Hotel. Someone had told her that the lobby at Christmas time would create an image no one could forget. She had only stepped a few feet inside and was completely captured by the tunnel-like appearance formed by brightly lit branches that curved over the central walkway and reflected off the floor. The chandeliers looked like a person could live in one because of their size. The entire scene seemed to have its own heartbeat. Classical Christmas music played in the background. She slowly entered and discovered a different scene around every corner. Figures of angels floated above her, suspended from the ceiling. The center of the lobby was host to the biggest Christmas tree she had ever seen. Words seemed to come to her lips so silently, yet with such clarity, *"Mama, can you see what I'm seeing?"* She was all alone, but what her heart felt and her eyes saw told her she was loved. By whom, she wasn't sure, but the feeling was warm and visceral.

Sparse as they may have been, Christmas times at home had a warm, sensitive spot in her heart. Her father would always let her pick out a small tree from the woods, and sober or not, he would manage to cut it down and drag it home. When it reached the back porch, Joshua's holiday obligation was done. Emma would have a bucket full of sand in the corner of the living room, which became the base for the tree. Colored ribbons and popcorn on thread, placed and rearranged as best as a young girl could do by herself, was the extent of the tree trimmings. In New Orleans, the whole city seemed to pulse with blinking lights and music from every corner. Street performers wore Santa Claus hats. Some had small bells on their feet, which added a bawdy holiday flavor to their dance.

The cafe was dim and smoke-filled. Plastic holly branches in vases adorned each table. As soon as Emma had found her usual corner, a man's figure with a familiar walk came across the floor toward her. Brock's voice was subdued.

"I heard you tried to call me," he said.

"Yeah, I did. You eat yet?"

"No, I thought I'd wait for you. I knew you'd be by sooner or later. You shouldn't skip meals. That baby's as hungry as you are."

"I had lots on my mind."

"Is that why you called me?"

"Yeah. Brock, am I safe where I am? Does Mr. Carlucci know what happened today?"

"He knows. What I'm curious about is what do you think happened today?"

"Brock, you weren't there for the whole thing. Some guys have been getting into my studio whenever I'm out. They seem to know when I'm not there. I think they're watching me. How else would they know?"

"You have a point. Mr. Carlucci is aware of that very thing as of today. But what do you think they were up to? Is there any clue that you haven't told me?"

"Brock, I haven't held anything back. Mercedes says—Brock, you don't think she had anything to do with this, do you?"

"No, I don't. But she a very perceptive woman. She may have not told you everything she suspects. What'd she tell you?"

"She wanted me to move today. But I told her I wasn't going to let this scare me. All my customers know where I am. I'd have to, like, start all over, wouldn't I? Besides, I knew you would be around. That's what I told her."

"Did she say where you should go to?"

"No, but she was pretty upset when I said I wasn't. I think she's really worried."

"She's a mother hen. I haven't seen her so protective over anyone as she is with you." Brock reached across and gave Emma a gentle pinch on her face. "Okay, I'll tell you this. Mr. Carlucci is also upset about these guys coming in and out of your place. Tomorrow, we change all the locks. Then, we also get a crew to clean out that empty room, and your studio will suddenly double in size. Well, almost. We've also got more people keeping an eye on you. If you start seeing new faces on your block, don't worry. That's probably our guys." He paused and looked at her. "Feel better now?"

Emma rubbed her eyes and nodded. The waitress saw Brock look up at her and then approached with menus.

After they ate, Brock walked her back to the studio. At the door, he held her face in both hands and kissed the top of her head.

"I'll be here to pick you up tonight for the party, okay?"

"Yeah, sure," she said softly.

Once Emma was inside, Brock walked to the next intersection, where a silent figure in a police uniform met him in the shadows at the entrance to an alley.

"So, what did she decide?" the officer asked.

"She's staying."

"What does she know?"

"Nothing. And she doesn't need to know."

"Don't worry. We'll keep an eye on her."

A pair of ears behind a stack of garbage cans listened intently to the conversation.

Two weeks went by. Customer traffic through the little studio was at a peak. Emma had decided the only way to be part of the seasonal atmosphere was to decorate the studio. She put lights around the window with green garland and a big wreath in the center. Her pictures took on more of a festive slant. She had decided to keep the mystery door propped open permanently to give her more room to keep her works on display. Following Mercedes' advice, she set up a place to sit at a small table near the front door to keep an eye on anyone who may try to browse a little too seriously and leave with something tucked under a coat or a jacket.

At noon, near the end of the week, Mercedes came by at her usual time. Emma could almost set a watch by Mercedes' schedule. Today, however, there was a look of concern on her face.

"You seen Brock?" she asked.

Emma didn't look up but just shook her head.

"I'm worried," said Mercedes.

"Why? You always told me not to worry so much," Emma answered vacantly.

"Carmen don't even know where he is. Hmm."

Upon hearing this, Emma laid her brush down and turned toward her friend. "What do you think happened? That's not like Brock to just disappear." Emma pondered for a few seconds, then said with resolve, "Yeah—but you know how Brock is. He's probably run off for a day with some old girlfriend. Probably something like that. He'll be back. You want to go get some lunch?"

Mercedes just nodded in agreement, rubbing her chin.

The two walked in silence toward Emma's now habitual eating establishment. She noticed how distracted Mercedes seemed.

"You really worried about him, aren't you?"

"Uh-huh."

"Well, he'll sure have some explaining to do when he gets back, won't he? Say, you want to eat some place different today?"

Hearing no answer, Emma looked up toward Mercedes just in time to see her break away and cross the street. A man in an old army-issue jacket waited for her on the corner. Emma saw Mercedes lend an ear to the man, then jerk her head up and look directly at Emma. She said something in reply to her informant and came back toward Emma in a hurry.

"No time for lunch, honey. We got things to do. Remember what I told you a few days ago? I told you that you got to move. Now, I mean it."

Emma gave her undivided attention to Mercedes.

"They found Brock. He was floating face down in the river under one of the piers. One bullet hole in the back of his head. C'mon, we got to pack you out of here."

Emma's scream was muted by Mercedes' quick hand over her mouth.

Later that day, Emma went to the bank as she usually would. Her transaction was different on this day, however. That night, with Mercedes's help, she put all her things into a variety of containers: paper sacks, pillowcases, a laundry bag, anything they could think of. Starting shortly before 2 A.M., a succession of silent figures passed by the studio at regular intervals, and each picked up a single parcel waiting outside the front door. When one parcel was gone, the studio door opened quietly, and another replaced it. Within two hours, the place was empty. In the darkest hours of the morning, the two women left the studio and locked it for the last time. They walked several blocks without saying a word until they reached the bus station. Behind the station in a narrow alley, all of Emma's belongings sat neatly boxed up in two large, old trunks and one suitcase. All three items looked like they had been residences for a million rats, but they each were held together in one piece—with a little help from some tape, some twine, and a couple of old belts. Emma stood at the ticket counter, feeling the weight of the first real crossroads in her life. The first outbound bus that morning left at six o'clock. Mercedes stood at the corner, tearfully waving good-bye.

Oscar Carter was relaxing after a full supper from Lavenia's kitchen when the phone rang. Lavenia was at the other end of the house, so Oscar got up and answered it.

"Hello. Say what? If—but—who is this? Who? Where are you? Where?"

Joshua Parker shuffled through his house, mumbling to himself. The breakfast dishes still sat in cold water from that morning. Supper dishes and utensils still lay scattered on the table. He stared at them as though he could wish them clean and stacked. The phone rang.

"Yeah, who's this? Oscar? Do you know what time it is?" He listened and replied, "So go ahead and tell me! What's the big secret?"

The line went dead.

Joshua mumbled to himself. "Where in the hell does Oscar think I'm gonna' be this time of night? If he's got something to say, just say it. That's what the damn telephone is for! Naw, he's got to come over here to tell me something and see me trying to clean up the kitchen, then he'll go back and tell that wife of his, then she'll be coming over here, worrying about me. Just a few damn dirty dishes."

The fire in the old fireplace had burned down to just hot coals while he had dozed off in his rocking chair. The harsh ring of his phone had awakened him with a start. Some weeks ago, he decided he needed some way to keep up with the outside world. So, the phone seemed a logical decision. Besides, Mr. MacArthur suggested he get one, in case he was needed to fix something at the school. In return, the school board had paid for the installation. When it first rang tonight, he hadn't known what it was; it rang so seldom. Being half groggy with sleep hadn't helped either. It had been Oscar calling to make sure Joshua was at home. He had something to tell him and insisted on telling him in person. Said it might upset him. These days, nothing could upset Joshua.

He had time, so he filled a kettle with water and put it on the stove to heat. The scraps he saved for his new four-legged companion, Butch. Butch had appeared on the schoolyard about two months before, obviously abandoned as a half-grown puppy. From the looks of him, Joshua figured he was about six or seven months old. Butch had followed the schoolchildren around the playground and tried to go with them into one of the classrooms. In fact, he tried for the better part of a week to follow the children anywhere they went. The lunchroom staff started feeding him outside the back door until finally, Mr. MacArthur asked Joshua if he could remedy the situation. Butch came home on a Friday afternoon, and by Monday, Joshua had a makeshift pen built to keep him locked up during the day. At eight months, he weighed about thirty pounds, and Joshua aimed to make a squirrel-hunting dog out of him. He'd have to wait until next year, though. The season would be over in a couple of months, and Butch was still too playful to be serious about training for anything.

"Butch! Boy, did I forget to feed you? Here we go, cornbread and beans with a little bacon juice." He watched the pup bouncing on the floor. "Awright, I'll slice off some of this salt pork and throw it in there."

Butch started gulping his leftovers down before Joshua could put the bowl on the floor.

"You know, you are one privileged son-of-a-bitch. You are the first dog I ever let come into my house. Maybe I ought to get you one of them charity jobs. You can't read or write, and all you do is sleep, eat, and crap in the yard. You ain't worth a shit, but you're all I got."

Oscar never could sneak up on anyone. After years in the sawmill, his voice boomed but sounded perfectly normal to him. The driver's door of his old car uttered a loud squawk, which Joshua barely heard. Butch barked at the sound of it.

"Mr. Josh! You home? It's me, Oscar!"

"Who else? Of course, I'm home! Didn't you just call me?"

"Yessuh. Mr. Josh, could you come out here? I need to talk to you."

"Well, come on in! I'm just cleaning up the supper dishes."

"Nawsuh, I need to talk to you out here."

"What the hell? Since when do you need to talk to me on the front porch when you know -? Joshua peered out the screen door and flipped on the porch light. Oscar stood in the middle of the yard with his arms folded. His face had a worried look.

"Okay," Joshua said from the porch. "I'm out here, and it's cold. What is it?"

"Out here in the car. C'mon, I'll show you." He turned around and looked at Joshua, who hadn't budged from the porch. "Mr. Josh, I ain't gon' say it again. You need to see what come in the mail today, but don't be upset." The tone of his voice now had Joshua's temper a little aroused, but it was overcome by curiosity.

Joshua walked toward the gate, and Oscar stepped aside to let him pass. The two men stared at each other for a moment, then Joshua went through the gate. "In the back seat, there. Go ahead. Look what come in the mail!"

The interior of the old Plymouth was only partially illuminated from the porch light, and Joshua noticed the window was rolled down. He approached the car and took one more look back at Oscar, who motioned him to look inside. As he stooped over to get closer, a face—Marcia's face—slowly emerged from the shadow on the opposite side.

"Papa, I missed you."

Chapter 22

Joshua stood looking amazed into the face of someone resurrected. As she slid across the seat to get out of the car, he stepped back to give her room and tried to quickly sort out his thoughts. She stood in front of him in a tan trench coat and silk scarf around her neck with minimal but tastefully applied makeup. He was still dumbfounded and unbelieving of his own eyes. Gently, he took both of her hands and, like he had never seen such beauty before, spread her arms and looked at every inch of her, from her carefully styled hair down to her brown leather pumps. It took a full minute for him to find his voice.

"My dear Emma," he said in a whisper. "Just look at you!" his voice got louder. "Look at you! My baby girl! Where have you been? Thank you, God! Oscar, thank you so much for bringing her home."

Oscar declared, "All I done was pick her up at the bus station, Mr. Josh. She called me from there, and then I called you. I was gonna' tell you on the phone, but I figured a surprise would be better." Oscar was beaming at the sound of his own words.

Joshua didn't know what to say next and shifted his gaze nervously between Emma and Oscar. Finally, he said, "Well, let's don't just stand here in the cold. C'mon inside, both of you."

He wrapped his arm around Emma's shoulder and walked toward the front door with Oscar close behind. Once inside, Emma took the scarf from around her neck and unbuttoned her coat. Beneath it, Joshua saw a finely tailored gray maternity dress and jacket with a delicate white blouse. Never had he seen such finery on his daughter.

"Here, let me take your coat," he said with enthusiasm. "Are you hungry?"

"Maybe later, Papa. I just need to sit down for a while. It's been a long day."

Oscar remained by the door, watching the two Parkers come to know each other again.

"Oscar, come on in and sit with us."

"No suh, I better be going. Uh, Miss Emma, we still got yo' stuff in the car."

"Oh, I can't forget that," she replied. "Here, I'll help you."

"You sit. Mr. Josh and me, we git it."

The two men walked back out to the car, and as they passed through the gate, Oscar looked back at the house and said to Joshua, "Don't she look good, Mr. Josh?"

Joshua only opened his mouth and shook his head in disbelief, not saying a word. He looked back at the house, then at Oscar, and wiped his eyes.

Oscar opened the trunk of the car, and Joshua's eyes got big. "She came home with all that? Oscar, where has she been?"

"New Orleans, Mr. Josh. But let her tell you about it. She done good down there. Lavenia can't wait to come over tomorrow and see her." He stopped and asked, "Would that be okay?"

"Oscar, I've never kept you from my house before. I'm not going to start now. Lord, that stuff looks heavy."

Emma heard the men coming up the porch steps. "Papa, just leave the trunks on the front porch for tonight. All I need inside is my suitcase."

"Open the door for us, Emma. We'll put this is the other room for now. We can't just leave stuff like that out on the porch."

"That's right," Oscar chimed in. "We not just po' white trash."

Hearing Oscar's words, Joshua rolled his eyes and almost stumbled.

Back into the living room, Joshua said, "This is going to take two trips. Be right back."

Both men went outside again. As they were lifting the second trunk and the suitcase out of the car, Oscar asked, "Mr. Josh, you two gonna' be okay?"

Joshua straightened up and looked at him, puzzled. It took him a second, but then his face became firm. "Oscar, you're a good man for worrying about us. We'll be fine. I'm so glad to get her home, I can't be angry about any of this."

In the dim light, Joshua saw Oscar's broad grin full of white teeth. They deposited the last of Emma's things, and Oscar bade them good-bye. Emma walked him to the door and gave him a big hug before he left.

After the door closed, Joshua and Emma sat on opposite sides of the room, Emma on the couch and her father in a chair. Emma folded her hands in her lap and said, "Where should I begin?"

"It doesn't matter to me. We can just pretend you left yesterday. I just couldn't believe my eyes when I seen you in that car."

"Papa, we can't pretend about anything. I've been gone, and I'm going to have a baby. We can't ignore that."

"Okay, tell me where you been."

"Not like this. You come over here and sit beside me, and I will tell you the whole story."

Joshua realized he was keeping a safe distance and almost tripped over his own feet in his haste to get to his daughter's side. Once seated, he took her hand and said, "Before you start, I want you to know how much I missed you. I do love my little girl very much." He slowly reached across, and she leaned toward him. Arms around each other for several moments, they both wept. He sat back, wiped his eyes on his sleeve, and added, "But you talk different. What happened?"

"Papa, it seems we've both changed. What is that over there? A telephone? I heard Oscar saying something about calling you. When did we get that?"

"Well, I knew we could afford it. Uh, I got me a real good, steady job. And I didn't want to be out of touch, in case somebody found, uh ..." his voice started to crack.

"In case someone found me?"

He simply nodded in agreement, squinting his eyes and blinking back more tears.

"Papa, I'm back. So, stop worrying." She gave him another quick squeeze. "So, when I left back in September, I caught the bus to New Orleans. I had no idea what I was going to do there, but that's where I went…"

An hour later, Joshua sat looking astonished and exhausted from listening.

"You spent the first night in a cemetery?"

"I had some good people looking after me."

"So, all of them new clothes in those trunks come from selling artwork? Well, I think that's wonderful!"

"You sure you're not mad? You once told me I couldn't even do my drawings, much less sell them."

"It reminded me too much of your mother. I've been trying to pretend all these years that she wasn't dead. I've been livin' in a dreamland, honey. A drunken dreamland."

"The house looks nice. You must be taking good care of yourself. You mentioned a job."

"Yeah, I—I done okay, I guess. Yeah, Mr. Mac give me this job at the school. Same one I had when you left, only it's full-time now. I got to know lots of the kids. I think they really like me. Most days, I work in the lunchroom, and that's where I see 'em." He nodded and smiled at his own words.

Emma continued, "I've been thinking, maybe I'll go back to school after the baby's born. I know I can't go back now while I'm pregnant. Besides, I've missed too much. I'll have to start the year over."

Joshua shifted uneasy in his seat beside Emma. She saw he was trying to form a question but was unsure of himself. Emma patiently waited.

"I need to ask you about, uh, the father of, you know, like—who is it?"

"Papa, his name is Hugh Giles. He's from Houston. He was staying with the Ruckers while his parents were traveling abroad. I was about to get in touch with him down in New Orleans when I had to leave town in a hurry."

"Get in touch, how?"

"I have a phone number."

"You want to call him now?"

"No, it's too late, and I'm too tired. I thought about it on the way home. I'll try tomorrow."

"Does he know? I mean, does he know about the baby?"

She shook her head.

"How old is he?"

"He's in his last year of high school. I don't know what plans he has beyond that."

"I kin think of some plans right off the bat! Why don't you call him now? That's long distance, ain't it?"

"No, all I have is his daddy's office number. There's no one there at night. Don't worry, I've got money for plenty of phone calls. Which reminds me, would you help me find a place around here to set up a little art shop? I mean, not here in the house, but in town somewhere?"

"Emma, just name it. You can have one here in the house, in town, anywhere you want. We'll look tomorrow. We gonna' give that boy a call first."

She patted his knee and gave it a squeeze. Emma suddenly felt the fatigue of the day's events.

The next morning, Joshua was up before sunrise. Emma smelled bacon cooking and heard Joshua in the kitchen, talking. She sat on the edge of her bed and reached for a robe.

"Papa, who are you talking to?"

At the sound of her voice, Butch came bounding into her room and leaped onto the bed, covering her with wet licks.

"Butch!" Joshua's voice resounded from the kitchen. "Butch, git in here! Leave Emma alone!"

Emma came out in a long nightgown and robe. Joshua was taken aback at his daughter's mature appearance and noticed her middle bulging.

"Sorry if he woke you. I didn't have much company in the house, and I guess I sorta' spoiled him, letting him come inside like this. Hang on, I'll put him back in his pen."

"That's okay. He's alright in here."

"Naw, he makes a pest of hisself when I'm eating. I always put him up at mealtime. I'll be right back."

Joshua took Butch by the collar and led him out the back door. Emma followed them to the back porch and stood looking at the yard. In the daylight, she could see the weeds were gone; the fence was upright, in need of paint, but standing. All the broken appliances were gone. She walked back through the house to the front and saw that it was the same way. The old truck remained, however.

Moments later, she heard Joshua coming back into the house. She went to the kitchen table and sat watching him cook.

"Papa, how much would a car cost?"

"You mean new or a used one?"

"I don't think it matters. Just something for us to get around in."

"Well, Hershel Stuckey has a '49 Ford pickup for sale parked over by the gas station, but he wants eight hundred dollars for it. We ain't got that kind of money."

"Is it a good one?"

"Yeah, not too old and low mileage, but like I said—"

He turned to continue talking, but Emma had left the room. Quickly, she was back with cash in her hand.

"Here," she said. "Go buy the truck."

Joshua looked at her with astonishment. He turned the stove off and walked to the table where she was sitting. "Where did you git that?"

"I told you last night. It's all honest money, Papa. Go buy the truck before somebody else does. We need it."

"How much money you got?" he asked with a quizzical look.

"There's more. Don't worry. But I need most of it to set up my shop. Once I do, there'll be plenty more coming in."

"Emma, you got any more amazing things to tell me, or is this all for now?"

She laughed and said, "Let's eat so you can go buy that truck."

Emma waited about an hour after Joshua left and looked at the phone. Should she try the Giles Oil number again? Three times she reached for the phone and put it back. She had even placed the call and heard it ring, then hung up. She sat wondering what to say. Finally, she picked it up again and dialed the operator. She told her what number she needed in Houston.

"Ma'am, did you just try to call this number?"

"Yes, but I had to hang up. Could you try it again, please?"

The Houston number rang three times. A familiar voice answered, "Giles Oil, may I help you?"

"Mrs. Dominguez, this is Emma Parker. I called you, when was it, a couple of weeks ago? Do you remember me?"

"I'm trying to think; I get so many calls."

"I was looking for Hugh. Do you recall that?"

"Oh, yes! I gave him the message, and he called me back about an hour later, saying he couldn't get through on that number."

Emma's heart was pounding. He had really tried to call her back.

"Emma? Are you there?"

"Yes, I'm sorry. My mind's in a whirl right now. I'm not in New Orleans anymore, and I wanted to give Hugh my father's phone number."

"Great! I'm sure he will want to have it. He's home today, you know. The schools are out for the holidays. Wait, could you hold a minute?"

Emma heard the line go silent and thought she had lost the connection. While she pondered, Rosa came back on. "Hi, I'm back. Give me the number, and I'll call him right now."

Her voice was shaking as she read the number off her father's old phone. *God, I hope this is the right number,* she thought after remembering the mix-up in New Orleans. Before she hung up, one more thought occurred to her.

"Mrs. Dominguez, how is your daughter, Angelina?"

"Oh, thanks for asking. She's fine. Good news, she's decided to apply to Baylor, and folks say she's got a good chance."

Emma chewed her thumbnail and remembered Hugh mentioning Baylor. "That's great. Has Hugh applied there?"

"I don't know what he's going to do. He's looking for a basketball scholarship somewhere. Hey, I gotta' go now. My other phone lines are blinking at me. I'll call Hugh for you. Nice to talk to you again."

Emma hung up and realized her palms were drenched with perspiration. What will she tell him? What if he doesn't call? But he had to! Rosa had said he tried with the other number. She felt so close, yet so far. For several minutes, she stared at the phone as though she could will it to ring. When it did, she jumped as though something had grabbed her.

"Hello?" She could hear her own voice trembling.

"Emma, I got the truck. Boy, you ought to see her! I got some paperwork to do, then I'll be home." Joshua sounded jubilant.

Emma couldn't decide whether to talk to her father or urge him to hang up. "Papa, don't hurry. Enjoy yourself. Find someone who will come get the old one."

"Yeah. That's taken care of. Man, this thing is a beauty. I sure do thank you."

"Okay, Papa. You enjoy yourself. Bye."

Quickly, she hung up. Trying to regain her composure, she left her hand on the receiver. It rang, and she let out a small yell. She let it ring a second time and picked it up.

"Hello?"

"Emma? Emma, It's Hugh."

Emma felt herself melting inside. It was as though all her strength was being sucked into the phone. The voice was the same. She could picture him standing on the trail in the woods, feel the way he had kissed her. She couldn't think of anything to say.

"Emma, you there?"

She stammered, "Yeah, I'm here. Hugh, I've missed you so much."

"Hey, I miss you, too. So, what you been doing? Were you in New Orleans? That must have been great!" His voice sounded youthful and full of energy.

"Uh, yeah. I was down there for a while. You sound good, Hugh. School's okay?"

"Yeah, just great! We won city champs in basketball. My coach sent a letter to a bunch of colleges. He thinks I'd be a good recruit. Maybe I could get a scholarship."

"Hugh, why do you need a scholarship? Doesn't your daddy have the money to send you?"

"Yeah, but he said it would look better on a resume' if I had a scholarship. Dad says maybe he might try to get me an appointment to one of the service academies. He knows a bunch of politicians that owe him favors, and that's how you get in." He paused. "So, how're you doing? Your school okay?"

She struggled to keep sounding upbeat. "I'm fine. Everything's fine. I hope you don't mind my calling your dad's office. Rosa was really nice to help."

"Yeah, she's worked for Dad a long time. Did she mention her daughter, Angelina? I went out with her a couple of times. Rosa thought I was getting serious with her daughter, and she got all excited.

She felt herself grip the phone tighter. "So, what happened?"

"Actually, I was just doing it as a favor for a friend of mine. He wants to keep playing the field, and Angelina is the type who wants to get married right out of high school. He just needed some distance from her."

That didn't sound like what Rosa had told her. "So, how did you—how did you—get Angelina's mind off her old boyfriend?"

"Nothing to it. Just took her out a couple of times, like I said. Showed her that there were other guys to notice. I even introduced her to some of my other friends."

"That was so very kind of you, Hugh." Her sarcasm went unnoticed.

"Hey, are you okay? You sound different."

"Uh, yeah. Well, it's been a while, Hugh. I'm sure it sounds different over the phone. I have a question for you. Did you get any letters from friends of mine while I was in New Orleans? Maybe even a telegram?"

"No, don't think I did. Who would have sent it? By the way, were you in school down there?"

The sound of squeaking brakes in front of the house caught Emma's attention and broke her concentration. She tried to conceal her agitation.

"Hugh, I want to talk some more, but I can't right now. Please call me back later."

"Sure. Are you sure you're okay?"

"Yeah—Yeah, couldn't be better."

"Hey! That's great, button. Had me worried there for a minute. Yeah, I'll call you back sometime over the holidays. Maybe some evening when we can talk longer?"

"I do miss you, Hugh."

"Yeah, sure. Same here! Gotta go!"

Emma glanced out the door to see who had stopped in front and saw Lavenia, purse strap over her arm, making long strides toward the front door. Emma slowly hung up the phone and walked out onto the porch.

"Emmmaaa! My baby girl! Where have you been, child? Oh, don't you look grand!" Emma met her halfway in the yard and Lavenia wrapped her in a bearhug.

"Lavenia, I think I missed you more than anybody. Come inside. I'll make some coffee."

The two women talked incessantly for almost an hour, each telling what had happened in the other's absence over the past few months. Lavenia was both enchanted and horrified by the events that took place in New Orleans. Emma was totally engrossed in what Lavenia told her about the apparent metamorphosis that Joshua had undergone.

"So, did you ever git 'hold of that boy, Hugh?"

"I was talking to him just as you drove up, Lavenia."

"Oh, I come at the wrong time!" She put her hands over her mouth, then leaned forward and asked, "What did he say?"

"About what?"

"About the baby, of course!"

"I didn't tell him."

Lavenia looked at her in amazement. "He don't know? What you waiting for? It's time he acts like a man and do what he ought! Call him back. Right now, call him back!"

"I, I don't know his number. But he said he'd be calling me again. Maybe I can tell him then."

"What you mean, 'maybe', huh? He got to know, don't he?"

Unaware of it, Emma had started to wring her hands. "Lavenia, it was an accident. It was as much my fault as it was his. He's got such a bright future, and how can I put such a burden on him?"

"All I hear is what's good for him! Don't hear nothin' what's good for Emma or her baby!" She stopped and looked hard at her young friend. "You ain't gonna' tell him, is you? You not gonna' make him put on his big-boy britches and answer for what he done?"

Emma didn't answer. Finally, she said, "Maybe I love him enough to let him go. He's got that rich family, and I don't think they want me in their lives."

"What kinda' nonsense is that? This ain't no storybook tale, girl! This is for real!"

Emma just shrugged.

Lavenia sat in silence, knowing that this was not the time to press the issue. Maybe later. Maybe never. But not now.

Several seconds went by. "Miss Flora know you back?"

"Papa went to town to buy a new truck. I'm sure by now the whole town knows I'm back."

"You gonna' go see her?"

"I'll get around to it. I need to figure out how to tell her or anybody, for that matter, who the father of this baby is."

Lavenia raised her eyebrows. "I think Miss Flora know. Tha's why I asked if she know you back."

"How could she know? Who would have told her? Who else knew except me and—Lavenia! What did you tell her?"

"Child, you was gone, disappeared off'n God's green earth! Nobody knew where you went off to. We called all over town, drove all over the place, everybody worried about you. I ask Miss Flora if she seen you and she say, 'No'. Then she ask why you gone run off like that, and I said—I said—Lord, what did I say? Well, it don't matter what I said. She know about you and Hugh and the baby."

"And she probably told Mr. Rucker, who probably told Hugh's parents. No wonder he didn't sound like the same Hugh on the phone."

"How you mean, not the same?"

"Like he didn't care if I was pregnant."

"Wait, wait. I don't like what he done, but let's talk about this before we send the boy to hell and damnation. What did he say?"

"It's not what he said; it was how he said it."

"Don't keep me guessing, child. Like how did he say whatever he say?"

"Well, when he was here, he was—I mean, he said wonderful things to me. He made me feel good. And today, he just, well, like none of those things happened. It was like there was nothing between us."

"Time done passed by. Young kids, they go on to other things. He probably figured you gone on to other things, too. Be different if'n he know'd about that." She pointed to Emma's tummy. "Look, Hugh be back in his own world. All this time I been calling him 'boy'. Got good reason to. That's what he is, jes' a boy. You wantin' him to act like a man. He can't, 'cause he ain't one yet. Best growin' up he gonna' do is when he finds out you got his baby. But, no, you didn't tell him! Now you want him to act like he knows. He probably don't know!" Lavenia looked down and scratched her head. "And now we back where we started. How did I do this?"

"So, half the town probably knows by now." Emma had never felt such a burden. "So many people had seen us together."

Lavenia was rubbing her forehead. "Let me think a minute. Mr. Rucker, he don't have many kind things to say about his sister, Right? That's what you told me before, right?"

Emma nodded.

"So, if he called his sister—and told her—she would be mad at him, not at the boy, right? So, maybe he ain't told her. And if he did, she probably wouldn't tell the boy if they thought you was off and gone!"

"So, maybe he doesn't know!"

"Emma, it ain't nothin'! So what if'n folks in town know? If this baby is half as pretty as you and Hugh put together, it gon' be one fine baby. Everybody be jealous of you and that good-lookin' baby. You'll see." The look in Lavenia's eyes didn't agree with her words, however.

"Lavenia, you're sweet to say those things. But I wanted to start my own business like I had in the French Quarter. In a little town like this, though, I don't think anyone would buy anything of mine now."

"Just because the baby come from Hugh? You think Hugh that special? Maybe to you! Most folks don't care. He come here for a little while, then he gone. So what? Only person he matters to is you."

"But he was so popular and well-liked."

"Sure. The kids at school liked him. You gon' sell pictures to kids?"

"Maybe you're right. I'm all mixed up now. I don't know what to do."

"You take one step at a time. The baby come when it come. Can't change that. You want a shop? Do it! What happened to that girl who was always seeing the good side of things?"

"I've seen a lot of bad things in the past months, Lavenia. Stuff I didn't know about."

"And the good things still there, too. And lots of them you ain't seen yet. Don't worry 'bout tomorrow. The bible say that. You go to church while you down there?"

Emma just shook her head.

In the distance, they heard a car horn. Lavenia looked out the window and said, "Who's coming in that pick-up truck? Man, that's what I call a red truck! Is that Mr. Josh? It sho' is! Look at him! Hey, Mr. Josh!"

Emma and Lavenia were at the gate when Joshua pulled up to the yard. The road was dusty despite yesterday's rain, but Joshua didn't care.

Lavenia turned to Emma. "Honey, I got to go. You think about what I said. We gon' open your shop, don't you worry."

Joshua leaned out of the window and greeted Lavenia as she walked to her car. He looked at Emma and said, "Go for a ride? How you like the color? Ain't she a pisser? C'mon, hop in."

As they started back towards town, Joshua asked, "So, did you and Lavenia get caught up on all the latest?" The open windows made a blast of wind through the cab, and Joshua had to shout to make himself heard.

"Yessir. Where we going?" she yelled back.

"Got something to show you." Joshua was all smiles.

The engine in Joshua's new truck purred and growled as he shifted the gears, sometimes more than he needed to.

"I talked him down, you know," Josh yelled.

"That's good," Emma answered in a strained voice. "How'd you do it?"

"I told him I wanted to trade in our old truck. He said he could use it for spare parts. That guy's got two of everything. Took seventy-five dollars off the price. He's coming tomorrow to git the old truck."

"Good! You still haven't told me where we're going!"

"Just around the corner. Right there! There she is!"

He pulled the truck off the road onto a gravel driveway about a stone's throw beyond the post office. The driveway led to a small one-room building about twenty feet wide and equal in length. The one and only layer of paint had long since peeled off, leaving the wood siding to turn weathered gray but still substantial and sturdy. The roof sagged slightly, and the narrow front porch seemed to droop at the corners.

"There's what?" she said. What're you talking about?"

"Girl, you lookin', but you ain't seeing. What's that right there?" he pointed straight ahead.

"That building? I don't know. I've always seen it there but never knew what it was. Never seen anyone in it." she paused and looked at her father carefully. "Papa, tell me what's going on."

"It's the payroll shack, we called it. The only thing Whitmyer ever used it for. Twenty, thirty years before you were born, this place was workin' alive with sawmill folks on payday. They always paid everybody in Kisatchie every two weeks. The brothers wanted payday separated between the two mills, but the old man wanted all his folks to come together on payday. After he died, the brothers did as they pleased. Paid their men at the mills and never used this place again. This little symbol of prosperity is probably fifty years old. Maybe more."

"Interesting. I still don't understand why you're showing it to me?"

"Honey, child! Who's in charge of all Whitmyer's stuff? Me! They never told me what to do with the payroll shack, so I made a decision about it just today! Come look inside!"

Joshua pulled out a wad of old rusty keys and searched for the one he needed. It worked on the first try. The door creaked as he opened it, and the air of a half-century slowly rolled out. Cobwebs almost obscured the entrance, and a measurable amount of dust rested on every surface. Small, delicate swirls came up from the floor in response to the door's opening. A window on each side let in sunshine through cloudy panes of dirty glass.

"You think this will work, honey?"

Emma had never seen her father so animated and excited, almost like a young boy showing off the first gift he had ever picked out all by himself.

"Tell me what you had in mind, Papa. It would help if you told me more."

"It ain't enough room, is it? I can tell by the way you said that. It come to me while I was driving the new truck around, trying to decide if I really wanted it. I remembered nobody's using this building. I figured you could hang your finished pictures up here on the wall for sale and keep the ones you was still working on over in this here closet. I know a fella' who can make you a sign, but we'll find a better place. This 'uns too small. You're right."

"Papa, I haven't said anything yet. I just realized what you're talking about! This would make a perfect studio! This is bigger than what I had in New Orleans! Are you sure we can use it?"

"It's mine to do with as I see fit!" He looked at his daughter gleefully. "You mean, you want it?"

"Papa, this will be great! Oh, I can't believe this!"

"You damn right, it'll be great! We'll make a nice little shop here to start with, then we'll add on some more rooms when things get going good, and then—"

Emma wrapped her arms around her father and hugged him tightly. Pressed against him, Joshua could feel the bulge in her middle. Years before, he had known how this felt. Deep inside, he hoped for the best. He wasn't sure what the best would be, but he felt so alive right at this moment that he'd kill anyone who got in the way.

"So, where do we start?" he said, looking around and realizing the enormous task ahead just cleaning this one small room. "I know. While you're thinking about it, I got a broom in the back of the truck. I'll start knocking some of these spider webs down."

Emma nodded, "Okay. We'll need a mop and a bucket. Let me go next door to the store and get them. I'll get some stuff to go in the mop water."

Emma walked the few yards to the front of Rucker's store. She stopped and took a deep breath before going in. Her back was turned when Tom Rucker approached her from behind.

"Help ya', ma'am?"

Emma turned around and saw the blood drain from Tom's face. He stared for several seconds before realizing what he was doing. Emma finally broke the silence.

"Hello, Mr. Rucker. You look very good."

Tom wiped his hands on the apron he was wearing and shifted his gaze to the floor. He mumbled something unintelligible and walked toward the back of the store. Emma proceeded to look for what she needed. In about three minutes, she was standing at the register with her purchases, waiting. Loud whistling came from the back of the store, and she heard the rear screen slam shut. Lonnie spotted her as soon as he rounded the corner and stopped in his tracks.

"My God! Look at you! I heard you was back. Spent some time out of town, did you?"

Emma let a few seconds tick by before answering. "Yes, I was gone for a few months. How are you, Lonnie?"

Lonnie gestured like he didn't know what to do with his hands. He took a few steps closer.

"You, I mean, you look like you've - Emma, I knew you was back, but nobody told me what a change had come over you."

"Change? Like what, Lonnie?"

"Well, you look great! What have you been doing?"

"I had an art shop in New Orleans."

"An art shop? Okay, seems to have done you well. You must have been hanging out with some classy people."

"No, just some people who honestly cared, Lonnie. I'd like to buy these things if I may."

As if on cue, Tom Rucker emerged from nowhere. "Lonnie, remember what we said about accounts and so forth." With that remark, he retreated to whatever corner of the store he had been listening from.

"Uh, Emma, we aren't opening any new credit accounts, and Mr. Rucker is trying to collect on old ones, so could you pay cash today?"

"I had no intention of charging today, Lonnie. Once I get my new business going, I will close out Papa's debt completely."

She reached into her dress pocket and brought out a small coin purse. Lonnie could not help but notice that it was full of bills, not coins. She carefully pulled the creases out of the bills before handing them to him.

He took the money and said thoughtfully, "What kind of business?"

"Same as I had in the French Quarter. It'll take me a few days to get set up."

"Another art shop? But if you were doing so well, why did you leave New Orleans?"

"I came home, Lonnie. That's why. It was just time to come home."

With that, she turned and walked to the front door, where she stopped and looked back at Lonnie. Tom had stepped back out into the open and was standing next to Lonnie.

"Maybe the two of you could be my first customers."

The two men said nothing as she left. Finally, Lonnie remarked, "Did you see that wad of bills she had? What kind of business was she in? Nobody makes that kind of money selling pictures!"

Later that evening, Tom Rucker made a phone call while Flora was out of the house for a few minutes. The Houston operator made the connection, and a voice at the Giles residence answered. Isabella was about to leave at the end of the day when the phone rang.

"Giles' residence, this is Isabella," She answered in a clipped accent. "Mr. Rucker, good evening. Mrs. Giles? Let me see if I can find her."

She laid the phone down and located Rose Giles in the bedroom, sitting at her dresser.

"Mrs. Giles, your brother is on the phone. Your brother in Louisiana…"

"Yes, I know where my brother lives! What does he want?"

"No se, he wants just talk to you." In her nervousness, Isabella often mixed her English with Spanish.

Rose picked up the extension. As Isabella was leaving the room, she heard Rose say, "No, Thomas, Hugh didn't tell me about some girl in Kisatchie. What? WHAT?" She hesitated and listened. "No way! No damn way! Listen to me, brother of mine, not a word of this to my son! You hear me? Not a word! In fact, you've seen the last of him! I asked you to look after him for just a few weeks, such a simple thing, and now this?"

In the parlor, Isabella put the phone to her ear and then quietly hung up. Rose heard background noise, then the telltale click as the receiver went into the cradle. Isabella was fired that night.

Chapter 23

Joshua Parker had been catching a nap on the couch one Saturday afternoon in early May when the phone rang and rudely rattled him into wakefulness. Emma had gone to a perspective buyer's house with some of her latest work, leaving Joshua by himself.

"Hello!" he said roughly.

"Mr. Josh, that you?"

"You called me, didn't you? Who'n hell is this?"

"Mr. Josh, this is Hershel Tulley at the gas station. I thought I ought to call you about something."

"Okay."

"I mean, I know its Saturday and all, but I figured I should–"

"Hershel, what is it?"

"Well, there was this big, long car come here a few minutes ago. Black one. Longest car I ever seen."

"Okay."

"Must've had five winders on each side."

"Hershel!"

"Okay, I'm getting to it. I just didn't want you to get excited when this thing pulls up to your door."

"My door? It's coming here? Who is it?"

"That's what I been trying to tell you. They stopped and asked directions to your house, and I wasn't going to tell them, but two big ol' boys got out of the car, and they didn't look any too friendly, so I told 'em where you live. I hope that's okay."

Joshua was rubbing his eyes. "How long ago did you talk to them?"

"Oh, it was ten, maybe fifteen minutes ago."

"And you just now calling me?"

"Like I said, Mr. Josh, I weren't too sure."

"Hang on, I hear someone at the door."

Joshua walked to the door and peered through the screen at two heavy-set men in dark suits. They wore ties and wingtip shoes. Neither one smiled.

"You fellas need something?"

"Emma Parker live here?"

"Depends on who's asking?"

"You Joshua Parker?"

"Like I said, it depends on who's asking. Hang on a second." Joshua went back to the phone and sat down. "Hershel, did these guys say they was lookin' for me or someone else?"

Before Hershel had a chance to answer, a huge hand took the phone from him and hung it up. Joshua snapped his head around to see not two, but three men standing in his living room. The largest of them said, "Pardon the intrusion, but our boss doesn't like to be kept waiting."

"What the hell you think you're doing? You just walk into my house like you own the place? Git outta' here!" Joshua knew exactly where his shotgun was but also knew he couldn't get to it in time. "Who are you, anyway?"

"That doesn't matter. We're looking for Emma Parker. We have something for her."

"She ain't here!"

"So, you are Joshua Parker?"

"Could be."

"We'll take that as a 'yes'. We'll wait for her to get back from wherever she is. When do you expect her back?"

"Maybe never!" He tried to get out of his chair, but one of them stood directly in front of him. He tried again, and the man politely sat him back down.

"Yeah, I'm her father, and I ain't lettin' anyone like you just come in here and sit in my living room without an invitation. I may be an old man, but I'll give you the fit of your life before I let you push me around. If I was forty years younger, they'd be scoopin' all three of you up with a big shovel!"

The three men backed off and gave him room. Joshua felt a little relieved.

"You can wait for her, but you'll do it out there in that crazy-lookin' vehicle of yours!"

The biggest of the three men turned to the other two and said, "You know, maybe we should do that. It's hot in here. At least the car has air conditioning. No telling how long we got to wait."

"Yeah!" Joshua yelled, starting to feel in control again. "Hell might just freeze over first!"

The three men walked back toward the front door, and the last one turned around and said, "We heard you had a temper. We also heard you got a real sweet daughter, though." Joshua felt his face turning red.

As the visitors walked back to the car, the phone rang again. It was Hershel.

"Mr. Josh, you okay? You hung up awfully fast a while ago, I wasn't sure what happened. Did them guys git there?"

"Yeah, they're here. Hershel, did they ask you any questions about Emma?"

"No, sir. They asked for you by name. Why would they want anything from Emma?"

"I don't know, but I'm sure I'll find out. Listen, don't say nothin' to nobody about this until I get it all straightened out." He hung up the phone and went to his closet. The old double-barrel shotgun seemed to leap into his hands. He loaded both barrels and put several 12-gauge shells in his coverall pockets. To make his message plain, he walked out on the front porch and sat in the old rocker in plain view of the limousine. After a minute, he gave a shrill whistle that brought one of the car windows down.

"Nice car you got there!" he yelled. Makes a big target! Now, why don't you start explaining to me why you're here and what you want with my daughter?" He slowly raised the shotgun and took aim at the driver's door.

Joshua saw the window go back up with a faint machinery noise. He stood and craned his neck to see what would happen next. Finally, a door on the opposite side opened, and a woman stepped out. She was tall and the color of coffee with cream. Lots of cream. Her cheekbones were high, and her shoulders wide. The car blocked his view of the rest of her from the shoulders down. The top she wore was bright orange mixed with large floral print. A matching turban wrapped itself around her head several times. She stepped out from behind the car, and Joshua saw the most full-bodied woman he had ever laid eyes on. She walked toward the gate, and as she approached, he began to fully realize how tall she was. A belt of large beads encircled her waist and hung by her side. Her feet were bare.

"Say, you Joshua Parker, no?"

Joshua couldn't find his voice. He didn't even hear the distant crunch of tires as the red pick-up came slowly toward the house. Emma had learned to drive but always did it like it was her first day. The truck stopped behind the limousine. All eyes were on Emma as she planted her feet on the ground and shaded her eyes from the sun. She filled her maternity dress with no room to spare. She took careful steps toward the limo and finally spoke.

"Mercedes? Mercedes!"

Both women ran toward each other in an awkward shuffle, one from age, the other from added size. Mercedes had to bend forward to hug Emma. Emma clutched her with strength that surprised Mercedes.

"My God, Child! I thought I'd never see you again!"

Emma's joy was without words. Her mentor, her savior, her best pal, was here in front of her house. As tears streamed down, an awesome feeling of comfort enveloped her, making her feel whole and loved. They walked arm in arm toward the house. Mercedes turned and shouted to the men in the limousine.

"Put my stuff on the porch! I call you later, yeah?"

Her words did not sink in with Joshua until he realized the limo was pulling away and her bags were on the porch of his house.

"Hey! Where're they going?"

"Don't worry. They be back in about t'ree months."

"Hey, wait a minute! Are you staying? I don't even know who you are!"

"Sure you do, Papa. I told you all about Mercedes. She found me outside the bus station in New Orleans.

"The cemetery gal? The mango thief?"

Mercedes stopped and glared at Emma. Then, both women erupted in laughter.

"Mercedes, what are you doing here?" Emma asked.

"At's what I want to know," said Joshua. "And what kind of fellas were them that brung you here?"

She looked at Emma. "I don't know how much you told your papa. Those were some of Carmen's guys. New fellas."

Joshua kept looking back at the disappearing taillights of the limo. He turned to Emma and said, "So, they're really leaving?"

"You miss them already?" Mercedes said.

"No, I just hadn't planned on - I mean, how long did you say you was staying?"

Mercedes laughed and walked toward the house with her arm wrapped around a jubilant Emma. Joshua stood on the porch in disbelief. Inside, the two women sat on the couch, facing each other.

"So, what made you come?"

"Hey, I can count. You tol' me when this baby got started, so I count me nine months, and it looks like I come just in time. Where you gonna' have it?"

"Right here, I guess. I suppose I could go to the clinic in the next town, but that's expensive."

"You got money, no?"

"Well, the art trade here isn't the same as in New Orleans. People aren't exactly leaning in that direction. But I did sell two pictures today."

"I tell you, I got a couple more reasons comin' here. Lemme' get my bags."

Mercedes walked onto the front porch to retrieve her belongings, and Joshua was still standing there. He barely turned around when she walked through the door. She hoisted her load with one arm and went back inside. Through the screen door, she spoke back to Joshua. "May as well come inside and see what I brought. Got to come in sooner or later, anyhow. Your house!"

She sat cross-legged in the middle of the floor with her huge duffle spread open in front of her. An assortment of clothes and strange items found their way to the floor. More beads, a leather pouch, and a coin purse. Joshua had finally walked in just in time to see the little derringer appear. He paid closer attention after that. Finally, a heavy cardboard tube came out, which she handed to Emma.

"Go ahead, open it. They all your stuff."

Emma reached two fingers into the tube and gently pulled out a cluster of rolled-up drawings. Her drawings. Her best.

It was as though she were looking at old companions, lost for countless years and returned to her in one act of redemption. Her eyes widen at first, then grew moist as she remembered the thoughts that brought her to create them. She looked at each one slowly, soaking in every detail, re-living every moment. Her favorite was that of a young woman holding a child by the hand, viewed from the back. The child in the picture was looking up at the woman, who, in turn, was looking at a young man off in the distance. The young man was casting a glance over his shoulder, but his arms were pumping as someone in a hurry to get somewhere else. Emma lingered silently over this one for several minutes until Mercedes finally spoke.

"You talked to him? You told him, huh?"

Emma just nodded.

"You told him?"

"I talked to him. But, he doesn't know."

"Bullshit!" Mercedes proclaimed. "Somebody knows!" She held up four envelopes.

"What's that?" asked Joshua.

"This from Giles Oil Company. They all addressed to you, care of Carmen Carlucci. First one come right after you left in December. I got my guesses what they are." She handed the envelopes to Emma.

"Giles Oil? What—why would they be sending me anything?"

"I think I know why. Question is, how much?" Mercedes' look of determination faltered when Emma looked at her inquisitively. "Well, if you hold it up to the light, you can see some of it."

"Mercedes, you've been reading my mail!"

"Oh, hush up and open it!"

The first envelope contained a check for one thousand dollars. The remaining three were identical, dated one month apart. The signature was illegible, but it certainly wasn't recognizable as Hugh's.

"I just found out about these a week ago," Mercedes said. "Carmen knew about them. He knew it was important because nobody don't send no love letter in an envelope like that. Carmen's lawyer had these, and Carmen asked me where you be. I told him nothing, but I told him I bring it to you."

"But now, Carmen knows where I am. I don't want him around me after what happened. Remember the white powder and what happened to Brock?"

"Honey, Brock didn't know nothing about the powder. He was good as gold. Them other fellas, they had your key, but Brock didn't know it. They got caught about a month after you left. I told you how Carmen always got a back door, didn't I?"

"But look what happened to Brock. And Carmen was using me! I can't forget that."

"Honey, Carmen would use his own mother if he had to, but he watches close. He never let nothin' happen to his family and friends. He asked me the day you leave; he says, 'Hey, Mercedes. We got to move Emma. She gettin' too close to the action and don't know it.' He really was looking out for you. Then I told him you knew about Brock and how he died. Carmen, he was really upset. But you did the right thing. Leaving was smart."

"I just did what you told me to do."

"Yeah, and I'd tell it to you again, but Carmen don't need to know that."

Joshua had remained silent as long as he could stand. He tapped Mercedes on the shoulder and said, "Emma told me all the details." His voice got louder. "It was you that introduced her to this gang family and almost got her in hot water! What if the police woulda' come in? Who is Emma to them? Just a little country girl from Grant Parish. Easy pickin's." He could feel his temper rising. "Blame everything on her. You put my little girl in harm's way, you bitch!"

She barely glanced up at Joshua. "Call me what you want, old man. She run from you, and Mercedes took care of her!"

"I shoulda' never let you come into my house!"

She tried to stand but lost her balance from where she was sitting. She fell backwards and immediately sat back up, the derringer in her hand aimed at Joshua's belly.

"You want to die real slow, old man? This little piece not much, but it do the job. She came to me because she left this place. Why she leave here, huh? What you do to her, make her leave like that, huh?" Carefully, she watched Joshua's expression melt from bristling anger to shame; then, she lowered the tiny gun.

Joshua took a step back and disappeared into the kitchen. Emma followed him. "Papa, look at this. It's four thousand dollars! Think what we can do with it!"

"Honey, don't you see what that money is for? It's tellin' you to stay away - his family is paying you to stay away. The next time you try to contact him, they'll probably send a court order. If they wanted to get the two of you together, they would have sent an invitation, not money!"

"He's right," said Mercedes from the kitchen door. "Much as I hate to agree with you, old man, you right. Emma, you sure he don't know about the baby?"

"He would have said something about it."

"So, only his folks know about it," said Joshua.

"Yeah, his folk and whoever signed these checks. Probably Giles' lawyer."

"Papa, you gotta' understand something. Mercedes got me involved with Carmen Carlucci and his family, but she pulled me out as soon as she saw something was wrong."

Joshua thrust his hands into his pockets and looked at the floor. He pondered for a moment, then said apologetically, "Okay, you helped Emma when she needed help, and I thank you for that. You helped her make some money and kept an eye on her. I thank you for that. But I still don't have it clear how you two ever got together."

"I knew she was coming," Mercedes said in a matter-of-fact tone.

"You knew? How? Who could have told you?"

"Marie. Marie and Orum. They told me."

"Who in the hell are they?"

"Papa, this is fixin' to get complicated. Why don't we think about supper first. We can put Mercedes' things in the far bedroom."

Joshua bit his lip and looked quizzically at his daughter without saying anything.

"Yes! She's staying!" she said.

Supper was quick and mostly silent, except for exchanged glances and a few words to get the food passed around. Joshua had revitalized Marcia's garden, and fall vegetables were in storage and plentiful. Mercedes wolfed down her meal and asked for more before Joshua and Emma were half through with their first helping. She slugged down a full glass of milk and wiped her mouth with her bare hand. Joshua missed nothing, but knowing Emma's feeling toward Mercedes, said nothing. When the meal was over, Mercedes rose and collected her plate, along with the others.

"I'll get that, Mercedes," said Emma.

"No! From now on, this my job."

Joshua looked at Emma and mouthed the words, *From now on?*

As though she had eyes in the back of her head, she said, "That right, old man. I be here for a while."

"Now I've heard enough!" Joshua roared. "We've had our little spat with words, and I know that little pistol of yours is in the other room. It's time to answer me one question. How long do you plan to stay, woman?"

"My name is Mercedes!"

"And mine is Joshua! I've even been known to answer to Mr. Josh or Mr. Parker! So, no more of this 'old man' shit from you, you hear?"

Emma froze and looked back and forth at the two of them. Mercedes calmly kept on washing dishes and gave a weak smile over her shoulder. "Joshua. I like that. Joshua was a soldier in the Bible. Okay, Joshua. Emma gonna' need help havin' that baby and gon' need help after it come. One month, two months, we see how it go. Good enough?"

"Emma don't need no help."

Emma asked quietly, "Papa, who helped Mama when I was born?"

Joshua pondered for a moment. "Well, there was quite a string of lady friends comin' in and outa' here, but they was just bein' sociable."

"And where was you when they bein' so nice to your lady?" Mercedes asked.

"Men gotta work, woman, uh, Mercedes. I was at the mill!"

"So, you don't really know what they be doing here, huh?"

"Papa, you just don't remember," Emma interjected.

Joshua was breathing hard. "How could you?" he said. "You were just a newborn."

"I know. It was a long time ago. But the fact is, women need help when they have babies."

"You think I don't know what your mother needed? I gave her everything she asked for! I gave her everything she needed! Everything! And I can help you! Why do we need HER here? This is my house! My family! My grandchild! I *will* provide for them!"

The two women remained silent while Joshua chewed on his own words. He waved his hands like they were appendages he didn't know what to do with. His eyes darted around the room as though the answer to some question would spring out of the woodwork.

Emma walked to her father's side and took his arm. "Papa, Mercedes is here to help for just a short time. I really appreciate her coming. I really do. I can't ask Lavenia because she has her own family to look after. Yes, this is your family. Always will be. She's just here for a little while. We need you for the long haul." She held his hand on her tummy as she said it.

He took Emma in his arms as he had become accustomed to over the past few weeks. "You hear that?" he croaked, directing his words at Mercedes.

"Yeah, man. I hear. Once Emma on her feet with that baby, I'm gone. All it takes is one phone call."

The next morning, Emma walked into the kitchen just as her father had looked out the window and let out a war whoop.

"Hey, what's she doing? She's in your mother's garden! Look!"

Emma walked to the window. "Looks like she's chopping down some weeds, Papa. You gotta admit; it needed it."

He walked away from the window, shaking his head. "That's one strange woman. Does she ever take that thing off her head?"

"The turban? I've never seen her without one. But it's not always the same one, so she must change it sometime."

"Well, something's really different about her. I got up last night, and her door was open. I mean, I wasn't trying to look, but I couldn't help but see. She was sleeping on the floor! Perfectly good bed, and she sleeps on the damn floor!"

"Papa, her room is down the hall. What do you mean you couldn't help but see?"

"Well, I saw the door was open, and I wanted to make sure that - hell, I don't know why I went down there and looked! The point is not why I looked but what I saw. She was sleeping on the floor!"

"I know. She stayed with me a few nights in New Orleans and did the same thing. Don't worry about it. And stop peeking in her room!"

A week went by, and Joshua was becoming used to the presence of Mercedes in the house. She couldn't cook, but she knew how to clean. Joshua found all his dirty clothes washed and folded on his bed one day. He was going to protest, but Emma stopped him. Emma knew they had crossed a huge hurdle later one evening after dark when she walked into the living room and heard voices on the front porch.

"Orum and me, we got married in New Orleans - seems like so long ago. He worked at the river dock. He loaded ships, you know."

"How long did you know him before you got married?" Joshua asked.

"Oh, 'bout six days! HA!"

"He must have been quite a man."

"Yeah, he like to think that. He always sayin' he going to buy me 'dis and buy me 'dat. I tol' him; all I want is him. Just him. I make him happy, and I told him he make me feel so good. Don't need to go buy things all the time. But he still tried."

"Where did you live?"

"We had an apartment in Chalmette. One bedroom. One room to sit. Kitchen, bathroom, that's all. Enough for me. Orum, he always talked big, like someday we have a palace. Always dreaming, that man."

"No kids?"

Mercedes hesitated and looked at the floor for what seemed to be a full minute before answering. She sighed heavily and said, "Yeah, we had one. But she die. She die in the fire we had."

Joshua shifted uneasily in his rocker. "I'm sorry. I didn't mean to bring it up like that."

"Is okay."

"What happened to Orum?"

"He die the same day as my baby. Orum, he tried to make money fast, and he start making deals with some really bad guys. One day, it went bad, so bad they kill him and set fire to our apartment. Firemen, they came and carry me out, but our baby die."

"That's terrible. Must have been a bad fire."

"It was. That's how I got this." Mercedes reached up and pulled her turban off. In the dim light, Joshua could see horrible, disfiguring scars on her moth-eaten scalp. "I don't show this to many people. You may as well see it. You would sooner or later." She wrapped the turban back on her head.

Joshua was speechless. He had seen sawmill accidents but never the aftermath of a burn. Finally, he managed to find words. "I know what it's like to lose someone you love. How old was the baby?"

"Only one month. I miss her. But I really miss my Orum. I still talk to him. Almost every night."

"Yeah, I do that, too. Me and Marcia, we talk. You ever had anybody else after your fella' died?"

A sly gleam came into her eye. "Wouldn't you like to know?" She finished with that deep chuckle Emma had come to recognize. "How 'bout you? You got any old flames still comin' around?"

"If there were, they'd be nothing but ashes by now. No, I only had one flame. I forgot you had to feed the fire to keep it going."

As Emma listened, how she wished she could have known her mother better. Losing someone she loved, she knew about that part.

The next morning, from his bedroom window, Joshua saw Mercedes leaving the house just as the sun was coming up. She had started taking long walks in the woods in the early morning hours. She was truly not the problem he had thought she would be. He walked into the kitchen and began fixing a pot of coffee. The pot still held grounds from the previous day, so he walked to the back door to toss the grounds out. As he did, a faint cry from Emma's room reached his ears.

"Papa! Come quick!"

Joshua shuffled back into the house as fast as his bare feet would carry him. In the doorway of her room stood Emma, a puddle of water at her feet. "It just started," she said weakly. "Where's Mercedes?"

Joshua took three steps toward Emma, then started to go back toward the kitchen. He reversed himself again and said, "What can I do?"

Clutching her belly and bracing herself again the wall, Emma said, "Go get Mercedes. Where's Mercedes?"

"She went for a walk! I'll—I'll go get her. Wait, you go lay down first! Here, I'll get some pillows—"

"Papa, go get Mercedes!"

"Uh, yeah, I'm going. Be right back. I'm going!"

Joshua jumped into slippers and crossed the back porch in big strides. He planted a foot on the top step and hit the ground with the other. Running down the trail he had seen her take, he headed toward the mill pond. He tried to call out, but his breath was coming in big gulps, so he just kept moving. The mill pond wasn't visible until he negotiated the last turn, whereupon he stopped sharply, trying to breathe. His mind was so preoccupied with Emma it didn't register that his eyes were showing him Mercedes, with her dress gathered up almost to her hips, stepping off into the shallow water. In a few heartbeats, his eyes connected with his consciousness, and he huffed out, "Mercedes!"

Mercedes whirled and yelled, "Joshua!" she screeched. "Why you sneak up on me like that?" It was then that she saw the distress on his face. "Emma?"

"You go! I'll catch up!" he said in gasps.

As Joshua came out of the woods and struggled up the steps of the back porch in his wet slippers, he heard them talking. He kicked off his footwear and quietly walked to Emma's door. Mercedes was sitting on the side of the bed, holding Emma's hand. She didn't seem to be in any distress at the moment, and she noticed Joshua standing in the doorway. She smiled and waved. Joshua's insides were about to burst from anxiety and exertion. But he was happy.

"Joshua, call Lavenia," Mercedes said calmly. "Tell her Emma's water broke, but we still got a few hours. She knows what to do." Emma had made sure that Mercedes and Lavenia had met each other. The two women had struck up an immediate friendship despite their vast differences. One thing they both knew about was midwifery. It was great to have not just one but two like them.

"Let me go get some things ready. Joshua, you called Lavenia yet? That the only thing I said for you to do, and you just standing there."

"Have you ever done this before?" he asked.

"Joshua, I birthed more babies than you ever see. Street people have babies, too. Somebody got to help, no? Lotsa' years, I been doing this. Now stop worrying and go call Lavenia. And on your way back, bring a mop."

Lavenia arrived about an hour later, and all three women banished Joshua to the kitchen. Emma's contractions were about thirty minutes apart, and everyone seemed rather relaxed at this point. Within the next two hours, the interval decreased to twenty minutes, then fifteen. Joshua kept pacing back and forth from the kitchen to the bedroom door. Each time, he saw the three of them talking and laughing as though it was a ladies' social gathering.

By noon time, things were progressing. Her contractions were less than two minutes apart, and the women were doing less talking. Joshua couldn't stand being in the kitchen any longer and stationed himself in the hallway across from the open door to Emma's room. Emma had several pillows stuffed under her head and shoulders, and her knees were propped up under the sheets. Lavenia sat on the side of the bed talking to Emma, and Mercedes was at the foot of the bed, taking care of business.

Lavenia said, "Now, when the next one come, you do like I told you. Emma, you listening to me?" Lavenia saw that Emma was looking through the open doorway and smiling. A glance upward, and she saw Joshua standing there, a forced, plastic smile on his face, but not enough to hide his feelings of concern. Lavenia got up from the bed and politely closed the door. "Now pay attention, Emma."

All Joshua heard from the room were the soft tones of Lavenia and Mercedes, along with Emma's muffled groans for about the next hour, although it seemed like a year. He pulled a kitchen chair to the spot in the hall and sat. From the kitchen, he retrieved a cup of coffee and a piece of leftover cornbread. The coffee was lukewarm, and the cornbread was dry, but he didn't seem to notice. Twice, he heard Emma's voice with a twinge of pain, maybe even panic. Both times, he slowly opened the door to look and quickly shut it.

It was suddenly dead quiet. A minute went by, then two. He was about to rise from his chair again when a small voice uttered a squeak from the closed room. The squeak became a yowl and then a wavering little howl. He waited as long as he could, then opened the door as though to dare anyone to order him out. Lavenia met him at the threshold with a small bundle.

"Mr. Josh, you have a grandson."

He looked beyond the woman and said, "Emma, sweetie, you okay?"

"I'm fine, Papa. Just a little tired."

"Can I see him?"

Slowly, almost reluctantly, Lavenia handed the baby to Josh. She saw tears well up in the man's eyes. "Emma told us about an hour ago that if it was a boy, she liked the name of Brian."

"Look at that!" Joshua exclaimed. "Mr. Brian Parker! We gonna' have another man in the family!"

After Lavenia went home, Mercedes and Joshua let Emma rest, and they went into the living room with the baby. As soon as they sat down, Mercedes said, "I got something I need to tell you.

Bringing this baby into the world is one reason I come here. There's another reason.

"There are some really bad folks in Gretna. That's across the river from my city. They startin' a baby thing. They sellin' babies. Street babies from Gretna. Mama gets five hundred; they get five thousand when they sell it. Had their eyes on Emma and her baby."

Joshua shifted nervously in his seat.

"My friend, Brock, he gets wind of it and go tell Carmen. Carmen got some police friends, so he tell them. They ask Brock to be a witness, and he say yes. Next day, they find Brock dead. I never seen Carmen so upset. He tell me to get Emma out of town, and then later he tell me to come here. Carmen sent me here."

All Joshua could do is listen and blink his eyes. "So, what do we do?" he asked.

"For next couple months, one of us always stay with Emma," she answered. "No need to tell her about any of this. Couple of months, it'll all blow over and be done."

Two months later, Mercedes kept her promise. As she was leaving, she gave Joshua Parker the first real kiss he could remember in almost a decade.

Chapter 24

Three Years Later...

Brian played on the floor of his mother's studio in the payroll shack. In four months, he would be three years old. He had just gone through his third Christmas and was old enough to imagine the mystery and the beauty that only the mind of a small child could appreciate.

The trees were bare, and the daylight hours in January were short. Winter had arrived cold and crisp. For Emma, it helped her with an idea she came upon from watching other artists in New Orleans. In most shops, there had been at least one nude painting, but she never had the courage to try one. She had developed a friendship with a New Orleans woman who had done one and sold it for a hefty price. Embarrassed to talk about it at first, she finally asked who had posed for the picture. To Emma's surprise, the woman revealed it was her own body drawn with the aid of a mirror but the face of someone else, created from her own recollection. Emma's little art shop in New Orleans was on a street that was constantly busy, even at night, and never did give her the seclusion she needed to overcome the self-consciousness of trying it herself. But, when darkness came to Kisatchie, especially in the chill of winter, nothing stirred.

"Brian, line the dominoes up and make a fence," she said. "Put your farm animals in it." She knelt beside her son and showed him how to make a game of the animals he was playing with. "See, you make a pen for the cows, and the pigs, and the horses."

"Ducks!" he exclaimed, holding up a small figure of a duck with several ducklings. The spring before, Emma had taken him to the mill pond as was her routine each morning, and a flock of mallards had nested nearby with their half-grown ducklings. From that day on, he persisted in asking for a duck of his own. Christmas brought the next best thing for him; a set of plastic farm animals, among which were his prized ducks. He carried them in his coverall pockets everywhere he went.

As soon as he was thoroughly occupied with his toys, Emma pulled down the window shades and started to slip out of her clothes but stopped. This was too bizarre. On a sketch pad, she tried to imagine what it might look like, and the mere idea of it made her blush inside. After several pages lay on the floor, she thought she could do this without disrobing. Maybe. First, she decided what was the most convenient arrangement of paint materials on the floor. Then she laid down next to a long dressing mirror she had bought just for this purpose. It lay horizontal on the floor, propped up against a chair. She positioned herself so she could easily glance over the mirror and keep an eye on Brian.

The hardest part at first was separating herself from the fact that it was a self-portrait. Her instinctive approach to art was always an expression of the beauty she saw in the world around her, in the faces of other people. She was now looking at herself and had never thought of her own human features as unique and beautiful. There had to be flaws that made her an unsuitable subject. It immediately came to her how the picture should look, but she needed a few seconds of visual reality.

Off came the dress. The form of a nude woman laying on her side developed on the landscape canvas. Beside the woman was a child looking at a small bird. She first had wanted to position the child in front of the woman's hips to make the scene somewhat modest but changed her mind and, instead, drew the child at the woman's knees. Brian stood to get a better look at his imaginary farm. He innocently looked at his mother.

"Hi!" he said with a wave.

Emma waved back at him. "Hi, big fella'! Play with your toys now. Mommy's busy, but I'll be done in a little bit."

A few more minutes went by, and Brian again stood and got his mother's attention.

"Hi!" he said again with a big smile.

She needed to create a distraction for him. "Brian, you want to sing with Mommy?" Emma knew he loved it, and it always settled him down when he acted restless. "Okay, here we go..."

"You are my sunshine, my only sunshine."

"C'mon, sing with me…"

"You make me happy when skies are gray."

Brian's little voice joined in with poorly formed words, but his tone was perfect. It was his favorite song. He quickly went back to his toys while he was singing. At an age when most children are very self-centered, Brian was a joy to be around. He entertained himself easily and was happy with the simplest of playthings.

Emma returned to her work and was totally focused on developing the woman's face when she heard a rustling sound from the window and realized that Brian had pulled one of the shades away from the glass. He was looking out the window.

"Hi!" he squealed gleefully and pointed outside through the glass. In his excitement, he jerked the shade, which recoiled out of his hand and quickly wound up to the top. A strange face looking in the window quickly disappeared. She screamed out of reflex and, along with the sound of the window shade flapping on the roller, Brian became frightened and started crying. Crouching on the floor behind the mirror, she struggled momentarily with the conflicting thoughts of hiding or grabbing Brian.

"Brian! Pick up all your toys! We have to go home!" Emma threw her dress on and scooped Brian up. Ignoring the chilly wind, she carefully stepped out onto the porch and looked in both directions. In his mother's firm grip, Brian turned to look back inside through the open door, and slowly, his lower lip protruded more and more. He sensed his mother's anxiety but was more concerned with the toys he had left on the floor. A small wail that began from deep inside slowly emerged from the child as he pointed to his possessions back in the studio. Emma suddenly realized she was prepared to leave without gathering her things or even locking the door.

"I'm sorry, Brian," she said as she walked back inside and let him back down to the floor. "Help Mommy put everything away. Let's go home and see what Grampa's doing. We can play some more when we get home."

It was then that she noticed some of her preliminary sketches had blown across the floor and were outside on the porch. She picked up three pages and wondered, *Only three? Where are the others?*

Emma had an overwhelming feeling of child-like embarrassment. Who was that at the window? She couldn't be sure. How long had he been there? Was this the first night he had tried to look in the windows? Why had she picked tonight to try this idea? It was just art. She was just trying to do what she did best. The window shades had been drawn shut and the door was locked. It was her privacy, hers alone. And she hadn't tried to involve anyone else. What she did was her own business. Still, someone else had made it their business and now she must be ready to deal with the small-town consequences.

She drove homeward slowly with Brian on her lap. Not a single car moved on the road except the red truck. She arrived in less than ten minutes. Joshua was sitting in the living room, listening to the radio. He had developed an insatiable appetite for *'The Amos and Andy Show'*. Even though the front door was shut, Emma could hear him laughing as she came through the front gate.

"Hey, you two! Come listen to this! I been bustin' my guts for the past twenty minutes." He paused to look closer at his daughter. Brian squirmed in her grasp, wanting to be let down.

"What's wrong?" He turned off the radio.

Emma took a deep breath and sat across the room from her father. Joshua was patient, but only for a few seconds.

"Emma, you look like you seen a ghost or something. What happened?"

"I can explain. I just need to think a minute."

"No, you don't. Just spit it out. What's the matter?"

She took a couple of deep breaths and said, "Papa, this wasn't my fault. It wasn't like I tried to start anything, but—"

"Just tell me what made you come in here looking like all the blood drained outa' you."

"Okay. Papa, you ever seen pictures of—well, okay - let me start over. I was working on a picture, and somebody came looking in the window of the shop."

"Looking in the window? Who?"

"I don't know. I looked up, and there he was, and then he was gone. I never thought there would be anybody out there after dark. I got really scared, and then I was worried about Brian, and I hurried home. I felt like I was a million miles away from you. I haven't felt that way since before Brian was born."

Joshua rose out of his chair and stood next to Emma. "Honey, I'm sorry that happened. Probably never happen again. Tell you what, next time you want to do some work after supper, me and Brian will play some poker while you do what you got to do right here in the house. It was probably some hobo off the tracks. That kind just pass through. Don't worry anymore about it." He patted her on the shoulder, and she squeezed his hand. "So, what were you working on?"

Emma looked down from her father standing beside her. "Just a lot of stuff. A picture of myself and some other things."

"You know, your mama always had something she was trying to finish. Maybe you don't know how much you take after her. She had the same gift. She could make a picture outa' anything. Tried to draw me, but I wouldn't let her. She had all kinds of books with paintings and such in 'em. She'd try to get me to point out my favorites. I'd always tease her and turn to the pages with pictures of the ladies. I know she liked that kind of teasing occasionally. We were lots younger then." Joshua's voice got softer. "Your mama was so pretty. I sometimes wondered how she would look in one of those pictures. But - hell! What am I telling you this for?"

"Well, Papa, I'm a grown lady now. I can talk about things like that. Wouldn't hurt a thing."

He gave her a warm smile. "Hmm. You're always my little girl. Hard to think of you as anything else." He looked down at Brian. "Hey, partner! What say you and me get some ice cream?" With that, he swung Brian onto his shoulders, and the two of them galloped off into the kitchen.

Two days later, Emma and Joshua were driving to town. Joshua dropped Emma at the post office while he and Brian continued to the gas station. As children will sometimes do, Brian made no pretense about who he liked and who he didn't. Adult opinions had no vote in it, and he had decided that Hershel Tulley was the most fascinating person he had ever seen. Hershel always made him laugh and always had small toy trucks and cars for him to play with on the floor while Joshua talked and bragged on his grandson. Emma always complained about the grease Brian brought home on his clothes every time he went to the gas station and finally learned it was easier to put old clothes on him when she knew they would be stopping at Hershel's.

She dropped two envelopes in the mail slot and went to her mailbox. As she dialed the combination, she noticed a group of three young men standing in the corner. One of them was Greg Spears, who worked as a roughneck in the oil fields nearby. He was the younger brother of Woody Spears, her old nemesis from a few years ago. She tried to appear preoccupied with her mail delivery, but from the corner of her eye, she saw Greg lean his head toward the other two and say something, but without taking his gaze away from her. Whatever he said, it brought big grins to the faces of the other two. They finally started walking toward her in a slow swagger.

"Hey, Emma!" said Greg. "How's it going? I hear you a regular businesswoman now."

Emma held her mail in both hands and looked straight at Greg. All three of them wore hard hats and heavy boots. "I'm fine, thank you. Business is a little slow, but it'll pick up, I'm sure."

"My buddies might be interested in what you got, you know? They don't look like it, but these are very sophisticated people when it comes to things like art. Ain't that right, fellas?"

"Yeah. I like stuff that makes me horny," said the one nearest to Emma.

The other one spoke up and said, "Man, you horny all the time. Don't he look horny to you? See? His tongue kinda' gets in the way when he gets like that."

"Excuse me, I need to be going."

First one, then the other two shuffled their feet and formed a circle around Emma. "Wait a minute," said Greg. "We trying to do business here."

"If I wanted to do business in the post office, I wouldn't go to the trouble of setting up my shop. Now, please excuse me."

"I hear you keep late hours sometimes," said one of them.

"Sometimes I have to. I need time to get things done. Like right now, so please let me by!" Her voice gave a faint echo within the small building. Gladys Summers, who had worked for the postal service for more years than anyone could remember, looked through the bars of the cashier window and said, "Hey! This here's a federal building, and if I have to come out there to break this up, you guys are going to see y'all's pictures on that bulletin board up yonder. Now git on outa' here! Not another word!"

Emma immediately took advantage of the distraction to slip through the makeshift human blockade. One of them, however, saw her intention, leaned toward her as she left, and gave her a smack on the rump as she passed. She felt it but held her reaction to only a blush and took quicker steps. She hurried down the walk past Rucker's store and to the gas station. Joshua and Hershel were in deep discussion when Emma walked in. Brian had a pile of nuts and bolts on the floor. As she entered, she saw Brian put one of the small bolts in his mouth.

"Brian! Spit it out! Give it to me!" The child complied immediately.

"Papa!" She said as she laid the saliva-coated object on the greasy countertop. "If you're going to bring him in here, you have to watch him. He could have swallowed that thing!"

Joshua was startled by Emma's entrance and immediately felt guilty for not paying closer attention. He started to speak, but Emma cut him off.

"Brian, let's go. We have to go to the shop." She whisked the child up into her arms and left through the door.

"Hershel, I better see what's bothering her. I'll be back later."

Joshua hurried to catch up with his daughter. When he was several paces behind her, he said, "Emma, wait. I'm sorry. I *was* watching him except for that very moment when you come in. He tried before to put one of them things in his mouth, and I made him stop. I took my eyes off him just for a second!" Emma kept walking. "Emma Parker, will you stop and turn around?"

When Emma turned and looked at her father, he could see the distress in her eyes. "This ain't about Brian, is it?"

"Let's go to the shop, daddy. I need to talk to you."

Joshua knew she had something profound to tell him. Throughout her life, she rarely ever called him 'daddy'. When the shop came into view, Emma slowed down and said, "I didn't tell you everything about the other night. I was afraid to. Now I'm afraid not to. I need to show you something."

She unlocked the door and opened the shades to let the natural light in. Joshua lit the small kerosene heater. Brian knew exactly where his crayons and paper were and set to work on a meaningless swirling, crisscrossing collage of colors. Emma unlocked the small closet and reached behind a stack of boxes. What she brought out stopped Joshua in his tracks.

"This is what I was working on the other night when somebody looked in the window."

Joshua took the drawing in his hands and studied it carefully. The woman in the picture was reclining on a blanket under a tree with a basket of flowers nearby. A small child, a boy about Brian's age, sat at his mother's knees, looking into the background. The woman's breasts were full and slightly pendulous. Her top leg was bent and angled forward to give a sense of dignity. The hips were smooth and had slight creases in the skin where the leg flexed. Her neck had flowing lines that outlined the muscles as she held her head up. She had a face without blemish, blue eyes, a small nose, high cheekbones, and jet-black hair.

Joshua said nothing for several minutes, then spoke with a low tone. "I didn't know your work had gotten this serious." He looked up from the picture at Emma. "What's this got to do with the other night?"

"That's what I was working on when Brian accidentally opened the shade. That's when the face was there at the window."

"And whoever this face was saw the picture, right?"

"No, Papa. He saw me. That's me in the picture."

"He saw a picture of you?"

Emma shook her head and said, "Papa, I love you so much. You just can't imagine what I'm really talking about. Here, I'll show you." She pulled the old mirror out of the closet and positioned it as it had been that night. Then she put the picture on the floor and laid down beside it with her head propped up on one elbow. Joshua walked around behind her and stooped down to look in the mirror. The truth finally dawned on him, and he stood up.

"Well, you did say it was a picture of yourself. I guess I didn't get the whole message when you said it."

"So, when the guy looked in the window—"

"Uh-huh. He got an eyeful, right?"

Emma nodded, and Joshua pulled up a chair and sat down.

"Lemme' think about this for a minute." Joshua held the picture carefully, took a deep breath, and let it out slowly. Brian toddled over to his grandfather and climbed up into his lap. He looked at the picture and pointed to it.

"Mommy," he said.

"Yeah, that's your Mommy, son. And it could be her Mommy as well." Joshua gave Brian's hair a tousle with his big, rough hands. "So, this is what you're upset about?"

"I should have told you."

"I think you would have, sooner or later. It's good work, honey. Maybe you better do this sort of stuff at home from now on. This payroll shack ain't no place for privacy." He handed the picture back to her. "Anything else I need to know?"

Emma began to wring her hands. "I think there may be others in town who know about this, Papa."

"What makes you say that?"

"I lost some of my sketches. The wind blew them away, then some guys stopped me in the post office and were talking about it. They made me feel—"

"And that's when you came to the gas station, and so forth, I see." He leaned forward and asked, "Who were these guys?"

"I know one of them, but please don't say anything. It'll only get worse."

"Who was it? Are they from here?"

"They looked like oil field workers."

"And you knew one of them? I'll find out in my own way, so you may as well tell me."

"Promise you won't stir up anything?"

"I ain't promising nothing."

Emma's eyes darted from one corner of the room to the other, searching for a diplomatic escape. There was none. He was still Joshua Parker, her father. "The one I knew was Greg. Greg Spears. I don't know the other two."

Joshua clinched his jaws and never took his eyes off her. He just nodded. "Don't worry. It won't happen again."

"I'm sorry about all this. I should have been more careful."

"Emma, this ain't New Orleans. People don't understand. C'mon, let's go home."

"I need to stay, Papa. A couple of ladies said they wanted to come by this morning to look at some of my stuff. They might even buy some. Now that you know, I'm not afraid. I'll be fine. You and Brian go ahead. Come get me after lunch, okay? About three O'clock?"

Joshua agreed and left with his small partner perched on his shoulders.

That night, Joshua disappeared from the living room. Emma could hear him rummaging around in a distant closet. She was about to go see what he was doing when he came out with a box covered in dust and spider webs.

"Let me take this outside and brush it off first," he said. "I got something I want to show you." In a few minutes, he returned and sat the box on the floor by the kitchen table. "You ain't gonna' believe this. Everybody thought I got rid of all of 'em, but I didn't."

"All of what?"

"Come see. Dig in there. Start pullin' stuff out. There's things in there older'n you are."

Emma saw that the box was filled with something very flat. The top layer was nothing but newspaper, which she pulled out carefully. Beneath were sketches of their house, of gardens, scenes from the sawmill, and ladies in bonnets and full dresses. In the bottom corner of each one was a signature, Marcia P, written in a swirling, bold script. She laid a dozen of them out on the table and looked at them as though she had just discovered the Rosetta Stone. They were treasures, a window to someone she vaguely remembered. She traced the edges with her fingers as she drank in every detail. It took her several minutes to look at the first group she had laid out. Joshua sat by patiently, not saying a word. His eyes were on his daughter, watching her drink in the unspoken story of her mother, told by what she had chosen for her own expression of beauty and how she chose to depict it.

Emma said in amazement, "Look, this one of the churchyard and the horse carriages in front. She put azaleas in front of the church and a dogwood tree. So much color. She paints like Monet."

"Well honey, I don't know about nobody like that. I just know she found something beautiful in everything, even in people. I don't think she had an enemy in the world. I could always tell when she was enjoying herself and her art stuff. I could hear her singing. Nothing loud, just to herself."

"Did she go to church?"

"Yeah, sure. Took you until she got too sick. I'm surprised you don't remember that part. You had a frilly dress and a bonnet. She tried to drag me along, but I think I scared the folks off." He uttered a low chuckle. "Folks back then was so easy to steer. I coulda' told 'em all they had to go to church, and that collection plate woulda' been running over. Naw, I didn't git into none of that. Never got into the habit. Didn't see no need."

"Papa, I feel like I should know her so well, and yet I don't know anything about her. I don't remember what she sounded like when she laughed, and you told me she did that a lot. I don't remember what colors she liked, or what she ate for breakfast, or what perfume she wore. Oh, jeez, I don't remember!"

Emma felt like someone had opened a gigantic void in her soul. Everyone said she was so much like her mother, and yet, when she tried to latch onto it, there was only a bottomless pit. A freefall into nothing, with no hope of grasping anything as an anchor. She looked at the pictures again and felt her mind searching again, beyond her own control, detached from her own will, looking for a safe harbor. Suddenly, one picture reached out and snared her in an irreversible grasp, like talons in a prey. In the picture were a mother and daughter, both with mixing bowls in hand, standing next to a wood-fired stove. A small kitten sat in the background, licking its paw. The mother's face, as she looked at the girl, was soft and kind and patient. The child had an inquisitive look that asked a thousand questions.

"She did that one right before she got sick," Joshua said.

"I remember her kitchen! I remember what it smelled like! Why do I remember that? It's like it was yesterday! Oh God, I do remember!"

Joshua watched his daughter try unsuccessfully to control herself. What was happening was important, and he only wished he had shown all this to her sooner. But who's to say when is the right time for anything? A year ago, three years ago, it might not have meant the same to her.

Finally, her father asked, "Okay, what did it smell like?"

"Like coffee and buttermilk."

"Like what?"

"In the mornings, she always made biscuits with buttermilk, and she made a pot of coffee. Then she fried bacon and eggs and made a big pot of grits."

"Yeah, she did, come to think of it. What we couldn't eat, she made me take to the mill 'cause she knew there were men who came to work without breakfast."

"And then there would be cornbread and butterbeans cooking for lunch with chopped-up ham, and we'd slice tomatoes from the garden—"

"And then she'd fry chicken for supper. Well, not every day, you know."

"No, not every day, but that's what I remember. I always felt so good when I could walk into her kitchen and smell all those things because I knew it was going to be a good day." Emma's voice became louder and faster as though her memories were crowding in, taking control. "And cinnamon rolls! Remember those? The whole house would be like one big cinnamon bun, and they'd come out of the oven all hot and sticky, and we'd eat 'em so fast we'd burn our tongues - and God! I miss her! Why did you show me these pictures? Why?"

Emma just dropped her face to the tabletop and tried to control the tears. She raised up and said, "Papa, I love my little Brian so much. But he came at the wrong time in my life. Mama could have told me all about these things. It wouldn't have happened if she had been here. I've been so stupid all these years!"

"Emma, your mother is gone. Not your fault. No one could have kept it from happening. She had cancer all over her body. It was her time to go. We had to do the best we could without her."

"The best we could? Did we? Did we do the best we could? Look where we are now! What future do we have?"

"Future? I don't have much of any left for me. You? You're coming up on twenty years old. You've still got a whole life ahead of you."

Emma rose from the table. "I'll be right back."

"Where you going?"

"I said I'll be right back."

"Oh."

Emma disappeared out the back door and was back in less than three minutes, looking more composed. As she sat down at the table, she said, "Papa, I want us to get an indoor toilet in this house. This is 1955 and we're still living like a bunch of pioneers!"

"Yes, ma'am. I'll have it done before dark."

Her father's dry wit brought reality back to center stage and made her smile. He reached into the box and brought out more layers of paper. "Now, these are really special. Your mama did all of these just to get my goat; only it backfired on her."

"What do you mean?"

"Take a look."

The next stack of pictures was a shock to Emma. Every one of them were of nude women. They all were posed in a dignified manner of one sort or another, and all were in some tasteful setting. There were some in wooded meadow scenes, some in elaborate bedrooms, and a rather spectacular one of several women cavorting in a pool of water with a gentle waterfall in the background.

"Your mother and me are the only ones ever seen these."

"Why did she do this?"

"Well, she come in one day and asked me what I thought of nude paintings, and I told her I seen one over a bar in Texas that looked right nice. Well, that done it. She set right then to fix my wagon and show me that nude pictures ain't something to be thought of as dirty. Not that I ever did, but I guess my joking made her get so god-awful serious."

"And she did all these because of that?"

"Well, she wouldn't let me see none of 'em until she was done. Then she laid it on me in one swipe. She called me into her little private room there and says, 'Now, do these ladies look like bar room hookers to you?' That's what she said. Your mama was a real pistol, and I think I'm the only one who knew it. Yeah, she could be a real tart when she wanted to be."

"You said it backfired on her."

"Well, not really. That was the wrong way to say it. What I meant was it had an effect she wasn't counting on."

"What?"

"You! Nine months later!"

"Papa! I can't believe you're telling me this!"

"Hey, you wanted to know about your mother. Right now, you're older'n she was when I married her." His eyes gleamed like Emma hadn't seen in a long time. "Yeah, yeah. Heh! You know, this has been good for me. I haven't felt this good in ten years. Make it twenty years!"

Emma laughed. "Well, I'm sorry I didn't tell you the whole story at first, but how could I know what a spicey life you and Mama had?"

"Sometimes the best things come at the most unexpected times. We'll remember this evening for a long time, won't we, honey?"

The conversation continued long into the night with the hopes of a different day come morning.

Chapter 25

It was close to midnight. Emma said, "Papa, you never talk about your parents."

Joshua stared off into a distant world. "Mama died when I was too young to know, and my daddy was the meanest sonofabitch in Texas. Used a wide belt on me to keep me in line. I left home as soon as I was old enough to figure out a way. That's all there is to know."

"That's it?"

"That's it. And by the way, them oil field fellas won't be bothering you anymore."

She looked at her father rather astonished, with the question written all over her face.

"Don't ask," he said. "And don't worry. No one got hurt. Just some attitude adjustment that needed to git done."

"What did you do?"

"It was right after I left you in your shop. Remember you told me to come back after lunch? I found those three standing outside Rucker's store. We just had us a little 'Come talk to Joshua' meeting. Felt like old times again. I know some old boys who work the oil fields, and they tell me stuff. Them other two guys? They were from Monroe. Just got outta' jail. I told 'em they'd find themselves right back in there if they weren't careful! And Greg? Ha! That piss-ant got the spine of a jellyfish. Just like his daddy."

Emma felt assured that no harm had come to anyone. Gradually, she was beginning to see the facade her father held in front of himself like a shield. To some, it was worth believing. To others, like her, it was an old man hanging onto the past. She had no doubt it had worked this time, though.

Tonight's conversation was too rich to put away, however. "What church did Mama go to? Was it here in town?"

"Baptist. Over on the north edge of town. Used to bring bunches of church ladies in here with their Bibles. Sat in a circle right here in the kitchen and read stuff. They'd meet in the late morning, and sometimes they'd still be here when I come home for lunch, sittin' there all pious and righteous, your mama acting just like one of 'em. But none of them knew your mama like I did."

"Today's Friday. Could we go to church on Sunday?"

"Aw, Emma, I don't know. Your mama tried to get me to go, but that just wasn't for me."

"Just once. Just once. If you don't like it, we won't do it anymore."

"Well, you can go all you want, but I don't think I can—"

"What do you recall about Sundays with her?"

"Sunday dinner. We'd eat a little later than usual. About two in the afternoon. She'd come home from church all stirred up, talking about the sermon, trying to get me pulled into it, but I just sat there and listened. Then she'd start hummin' and cookin'. The kitchen was the best place in the house."

"I'll cook you something special if you go with me just this once."

"Oh, alright! Just once, but don't go trying to get me baptized or nothing. That's just not for me."

"How could I? I'm not exactly a regular. Can't remember the last time I went there. I really can't. I don't even know if I was ever baptized. Was I?"

Her father didn't have a clue.

Two days later, they sat on a back row of pews of the First Baptist Church of Kisatchie. Joshua insisted they sit in the truck until it looked like most everyone was inside. When the three of them entered, all the back rows were filled. Brian clung to his mother's dress. Joshua simply looked at one man, and his whole family rose to their feet and moved to the other end of the pew. Emma could only offer a weak smile as an apology. Joshua's expression never changed. Someone offered a prayer and then the choir sang a special number. After a couple of hymns and some announcements, Brother Raymond Howell approached the pulpit. He was a middle-aged man who had come to Kisatchie only a month before.

He stood silent for several seconds, bowed his head, and said a silent prayer. When he finished, he looked up wide-eyed as though something had startled him.

The minister's sermon began like a gunshot. "Hear the words from the Book of Hebrews, chapter 13, verse 2. It says, 'Let brotherly love continue. Be not forgetful to entertain strangers: for thereby some have entertained angels unawares.'"

"I tell you, no truer words have ever been spoken. Faces, human faces, like so many other things, can be looked at and yet not seen. In most places, we are surrounded by individuals, but how many times do we truly see them as unique individuals? Occasionally, we may catch some momentary eye contact, but that is all the time it lasts. A moment, nothing more. Minutes later, you cannot remember what color shirt that person was wearing, but you recall he was looking at cornflakes on the grocer's shelf because that is what you were looking at. These faces have no personality, no history that you know of, no complexities to dwell on. They are anonymous strangers, and for all you care, at the moment, they don't matter in your life. For it to matter would require that we stop and ponder many things, and we just don't have time. If we took the time, we might discover amazing things. All faces hold stories, stories sequestered in secret recesses of the human mind. Stories of the joy and pain of life. Stories told only to the closest of friends, if at all."

The congregation all nodded in agreement.

Brother Howell looked around with a large smile and said, "For those of you who don't know me, my services are a little different from what you're used to."

"I ain't used to nothin'," Joshua whispered.

"What I just gave you was food for thought. We'll come back to that later. I like to stop occasionally and get some comments from all of you. Any thoughts on this scripture?" The minister's eyes scanned the congregation. "Speaking of angels, I see some new faces among us. I'm going to pause here while you are thinking and acknowledge our visitors. Could you tell us who you are? Let's start over here, on the left side."

Several couples stood and told the congregation who they were and where they came from. Brother Howell shifted his view toward the Parkers. Joshua saw it coming. "Aw shit," he said under his breath.

"The couple in the back - sir, you with the young lady and that fine-looking boy, could you introduce yourselves?"

"How did you git me into this?" he whispered to Emma without getting up.

Emma sat for a moment and then stood while her father just shook his head. "I'm Emma Parker, and this is my father, Joshua, and my son, Brian. We've lived here all our lives. Just visiting today."

"*They* know who we are," Joshua said in a loud whisper. "Just that *he* don't!" He motioned toward the pulpit. "But give him time."

"Well, thank you," said the preacher. We're always glad to have new souls among us. As many of you know, we're having a covered dish gathering after the service in our social hall, and all of you visiting us will be more than welcome to join in. Brother Edwards, please lead us in a word of prayer and give thanks to God for these new friends."

One of the deacons stood and began a prayer of thanksgiving. Joshua bowed his head, then shot a glance over at Emma. "I can't believe I'm in church," he said softly.

"You want to stay for the picnic?" she whispered.

"Hell, no." A few heads turned and looked at Joshua. He simply returned their stare.

"It might be fun. You said you met Mama at one of these picnics."

"I'm too old to be looking for another wife."

"You said my life was just beginning."

Joshua's gaze dropped to the floor and nodded in agreement just as the deacon finally said, "Amen!"

Brother Howell finished his sermon, and the organist played a music finale. He walked down the aisle with the choir director and stood at the door. From the back of the congregation, he pronounced the benediction with arms stretched wide, his voice almost in a tremble. Suddenly, the room was full of conversation as people left their pews and filed toward the door where their pastor stood, waiting to shake each hand going by. Joshua and Emma were quick to reach the door.

"Mr. Parker, I don't think I've ever met you in the short time I've been here. And this is your lovely—"

"Daughter," Joshua quickly asserted. "And my grandson. No, you ain't never met us because we don't go to church. At least, I don't. These two might get started." he nodded toward Emma and Brian. "So, where's the picnic?"

"In the social hall in the rear. Door's around back. You'll see it. Be starting shortly. So glad to have you." The pastor watched Emma closely.

They descended the few steps from the church door and turned to walk alongside the building. Joshua stopped and looked across the church property.

"Nothin' changes," he said. "I met your mama under that oak tree. It was in the evening, it was. Toward dark, a bunch of guys built a bonfire over there behind that big rock, and a group of 'em got around it, singin' songs. Your mama was sittin' on a little stool she brung with her. I seen her across there on the other side of the fire, and I noticed she kept on looking at me. I wasn't sure, so I moved over a few feet. When I saw her turn her head to follow where I had moved to, I was sure she had something on her mind. Took me a few minutes, but I walked over to her and started talking. That's how it happened."

"I wish I'd brought something," said Emma, looking at the prepared dishes others had brought.

"Don't need to. We're visitors today, remember?"

Joshua and Emma entered the back room used for such gatherings and watched as a few men of the church began setting up tables. Out came tablecloths, and a few covered dishes appeared. No one approached them or even spoke. Emma saw fleeting glances in their direction from some of the women. One elderly woman who was almost blind shuffled up to Emma and spoke.

"Hi, I'm Edna Thornhill. Don't think I've met you folks." She stood very close and spoke loudly. Emma noticed she had a hearing aid and very thick glasses.

Emma started to answer when a middle-aged man came up to the old woman and guided her away to a chair.

"Mama, let's sit you down over here," he said.

"But I was talking to those nice people back there," Joshua heard her say as they walked away. Her son leaned toward her ear and whispered. The old woman stopped and turned around quickly to look back at Emma and Joshua, then continued to her waiting chair with no more objection. She refused to make any more eye contact with them.

"I ain't staying for this," he said. "I don't stay where I ain't wanted. You can if you like. I'll be back in a couple of hours to get you."

"No, I promised you a nice Sunday dinner. Let's go."

They were almost to the door when the pastor came in. His face was all smiles. "You're not leaving, are you? We haven't even begun."

Joshua said with a slight chuckle, "Preacher. Looks like most folks didn't listen to your sermon."

"Brother Howell," someone from the crowd said. "This is my Aunt Peg from—"

"I'll be there in a second." He turned back again to Joshua and Emma. "Really, I was hoping you would stay." More folks were coming through the door. The pastor stopped one man and said, "Mr. Foster, do you know the Parkers? They're visiting with us today."

"Sure, I know Joshua Parker," the man said. "Everybody does. Don't turn your back on him, preacher. And don't let him go near them collection plates. Never can tell with some folks." With that, the man disappeared into the crowd.

"I'm terribly sorry about this, "said the pastor. I didn't know he knew you so, uh, so well." He finished with a weak smile.

"Well, hello!" said a voice behind them. "Look who's here?" They all turned and saw Alton MacArthur walking toward them with his cane. Alton had helped Emma accumulate enough credits to receive her high school diploma. It seemed to be his last goal before he retired. A minor stroke a year ago had left him with a barely noticeable limp, but enough to require the cane. His wife, Maxine, kept her fingertips at Alton's elbow. He said to Brother Howell, "I see you've met some of my favorite people. Mr. Parker used to work for us at the school. Emma has a thriving art business now. Must be thriving; she supports the whole family now, don't you, Emma?"

Brother Howell was noticeably relieved at the reception Mr. Mac was extending to the Parkers. "Don't worry about some of these old-timers," said Mr. Mac. "They come to church and hear all about forgiveness, but they can't put it into practice. Why don't the three of you come sit with my wife and me so we can talk? I haven't seen much of you folks lately." Alton and Maxine had developed a strong affinity towards Brian. On certain occasions, Emma had allowed Brian to stay with the MacArthurs while she tended to other necessities. They had no children of their own. Maxine gave the boy a wide smile and patted his head.

Alton continued, "Looks like you and your wife have your work cut out for you, pastor!"

"I enjoy a challenge," said Howell. "By the way, I'm not married."

At those words, Joshua turned and looked at Emma.

The Parkers and the MacArthurs were halfway through their meal together when Emma noticed a small girl, no more than four or five, standing just a few feet away with a quizzical look. When Emma tried to speak to her, she stepped closer and stuck out her tongue. She was about to say something when her mother appeared and quickly picked her up.

The whole exchange didn't take more than thirty seconds. But it was enough for Joshua to decide it was time to go home.

"Oh, stay for dessert," Maxine insisted. "There's pecan pie and turnovers and …"

The mention of the desserts caught Joshua's attention. He rose from his seat and said, "My treat. Who wants dessert?" With that, he headed for the sweet table. When he returned with his hands full, he saw Emma standing away from the table with a look of distress on her face. Brian was standing beside her. In his chair next to Emma's sat Jack Spears, taking a final draw on a cigar. He smashed the stub into the leftover food on Joshua's plate.

"You're in my seat," Joshua said slowly as he unloaded his hands.

"I didn't see your name on it," Jack spewed out.

"Get outa' my chair."

"Go piss up a rope, you dumbshit."

With one sweeping motion, Joshua jerked the chair from under Jack, who landed with a thud on the floor. He collected himself and stood, a little unsteady.

"I'll see you outside," Jack hissed. The room was suddenly silent.

"I'm in no hurry, Jack. I just want to enjoy my dessert."

The next several minutes then passed as though nothing had happened. Joshua managed to make small talk with those who remained at the table, all the while keeping a close eye on the outside door where Jack had exited.

The Parkers and MacArthurs stood outside the door saying goodbye when someone tapped Joshua on the shoulder. He turned to see Brother Howell with a young man who looked to be in his early thirties, wearing a suit that was grossly wrinkled and a tie loosened at the collar. He carried a briefcase.

"Joshua Parker, do you remember who I am?" the young man asked.

Emma was caught off guard. Joshua looked with his eyebrows arched, then with an ever-deepening frown developed as faint memories began to creep to the forefront.

"When I went by your house, and no one was home, I thought this might be where I could find you. I'm Eugene Stockman", he said. "From Giles Oil. I defended you when you were in jail in Colfax."

Houston, Texas

Hugh Giles was a senior at Rice University, about to enter his last semester before graduating. He had just found a table at a coffee shop on the edge of the campus, where he was waiting for several friends to join him. The waitress, a middle-aged Hispanic woman, approached his table and uttered an audible gasp.

"Señor Hugh! Is that you? I no see you for so long!"

"Isabella? Oh my gosh! It's been, what—three years? I just woke up one morning, and you were gone! No one told me why you left or where you went. How are you?"

"We are fine, gracias, just fine. My husband, he come here last year and find good job. My children all grown up like you." Her face was beaming. "You in the school at Rice?"

"Yes, one more semester, and I graduate. Then the job hunt starts." He craned his neck to see if his friends were approaching.

"You wait for someone?"

"Yes, some friends of mine. They never are on time."

"You want me to come back in a few minutes? That's okay. I come back later." She hesitated and then continued, "That girl you met in Louisiana, you hear from her?"

"No, that's old history. I guess she's gone on to other things. She stopped answering my letters. I really did like her, though. She was a genuine person."

Isabella stood fixed, looking at Hugh with indecision on her face. Twice, she started to say something and changed her mind.

"Isabella, what's wrong?"

As though the words were a heavy weight being pulled up from the depths of a bottomless pit, she finally spoke.

"Señor Hugh, we must talk."

Chapter 26

Emma felt suspended in mid-air. The words, 'Giles Oil' echoed in her ears like a message sent across a wide canyon years ago. It felt as though she had heard that name from a former life.

"Mr. Stockman, what are you - I mean, how good to see you," Emma exclaimed. "It's been so long, I—uh, we—we weren't expecting to see you ever again."

Joshua's memory was slower, but his scowl gradually became a smile of gratitude. He was silently nodding to everything Emma said and stood with his hands thrust into his pockets, shifting his weight from one foot to the other like a child who was anxious for his turn to speak.

"Young fella', I never did git the chance to thank you. Them sonsabitches woulda' railroaded me right into prison if you hadn't come along."

"Well, you can thank the Giles family for that. Emma, I assume everything is okay with the checks you've been getting?"

Emma just shrugged, unsure of how to respond to the question.

"You have been getting the checks, haven't you? I know they went out because I signed every one of them."

Emma turned to her father and said, "That's the name on the checks! Eugene Stockman! We couldn't figure out who it was!"

"Yeah, that was me. With my handwriting, my mother says I should have been a doctor." He looked down at Brian as he spoke.

"Brian, say 'hello' to Mr. Stockman," Emma said. "Go ahead. He's a good friend. We haven't seen him in a long time. He's never met you."

Stockman squatted down in front of Brian and extended his hand, and Brian retreated to a vantage point behind his mother.

"He seems attached to you," Stockman said.

"Yeah, he's mine."

"He's yours? I didn't know you had—he's yours?"

There was a prolonged moment of silence. Emma looked away and spoke as though she didn't want to see Stockman's reaction to her next words.

"How's Hugh, Hugh Giles?"

Only when he didn't answer immediately did she look back at him. Perplexed, he said, "I wouldn't know. He's enrolled at Rice. Did you know Hugh?"

Alton MacArthur had just walked up to the group and heard Stockman's last few comments. He motioned to the lawyer, and the two men stepped aside a few paces. The young lawyer was listening intently and then suddenly looked over at Emma and Brian.

Stockman was beginning to panic. He had entered a forbidden arena totally by accident and clearly saw that there was no way out of it. He glanced around the churchyard and spotted an old, abandoned picnic table. "Why don't we go sit over there?"

"Why don't we stand right here, and you tell us whatever it is you came here to tell us?" Joshua's tone carried a clear message. Stockman immediately recognized the cold eyes he remembered from the courtroom. It had been a few years, but some visual memories stuck. Gathering his wits, he looked at Joshua, then Emma.

"I didn't come here to tell you anything. I don't know what communication you've had with the Giles family. They just asked me to drop by and bring you these checks that have been accumulating and—"

Joshua took a step closer, but Emma put her hand on his arm. He could feel her hand trembling.

Stockman looked down at Brian and carefully thought before he spoke. "It seems like I have found myself in a very awkward place right now. We have other attorneys in our company, and I am a mere junior staff member. I just do what they tell me to do. We're opening a branch office in Alexandria. I was on my way there, and folks thought it would be convenient for—well, okay, I brought your checks. That was my task to accomplish." He stopped for a moment. "I didn't know about this child."

"Does his daddy know?" Emma asked.

Taking a deep breath, Stockman continued, "Hugh is about to finish his engineering degree at Rice University. He's making wedding plans. To my knowledge, he doesn't know about your child."

"His child, you mean!" Josh thundered. "Somebody in Houston knows! That's what them checks are all about! Why didn't they tell him?"

Emma clutched at her stomach and glared at Stockman in disbelief. At first, her expression was blank. She felt the blood drain from her face and sensed a curtain of darkness surrounding her. After several seconds passed, her legs suddenly felt like limp spaghetti, and she dropped to her knees. Her head bowed, she sobbed silently. The hem of her dress became soaked with tears. Stockman was almost in tears himself. Joshua knelt on the ground beside her and put his arm around her. Little Brian walked around the couple and innocently held his arms up to Maxine MacArthur, wanting to be picked up. The child sensed his mother's emotional plight and began to cry, too.

For several minutes, Emma could not be consoled. The church crowd was slowly filtering out of the building and saw Emma's sobbing figure clutching at the dried grass. They saw Joshua beside her speaking softly and a perplexed young man in a wrinkled suit with a briefcase. No one stopped. The crowd made a wide circle around them as each one found their way to the parking lot.

From the back of the crowd, a mocking voice cackled. "What's wrong with the Parker tribe? Too much of the Holy Ghost for you?" Joshua immediately recognized the voice of Jack Spears, a sound emblazoned on his memory. Jack came to church only when there was the promise of free food and a crowd full of ripe gossip to take home.

Joshua stood and muttered forcefully, "Shut your damn mouth, Jack! When are you going to learn? You don't know what the hell is going on here!"

"I don't need to. All I see is a bunch of squawlin', bawlin' Parkers. Does my heart good!"

"Shut up, Jack!"

Jack Spears walked around the crowd and approached Joshua from the rear. He stood only a few feet away.

"How's that little bastard grandson of yours? You gonna' teach him to be an asshole like you?"

Joshua looked over his shoulder and growled, "I shoulda' killed you years ago!"

"Couldn't do it then, and you can't do it now, you old fart!"

"I'll see you in hell!"

Joshua turned and closed the distance between himself and Jack in two steps. Jack's son, Woodrow, stepped in front of his dad and threw a punch. Joshua skillfully dodged the young man's fist and connected with his own, sending Woodrow staggering backward. Jack was within arm's reach, and Joshua placed an iron grip with both hands around the man's throat. The two ancient combatants went down and rolled on the dusty ground, Jack flailing away at Joshua's face with the palms of his hands and Joshua tightening his grip. As he felt Jack begin to weaken, he released his grip and pounded the man's face with his fists. The crowd was stunned by the sudden outburst of violence.

"Someone stop them!" a woman screamed.

Joshua continued to throw punches into Jack's body until Brother Howell and two other men grabbed him by the arms and pulled him off. The crowd gathered around the scene and saw the bloody remains of what had once been Jack's face. Joshua stood and took a step back. Jack lay motionless for a moment, then slowly got to his feet with the help of those around him. He was gasping for breath and holding his ribs. Eugene Stockman pushed through the crowd and shuddered when he saw the damage. He quickly took

Joshua by the arm and pulled him away. Woodrow Spears had regained his balance and composure and stood beside his father. A murmur began to roll through the crowd.

"Get out of here," Stockman muttered to Joshua. "Go now! Take Emma and disappear!"

"Go to my house," Alton MacArthur said to Joshua in a half-whisper. "You'll be better off in the middle of town with us for a while until this cools off. My wife and I will have Brian."

"Daddy, look at what he done to you!" wailed Woodrow. We gotta' git him to a hospital! That old bastard, look what he done! You all saw it! Call the Sheriff! Where'd he go? Where'd he go, damn it? There—there he is!" Woodrow started in pursuit of Emma and Joshua when suddenly a mahogany cane was thrust between his ankles, sending him sprawling for the second time.

Alton MacArthur began apologizing immediately. "I'm so sorry, son. How clumsy of me! I was trying to catch my balance. Please, someone, help him up." He quickly turned to face Emma and whispered forcefully, "Emma, get out of here. Go! You and your dad go to my house. Stay there until we get home. We've got Brian, and we'll figure out something."

The crowd began to mill around, people gasping at the sight of Jack's bloody face. Within seconds, everyone heard Parker's truck start and gravel fly from beneath the rear wheels. When it reached the pavement, the tires uttered a loud squeal for an instant as they sped away.

Brian was squirming in Maxine's arms. She turned to her husband and asked, "Who is that young man? The one with the briefcase?"

"I don't know, but I think he's someone we'd better talk to." Alton navigated his way to Stockman and said, "Excuse me, sir. We're all trying to figure out what happened here, and we don't seem to know who you are."

Stockman looked pale. "I'm Eugene Stockman, attorney from Giles Oil. I guess you could say I'm a friend of the family. I defended Joshua a few years ago. Looks like I stirred up something."

"Maybe not. I think Josh is going to need all the help he can get right now. Look, I told Emma to take her dad to our house. Let's go home and connect up with them. Mr. Stockman, just follow us in your car. We have some things to discuss once we get there."

At the MacArthur house, Joshua and Emma were looking out the front windows, waiting for the MacArthurs, Stockman, and Brian. They arrived and had barely gathered in the living room when suddenly the phone rang. Maxine answered. Her eyes told the others that something was wrong.

"He's what? How did it happen?" Maxine covered the mouthpiece and whispered to the others, "It's Patsy from next door. She heard that Jack Spears is dead!" She returned to the phone conversation. "Please find out. Well, it's important that we know. Yes, call me as soon as you can."

Maxine continued talking for a few seconds as the others huddled and murmured about what this could mean. None of them saw Joshua slowly back away and quietly move toward the back door.

When Maxine hung up, she was pelted with questions from the others about the phone call. It took several seconds for them to realize someone was missing.

"Where's Joshua?"

The entire group turned and saw that he was gone. Emma walked into the kitchen. "Papa? Papa, where'd you go?"

"He's probably in the bathroom," said Alton. "I'll go check."

The rest of the group resumed the discussion about Jack Spears. The caller had not given Maxine any details, only that Jack was dead. Alton came back into the room with a worried look.

"He's nowhere in the house. I've looked in every room."

"Why would he leave?" asked Stockman. "Wouldn't he want to hear the details?"

"What details?" said Maxine. "We don't have any. Jack's dead, that's all we know. You don't suppose someone will try to blame Joshua for this?"

"No, I know my Papa," said Emma, "Right now, he's afraid someone *is* blaming him. Doesn't matter what the connection is. Someone will try to put Papa in the middle of it."

"Maybe he died from the fight," said Stockman. "You know, one of those delayed reaction things."

"Oh, God. You don't think that could be it?" Emma blurted out. "I got to find him before he does something crazy! He'll think the whole Parish is after him!"

Emma ran out the door and saw the truck was still in the driveway with the keys in the ignition. As she pulled away from the house, the phone rang in the MacArthurs' living room. Again, Maxine answered.

"Yes, Patsy. What did you find out? A wreck? Was he alone? Woodrow was driving - where were they going? I see. Yes, that's terrible. Yes, they're all here. Well, I don't know if we can stand any more news, but call us if you hear anything else. Okay. Bye."

"Woodrow was driving his dad to the hospital," Maxine reported as she was hanging up. "He was apparently going very fast and lost control of the car in a curve. He hit a tree, and Jack went through the windshield. Jack's dead, and Woodrow's a little banged up, but he's telling everyone he was driving fast because he was worried about his father. Emma was right. Someone's going to try to blame this on Joshua."

"So, what can we do?" asked Alton.

"Nothing," said Stockman. "We just sit here and wait for Emma or her dad, either one, to come back."

"Shouldn't we be out looking, too?" asked Maxine.

Alton shook his head. "Emma knows where to look - better than we do. Mr. Stockman is right."

A moment of silence passed before Stockman spoke. "So, while we have time, it might help if someone could bring me up to date on what has transpired since the last time I was here?"

Stockman sat amazed at what the MacArthurs were telling him. An hour later, Alton was giving him the last of the details.

Eugene Stockman was trying to comprehend it all in one gulp. "So, you say she came back from New Orleans, set up her shop, and Brian was born. I don't know if she heard from Hugh after she came back from New Orleans. Who do we know that can fill in the gaps here?"

"What about the Carters?" Maxine asked. She turned to Stockman and explained, "That's a family that lives close to them. They befriended Emma when she was just a child. I think she still sees them often."

"Or we could just wait for Emma and ask her," said Stockman.

"What a minute, folks," Alton said. "This is not the time to be doing all this. She's been hurt today. She needs comforting right now, not interrogation."

"Yes, yes, you're absolutely right. I'm too busy acting like a lawyer. But, in defense of my own apparent ignorance, I had no idea that Hugh had a child. In fact, I'm fairly certain he knows nothing about it. The Giles family sent Emma a check about once a month for a while, then about once a quarter. I always wondered about it, but they never told me what it was for. Lots of checks go out, and I just sign them and send them wherever they tell me to. It just wasn't my place to ask about too many details."

Two hours passed. Maxine served coffee and snacks while they waited.

A heavy car crunched through the gravel in front of the MacArthur house. When Maxine went to see, she came back with a worried look.

"Alton, the sheriff is here. Tom and Flora Rucker just pulled in behind him."

Alton pushed himself to his feet. "You stay here, Maxine. I'll see what he wants."

He had barely made it out of his chair when Flora walked into the room with Tom and a deputy behind her. Incredulous at their boldness, Alton simply sat back down.

"I hope you don't mind my letting myself in," Flora said. "I knew you were home and, well, I'm so worried. I called the Sheriff as soon as I could."

"I'm confused," Alton said. "What do you mean, you called the sheriff? About what? The fight?"

"No, something else. As soon as we found the truck, I called. I didn't know what else to do!" Flora's eyes danced nervously.

"Found the truck?"

"We missed church today because we had to go visit someone. We were driving back across the Little River bridge near Oak Point and saw part of the guard rail was missing. There were skid marks on the bridge that led right up to the, you know, the missing rail. So, we got to the other side and pulled off. I looked, and there was the red truck sitting on a sand bar in the middle of the river. There was an injured deer struggling to get deeper into the woods. We got to a phone and called the sheriff's office, then went back out to the bridge and waited."

The deputy interrupted. "The sand bar was shallow and led up to the bank, so we were able to walk right out to the truck to investigate."

"And?" Alton said with anticipation.

"We found Emma Parker under some buttonwoods on the bank. She was unconscious, so we called an ambulance. She's on her way to Alexandria right now."

The silence and shock in the room were palpable.

The deputy broke the silence. "I hate to ask at this point, but is Joshua Parker here? I need to reassure him that Jack Spears' death was not his fault. His son has clarified that and is now worried about his own charges of reckless driving."

"He's not here," said Stockman.

"And your name, mister?"

"I'm Eugene Stockman. I'm Mr. Parker's attorney."

The deputy chuckled, "That was quick. How'd he get a lawyer so fast if he's not here?"

"Is that part of your sensitivity training, Deputy?"

"Naw, I just thought it was strange." He gave another soft chuckle.

"Then have some respect for this group. My relationship with Mr. Parker will come out sooner or later."

"So, you say he's not here?"

"I don't just say it. I'm telling you, he's not here. We can pass the good news to him when we find him. In fact, you could help us find him. But just know that he still feels like a fugitive."

"Mind if I look?"

"Go ahead," Maxine said. "Go ahead and look. He really isn't here."

"We need to go check on Emma," Alton said. "Then we can be looking for Joshua."

The deputy finally left, and they all tried to find the words to start what was a crucial discussion. Tom Rucker offered, "Let the sheriff find Joshua. Let's go to the hospital. But then there's the third issue."

One by one, they looked at Brian, who had found a magazine and was on the floor, propped on his elbows and flipping pages.

Finally, Stockman spoke. "May I use your phone?"

Maxine showed him to the kitchen phone. She lingered long enough to hear him ask the operator for assistance in placing a collect call to Houston. He spoke in hushed tones for almost a half-hour. The MacArthur living room had the atmosphere of a funeral home.

Holding the phone to his chest, Stockman said, "Mr. Rucker, your sister wants to talk to you."

When he hung up, Tom said, "Flora, I need you to hear what I'm saying. The Giles family has asked that the boy, uh, Brian, stay here with us until we can decide what to do with him. Can we do that?"

Flora gasped. "What a mess!" she exclaimed. "And our nephew knows nothing about this little fellow?"

"That was one of my reasons for calling Houston. Someone in his family has to tell him."

Alton chimed in, "First, we need to find Joshua."

Two days later, a car slid to a stop with a spray of gravel in front of Rucker's store. The startled look of the three men sitting on the breadbox was met by the driver's voice, "They found him! They found Joshua Parker! He's alive!"

Joshua had been discovered by a highway crew as they were searching for a means by which to extract Emma's pickup truck from the sandy bed of Little River. He was transported to Baptist Hospital by ambulance with a gunshot wound to his shoulder. Unfortunately, his age and the delay in treatment had taken its toll, and his condition was critical. Investigators believe he was shot at another location and managed to struggle to the place where he was found. The investigation was ongoing, and the details of it were published the next day in the Colfax Gazette, including a description of the encounter between Joshua and Jack and the death of Jack Spears. The article continued:

Tragic as it may seem, the story does not end there. Parker was found as a highway crew searched for a pathway to salvage his daughter's pickup truck from the sandy bottom of Little River. The location is aptly named Oak Point because of large oak trees that had taken root decades ago on a hillside overlooking the river. Recent heavy rains and high winds had uprooted one of the largest of the oaks, exposing a shallow grave containing a homemade casket, within which were skeletonized remains estimated to be that of a middle-aged woman. According to the medical examiner's office, cancer was the most apparent cause of death, as suggested by the moth-eaten appearance of most of the bones. Investigators are puzzled and amazed at the items found in the casket with the woman's body. A family bible was held next to her ribs. Jewelry of all descriptions laid among her bones and decayed clothing, including brooches, rings, necklaces, bracelets, and other finery. Her identity had remained a mystery until officials found a locket inscribed with the words, "To Marcia, with all my love." The remains are now believed to be those of Marcia Parker, wife of Joshua Parker. She will be given a proper burial in Kisatchie Cemetery despite a few objections from some town folk.

Chapter 27

The next day, the Ruckers and MacArthurs went to the Baptist Hospital in Alexandria, where they were allowed to enter Emma's room, where she still lay unconscious. The emergency room doctor said she had sustained a concussion and a fractured clavicle. The fracture was minor, requiring no intervention, and the only thing to do was wait until she regained consciousness.

As they approached her room, a man was leaving it. It took a moment for them to recognize Raymond Howell, the pastor of the Baptist church. He was walking in the opposite direction and did not see the group of visitors in the hallway. Flora insisted they leave their home number in case her condition changed.

A week later, Tom Rucker received a phone call from Eugene Stockman. With all the legal and compassionate words he could employ, he had convinced the Giles family it was in their best interest to tell Hugh he had a son. When they approached Hugh with the news, he informed them he already knew and was preparing to go to Louisiana, with or without their permission. His mother was about to call his decision ridiculous when Stockman asked if he knew of the latest development. Risking his job, Stockman proceeded to tell Hugh the entire story, including the incident at the church, Emma's accident, and Joshua's injury. There was no stopping Hugh at that point. When Hugh broke the news to his fiancé, she just shrugged, returned the engagement ring, and called off the wedding. "This is not what I signed up for," were the last words she said to him.

Hugh spoke with his college counselor and was given an academic sabbatical for one semester. The next day, he found himself in the passenger seat of Stockman's car, crossing over the Louisiana State line. They reached Alexandria a few hours later.

"We've been treating them both as charity cases," the hospital administrator said to Eugene and Hugh. She is still in a coma, and she has no insurance. Her father is barely hanging on. It is a very difficult situation for us."

"What does she need? Round-the-clock nursing care?" Hugh asked.

"Talk to her doctors. They know the problems she could face."

After waiting what seemed like hours in the lobby, they saw a man in a scrub suit and white lab coat approaching them.

"I'm Dr. Peterson. Are you Emma's family?"

Eugene Stockman said 'no,' and Hugh said 'yes.' The doctor looked puzzled.

"Okay, let me ask again, are you Emma's family?"

Eugene gave a general explanation, leaving out some of the details, especially that of a child back in Kisatchie.

"So, who makes the decisions for her?" the doctor asked.

"I do. I'm the attorney for the family. I have been for some years now." Quietly, he hoped this would open up the discussion.

"That will help things. Her father is on this wing in critical condition and is not able to discuss treatment options for her. Miss Parker is being attended to by the nursing staff right now. I suggest you see her father first. We tried to find out who shot him, and the sheriff just said the list of possibilities is too long to mention. I have no idea what he meant by that."

Hugh plodded down the hospital corridor, not knowing what he was going to find in the room at the far end. Stockman waited in the hall. Joshua Parker lay in his bed with an array of intravenous infusions attached. His injury included both entrance and exit bullet wounds and a shattered scapula, apparently the result of a high-powered rifle. The Sheriff's department, ironically, was interested in finding the shooter, but Joshua had not been forthcoming with information. He did not see who shot him and could not remember where he was when it happened. The delay in finding him and receiving treatment had allowed a stubborn infection to invade his chest cavity. He was barely responsive, but he heard Hugh come into the room.

The two men, one an ancient fossil and the other a bundle of youth and promise looked at each other with a common thought. Hugh introduced himself.

"You're my grandson's daddy?" Joshua's voice was a bare whisper.

"Yessir. It looks like it. You and I met a few years ago."

"Have you seen him?"

Hugh leaned closer to hear what he was saying. "No sir, not yet."

"He likes trucks, you know, toy trucks. He sings like his grandmother. Got a great voice." A raspy cough interrupted Joshua's comment.

Hugh waited until the right moment and spoke with a nervous chuckle, "Mr. Parker, I'll take good care of him. I can't deny who his daddy is."

Joshua didn't take the bait of humor. "C'mere, son. I need to tell you something."

Hugh moved closer to the bed, unsure of what to expect. "I'm right here, Mr. Parker."

Joshua's voice came in interrupted gasps. "You take care of my little girl. She's the spittin' image of her mother, and she deserves better than what I give her. Love her like I did her mother. You promise?"

"I hear you, Mr. Parker."

Joshua grabbed Hugh's shirt and pulled him close. "I know you heard me. I asked do you promise me?"

Hugh was shocked at the old man's grip in spite of his weak condition. "Yessir, I'll take care of her."

"That's not what I asked you, son! Do you love her?"

Hugh looked deep into the old man's eyes. Pleading eyes. He answered, "With all my heart, yessir." He watched as a weak smile appeared on the old man's face, and a small stream of tears from one eye inched its way down to his chin.

Back in the lobby, Hugh and Eugene continued their conversation about Emma. Dr. Peterson seemed to have a plan in mind. "Okay, she needs to be moved in a few days, but not too far. There are nursing homes all over this Parish with empty beds. They don't do charity work, but it's less cost than a hospital room. I'll drop in to check on her after she's been moved."

"Expense is not the problem," Hugh blurted out. "When can I – when can we see her?"

The doctor looked at the young man and could sense the urgency in his voice.

"Let's go right now. I'll walk with you. Just so you know, she's going to look awful to you. The staff sees this kind of thing all the time, and we're used to it. Just prepare yourself."

They entered the room, and a nurse was standing by the bed near Emma's head, blocking Hugh's field of vision. The doctor motioned to her, and she stepped away. Hugh gave an audible gasp and stepped closer to the bed. One side of her head and face was horribly bruised and was a collage of colors.

"We took her off the ventilator yesterday," the doctor said. "She had some swelling in her throat, and we were afraid it might restrict her airway. But she's okay now, at least on that concern."

The two men saw that Hugh was struggling to keep his composure. They stepped into the hallway and gave him his moment with Emma. Flowers from the Kisatchie A.M.E. church filled a vase on the windowsill.

Hugh felt bewildered. The scene was beyond words, and he wasn't sure if he had the right ones. "My dear Emma," he whispered. "I am so sorry about all of this. After all this time, I didn't know about the baby. I swear to God, I didn't know. If you had just told me, none of this would have happened. I guess you had your reasons."

He looked for a response and saw none. He gently touched her hand and pleaded, "Please don't hate me. You have every reason to. That girl I was engaged to, I—I didn't really love her. My family was pushing us together. Her parents had their eyes on my dad's money, and I should have known. I'm going to do whatever it takes to get you out of—out of here and …" His voice choked. "I swear to God!"

He leaned on the side rail with his hand on her arm and quietly sobbed until he heard a voice from the far corner of the room where the lighting was dim.

"That's a prayer if I ever heard one."

He turned and saw Pastor Raymond Howell standing in the shadows.

"I'm glad to finally meet you," the pastor said. "Maybe we can meet later and get to know each other." He took a step closer.

"I think God has given you a task." Howell's words seemed to have a balm to them. "We all have a secret, holy place in our hearts that only God knows about. He's asking you to reach into that holy chamber of this young lady and help her restore some sense of order to it. It's a daunting task, but there's so much joy to be had when it's done. You both are in my prayers."

Hugh wiped away his tears and simply nodded. The pastor said nothing else and left quickly.

In the doorway, Hugh saw Tom and Flora Rucker standing close by, close enough to have heard Hugh's pledge to Emma. Both were misty-eyed. He had not seen them in over three years.

He took a step toward the couple, and with red eyes full of tears, he hissed, "Why didn't you tell me? Why didn't someone tell me I had a son? Did everyone think this would just go away like a bad dream?" His voice got louder. "Uncle Tom, you've had almost three years to tell me! Does my mother hold that much sway over you? Doesn't anyone in this family trust me enough to make my own decisions? Huh? Goddamn it, say something!"

Flora and Tom were stunned by Hugh's visceral words.

An hour later, Hugh and Eugene drove to the Rucker's house. Tom gave Hugh a stack of letters he had written to Emma, yet undelivered as per Rose Giles' instructions. Alton and Maxine arrived with Brian a few minutes after that. Hugh stood at the front steps and watched as an almost three-year-old replica of himself approached on the walkway. He knelt when the boy was just a few feet away and saw a mop of blond curly hair and blue eyes. The boy held onto Maxine's hand but reached out with his free hand and touched Hugh's nose with his finger.

Hugh's face was a mixture of amazement and disbelief. He was gazing at a treasure he didn't know he had. Softly, he said, "Hi, my name is Hugh. What's your name?"

The boy stood with a nervous twist in his legs and one finger in his mouth. He looked at Hugh for several moments, and just when it appeared that he was not going to respond, he pointed toward his father and giggled, "Hi!"

That night, Joshua Parker died in his sleep.

Giles Oil was expanding into central Louisiana as a satellite of their efforts in the Gulf of Mexico. It became obvious that a branch office was needed in Alexandria where staff members could be in contact with companies that supplied drilling equipment. The branch included a legal office, and Eugene Stockman was the natural choice due to his experience in Louisiana law.

Eugene and his wife, Jill, had found a beautiful old home on Jackson Street, and Hugh was made to feel welcome there. It was closer to Emma than the Rucker's house. Although the child stayed with the Ruckers, Flora had assured Hugh that his priority was Emma's recovery. He could form his bonds with Brian later. He had found a used car to buy, and every day, he would drive to Bayou Manor Nursing Home, where Emma was now in residence. He would talk to her, read to her, sing to her—anything to get a response. Had she been able to hear him, she would have learned about the entire story of Giles Oil and the Giles family, the history of Texas, football games at Rice University, and every boyhood adventure Hugh could remember. At one point, he read the local phone book to her. Sadly, she remained in a comatose state. The staff began to recognize him as a familiar fixture. After six weeks, however, his hope began to waiver. He found himself looking for any small glimmer of change, only to realize, again, that the outcome was still unpredictable. Hope and depression swept over him in increasing waves. His appetite waned.

Eugene and Jill encouraged him to take some time for himself to change his routine. They saw how his clothes were beginning to fit a bit loose. His daily morning shave and shower routine were now once, maybe twice, each week. They saw a hollow look on his face. Taking their suggestion, he decided to drive back to Kisatchie and Pittman. Maybe there was something there, something in the realm of hope, something to latch onto. With his hosts' blessings, he filled the gas tank, found Highway 165, and aimed the car towards Grant Parish.

Thirty minutes later, a gas station came into view. A railroad track lay parallel to the highway. A sign pointing to the right read, 'Kisatchie - 1 mile'. He felt the pavement change as the car turned off the highway onto an aging asphalt road, which was bleached and fissured by years of sun. The surface was uneven from a patchwork of repairs. He crossed another rusting railroad spur and came to a cross street that was further layered in history. It was hard to tell if the composition of the road was pavement or gravel. Maybe both. A turn to the left led past the front of Hershel Tulley's gas station, now out of business. The rounded gas pumps with crank handles were faded orange, and the gauges were caked in rust. A few yards further, Rucker's store came into view.

The store hadn't changed much. The outside was the same, and the breadbox hadn't moved.

It was a town of old, tired buildings with faded, peeling paint and rusty signs. What few people he saw didn't seem to be in any hurry to go anywhere. Up ahead, he saw the charred remains of a small building; the support piling and one corner were the only evidence that it once was a structure. This had been Emma's art shop that had burned the day after Joshua died. The cause was never investigated. He had never seen it as she had used it, but he knew about it from his Aunt Flora.

He sat in silence, looking at the blackened stumps of the foundation poking out of the ground. Like so many other landmarks in the town, what little remained was being swallowed by nature and time. Vines had started to obscure the gravel walkway, and grass with tall seed heads hid the rest.

He considered going to see the boy. "I wouldn't know what to say to him," he said to himself. The image of the youngster piled on top of family conflict, and the emotional avalanche he was going through was almost unbearable. So many things at stake, and he hadn't the faintest idea where to start.

"Well, enough of this," he said to himself. As he wheeled the car around to leave town, a thought occurred to him. He headed straight for the old Parker house in Pittman.

It took exactly five minutes to get there. It occurred to him that in the time he had known Emma, he had never been in her house, only in the yard. Standing outside the car, he noticed the front door stood partly open, and he crossed the threshold.

A layer of dust covered everything. Someone had covered all the furniture, probably Oscar. He thought, *Who else would have cared enough?* He could only imagine the sounds, the thoughts, the lives that had filled the old house when it wasn't so old. Which room had been Emma's? Was there evidence of Joshua's fury still engraved into the walls? Where had Marcia entertained her lady friends? Which room did she lay in while she suffered? The kitchen was almost the largest room in the house. Empty cabinets with muted tones greeted him. Hugh took out his handkerchief and began to wipe the front of one. After several strokes, a rich cherry color began to emerge. He tried another with the same result. Countertops gave off a cloud of dust when he blew on them, then gradually unveiled their deep colors. A huge walk-in pantry was crisscrossed by dangling spider webs and floating dust balls, which seemed suspended from nowhere. Outside in the backyard, he saw the faintest remnant of Marica Parker's thoughts as he gradually understood the layout of her garden. The only hint of planning was crumbling fences and lines of flagstone leading from a tumbled bird bath to a sundial and then to a gate overgrown with climbing roses, still blooming. Were these her efforts or Emma's? Two women had called this place home. Two women had had a child here and could lay claim to it. Two had blessed it with their nurture, love, and patience.

"My God, if these walls could talk," he said to himself.

He re-entered the house and walked slowly down a long hallway. At the end of the hall, daylight was coming from an open door that led to a small bedroom. Inside, a closet door drew his attention.

He yanked on the old wooden handle, and it came off in his fist. Using his fingertips and a pocketknife, he worked the door loose, and it popped open with a cracking sound that vibrated in his hand. The hinges creaked as he slowly swung it open wider.

In a far corner was a small bundle of denim fabric. When he unfolded it, he saw the smallest set of coveralls he had ever seen. There were still grass stains on the knees.

"Well, I'll be damned!" he said out loud. "These must have belonged to Brian. Probably don't fit anymore."

He held the coveralls by the straps and immediately thrust his fingers into all the pockets and felt something he couldn't readily identify.

With two fingers, he extracted a molded toy duck about an inch high. It was anchored on a base with three ducklings in the rear, all marching in a straight line.

He stood there and turned the toy in his hands, looking at it from every angle. Gazing around, the house spoke to him as sure as human voices could speak. He folded the little coveralls and walked back to the car, carrying the bundle under his arm.

As he drove back toward town and the railroad crossing, Oscar's house came into view.

Oscar Carter's house was beginning to match the condition of many others in Kisatchie. The old wood siding was weathered and had streaks of rust streaming from the nails. Individual pieces were warped, giving the house a wilted look like it needed to be starched and ironed. The low roofline sagged at the peak. From a distance, the roof looked reddish orange. Up close, he saw it was that color indeed, of rust, not paint. No shrubs grew around the house. In the front yard was not a blade of grass. The Carters had owned no lawn mower, so, like many of their era, they had worked for years maintaining the front yard as bare sandy soil. Raking daily kept it looking cared for. As he approached the house, a tall, grey-haired man stood by the gate, rake in his hand. He waved, as all people do in Kisatchie when a car goes by. Hugh hit the brakes suddenly and jammed the car into reverse. He stopped even with the gate.

"Oscar?" he asked.

"That's me," came the reply.

"Oscar, it's me, Hugh Giles. Remember me?"

A big smile blossomed on his face. "Yessuh, I heard you was back around these parts. How you been?"

"I'm staying at a friend's house in Alexandria. I go to visit Emma every day at the nursing home. She's still not awake yet." He studied the man's face for a moment. "How's Lavenia?"

Oscar slowly frowned and said, "She ain't around no more. She passed last month."

Hugh shaded his eyes and said, "You lost someone you loved. I'm so sorry."

"Yeah, my kids is all grown and gone. Looks like I'm the only one left in Pittman."

Hugh was at a loss for words until he said, "I was just heading back, but I'll stop by again when I have more time," he said.

"Hang on, before you hurry off like that, I got something you might want. Hang on, I'll get it."

Oscar disappeared and emerged from the house carrying a large, flat object wrapped in brown paper. He handed it to Hugh through the car window. Carefully, Hugh took the paper off one corner and then uncovered the whole thing. It was a framed painting of a landscape with three people on a road. A barefoot woman stood in the middle, holding a child with one hand and waving with the other to the third person, a young man in a coat and tie. He was running far ahead of the mother and child and was looking back at them over his shoulder. Alongside the road, dogwood trees bloomed. In the bottom right corner, the single word, 'Emma' was printed.

"I don't know what to say, Oscar. Thank you. This means more than you can imagine."

"Lots of people had their hands on it. It finally ended up here with my wife. I been looking at it a long time, and I still don't understand what Emma was thinkin' when she painted it."

Hugh sighed. "I think I know. Pretty sure of it."

The nursing home was near an intersection folks called the 'Crazy Quilt'. Several highways came together from places like Pineville, Alexandria, Winnfield, Shreveport, and Tioga, forming a five-way intersection. Some speculated maybe the contractors were drunk when they designed it. The nursing home was on the Shreveport Highway, set back about fifty yards among some pine trees. Hugh knew the roads now by memory and swung into the parking lot.

Inside, he noticed a sense of urgency and excitement among the staff. One of the nurses recognized him and shouted, "Hugh, go to Emma's room! Go now!"

He sprinted down the hall, almost knocking over a patient in a wheelchair. Several staff members were crowded around Emma's bed.

"What's wrong?" he asked.

They parted and gave him a full view of a young woman trying to sit up. Her eyes were blinking with a distant look on her face, staring but seeing nothing. Eyes he had not seen in three years.

Hugh was speechless. Her face was lined with wrinkles from sleeping so long, and her hair was unkempt, but she looked beautiful to him. The staff motioned him to come closer. He approached and spoke softly.

"Emma? Emma, can you hear me?"

He turned to the nurses and asked, "What am I supposed to say to her? Does she know me?"

"Just keep talking to her," one of them said. "We'll leave one of the nurses here with you in case she needs us for anything."

With that, the nurses and aides began to exit the room and left Hugh standing, amazed by the bed.

"Emma, Emma, honey … It's me, Hugh. Do you see me? Can you hear me?"

Chapter 28

Hugh was torn between staying at the bedside or rushing to a phone to call someone—anyone. He found it almost impossible to contain his excitement.

He turned to the nurse who had stayed in the room and said, "Can you make a call for me?" She agreed, and Hugh quickly wrote down Stockman's home phone number.

Word of the revelation traveled swiftly from Emma's room to Eugene and Jill, to the Rucker house, and from there to all of Kisatchie. Hugh skipped lunch and stayed glued to Emma's bedside for the rest of the day. He left as darkness was approaching with high spirits, like a man who had discovered an enormous treasure. In fact, he had.

That evening, he was strangely quiet, but Eugene and Jill could see his mind working. There was a permanent smile on his face.

The next morning, he gulped down breakfast, took a quick shower, shaved, and hurried to the car. Eugene and Jill promised to come join him later that day. What would he find when he got there? How much had she progressed since the day before?

The receptionist at Bayou Manor greeted him with her usual smile. The corridor to her room seemed so long today. He couldn't get there fast enough. A nurse met him at the door.

"Not yet, young man. Can't go in, not just yet. They're getting her cleaned up and in fresh clothes. Just give them a few more minutes."

When he finally entered the room, he didn't know what to expect. The head of the bed was elevated, and she was staring at the far wall.

"Emma? Emma, good morning," he spoke softly.

She turned her head in his direction with a blank look.

"Hey, girl! Let's go for a walk in the woods, huh?"

No response.

"Emma, c'mon. Talk to me."

Nothing.

An aide came in with a small cup of applesauce. She said, "Let's see if she can eat. That would be a big step in the right direction."

The aide scooped out a small spoonful and touched it to Emma's lips. "C'mon, sweetie, have a bite of this good stuff."

"Let me try," Hugh interjected.

"Okay, just make it small bites."

He followed the aide's example and touched her lips with the spoon. Her lips barely moved. "It's okay, Emma. This is good stuff. Try it."

There was no response. Hugh turned and looked at the aide in desperation, but the aide never took her eyes off Emma's face.

"Look, there it is. Do it again," she said.

"There WHAT is? What?"

"When you looked away, she moved her tongue. She tried to lick her lips."

This time, Hugh made more effort to put some of the applesauce where she could taste it. He gently parted her lips with one finger and deposited a minute amount in her mouth. A slight quiver of her mouth caught his attention. She made a barely perceptible smacking sound.

"She got it! She got it!"

Over the next fifteen minutes, Hugh managed to feed her about an ounce of the simple meal. Once, she gagged a little and coughed. That was good, the nurse told him. It means she is regaining at least some normal function.

For the next two weeks, Hugh fed her every meal. He left the room only when the nurses came to tend to her. She still had not spoken but could make a few incomprehensible sounds. She was paying more attention to the room and her surroundings. She sometimes moved her arms and legs aimlessly. The staff decided it was time to see if she could walk.

It was clumsy at first, but within a few hours and after several tries, she shuffled a few feet before almost collapsing. She still had not recognized or acknowledged anyone, including Hugh. He eventually voiced his concern about this to the staff.

"When was the last time she saw you?" someone asked.

It was then he fully realized the impact of that question. It had been the day he cleaned out his locker at the school three years ago.

"I've got to find something to remind her who I am," he said. "There must be something."

They reminded him that her progress would be slow and that he was being an anxious young man. He was not in her immediate world, not after this amount of time. Her world was slow as molasses.

Within three more weeks, she was walking much better, mumbling, but not clearly. The staff said no one could predict how much memory and function she would recover nor how fast it would happen.

One day, Dr. Peterson stopped by.

"What else can we do to help her along? What does she need?"

"Reminders. She needs reminders," he said. "Objects she relates to, places, people, things in general from her past."

A flash of inspiration occurred to Hugh. "Hang on a second. Let me get something." He left the room and quickly returned with a pencil and pad of paper.

Thinking he was going to make notes to himself, Dr. Peterson was surprised to see him put the pad and pencil in Emma's hands. "What's that for?" the Dr. Peterson asked.

"No one told you what an accomplished artist she is?" Dr. Peterson shook his head.

Slowly, he adjusted the pad of paper in her left hand and the pencil in her right hand. He moved her hand so the pencil made lines on the paper. Slowly, her gaze lowered from the ceiling to the paper, and small, furrowed wrinkles appeared on her forehead. She gripped the pencil in a clumsy fashion but began to make slow, small, meaningless scribbles.

"Look! She's doing it! She's trying to draw! Keep going, Emma! Draw me something! Wait, I have something else!"

Again, Hugh ran from the room and returned with the picture Oscar had given him. Nurses had begun gathering outside her door. Hugh carefully unwrapped the painting and held it in front of her to see. Slowly, her eyes focused on the three figures in the picture.

A guttural sound escaped her mouth. She began slowly repeating it.

"What's she saying?" Dr. Peterson asked.

Her persistent sound became more emphatic and intentional. She began clawing at the picture with her fingernails as though trying to scrape the colors off. It was then Hugh noticed her attention was on the image of the young man in the picture, running away. An indecipherable babble came from her throat.

"Puddin'! Puddin'!" she grunted.

"Puddin'! That's what she's saying!" Dr. Peterson was smiling broadly but with a quizzical look.

Emma's clawing motion became more intense, and her voice grew louder, sounding like a mixture of moaning and growling. She began slapping and beating her fists on the picture, then threw it across the room.

"Okay, Hugh. Let's let her rest. She's remembering things, but they don't make sense to her. It seems trivial, but this took a lot of energy for her to do. Try it again later."

Hugh reached down and picked up the picture. "I think I know what she's remembering," he said. He suddenly felt unwelcome in her room.

"Brian!" Emma half-shouted.

"Oh my God! Oh my God! She said Brian!" Hugh was jerked out of his thoughts like a slap in the face.

"Who is Brian?" the doctor asked.

"He's her little—he's OUR little boy!"

"You're the father?"

"They didn't tell you?"

"I knew you were a relative, but I didn't know about this."

"The last time she saw Brian was in Grant Parish. What if we brought him here?"

"That's not a good idea. Not until she has a better grasp on things around her. Her reaction may be upsetting for the child."

Hugh tried another approach. "She's from a little ghost town called Pittman right next to Kisatchie. What if—what if we took her there? What if we showed her the mill pond behind her old house? What if—wait! I have something else in the car. Stay right there, doc!"

Hugh raced out of the building and came back moments later with a bundle of blue denim fabric. He carefully unfolded it and laid the coveralls on Emma's lap. Without looking, her hands touched the texture of the material; her fingers began exploring, searching, rubbing. She traced the seams, then fondled the shape of all the buttons. As though guided by an inborn map, she reached into a pocket and pulled out the plastic duck. They could see a puzzled look on her face, and then, without warning, a single teardrop formed in both eyes.

"Brian …"

At least thirty seconds went by, and she turned to the nurse and said, "Where's Brian?"

Hugh was almost crying himself. Dr. Peterson was jubilant.

"Where's Brian?" she repeated over and over. Flailing her arms, she tried to get out of bed.

Dr. Peterson said excitedly, "Let her go! Let her walk, but for God's sake, hold on to her!"

Emma was shuffling out into the hall when her legs finally buckled, and Hugh caught her in his arms. Scooping her up, he carried her back into the room and laid her in the bed. He stepped back and saw she was exhausted. Within minutes, she fell asleep.

"Now comes the hard part," said Dr. Peterson. We must watch her closely so that she doesn't try to do this by herself. She could fall."

"Don't worry, I'll be here. For as long as it takes, I'll be here."

Three more weeks went by. Her mobility improved dramatically, young woman that she still was. She noticed details around the room and pointed to them without saying anything. The window, the flowers on the bedside table, the pattern on her hospital gown. She focused on everything in the room except the faces of the people.

Hugh was there in his usual role when Dr. Peterson came in.

"Doc, I must ask something again. We talked about the possibility of taking her back to her old home, where she could see familiar things. Has she made enough progress to do that?"

"I must admit, she is coming along faster than I had imagined. Okay, tell me. What do you propose?"

Emma sat silently between Nurse Atwell and Dr. Peterson in the back seat of the car. Hugh had driven at a moderate rate of speed along the highway, paying close attention to the middle passenger through the rearview mirror.

"So, tell me," Hugh said. "You first met up with her in the emergency room, right?"

Dr. Peterson answered, "That's right. It was during the winter. I remember it well. She was - " He stopped for a moment and said, "Are we almost there? My goodness, I feel like we're out in the middle of nowhere, no offense intended."

"None taken," replied Hugh. "Here's the turnoff."

"Good. Slow down. Let her see the town. Let's see what she does from the safety of the car."

Emma was jostled in her seat when they went over the last set of railroad tracks. She turned her head carefully in both directions and squinted.

"Slower," said Dr. Peterson.

Hugh had the car moving at a crawl as they inched their way down the main street of town. The gas station provoked nothing more than a passing glance, but the Rucker store brought on a deep breath and darting eyes.

"She's thinking."

Hugh brought the car to a stop in the middle of the street in front of the store. Her breathing became ever more rapid, but only for a few seconds. The car inched forward. The burned-out payroll shack came into view, and a slight frown crept into her face, a look of question perhaps. The railroad station brought no response.

"Where's the house?"

"Back the other way."

"Turn around."

As Hugh wheeled the car in a circle, the Ruckers' house came into view through the trees. Her eyes widened, but no one in the car saw it. As they drove again past the store, a little boy's face appeared at the window.

Once out of Kisatchie and into Pittman, the car passed nothing but vacant landmarks that were overgrown by weeds and resembling nothing from decades ago. The car turned down the last street, and the Parker house came into view. Emma sat up straight in the back seat. The silhouette of the house swung into view with the morning sun glaring behind it. She stirred in her seat, and her lips parted. Hugh stopped the car, and all eyes watched her as images sorted themselves through her memory. She scooted to the edge of her seat and began a slow rocking motion, her hands on the seat back in front of her.

"This is crucial," Dr. Peterson said. She's processing a lot of information now, coming back to her. Let's get out of the car, but don't let her get away from us. You two are younger than me, so help me out here. I can't keep up with her if she runs."

"If she runs?" said Hugh with alarm. "She might run?"

"Just stay close is all I'm saying."

As they emerged from the car, she uttered a soft cry. Stumbling toward the gate, she held her gaze fixed on the roof of the house as though called by something visible only to her. She stopped at the edge of the porch, climbed the steps, then into the living room, and disappeared. Hugh quickly followed while the others tried to keep up. He suddenly reappeared at the door and said, "She's going through to the back. Meet us back there."

Hugh and Emma both emerged onto the back porch, then Emma turned around and went back inside just as the others were rounding the corner of the house.

"Come on in. We're in here," he yelled out to them.

When Dr. Peterson and the nurse finally caught up with them, Emma was sitting on the living room floor with her feet apart, staring into space. Slowly, she swayed back and forth, making a soft moaning sound. Dr. Peterson came closer and knelt beside her.

"Emma," he said. "What is it? Do you know this place?" He looked at Hugh and said, "Patients recovering their memory do this when they're feeling stressed about something."

As he spoke, she rose slowly to her feet and shuffled again toward the back door. She stopped only for a moment as the backyard came into view, then through the gate and into the woods with Hugh and the young nurse close behind. When Dr. Peterson finally caught up with them, she was standing at the edge of the mill pond, staring in wonderment. They all watched from a few feet behind.

"Be careful!" Dr. Peterson huffed. How deep is that water? I don't know if she can swim!"

"She can," said Hugh. "And she has. Right here, many times."

As though his words had meaning to her, she kicked off her hospital slippers and slowly waded out, feeling the sandy bottom between her toes. She stopped and swished the cool water with her fingertips. On the far side of the pond, a group of mallards slowly paddled between lily pads. Hugh leaned forward and cupped his ears.

"What did she say?" He turned to the others and said in a forced whisper. "She's talking!" He pulled off his shoes and socks and quietly waded next to her, close enough to hear yet keeping his distance.

"Ducks," she croaked.

Hugh jerked his head around and looked excitedly at the others. Dr. Peterson's eyes were wide open, and his mouth was gaping. "She's talking! This is marvelous!"

For five minutes, Emma played in the water, slowly kicking her feet and looking at the center of the pond. Gradually, she slowed down, then sat in the water, soaking her clothes, and mumbled something none of them could understand.

"Emma? What are you saying?" asked Dr. Peterson. "Say it again."

"What is she saying?" asked Hugh. "Sounds like just a grunt."

Within seconds, Emma had begun the same swaying motion, making another mumbling sound over and over. Hugh rolled his pants legs up higher and stood beside her. He leaned over and listened carefully, then stood quickly and spoke to the others. "Brian? I think she's saying Brian over and over!"

Before Hugh could answer, she said clearly and loudly, "Brian!" The head motion continued side to side, faster and faster. "Brian, Brian!" she said with each turn.

"For God's sake, answer her!" said Dr. Peterson.

"Emma!" he said, finally. "Where's Brian?"

Before Hugh could react, she plunged straight forward and went completely under. He grabbed the back of her gown and pulled her back quickly. They both stood, waist-deep, dripping. He tried to wipe the water off her face.

"Okay, we need to get her out of there," said the doctor excitedly.

As they came back to the pond's edge, he asked, "Doc, should we take her back into the house and see what else happens?"

"Frankly, I think she's had enough for one day!"

"Yeah, and what a day! Ducks and Brian!"

Dr. Peterson cautioned him, "Hugh, she said those words back in her room. She's just repeating what you said."

With limited success, they managed to dry her off enough to sit in the car.

As they pulled away from the house, Emma sat, dripping still, on the edge of the back seat, very focused on the scenery going past. They reached the turnoff to cross the tracks, and Emma suddenly grunted and pointed back at the main street of town. She gently bounced as she pointed.

Hugh stopped the car. "Emma, where do you want to go? What is it? Did you see something?"

"Hugh, we need to get back. I have patients to see."

"Doc, just give us a moment. Look, she's pointing over that way." Emma was pointing at the school. "We missed the school. It won't take but a minute."

Ignoring Dr. Peterson's last request to start back, Hugh turned the car and pulled into the schoolyard. It was mid-afternoon, and the school buses were loading students.

Emma's breathing became more rapid as they got closer.

"What's this about, Hugh?"

"I'm not sure, but I think we need to get out of the car one more time.

"Why? She's still soaking wet! She can see everything from inside the car!"

"It's not a matter of seeing; it's more than that. You know, someone at the nursing home asked me when the last time was that she saw me. It was here! The day I left! We have to get out!"

Reluctantly, Dr. Peterson and the nurse helped Emma out of the car, and they watched her as she closely studied the line of students boarding the buses. They all stared at her dripping wet hair and hospital garb. Her face was a picture of inquiry and concern, eyes searching every student that passed. She began to make a sound like she was quietly moaning in agony, slowly waving her hands slowly as she looked at the youngsters. Hugh walked around and stood in front of her. She stopped with her eyes wide open and gazed at him. Amazement was suddenly painted on her face like a baby seeing the world for the first time.

"What do you see, Button?"

She mumbled in low tones and continued to look at him closely.

"What's she saying?" asked the nurse.

"Get her back in the car," shouted Dr. Peterson, who was standing by the open car door.

Ignoring the doctor, Hugh held her hands in his and guided her fingertips to the buttons on his shirt. She gently fondled the fabric and began clutching it in her fists. She worked her hands up to his neck, then his chin. Her fingers traced the outline of his nose, his eyebrows, and his ears like her sense of touch had its own memory. Her breathing came in gasps, and she arched her eyebrows. She seemed puzzled, as though meeting a stranger for the first time. A stranger, but with a glimmer of something that glowed and kindled in her deepest memory, a small hint, a clue. It came into focus slowly as she heard the softness of his voice and saw his warm smile, the way his lips curled. Her chin quivered, and a sudden frown grew on her face as tears welled up in her eyes. She looked at him intently and shook her head.

"Emma, remember me? I'm Hugh Giles. It's me."

She continued to shake her head. "Hugh—gone."

"No, he's not gone. He's right here."

"Hugh—gone," she repeated.

"Button, I'm right here!" He was almost shouting. "Remember when you sewed my shirt? We went for walks in the woods. We'll do it again! I came back for you, and I promise I won't leave you again! I'll take you to New Orleans like we talked about, remember?"

Emma continued to shake her head. Hugh couldn't tell if it was in disagreement or disbelief.

Then he remembered what Joshua had said. "Emma, look at me. Listen to me." His voice almost croaked, "*Red sails in the sunset ...*"

Emma's eyes began to dart back and forth. Her mouth tried to form words, but nothing was audible.

He gently cupped her face in his hands and said, "Emma, I love you."

Her lower lip was clenched in her teeth, and she gently nodded. She was half-crying, half-laughing. Images tumbled through her brain, slowly finding their rightful place in her memory.

She finally spoke in a whisper, "*way out on the sea ...*"

Epilogue

The year is 1960. Two aging gentlemen sat on the breadbox outside Rucker's store. In gnarled, trembling hands, one of them clutched the latest issue of the Colfax Gazette with this article on the front page:

Grant Parish Update

The town of Kisatchie is experiencing an unexpected rebirth after more than half a century of slow stagnation and decay. A one-hundred-acre tract of lowland, stripped of timber years before by lumber giants, has been surveyed and will be configured to create a reservoir by damming up several creeks at a common point in the watershed. The engineering is underway by Giles Petroleum Industries, at the direction of their head environmental engineer, Hugh Giles, who will oversee the construction. The proposed area is surrounded by the vastness of Kisatchie National Forest, home to hiking trails, wildlife habitat, and picnic and camping areas. The reservoir will be stocked with a variety of aquatic species native to this part of the state, courtesy of the Louisiana Fish and Wildlife Commission.

With matching funds from the State and local Parish, Giles Petroleum Industries has agreed to erect a water tower and water treatment plant nearby to service all residents of Kisatchie and surrounding communities with water from the reservoir. Currently, there are plans for municipal water lines to be laid along all streets and outlying areas.

Interest in this public land has already attracted the attention of visitors from surrounding areas and as far away as New Orleans, frequently centered around the newly opened bed and breakfast lodging at what is known as the Parker House Inn, now owned by Emma and Hugh Giles. The home has been expanded and redesigned to include 25 private rooms, a spacious dining area, and an enlarged gourmet food preparation wing known affectionately as "Marcia's Kitchen." The waiting list for available rooms is growing steadily. The Giles live there in the master suite with their eight-year-old son Brian, and they are expecting their second child in three months.

Mrs. Giles maintains an art studio in Kisatchie, rebuilt and expanded at the site of her original studio where it was previously destroyed by a fire that was never explained. It now includes a small classroom where she teaches art to talented high school students.

One of the men sitting on the breadbox folded his newspaper and said to the other, "Why do you think that young fella' just picked up and left Houston? Left all that oil money? And look what he married into! I tell ya', it'll never last."

But that's another story.

Emma's forest is now safe. The blade of the woodcutters will never rape the land again. Every morning, she and Brian start her day with a walk in the woods behind the house and a conversation with Marcia. She has not forgotten the voices that live in the deep, moist shadows of the oaks and pines, all telling her that she is loved – loved by a power that transcends all powers, a power full of grace and truth that has spoken to so many down through the ages. People who may follow her path don't understand what she is hearing. But little Brian does. Like his mother, he hears the voices that tell him there is someone or something there. Whether he comprehends it or not, she tells him to remember the scripture her mother circled in her bible:

"Whether you turn to the right or to the left, your ears will hear a voice behind you, saying, 'This is the way. Walk in it'" Isaiah 30:21.

And she listened – and she did.